The Lady

ALSO BY K. V. JOHANSEN

Blackdog

The Leopard

The Lady

MARAKAND, VOLUME TWO

K. V. JOHANSEN

an imprint of **Prometheus Books**
Amherst, NY

Published 2014 by Pyr®, an imprint of Prometheus Books

Cover illustration © Raymond Swanland
Cover design by Grace M. Conti-Zilsberger

Inquiries should be addressed to
Pyr
59 John Glenn Drive
Amherst, New York 14228
VOICE: 716–691–0133
FAX: 716–691–0137
WWW.PYRSF.com

18 17 16 15 14   5 4 3 2 1

Library of Congress Cataloging-in-Publication Data

Johansen, K. V. (Krista V.), 1968–
    The lady / K. V. Johansen.
        pages ; cm. — (Marakand ; volume 2)
    ISBN 978-1-61614-980-2 (softcover) — ISBN 978-1-61614-981-9 (ebook)
    I. Title.

PR9199.3.J555L33 2014
813'.54—dc23

                                            2014023968

Printed in the United States of America

There's a gang that's been reading my stuff since—forever.
If they see shadows of a certain ancient character in both Holla and Ahj,
well, even literary characters have ancestors. Or descendants.
So, this one is for April, Marina, Chris, Tristanne, and Mum.

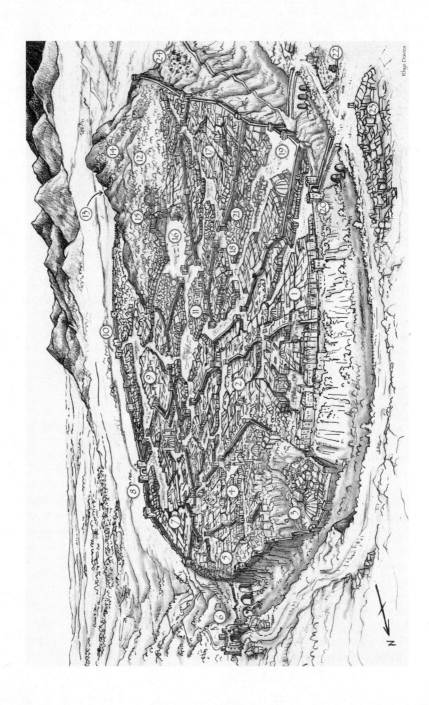

The City of

Marakand

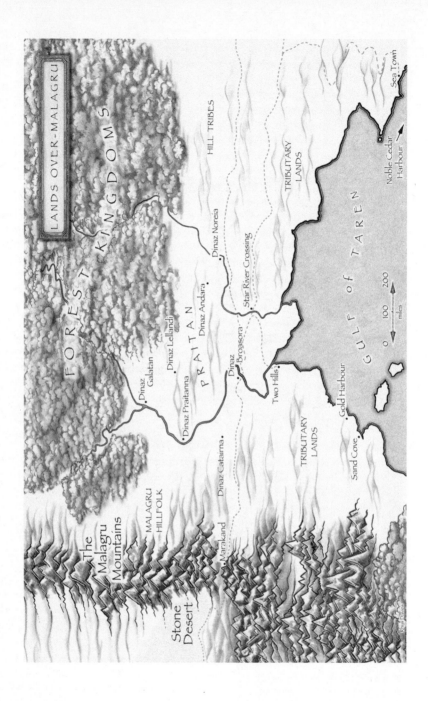

LANDS OVER-MALAGRU

FOREST KINGDOMS

The Malagru Mountains

MALAGRU HILLFOLK

Stone Desert

Dinaz Galatan

Dinaz Lellandi

Dinaz Praitanna

Dinaz Catarna

Marakand

PRAITAN

Dinaz Andara

Dinaz Noreia

Dinaz Broasora

Two Hills

HILL TRIBES

Star River Crossing

TRIBUTARY LANDS

TRIBUTARY LANDS

Sand Cove

Gold Harbour

GULF of TAREN

Noble Cedar Harbour

Sea Town

0   100   200
miles

DRAMATIS PERSONAE

Adva—The Serakallashi third wife of the Grasslander Ketsim, the Lake-Lord's governor of Serakallash, murdered with her daughter during the Serakallashi uprising.

Ahjvar—Surnamed the Leopard, a Five Cities assassin suffering under more than his fair share of curses; originally from Praitan.

Andara—Deyandara's god; god of the Duina Andara in Praitan.

Anganurth—A wizard of unknown origins, who became the devil Jasberek.

Arhu—A devout priest of the Lady, sent to speak for her in the Duina Catairna.

Arrac-Nourril—One of the Twenty Families alleged to have founded Marakand.

Ashir—A priest, the Right Hand of the Lady, husband of Rahel.

Asmin-Luya—A Grasslander man of Gaguush's caravan gang, killed in battle at Lissavakail, father of Zavel.

Attalissa—Goddess of the lake Lissavakail in the mountains called the Pillars of the Sky; foster-daughter of Holla-Sayan, formerly protected by the Blackdog.

Auntie—Midwife living with Talfan the apothecary; former nurse of Jugurthos Barraya.

Austellan—A blind Catairnan lord, ally of the Seneschal and Marnoch.

Aylnia—A sandal-maker's wife and diviner, taken by Red Masks.

Badger—A mastiff belonging to Deyandara, slain defending her against brigands.

Barraya—A Family or clan name in Marakand; one of the Twenty Families, supposed founders of the city.

Bashra— A Black Desert god, god of Gaguush's folk.

Beccan—Sister of Nour, late wife of Hadidu; she died in childbirth before this story began.

Belmyn—Senior-most patrol-first in the Sunset Gate company of the street guard under Jugurthos Barraya.

Beni Sessihz—An elderly senator of Marakand.

Bikkim—Serakallashi former member of Gaguush's gang; mortal husband of the goddess Attalissa.

The Blackdog—Thought to be a guardian spirit who bonded with a chosen warrior of Lissavakail to protect the goddess Attalissa; now the Westgrasslander caravaneer Holla-Sayan, free of Attalissa and said by Moth to be the damaged soul of a devil wounded and lost in the world in a forgotten devils' war.

Cairangorm—A king of the Duina Catairna in Praitan; some songs say he was murdered by his elder son, some by his young wife, on the Day of the Three Kings, about ninety years before this story takes place. The songs are still popular among the bards in Praitan, though they are not often sung in the royal hall of the Duina Catairna. It is believed the land and the folk have been under a curse of ill fortune since that day.

Catairanach—Goddess of a spring and patron of the Duina Catairna.

Catairlau—Son of Cairangorm's first wife, his heir, champion, and wizard. Alleged by some to have murdered his father; died not long after him on the Day of the Three Kings.

Cattiga—Queen of the Duina Catairna, aunt of Deyandara, murdered by Marakander envoys.

Chieh—A mercenary woman from the Five Cities, one of Ketsim's tent guard, wife of Lug.

Choa, high lord of—Ghu's former master, ruler of a province of northern Nabban.

Cricket—Deyandara's pony.

Costen—A lord of the Duina Catairna, at feud with Lord Hicca.

Dellan—A Catairnan lady, daughter of Lord Austellan and his representative with Marnoch's warband.

Demrios Xua—A senator of Marakand.

Deyandara—Illegitimate half-sister of Durandau, king of the Duina Andara and high king of Praitan. Niece and blood-heir of Catigga of the Duina Catairna. Sometimes called Deya.

Django—A member of Gaguush's gang, originally from the Stone Desert, brother of Kapuzeh.

Dotemon—One of the seven devils, otherwise the wizard Yeh-Lin the Beautiful.

Durandau— King of the Duina Andara and elected high king of Praitan; eldest brother of Deyandara.

Ead, "Young" Ead—A street guard of the Eastern Wall.

Elias Barraya—A senator of Marakand; wife of her cousin Petrimos Barraya; mother of Jugurthos. She was executed in the cages shortly after the earthquake.

Elissa—Praitannec lady, one of High King Durandau's wizards.

Ergos Arrac—An elderly sandal-maker of the suburb.

Ermina—Second daughter of Varro and Talfan.

Esau—Son of the priestess of Ilbialla and only person from that family to survive the earthquake and the subsequent slaughter of all priests but the Lady's. His name was changed to Hadidu and he was raised by the family of the Doves coffeehouse.

Fairu—A lord in the eastern part of the Duina Catairna.

Faullen—A huntsman of the Duina Catairna in Marnoch's service, later in Deyandara's service.

Feizi—One of the Twenty Families of Marakand.

Gaguush—A Black Desert caravan-mistress and gang-boss on the western road, recently married to Holla-Sayan.

Gelyn—A bard of the Duina Catairna.

Geir, Red Geir—One of the first three kings in the north, nephew of the wizard Heuslar.

Ghatai—One of the seven devils, otherwise the wizard Tamghiz, also known as Tamghat, the Lake-Lord of Lissavakail. Father of Ivah.

Ghu—Ahjvar's servant and companion; has been a slave horse-boy, groom, sailor, beggar, and other things besides in his life to date.

Gilru—Young son of Queen Cattiga, murdered by Marakanders.

Goran—A lord of the Duina Catairna, loyal to the Seneschal and Marnoch.

Gurhan—Hill-god of Marakand, formerly served by a clan of hereditary priests.

Guthrun—A Northron caravaneer, camel-leech in Kharduin's gang.

The hag—Ahjvar's name for the ghost which possesses him.

Haildroch and Hallet—Catairnan wizards, kinsmen of the bard Lady Gelyn.

Hassin—Street-guard captain of the Riverbend Gate garrison in Marakand.

Haukbyrgga—The lake-goddess of Varro's folk.

Heuslar—Red-haired Northron wizard who became the devil Ogada, uncle of Red Geir.

Hicca—A lord of the Duina Catairna, allied with Ketsim, aspirant to the kingship of the Duina Catairna.

Holla-Sayan—A Westgrasslander caravan-guard, who unwillingly became the host for the Blackdog of Lissavakail and foster-father to the goddess Attalissa; now one with the Blackdog and a free agent. Husband of Gaguush.

Hravnmod the Wise—One of the first three kings in the north, brother of Ulfhild, said to have been slain by her.

Hyllanim—Son of Hyllau, successor of Cairangorm and Catairlau as king of the Duina Catairna on the Day of the Three Kings.

Hyllau—Second (and much younger) wife of Cairangorm, King of the

Duina Catairna. She is said in many songs to have murdered her husband; died on the day of the Three Kings.

Ilbialla—Goddess of a well in Sunset Ward in Marakand, patron of Sunset and Riverbend Wards, served by a single hereditary priest or priestess.

Iris—Third of Varro's and Talfan's four daughters.

Itulyan—A clerk in the Sunset Gate company of the street guard.

Ivah—A wizard, daughter of Tamghat, who was the devil Tamghiz Ghatai, though Ivah did not learn this until after his death.

Jasberek—One of the seven devils, merged with the wizard Anganurth.

Jasmel—Eldest daughter of Varro and Talfan.

Jing Xua—A street-guard lieutenant at the Eastern Wall.

Jiot—A dog, black and tan, one of two strays from the streets of Marakand that have chosen to follow Ghu.

Jochiz—One of the seven devils, called Jochiz Fireborn; bonded with the wizard Sien-Shava.

Judeh—A Marakander-born caravaneer of Gaguush's gang.

Jugurthos Barraya—Captain of the Sunset Gate fort of the Marakander street guard; son of two executed senators and dispossessed heir of the main branch of the Family Barraya.

Jui—A dog, white and ash-grey, one of two strays that have chosen to follow Ghu.

Kapuzeh—A member of Gaguush's gang, originally from the Stone Desert, brother of Django.

Keeper—Moth's sword, forged by the demon wolf-smith, inherited from her grandmother. "Keeper" is the meaning of its proper name, Kepra.

Kepra—Moth's Northron sword. For the inscriptions on it, see "The Storyteller."

Ketsim—A Grasslander claiming to be warlord of the Orange Banners; formerly among the chiefs of Tamghat the Lake-Lord's *noekar*, or vassals, and the governor of conquered Serakallash, now a mercenary hired with his followers to take the Duina Catairna for Marakand.

Kharduin—A caravan-master from the eastern deserts, Nour's partner in business and otherwise on the eastern road.

Kurman—A temple guardsman, cousin of Lieutenant Jing Xua.

The Lady of the Deep Well, Lady of Marakand—The foremost of the original three gods of Marakand, served by a large number of priests and priestesses. Though the most-worshipped of the three gods, she never appeared to any but her priests. The Voice of the Lady was her intermediary in dealings with the city. About thirty years before this story, following a devastating earthquake, she, through her Voice and temple, assumed rule of the city.

The Lake-Lord—Title taken by Tamghat (Tamghiz Ghatai) as ruler of Lissavakail.

Lakkariss—A black sword, possibly made of obsidian, belonging to Moth.

Launval the Elder—Praitannec lord, High King Durandau's champion.

Launval the Younger—Praitannec lord, one of High King Durandau's wizards.

The Leopard—see Ahjvar.

Lilace—The Voice of the Lady, assassinated by Ahjvar.

Lin—A wandering Nabbani wizard who entered High King Durandau's service, also tutor to Durandau's sister Deyandara.

Lu—A Five Cities caravaneer and horse-dealer involved with Nour and Hadidu in smuggling the wizard-talented out of Marakand.

Lug—A Grasslander warrior, one of the mercenary Ketsim's *noekar* and tent guard. Husband of Chieh.

Lysen—Ketsim's second wife, a Grasslander, in grief for whom he neglected his duties as chief of the tribe and was driven into exile by his brother.

Maca—Ketsim's long-dead first wife, a Grasslander.

Mag—A Catairnan wizard.

Mansour—Member of the family of priests of the Marakander hill-god Gurhan; father of Zora.

Marnoch—Queen Cattiga's chief huntsman, son of Lord Seneschal Yvarr, warleader of the Duina Catairna after Queen Cattiga's murder.

Mikki—Moth's demon lover, a *verrbjarn*, or werebear, bear by day and man by night; his father was a Northron sea-raider turned homesteader, his mother a bear demon of the Hardenwald and the guardian of the grave of the devil Vartu.

Moth—A Northern wanderer, wizard, warrior, storyteller, sister and King's Sword of Hravnmod the Wise, allegedly his murderer; the devil Ulfhild Vartu, called Kingsbane.

Mother Nabban, Father Nabban—River and mountain, the only gods of the Nabbani empire.

Nour—Marakander wizard and caravaneer of the eastern road, brother-in-law of Hadidu, business partner and lover of Kharduin.

Ogada—One of the seven devils, bonded with the Northron wizard Heuslar.

Orsa—The goddess of a stream and swamp in the Duina Catairna.

Orta Barraya—A street-guard captain stationed at the Eastern Wall.

Pagel—A Catairnan scout and soothsayer of Lord Fairu's household.

Pakdhala—Name used by the goddess Attalissa as Holla-Sayan's supposed daughter.

Palin—A bard and prince of the Duina Catairna, alleged true father of Deyandara, brother of Queen Cattiga.

Pazum—A magistrate of the suburb of Marakand.

Petrimos Barraya—Senator of Marakand, husband of his cousin Elias Barraya, father of Jugurthos; executed in the cages shortly after the earthquake.

Praitanna—Goddess of the River Praitanna and the Duina Praitanna, one of the seven tribes of Praitan; regarded as the greatest of the seven patron deities of the *duinas*.

Rahel—A Marakander priestess, Beholder of the Face of the Lady, wife of Ashir. Killed on Zora's orders.

Rasta—The elderly master of a caravanserai in Marakand's suburb, where Gaguush's gang usually puts up. Fond of cats.

Rozen—Catairnan scout appointed as Deyandara's servant.

Sayan—A god of the Sayanbarkash in the Western Grass, Holla-Sayan's god.

Senara—Older lady of a northern region of the Duina Catairna.

Sera—Goddess of Serakallash, a town in the Red Desert on the western caravan road.

Sessihz—One of the Twenty Families in Marakand.

Shaugh—One of Deyandara's bench-companions, that is, a warrior of her household, among her personal guard.

Shemal—Young son of Hadidu, nephew of Nour.

Shenar—Master of a caravanserai in Marakand's suburb where Kharduin's gang is lodged.

Shiwasa Xua—A senator of Marakand.

Sien-Mor—A wizard from the southern ocean who became the devil Tu'usha; younger sister of Sien-Shava. Her body was consumed past restoration by fire, though some aspect of her soul lives on within Tu'usha.

Sien-Shava—A wizard from the southern ocean who became the devil Jochiz; older brother of Sien-Mor.

Siman—A Grasslander, leader of Ketsim's rebellious sons.

Storm—A bone-horse, a necromantic creation anchored to a horse's skull; Storm appears to have ideas of his own, which a bone-horse should not.

Styrma—Storm's name in Northron.

Surey—A lieutenant in the Temple Guard and an agent of Revered Ashir, the Right Hand of the Lady.

Talfan—A Marakander apothecary, wife of Varro, mother of Jasmel, Ermina, Iris, and an infant daughter.

Talwesach—One of King Cairangorm's wizards in the Duina Catairna, a century or so ago.

Tamarisk—A Salt Desert girl newly hired into Gaguush's caravan gang.

Tamghat—Name used by the devil Tamghiz Ghatai when he conquered Lissavakail.

Tamghiz—Grasslander chieftain and wizard bonded with the devil Ghatai; onetime husband of Ulfhild; father of Ivah.

Thekla—A Westron woman in Gaguush's gang.

Tihma—A Marakander magistrate of the suburb.

Tihmrose—A Marakander woman in Gaguush's gang.

Tulip—Adjutant (and mistress) of Captain Jugurthos Barraya of the Sunset Gate garrison in Marakand.

Tu'usha—One of the seven devils, called Tu'usha the Restless by the Northron skalds; bonded with the wizard Sien-Mor.

Ulfhild of Hravnsfjall—King's Sword of Hravnmod the Wise and his younger sister; wizard who became the devil Vartu Kingsbane. She, however, maintains she did not murder her brother. Once married to Tamghiz; their children were Maerhild and Oern; see Moth.

Varro—A Northron man in Gaguush's gang, married to the Marakander apothecary Talfan.

Vartu—One of the seven devils, bonded with the wizard Ulfhild; see Moth.

Viga Forkbeard—One of the first three kings in the north.

Watcher—The apothecary Talfan's watchdog.

Xua—One of the Twenty Families of Marakand.

Yeh-Lin the Beautiful—A Nabbani wizard, courtesan, general, and regent, or possibly empress, depending upon which history you prefer to believe; became the devil Dotemon. Ruled Nabban again at some point after she became a devil.

Yselly—A Praitannec bard with whom Deyandara travelled as an unofficial apprentice, died from an adder's bite.

Yvarr—Seneschal of Queen Cattiga of the Duina Catairna, father of Marnoch.

Zavel—A Serakallashi-raised Grasslander in Gaguush's gang.

Zora—A dancer and musician in the temple of the Lady, daughter of Mansour, the only survivor of the massacre of the priests of Gurhan. Given to the Lady to be possessed as her new Voice, she chose to bond with the devil Tu'usha.

PART ONE

CHAPTER I

The man had been like an older brother to him ever since his parents had got him hired into the caravan-mistress Gaguush's gang, but sometimes Zavel could hate the self-righteous bastard of a Westgrasslander. Like now. All he had wanted was the loan of a few coins, but no, he got a tongue-lashing instead. As if Holla-Sayan had never had a drink or two more than sat well the next morning, or gone with an easy woman. And if that wasn't what he was up to now, skulking down the street with his eyes running anxiously to those two slim figures who'd walked ahead and were now waiting arm in arm, a Grasslander caravaneer with the long braids of the road and another with her Nabbani-black hair cut short as a Marakander boy's. That one looked around, wondering where her victim had got to.

Zavel had Holla-Sayan by the arm, stopping the man just walking off on him, and now he dug in his fingers. Gaped wordless a moment. Couldn't be. And Holla had been right with them, a hand under the Nabbani's elbow, all friendly, when Zavel had spotted the threesome, the Westgrasslander and the two women, one of whom was—*Ivah*. The past year hadn't treated her well. She was gaunt and pallid, but cutting her long hair was no disguise at all; he knew the sly narrow eyes, yellow-brown as his own, the delicate features and tight little mouth, bruised black as it was. She knew him, too. He saw her eyes widen in shock, and damn if she didn't look to Holla-Sayan in some appeal.

"Holla!" He let go Holla-Sayan's arm, pushed away from him. "*Ivah!* You murdering, bastard whore of the Lake-Lord, you—" His knife was in his hand and he leapt for her, reaching to grab her by the front of her coat, to jerk her close and into the stabbing blade, but he choked, jerked backwards himself by the hood of his coat, Holla, damn him, and he spun around, slashing. Holla-Sayan knocked his arm aside and a fist hit his jaw. He heard the thud of it, felt the jarring clack of his teeth. Then nothing.

Sense returned in retching, in white lights smearing and streaking his eyes. Zavel hunched up and groaned, realized the man bending over him groping in his pockets was probably not trying to be helpful, and hit him, hard, low, and everything he deserved, the sneaking Marakander thief. He found his knife and staggered away, leaving the man groaning and retching in turn behind him.

No sign of Holla-Sayan or the women. Sera curse him, Holla, sneaking off with *Ivah*, of all people. Of all the girls he could go chasing when he tired of the boss's temper, he was whoring around with the damned dead Lake-Lord's thrice-damned and treacherous, murdering pet wizard, the woman who'd cut Bikkim's throat for him, or had haughty I'm-too-good-for-a-bondman's-son Shaiveh do it for her to keep her own soft fingers clean. He'd have expected Holla to tear the throat of her as soon as look at her and leave her broken in the street for the real dogs to feast on.

Maybe that's what Holla-Sayan had been about?

Not bloody likely, with that gentle hand under the arm he'd seen when he first glimpsed the man. Subtlety, sweet-talking her off into some private corner where he could kill her tidily out of sight, wasn't Holla's way. No, at the first sight, first *sniff* of her, the monster that possessed him should have taken over. The Blackdog should have been shaking her like a rat, had the throat of her there and then on the street without ever a thought for what danger that brought down on the rest of the gang from the Red Masks, the wizard-hunting mute priests of the Lady of Marakand. Even if they did hardly ever come out to the suburb.

The damned wizard had bespelled Holla-Sayan. That explained it. She had bespelled the whole gang, once upon a time, won herself a place with them, got herself made tutor to Pakdhala when they'd all thought her Holla's bastard daughter, not knowing she was the goddess of Lissavakail, not knowing Holla-Sayan had been taken and possessed by the Blackdog. Monster mountain-spirit or not, Holla-Sayan hadn't been immune to Ivah's wizardry then. He'd fallen to it again, obviously. And how was Zavel supposed to rescue him? He didn't want to end *his* life with *his* neck snapped like a rat's, and Holla, once the dog took him over, was quite, quite mad. Anyway, Zavel had no idea where they'd gone. In bed somewhere, he supposed and damned if he was going to start checking every inn and tavern to save the fool from himself. Holla would come to his senses in time. Surely. It wasn't like Ivah was even very pretty, to hold a man for long. Of course, you couldn't call Gaguush pretty, either, and he'd married her, so maybe that wasn't what Holla went looking for.

Zavel's jaw ached, his head ached, he was tired and alone and he had no money. Hardly any money. A few coins left. He'd already had to pawn his father's sabre, the only inheritance he had from either parent, because Gaguush refused again to advance him any pay on the next trip. They treated him like a child. At least he had enough for a bite to eat. He didn't think he could chew. His jaw throbbed, and damned if Holla hadn't loosened a few teeth for him. Something to drink, though, would settle his stomach, stop the spinning in his head, while he thought what to do about Holla.

A drink, and another, because the sweet thin wine did help, and the luck of the Old Great Gods was with him. He found a Marakander looking to play a game of tables, one of those who came out to the caravanserai suburb thinking the caravaneers all drunken barbarians with the wits of their own camels, and he won the first and third of the three-game match, made a decent purse off the game and more off the betting, which had mostly been against him. Made himself scarce thereafter, because he didn't like the way the loser was eyeing him. He wasn't so drunk as all that.

Zavel walked out into a battle.

Well, not quite. There had been an unusual number of people rushing in and out of the tavern, so he should have guessed something was afoot, but playing tables meant having your wits about you, and he had shut out the stir and fuss, though it had distracted his opponent to some advantage, in that last game.

The street, a crooked lane off the main road, was empty but for a couple of running caravaneers. Noise, though, cries and yells, and there was a reek of heavy smoke. He followed the running men, mostly to get himself away from the tavern as quickly as he could, with the pocket of his coat nicely heavy. He had the vague idea of heading for the pawn-shop, which was down along closer to the graveyard at the Gore, and an even vaguer notion of seeing what all the noise was, in case Holla was doing something about Ivah at last, but when he rounded the corner onto the main road it was to a scene of chaos that took him right back to Lissavakail, where his father had died, where everything changed, and sometimes it seemed he'd lost not only the dead, but the living.

The road towards the Gore was obscured by black smoke. Buildings burned, scarlet flames climbing high, the air roaring with them. Screams and cries, the clash and ring of metal, animal roaring, too, came from there. Nearer, a smaller battle raged, women of the suburb and women of the road close engaged with Marakander temple guard in red tunics and leather armour, a twisting, tight knot of desperation. He couldn't see who was winning, wasn't such a fool as to rush into it, either way. Fighting street guard never came to any good end and temple guard—if they hauled you off before the Voice of the Lady, no, some assassin had murdered her, and the Lady, the goddess of the city, spoke for herself now, they said—if they hauled you off before the Lady, you'd certainly better hope the Old Great Gods had their hands over you, because nothing short of a miracle would save you then.

The caravaneers, outnumbered, broke and surged back. Zavel whirled to run with them; it was that or be taken gawking there by the temple guard pursuit. Sera damn him for a fool, he tripped and stumbled along and missed his chance to dart away up the lane again when someone helpfully grabbed his arm to steady him. They didn't run far, just to get their backs against the corner made by a caravanserai's outthrust entryway. Its gate was firmly shut. Spears were levelled at the fore, a wounded woman shoved away to the back.

"Here," she gasped in passing, a Black Desert woman with tattoos the same red and black as the boss's, but not so thick and heavy. Her lips were going grey. She pushed her blood-slippery spear into Zavel's empty hands before staggering down, trying to bind up the wound in her own thigh with her headscarf. No one spared a hand to help. The temple guard came in a rush.

Lissavakail all over again, in miniature. Zavel chose his man and braced himself. He'd always had a good eye; the spear's point found the weak join he'd marked at the neck, bit, and he thrust and twisted, jerked back, but the damned thing stuck and the man was a screeching, flailing dead weight, pulling it down, and he lost his grip on the slick shaft. It was all close-in work by then anyway, sabres and the stabbing swords of the Marakanders. Not the place for his knife, but he slashed to fend off a Marakander boy, kicked and screamed himself, trying to weave his way back out of it, out of the way of those who had sabres and shields and some chance of surviving.

New yells, sweeping from behind. The caravanserai doors had opened and more folk of the road, Marakanders too, rushed out, all armed. They crashed against the temple-guard flank and the guardsmen fell away, running, outnumbered now, hah. Zavel grabbed up an abandoned short sword and joined the pursuit. A man fell before him, tripped and rolling, and Zavel swung aside to finish him. Flat on his back, the man drew his legs back and kicked him in the gut before he could dodge. He lost his grip on the sword and fell himself, doubled up, nearly lost what little he had in his stomach, gasping for air, and then they were grappling together, kicking and punching, both of them grabbing for lost swords. The man got him by the braids, dragged him, half-rising, and Zavel kicked him down again, jabbed a knee in his belly, found his knife, but the guardsman seized him by the scalp this time and slammed him down against the road. Red fire lanced across sight and his ears roared. Vision blurred. He squirmed sideways. The guardsman's two-foot staff was raised in his hand, teeth grimacing in a blood-masked face. The cudgel came down.

Someone was screaming in his dreams, shrill and terrified. His sister, Zavel thought, but he couldn't remember which one. He lurched to hands and knees, squinting at over-bright light and gulping against sickness. Not a girl screaming, not one of his little sisters, murdered by the men of Tamghat the Lake-Lord or taken for bond-servants or who knew what dire fate, but certainly lost, long lost. Not his mother, who had walked into a sandstorm in her despair. No, in his nightmares she never cried out at all, but beckoned, beckoned, and grinned, while the red dust of Serakallash whipped around her and her skin dried to leather on her face . . .

He was not dreaming at all. A woman was screaming, her voice rising piercingly over the wind-storm roar of other voices. Muzzily, Zavel blinked sense back into his thudding head. He was going to be sick. He had been. His mouth was foul and he lay in reeking filth, the dust of the road made muck with blood and bile and wine. If he'd fallen on his back he'd be choked and dead now. He pushed himself to hands and knees, shaking and shivering with cold, and crawled. He'd been lying close up against a wall. He got his back against it and just sat a moment, trying to sort out how bad it was. The screaming drilled into him and his empty belly roiled as fingers found the swollen lump of his jaw, the broken, sticky-crusted egg-lump on his head, far worse. He remembered the guardsman's cudgel. The man must have thought he was dead, or the Marakander bastard would have finished him. He'd had a sword.

No swords here now. There was his knife, though. He'd been lying on it. He crawled to pick it up, slow and shaky, found the sheath still in the big square pocket of his coat and the other still heavy with coin. That was something.

No Marakander guardsmen, street or temple, in sight. Whatever that boiling-over of rage had been about, the caravaneers must have won it. It was folk of the road mobbing the house across the street. He peered, blurrily. Desert folk and Grasslanders, Northrons and Westrons and Nabbani of the east. The woman screaming, she was Marakander, or at least, she was dressed like it, in a fine embroidered caftan, and they were dragging her stumbling down the steps. Not a shop, but a fairly grand, yellow-plastered house that would have looked less out of place in Palace Ward or by the Silvermarket. The porter lay limp before the door, and another, younger woman shouted, "Cowards! Traitors! Help her!" as she tried to struggle after the captive.

Someone stabbed the young woman in the midriff with a spear, and she just stood staring down at it, the dark stain spreading, till they jerked it away and she fell out of sight down the stairs, into the crowd, and a skinny man, another Marakander, staggered into the doorway, bleeding about the head. Mouth open, he slammed the door against the mob. Coward, too, or maybe wise. Zavel watched, a bit stunned, as if it were all a dream. That wasn't a fight; that was filthy murder. In broad daylight—murky, smoke-dulled daylight. In law-bound Marakand.

The older woman kept on screaming and pleading.

"Let me go! I've done nothing to you, I'm no priestess! Help! Someone help! I'm a magistrate of the city, a magistrate of the suburb! You know me, Old Great Gods witness, you all know me, I had no part in this, I knew nothing of it, I've wronged no wizards—" and then the threats, "You've murdered my clerks. The Lady sees, the Lady knows, the Voice will speak your names, you'll all die condemned in the cages for this, outlanders or no, you're not beyond Marakand's law . . . help! Help me!"

They dragged her away up the street, towards the city, and her cries changed again to wordless screaming.

Zavel staggered to his feet to follow, uncertainly, not even sure why, except that he didn't know what was going on, and the only way to find out was to follow. The threat of temple guard and Red Masks seemed past. He snagged the sleeve of a man with caravaneer's braids and Stone Desert tattoos.

"The temple—" he said. "They'll come. They'd better let her—"

"Didn't you see? The demons slew the Red Masks, and the Lady's put to flight!"

"What?" But the man pulled away from him, outdistancing his unsteady steps. "What demons?" Zavel called, but nobody answered.

There were bodies, far more than had been mixed into the fight he'd taken part in; the street stank like a butcher's market. Here the corpses were scattered like river-edge flotsam, in drifts and swirls amid the shops and warehouses and caravanserais just before the Gore, the triangle of land between the branching roads to the Riverbend and Sunset Gates. Zavel picked his way over men and women lying still, flies already settling in buzzing black carpets. Strange, how very still the dead, how different from the sleeping. You'd never mistake them. He wouldn't. Not anymore. Folk of the road. Folk of the suburb. Temple guard. Many temple guard, in their red tunics and armour, and Red Masks, in crimson-lacquered scale and masked helmets, but people were pulling the helmets away and dragging them into rows, and there was none of the crowing he would have expected, the exuberance of victory over the feared and hated mute priests, only a horrible solemnity. What in all the cold hells had been happening?

No flies swarmed on the slain Red Masks.

There was weeping. People were seeking their own slain. There was crying and moaning, prayer and pleading. The wounded, the dying. He ignored them, ignored the burning buildings, the shouting, the knot of fighting that broke out between Marakanders of the suburb and caravaneers. They weren't his dead, his wounded, his friends, he wasn't theirs; no one was left to claim him. If that temple guardsman had hit a bit harder, if Sera's hand hadn't been on him (if it was on him at all—his exiled Grasslander parents had never let their Serakallashi children be tattooed and claimed for the goddess of their birth), he might be one of those dead lying in the streets, and would Holla-Sayan have come looking for him, or Gaguush, or any of them? Probably not. Nobody had gone to look for his mother, when she walked into the dust-storm.

The gang dragging the magistrate took the northerly fork at the Gore and then crossed the bridge over the dry ravine to Riverbend Gate, where a sizeable crowd seethed and roared, beating against the timbers with what looked like the charred roof-beam of a house. There were street guard on the roofs of both the squat, square towers that flanked the gate, but they weren't doing anything. Not worried by the improvised ram. People clawed rocks from the road and hurled them. Nobody among the attackers seemed to have a bow. What were they shouting? *Murders, devil-lovers . . . Tamghati . . . ?* Ketsim, Tamghat's governor of Serakallash, had escaped, fled and formed a mercenary band from the Lake-Lord's surviving followers. The temple had hired them, but they'd all been sent east to deal with some barbarian tribe that menaced the city, or so Zavel had heard.

"Send out the Lady!" they cried. "Give up the necromancer!"

Necromancer?

"Open the gate!" a new voice roared, a Red Desert man gripping the magistrate by an arm. "Captain, open the gate, or we kill the magistrate."

The woman shrieked and tried to wrench herself away, but too many hands held her and she was flung back and forth like a child's doll that had fallen prey to a puppy. Her ornately piled hair had come loose, spilling about her face in wild hanks.

"Let us in!" someone shouted, and most took up the chant. "Let us in, let us in."

"We want the Lady!"

"Bring out the Lady!"

"Show us your false goddess . . ."

". . . necromancer . . ."

". . . devil!"

Devil? Zavel did not want to be here. Where was Holla-Sayan? Still off whoring with Tamghat's wizard? Did these fools think they could do anything against a devil, if it did come to the gate? He began to struggle away, but more than he had followed the magistrate's captors, and a crowd had closed up behind him, everyone shoving and shifting to keep their balance, trying to see, trying to hear. Many were taking up the cry of those closer to the gate, and the ones with the ram had propped the beam up like a ladder. Someone was inching up it like a cautious squirrel, though it didn't reach high enough for him to gain the arch over the gate unless he meant to perch atop it like a bird. For a moment attention was distracted. Soldiers in grey tunics and leather armour leaned from the parapet over the gate and shoved at the head of the beam with spears. It slid sideways with a terrible slowness at first, while the climbing man clutched it and cursed, curses changing to a shriek as it passed its tipping point and plunged. Zavel didn't see him hit, just heard the thump, the silence, the swell of roaring renewed.

"Devil's servants!" shouted the ringleader of the hostage-takers. "Let us in to the necromancer, or the magistrate dies and her blood will be on your hands!"

"I'll let you in," an officer called down, and there was silence. He was an old man, grey-haired, weary-faced, with two black ribbons trailing from his helmet and two wide black bands on the hem of his grey tunic. A captain. He stood in a crenel of the wall, exposing himself to any missile, a hand gripping the edge of a merlon with fingers like claws, as if he really, really did not like his perch. No one threw a stone. Yet. "You and the magistrate, no other. We'll talk about this."

"Open your gates!"

"And let drunken murder loose on the folk of the city? You know I can't do that." The captain was trying to sound reasonable, to pretend he thought the man making the demands could be reasonable. "I don't know anything of devils, but—"

"Open the gates! Open the gates!"

Zavel really did not want to be in the middle of this. His stomach churned and his skin was clammy, slick with sweat. He was going to be sick, he knew it. He needed to get out of this close and reeking crowd, get some air, a drink of water, needed to sit down somewhere quiet and let this damnable headache pass.

A couple of big Northrons had axes out and were hewing at the gate, long splinters slivering away. The crowd surged forward around a woman who'd got an improvised torch alight. They piled sticks and rags and dry dead weeds to kindle a fire. The ones about the magistrate were hurling her back and forth among them as she wailed like a baby, arms raised, clutching her head, trying to protect herself. They threw her to the ground and kicked her, took the butts of spears to her head and back as she rolled and hunched up small. The captain was gone from the crenel, and a spatter of arrows from above scattered them, left the ringleader lying dead, with others still or yelling, dragging themselves wounded. The magistrate tried to crawl but only flopped like a landed fish.

People shoved and shrieked and the guards above kept shooting, not a battlefield rain of arrows but carefully, picking targets. Zavel fell, unsteady on his feet, retching again, but he crawled anyway. Safer to keep low amid the legs. Someone walked on his hand, someone tripped on him, someone fell and didn't move, and he half rose and scuttled, yelling with the rest, but in his dizziness he'd gotten turned the wrong way and he tripped over the battered magistrate. She moaned, not dead, but her face was a blood-slick pulp with only one eye, which stared wide and unseeing in its terror. Zavel yelled again and rocked away. But nobody had gone looking for his mother. Too late, they said. The sand took her. He dragged the magistrate's arm over his shoulder, shouted at her, "Up, stand up, come on!" Somehow he heaved her up, though she dangled limp, feet fumbling. An arrow stuck the ground at his feet and he looked around wildly for shelter, any shelter, a bush would do. Nothing. Shouting. Guardsmen over the gate were dumping jar after jar of water down onto the fire, which hadn't done more than stain the gate with soot, and the ram-carriers had fled, though some of the mob were sheltering behind a cart abandoned on the bridge, whatever beast had drawn it gone.

"The gate!" someone was yelling. "Old Great Gods, man, the gate, now, hurry!" and it was him that she shouted at, a guardswoman up on the tower, gesturing.

Zavel looked to see one leaf of the axe-scarred gate drawn back, just a handsbreadth. He didn't for a moment understand, till the magistrate moaned again.

Great Gods, yes, the gate. He broke into an unsteady run, the magistrate a dead weight dragging half behind him. He caught a toe in the pit left by up-prised paving stones and fell, both of them striking heavily, struggled up and heard voices behind him. Looked back. Shouldn't have. Blood-crazed men daring the arrows, running to overtake him. Arrows from the towers took some, gave the others pause, but a hurled javelin bit into the magistrate's thigh as he dragged her on again, and then a man was hauling her from his grasp, another grabbing him, and he himself was pulled bodily through the gate as another thrown spear thudded against its timbers. It thumped shut again, the bars dropping home.

It was the grey-haired captain himself who had come out for the woman, and he swung her up like a child, running with her now, down the long arch of the gateway, turning through a dark doorway where guardsmen crowded. Zavel, with less urgency, was trundled after by other street guard.

He ended up in a windowless room with a table and a couple of chairs; they dumped him on a long bench along one wall, where he sat, a bit dazed. A watch-room, Zavel supposed, where the duty officer would be found and the clerks would scratch away at recording whatever it was the Marakanders were so keen on always writing down, yes, there were tablets and a big ledger on the table, and through another doorway a single, barred cell, the gate-fort's gaol, where brawlers and curfew-breakers would cool their heels overnight. Not, for a change, his destination. Someone pounded him on the shoulder and said, "Good man!" He clenched his teeth, which made his jaw hurt worse, and shut his eyes, holding his throbbing head.

That brought a woman's solicitous murmuring, and he was given a blanket, offered a cup of sweetened wine and a warm, wet towel for his wounds. Gentle, efficient hands bound up his head. It helped, at least when he lay down afterwards, eyes shut against the glaring clay lamps in the wall-niches opposite. He breathed carefully, to keep all within still and settled.

A hand on his shoulder shook him awake. Zavel rubbed his eyes. However long he'd been sleeping, it hadn't been enough. A fraction of a watch, no more, maybe, but now he had a stiff back to go with his sick headache. The grey-haired captain was sitting at the table, with a clerk beside him, stylus and tablet in hand. Typical Marakanders: you couldn't tell which folk their ancestors had come from. Like their languages and their very names, picked up bits of this and that. The clerk was a pug-nacious-looking bastard for a soft-handed scribe, with his crooked, flat-tened nose. He'd be the one to fear most if he had to bolt, Zavel was sure. A young guardswoman helped him to sit up, smiling anxiously, and pressed a cup into his hand. He smiled back. Thick-curling hair and a dark, heart-shaped face, well worth smiling at. He wasn't going to have to run. These were his friends, now. The cup was coffee this time, thick and steaming. He couldn't stand the stuff, but it wasn't exactly cheap, though even the poorest Marakanders made shift to drink it; it came all the way from beyond the Gulf of Taren and the Narrow Sea out of the south. You didn't give your prisoners coffee, so he murmured his thanks and sipped it. The sweetness seemed to settle his stomach some.

The captain cleared his throat. "I'm sorry to have to tell you, young man, that Magistrate Tihma has taken the road to the Old Great Gods, Lady bless her."

"I didn't—" Of course they weren't accusing him. "I didn't know her name," he amended, and added, "I'm sorry."

"Your courage is all the greater for that," the captain said earnestly. "To risk your life for a stranger . . ."

In the darkness behind him, a shadow stirred, and Zavel realized there was another man in the room, another guardsman. The other stepped forward. Temple guard, a man with a single ribbon to his helmet and a single dark stripe on his red tunic showing below the leather skirt of his armour. An under-officer of some sort.

"Captain Hassin would like to commend you," the temple man said. "But I would like to know what other part you played in the uprising and assault on the gates."

"None!" Zavel protested. "I—I was only passing by, I saw the—I saw Magistrate Tihma being pulled from her house and I followed. An old woman! I don't know what's going on, I don't know what's caused this madness in the suburb, it's nothing to do with me, but I couldn't let—it was just wrong, beating an old woman to death that way. I—I waited till I saw a chance I could help her. I—she made me think of my mother."

The temple officer nodded. "Naturally." He appeared to consider something, but Zavel had grown up in market bargaining and on the road; he wasn't wet behind the ears when it came to such things, and the man had already decided whatever it was he affected to consider. Zavel's stomach clenched.

"These are sad times for our city," the temple officer said. "The Lady has always looked on the folk of the road as friends of the city, and it will be a great sorrow to her that the outlanders of the suburb have been so misled by the lies of this wizard."

"Wizard?" Zavel asked, confused now. It had been demons, hadn't it, that the caravaneer had told him of?

"A Grasslander woman—or Nabbani, I've heard both. A great wizard commanding demons. For a lifetime the Voice of the Lady has warned of the evil wizards would bring and it's finally come to pass. We could use a man who might know how to keep his ears open—"

"Wait, this wizard. Sir. You said a Grasslander or a Nabbani? You don't mean Ivah?"

"You know of her? Is that her name?"

"I don't—probably. She's a servant of Tamghat. The Lake-Lord, the one defeated by the goddess Attalissa last summer in Lissavakail in the mountains. I was—" Probably best not to claim any closer acquaintance with Attalissa. The Lady was said to fear other gods, too.

Both officers fixed him in a keen stare, waiting, and the clerk scratched swiftly at his wax.

"I—I just heard. I met her once or twice."

"I came here to get a report on the assault on the gates for the Revered Right Hand of the Lady," the temple man said. "But your witness could be much more useful than what Hassin here's been able to tell me."

The street-guard captain frowned at this. He didn't like it. Well, if it came to a choice between street guard and temple, Zavel had a feeling the temple was the one to align himself with. Street guard were mere thief-takers, after all, and had to give way to the Lady's men. Look at this one-stripe man walking all over the gate-captain, and in his own fort, too. The clerk looked up, glanced at his officer, and went back to scratching.

"Captain Hassin would like to give you a pat on the back and turn you loose," the temple man went on. "I, however, think perhaps I should arrest you. You were clearly part of the assault. Perhaps you saw 'rescue' of the unfortunate magistrate as a way of ensuring your safety, when you realized the futility of storming the Lady's gates?"

"I never thought at all! I just—"

"And you seem to have great knowledge of the leadership of this uprising. You know their commander's name."

"I only guess—"

"In her inner counsels, perhaps?"

"That traitor? I'd cut her throat if I got close enough! If it is her at all," Zavel added hastily. "I never saw any evidence she was that great a wizard. A soothsayer, nothing more. But she was a liar, too. Probably she lied about that. And a murderer—"

"However," said the temple officer, "perhaps I do believe you. I could arrest you. I should arrest you. However, if you were to volunteer to come with me, the Right Hand would likely take that as earnest of good intent and honest goodwill towards the Lady. Any information we can put together about this wizard, now, is bound to be an offering the Lady will approve."

"If you can get me next to Ivah with a sabre in my hands, I'll even join your temple guard," Zavel said hotly. "I had nothing to do with whatever's going on out there, I'm an honest caravaneer—"

"We do need your name and gang, for our records," Captain Hassin said.

"No," said the temple man decidedly, "you don't. Young man." And he came around the table, taking Zavel's arm to help him up, a bit roughly. "That will be all, Hassin. Send your report to me—Lieutenant Surey of the second company—and be sure to include how Magistrate Tihma came to be murdered with an entire company of street guard looking on."

He swept out, dragging Zavel stumbling with him.

A change in his fortunes, definitely, but whether for good or ill, Zavel wasn't about to guess. If it gave him a chance at Ivah, though . . . and Holla was mad. Was he making war on a goddess now? It looked that way, if he was one of the demons the caravaneer had been going on about. The monster inside him had corrupted his soul and broken his mind, turned him against his friends and all right thinking. A devil in the city was lies and nonsense. Tamghati lies. Some scheme Ivah and Governor Ketsim had cooked up to turn the suburb against the goddess. Odds were Ketsim and his Tamghati mercenaries weren't off fighting in the east after all, odds were they were coming back up the eastern road and would be at Marakand's gates before you knew it. Ketsim and Ivah had been working closely together when they abducted Pakdhala—and the Lady's people would not only give him a chance to pay the lying wizard back for that, and avenge his parents' deaths, but maybe even reward him, if he could help them stop her. It wasn't like he had a gang to go back to. Gaguush had sacked him when he asked her for money yesterday, and in his heart of hearts he'd known this time she meant it. Besides, he wasn't happy bedding down for the night with a possessed madman sleeping so near, out in the empty desert, not at all. Holla's pacing and prowling in the dark was enough to give anyone the creeps.

They were always telling him to grow up and take a man's place in the world. Time he did.

CHAPTER II

A dozen men and two women stood before her, not one daring a whisper, not one daring raise eyes to meet the gaze of their goddess. They stood close-bunched and cowed before the high pulpit, the surviving officers of the company of the temple guard who had gone to the caravanserai suburb with the Lady of Marakand and her Red Masks, her silent, invulnerable, divinely blessed and protected warrior-priests. But those Red Masks had been proven very vulnerable indeed, to the magic of a yellow-eyed Grasslander wizard who rode into battle on a demon bear of the north, with what could only be the Blackdog of Lissavakail a tide of death before her.

That was neither here nor there. These, these had proven coward, all the temple guard had, faithless betrayers who broke and ran when they found the shield of the Red Masks did not protect them. They had failed their oaths, failed their faith, failed *her*, their goddess, when they found that the folk of the suburb, who ought to have been cowering unmanned and witless before the divine terror of her servants, were willing and able to fight. They had thought they went at no risk to themselves to arrest wizards made impotent and witless by the divine blessing of those same Red Masks, to take for the Lady's well even the least of the diviners who had thought themselves safe and outside the Lady's ban and reach, beyond Marakand's city walls. They were used to such easy tasks, secure in the shadow of the Lady's greater servants.

That the folk had lost their terror of the Red Masks—no, that the divine blessing of terror had been stripped from them by inexplicable wizardry—did not excuse the cowardice of the temple guards. To fail and flee because you found the enemy capable of fighting back was the mark of a bully, not a soldier. Zora had told them so.

No captain stood among them. He was dead, killed by caravaneers, outlanders. He had not been standing, no, that she had seen. He had died running, knocked down from behind, hacked and pummelled to death in the dust. A fitting end for a coward. The company's senior lieutenant, nearly unable to stand, one eye bloodied, cheek open and not yet stitched, had done no better, except that he had lived to make it to the gate.

As had she. She had fled with the rest of them.

That was different. That was . . .

. . . a sensible tactic. She had needed to remove her Red Masks from danger. Without them . . . without them the city might fall, without them she might fail, and what followed her failure. . . . She had been right to run, to take her damaged Red Masks out of reach of the wizard and her demons. Yes. She had brought them back to the temple, even the one stationed at the Eastern Wall to watch for Praitannec enemies, and the one at the Western. Did she dare leave the Eastern Wall unwatched by eyes she trusted? The first whisper of this, the first stir and swirl of a changing current, had not come from within the city. There had been a spy. Spies? The first Red Mask to die had died there. She had nearly forgotten. She had not been Zora then.

Doubt would cripple her. She had enemies all about her and she did not even know who they might be. She had sent her captain and his Red Masks, all who were not now in the city, east to Praitan, but death came from the west, from the north, not east.

North? No.

The sword of the ice. . . . She had muttered that aloud. She heard the words. Zora pinched her lips together.

A small sound escaped the huddled guards. One of the women, stifling a whimper. Weak. Other than the senior lieutenant, they were all patrol-firsts, the leaders of five-man units modelled on the patrols of the street guard. Leaders of their patrols. Examples to their men. These were the ones who had swept with their goddess through the Riverbend Gate.

Retreated. Fled. And some part of Zora's heart crowed, a part that might still be Zora.

Fool child. *I am we are Zora is we are the Lady of Marakand.*

The Lady, their goddess, surveyed them. Not vengeful. Not disdainful. Sorrowful, yes. Pitying their weakness, their frailty.

No. The Lady could not harbour the weak and the frail. Marakand must be strong. *He* would come against her, out of the west, and Marakand must be strong. Yes.

"The Lady sees your hearts," she said from the pulpit, and the fourteen, huddling together on the swirling mosaic floor on which she had so often danced when she was only Zora, when she was only the foremost of the temple dancers, when she was the hidden eyes, the spy of her father's stillborn rebellion against the tyranny of the Lady—they watched her, as the hypnotized bird watches the snake.

They had hope. The Lady was mercy.

Who says so? The Lady. Fools if you believe her.

Hush.

Behind them the priests and priestesses, saffron-robed, clustered. Fear was a rank cloud over them. Red Masks had died. The caravanserai suburb had risen against the Lady's arrest of wizards. The gates were under attack. Enemies, treachery, hidden wizards . . . disorder. They liked their safe order, her priests. She had taught them so.

"Never," she said, "has Marakand faced such danger as it does now. Rebels walk secretly among the folk of the suburb, of the city itself, spreading the poison of their lies. Foreign wizards and demons work against us. And what strength have we? Not the strength of arms, if the faith of those arms is weak. Weakness betrays us. Weakness *has* betrayed us. When the temple guard should have stood firm, to protect their comrades-in-arms, my chosen, my Red Masks, from appalling wizardry, from foreign demons and spirits and the servants of alien gods, they fled, squalling like children and about as much use."

Unfair. *She* had fled, had she not?

She must give them an explanation for that, a reason, an enemy, a plan. Not her own fear, her death in—

—the sword the ice is coming the road of the stars is sealed against the ice is coming—

Zora's hands clutched the pulpit rail and she licked her lips. She was not the Voice, the mad Voice, to spill the eddying mind of the goddess. She was not mad. Mad Sien-Mor was dead and burnt away. She was Zora now. Zora was not mad. Zora had not spoken aloud, the words echoed only her mind, she did not taste them on her tongue, she would not, she could not, she—

Be still, be still, be still.

"The Lady sees your hearts," she said. "The Lady knows your hearts. Your coward hearts. Your traitor hearts. And I say, treachery must be cut out. There is no place for such weakness and cowardice within my temple. When I say stand, you stand. When I say hold, you hold. You do not doubt. You do not break. You do not run. You stand and hold and die, if that is what serves your Lady's need. As it would have, this day, had you not been faithless."

No, no, *no no no—don't, I won't, I can't I must—*

She had no need for orders, for gestures. The Red Masks were hers, as her arms and legs were hers. The most faithful of her priests, so even the true priests believed, the holy warriors, with their vows of simplicity and silence, their isolated barracks where not a single servant attended them . . . fools. Even Zora, spying for the dead, had not penetrated to the heart of that secret, though she had wondered, she had known there was some truth that she could not see. A poor, lorn spy without a master to take her reports.

Still, for the sake of the priests, she raised a hand. It might have been a signal. But it was her thought that sent her attendant Red Masks, grim in their silence, faceless, to the unfortunate officers.

No need for their swords, for mess and blood and the fouling of the black-and-white floor on which she had danced. Like the street guard, the thief-takers, her Red Masks carried short staves at their belts. The white lightnings of her will, their wizardry, crackled as they struck, a blow to the back of the head, to the chest, a smashed face as the already-bloodied lieutenant turned yelling to flee. A single blow was enough to kill. The room smelt of scorching, of burnt meat.

Sacrifice.

"The remainder of the company," she said, when it was done, when a fainting priestess had been shunted aside amid her fellows' feet and a vomiting priest had made it as far as the porch before disgracing himself and her holy Hall of the Dome, "will be confined to their barracks. No surgeon will attend the wounded. Let them look to themselves, let the Old Great Gods choose their own. They will have barley-porridge and water and nothing more. They will purify themselves. Let them offer me prayers and face the truth of their own hearts, for three days. In three days, they will be summoned here to the Hall of the Dome to stand before their Lady, and she will *I will* give my judgement."

They would be redeemed and love her for her forgiveness, their redemption. She would appoint new patrol-firsts, a new captain and pair of lieutenants. She could not afford to lose so many men. But they did not need to know that.

"Revered Lady—"

It was Ashir who dared to speak, the Right Hand of the Lady, highest-ranking of the priests, a bald and bitter man, loving her, hating her. The Beholder of the Face, his wife, had died by her command, flung down the stairs to the underground chamber of the deep well. Yet he still loved his Lady, and he still served. But she did not love him.

"No," she said, to whatever it was. "I will not hear. I will speak no more. I will speak no more judgements today, I will—just go! Out! Out, all of you! Out from this place, out from here, out with your noise and your doubts and your coward fears, out and pray yourselves, and pray I am merciful, because I know not all the traitors of the city are without the temple walls!"

Her voice rose to a shriek in her own ears and her hands twisted together.

"The sword waits still, can't you see? Don't you hear me? The sword is ice, the ice is death and from the north it came to me for me not here not now does she not see, does she not know? I have trapped her held her she would have betrayed me she should have seen she should have known she should have come to me to stand with me—It is he it is not I she should fear we should fear she is nothing she is gone she is lost and trapped and gone and still the sword waits unsleeping it sees my dreams it whispers it sings the voice of the wind of the ice of the night—the stars, the cold and distant stars they see—"

She bit her tongue. The taste of blood shocked and silenced her.

The priests stared. They were used to the ranting prophecies of the Voice of the Lady, but she was not the Voice. She was the Lady made flesh, in the flesh of Zora, the dancer they would have given to be her new Voice. She was—

I don't know. I don't know anymore. Who am I who speaks?

"Get out!" she screamed, and the Red Masks moved.

The priests and priestesses fled.

The Red Masks began dragging out the bodies. Let the priests see to some burial, somehow. Let them prove their use by dealing with that one small problem, with the city gates sealed and no access to the grave-yard of the Gore.

Zora was going to be vomiting behind a pillar herself if she could not get out of here, into air, clean air, and space and sky and—

Up. Climb. Yes. To where she could breathe again.

The goddess, the Lady of Marakand incarnate, took the stairs so rarely used, cramped and dark, hidden with the walls, the passage left for workmen who might need sometimes to make repairs. She ran, forcing herself not to slow, revelling in the pounding of her soldier-booted feet, her racing heart. This, this was hers, this body, this strength, this lean beauty, this was she. She came out on the roof below the dome. There, for a moment at least, she had silence. Even in her own mind. Though not for long.

CHAPTER III

"**M**y wife!" the old man at the gate howled. "Gate-Captain, look! Witness! My wife!"

But what the old man held in his arms, staggering with the weight of it, arms and legs and long hair dangling limp, was the red-armoured corpse of a Red Mask. Jugurthos Barraya, captain of the Sunset Gate Fort, looked down from the northerly of his towers. He didn't know the man. Some small trader of the suburb, by his dress. He was surrounded—supported, maybe—by a score or so of others, Marakanders and caravaneers both. Even from the tower Jugurthos couldn't see what was happening around the bend of the wall to the north, but he had seen a band of temple guard and Red Masks rushing disordered to the east, and after them, pursuing, a surge of outlanders, armed, out of the smoking suburb. *Pursuing.* Red Masks *fleeing.* He'd sent a courier to Hassin at Riverbend Gate for news, but the girl hadn't returned yet. Nothing worse had befallen than that she was waiting on Hassin, he hoped, and not caught up in some assault. The all-in curfew had rung from Riverbend shortly after that, and his own bells had perforce passed it on. It shouldn't have kept his courier, though.

If what had rushed east along the main road past the Gore had been an attack, this small party that had peeled off to take the road to the southern bridge and his gate seemed peaceable enough, thus far. Grim, though, and angry, violence only a word away, not that the bare score below could offer the gates any serious threat.

"Witness!" the man called again.

"Witness what?" Jugurthos called down. "A Red Mask?" A dead Red Mask, and they were invulnerable, protected from weapon and wizardry by the Lady's blessing. They killed with a touch. What could touch them? That, indeed, needed witnessing. If it were true, and not some trickery, a corpse wrapped in a red cloak. Yet, that armour would be hard to come by and . . . there was a story going around that a Red Mask had died at the Eastern Wall not long before the Voice was killed. He had dismissed it as exaggeration, some mere temple guard murdered, even though he had heard it from Captain Hassin of Riverbend, who swore he had the story from his cousin, who saw the corpse, from some distance, before another Red Mask carried the priest away.

"What killed her? How?"

"My wife!" the man howled, and he laid the corpse down, kneeling over it, and stroked a dead, smooth cheek with his old, twisted hand.

Jugurthos felt his stomach turn. Surely—

"Don't you dare," his adjutant muttered beside him. "Captain, don't."

He looked down at her. Tulip only came up to his shoulder, a compact woman, young for her responsibilities, with the round face and straight hair of the mountain-folk. She hadn't even been a patrol-first when he appointed her his adjutant, and given her physique, which was rather better filled-out in all the right places than you'd expect of an unwanted bastard abandoned and farmed out on temple charity, everyone was fairly certain they knew why.

Useful to let them think so, of course. That, on the other hand, she *was* his mistress, was just a further obscuration.

Yeah, right, she would say. You really know how to make a girl feel wanted, Captain.

Jugurthos pushed away from the parapet. "I'm coming down," he called to the old man and strode for the stairs. Tulip, muttering imprecations, scurried after him. A patrol was just coming in; she drafted them as escort, grabbed a spear from his office—one of the few weapons not locked in the armoury—and glowered to the point that Jugurthos swallowed any protest.

There was no sally-port in either gate-tower; they had to haul back a leaf of the main gates enough for the seven of them to slip out, two by wary two, with Jugurthos, giving in to Tulip's common sense, in the middle. None of the mob beyond moved towards them, parting, rather, and standing back to give them passage. The old man had gathered the Red Mask into his arms again, held her on his lap, head lolling against his shoulder. He glared at them through tears, said nothing now but stroked the hair from her face.

A woman in her prime, which the old man was definitely not, dark-haired. Jugurthos had seen corpses enough, victims of family quarrels and drunken brawls, sullen, stealthy murders, and alley robberies. This was different. Old. Her skin was dry and tinged with grey, the staring eyes cloudy, the lips shrivelled, colourless. No stink of death, though, and not the greasy, horrid rot of that infant's corpse unearthed from a rubbish heap by stray dogs last winter. He swallowed against that memory and warily crouched, to put a hand to the face himself. Dry. Neither warm nor cold, like touching wood, cloth. The old man blinked at him.

"Your wife," he prompted, and fingered the slick lacquered leather of the armour scales, the crimson cloak, which up close was tattered, faded, and unexpectedly gritty to the touch, as if it had never been washed or even brushed clean.

"They took her," the old man said. "The week after they built that tomb for Ilbialla and butchered her priestess. You wouldn't remember, you're too young. You think there was always a tomb there in Sunset Market, but—"

"I remember," Jugurthos said. He was hardly so young as all that. Tulip put a warning hand on his shoulder. "Go on. Who took her?"

"Red Masks. They came—I worked with my brother in those days, and we lived up above his shop, at the back. Sandal-makers, he and I. Aylnia read the coins, the Nabbani divination, but it didn't bring in much, more just as a favour for neighbours, you know, and half the time nothing came to her and she just told them what she thought they wanted. Joking, almost, between friends. They came, Red Masks, and they took her as a wizard. We used to pray for children, we'd been childless so long. I've never prayed since, save to thank Ilbialla we had none. I wouldn't stay in the city after that. I moved out to the suburb." And all the while, he never left off stroking her hair.

"But the Red Masks take wizards for execution by the temple," Jugurthos said. "Condemned to death in the deep well, by the Voice's decree. They're priests, not—not . . ." He swallowed. "She can't be your wife. She's some priestess. She's not thirty yet, this woman." Stupid thing to say, stupid. The old man was manifestly not deluded. His eyes, though swimming with tears, burned. No confusion there.

"She died that day, or not long after," the sandal-maker said. "She hasn't changed, hasn't—she hasn't—" He wailed and bowed his head over her. "They said—when they killed her out there now they said—the temple—a necromancer—a devil. One of the seven." The words came out as half-strangled gasps, through sobs.

A devil?

"All right," Jugurthos said inanely. "All right." He put a hand on the man's shoulder. "All right, just tell me. What about necromancy and a devil? Who—no, to start with, what's your name?"

"Ergos," the man said, "Ergos Arrac." A very distant connection to the Arrac-Nourril Family, then.

"How did she die? This time," Jugurthos amended. "What happened out there, when the Lady came?"

"Bring him inside," said Tulip in his ear.

He nodded, recalled to sense. "Yes. Inside." Kneeling on the road before his gates with a riot or worse in the suburb was folly. But the men and women who had followed Ergos Arrac to the gate stood watching, menacing in their silence, and now murmured, hands, some of them, on weapons.

"I'm not arresting him," he said loudly. "I'm not going to make him disappear." Or let him disappear, if temple guards came for him? If Red Masks came? What choice would he have?

"Cold hells. Fine then. I do—" he grinned, a hand on his sword's hilt to stress that it wasn't their threat he bowed to. A couple of the Marakanders stepped back; no backing off on the part of the caravaneers, though. "—see your point. We'll all stay out here in the open. To witness. Tulip, go back. I want Itulyan out here, to set down everything that's said. And Belmyn, too."

Belmyn was the senior-most patrol-first. He didn't have to say, "Belmyn and her patrol as well as the clerk, and maybe a double patrol while you're at it, to make sure we can make it back to the gate, afterwards." Not to Tulip. She nodded understanding and strode away.

"Wait till my clerk comes," he told the old man. "Calm yourself. Get your words in order. We'll set them down fair. You wanted witness. You'll have witness. Testimony set down clear and true before the gods and the Old Great Gods."

And in the plural he betrayed himself, yes? "The gods" alone might have passed, been taken for "the Old Great Gods." Old Ergos didn't notice, but at his side a sharp-faced girl's eyes narrowed.

Ergos laid the woman down again, folded her hands above her breast, and tried unsuccessfully to close the clouded eyes.

The patrol hovered too close, their attention more on the corpse than the onlookers or the road. They whispered together. Jugurthos snapped at them to keep an eye to the bridge, and Tulip returned, with the clerk and three patrols, one of which, at a jerk of Belmyn's head, hung back at the gate. The onlookers gave a little ground but muttered.

Tulip's face was grim and she crouched to whisper in his ear again. "Courier's back from Hassin. The Lady's fled to the temple in disorder. The Riverbend Gate's being attacked by caravaneers. Nothing Hassin can't handle."

"Fled?" Jugurthos said aloud, checking his own bridge yet again and the footpath that hugged the wall. Nothing stirred there, no trouble spilling around from the north. The suburb itself, though smoke rose, seemed quiet.

"Don't speak to them," said a woman suddenly. "You were a damned fool to give your name, Master Ergos. We shouldn't have come here. They'll use your words against you. Come away while you still can."

The girl, the one with a face like a curious weasel, said, "No. You were right, Uncle. The city needs to witness, if we all die for it. Tell the captain."

But the old man was listening to neither, his eyes fixed on Jugurthos again.

"Tell me," Jugurthos said. "Itulyan, set his testimony down."

Because that was the law, wasn't it? An accusation needed to be recorded, witnessed, brought to a magistrate. There were a score of auditors here from the suburb and as many street guard, and he felt he was balanced on a bridge like a sword's edge, and the crossing—he would fall, they all would, disappear into the depths of the Lady's well. Red Masks would come for the record, for those who dared accuse and those who might have listened . . . but that was a Red Mask, vulnerable and dead, long dead if the old sandal-maker were to be believed, and Jugurthos would stake—was staking—his life the old man spoke honest truth.

A bridge like a sword's edge, and if crossed, if he dared—run, and don't look down.

"The Lady rode to the suburb with a company of Red Masks and temple guard," Jugurthos prompted. "What then?"

"They came for wizards," Ergos said. "There's always a few wizards among the caravaneers, there's diviners and such in the suburb, a few, in secret. But they killed—the temple guard started it, they killed honest tradesfolk for no reason, and the Lady looking on, and—and they accused wizards and the Red Masks took them and if their friends and kin tried to save them they died and then—and then the wizard came."

"What wizard?" Jugurthos asked. Itulyan's bronze stylus jabbed and flicked over the wax.

"I don't know. Outlander. Caravaneer. Someone said she was Grasslander, but she looked Nabbani to me."

A Grasslander who looked Nabbani, a Nabbani who looked Grasslander—one face came to mind at once. Old Great Gods, if the black-haired Grasslander Ivah, Hadidu's lodger, were not dead, then Nour, maybe Nour . . .

No one had ever escaped, once taken by Red Masks, and Ivah and Nour, both wizards, had been taken, staying behind to let Hadidu get his child and the young servants away, when temple guard and Red Masks burnt the Doves to the ground.

"What's this wizard's name?"

"I don't know. A great wizard. Sent to us by the Old Great Gods, maybe. She came out of nowhere, riding a bear."

"What?"

"A bear, a great demon bear, golden, a servant of the gods. And a giant dog like, like a nightmare of a dog, black as night, with them, and when they struck Red Masks, they fell. She broke the terror of the Red Masks," Ergos said, and gripped his wrist. "Captain, the wizard, she did that. Suddenly—we were afraid, all of us afraid, but it was our own honest fear and we could stand. We could think. We could fight the temple guard, we could dare. We could stand against the temple, then, and the Lady saw it and fled back into the city. And we—and people thought—they stripped the Red Masks and they weren't—they weren't—we thought they were priests and soldiers and they were— they were dead."

"Old dead," said the sharp-faced girl, with a look at Itulyan. "Not dead of the bear and the dog and the wizard. Set that down. My mother's aunt, since you're setting it all down for our deaths. I never knew her, she was arrested and executed before I was born. But *he* knows her, my uncle, my master. Don't you dare look him in the face and deny it."

"I'm not," said Jugurthos.

"The wizard said the Lady was dead, the true Lady, and a devil had taken her place," said Ergos, but someone at the back contradicted, "No, she said the Lady was a devil and a necromancer," and someone else said, "There was a devil in Lissavakail, and the goddess of the lake drove him out and he's come here."

Argument followed among caravan-folk as to whether that devil had been slain or driven away. The clerk Itulyan gave Jugurthos a harried look. He made a dismissive gesture. Enough, it was enough.

"The Red Masks are no priests!" the old sandal-maker shrieked, jerking to his feet, hands fisted. "They're dead! The enslaved dead! The violated dead! And the Lady of Marakand's the necromancer. I accuse her, I'll swear it to any magistrate, I'll cry it in the streets, I'll cry it from the Voice's own pulpit, from Ilbialla's tomb, the Lady is a devil and this is the proof if I die for it. This was my wife!"

His supporters surged up around him, shoving, and the patrol reached for their clubs. Tulip's knuckles whitened on her spear, but she only held it sideways, putting herself between Jugurthos and the throng.

"Will you come into the city?" Jugurthos said.

"Captain . . ." said Tulip in apprehension.

"Uncle!" the niece-apprentice cried.

"Bring her into the city. To the market square."

"*Ju!*" Tulip hissed.

He was running the sword's edge, and dizzy with it, and it might not even reach to the far bank of the chasm beneath.

"To the tomb of Ilbialla," he said. Where better?

The old man took a deep and shaking breath. "And what will that do?"

"I don't know. Let's find out. Belmyn, bring the—the sandal-maker's wife, the diviner, with due respect. Itulyan, I want—" Jugurthos made hasty calculations, "—ten fair copies of that testimony made at once. Draft every literate guardsman you need and dictate it, but ten at the very least."

"We don't—"

"Find them! Send someone to roust out a few scribes, then, folk who live near. Merchants' clerks from the warehouses. Go! Don't waste time."

Time would run through his hands. A lifetime waiting for what he had thought would never come, a vague *someday*. The Lady fled to the temple. The Red Masks—maybe not impotent. But proven vulnerable, proven—an abomination and a testimony against the temple, against the Lady.

Patrol-first Belmyn and three others used the Red Mask's own cloak to wrap and lift her, and the old sandal-maker let them, watching, with his niece—great-niece—standing arm about his waist, chewing her lip.

"Don't trust them," a tattooed Black Desert caravaneer urged. "They'll hand you over to the temple. They'll bury the truth."

"The Riverbend Gate's being attacked by the suburb," Jugurthos said. "They know all this?" A hand spread towards the body.

"We all know the truth, now."

"The city doesn't. The city's not your enemy. It's as much a victim of the Voice, the Lady, whoever and whatever this necromancer is, as you. It's been as afraid as you. Moreso. You can leave, caravan-man. We live here, with the Red Masks walking our streets." Not that they did so all that often. But there was always the one day they would come, and their terror would leave you helpless, broken and shaking as a beaten child. "We all need to know this truth."

"And then?" Tulip muttered. "Old Great Gods, Ju, what follows then? Riverbend's under attack, and it'll be a massacre if a horde of caravaneers out for revenge gets through."

"Law," said Jugurthos. "Law, the street guard, and the senate. We're Marakand. Not the temple. The suburb needs to remember that. Come inside, all you here. In. To witness, as you said. And then leave, leave freely, and rein in whatever madness for revenge is still brewing out there." He jerked a hand at the smoke-shrouded buildings beyond the Gore. "You all came here, with Ergos Arrac. You didn't go to Riverbend raging for blood."

"Some of that crowd would have torn her to pieces, dead as she was," sniffed the niece. "So we turned off. These just followed."

"The senate," remarked Tulip, to the sky, "is more or less appointed by the Beholder of the Face of the Lady."

"Oh," said Jugurthos. "I meant the other senate."

"There isn't another senate."

"No. But I think—since the Red Masks appear to have enemies who can destroy them at last—there will be."

A curt order and his patrols headed back to the gate, shepherding the sandal-maker and his niece with them. About two-thirds of the suburb-folk followed, more than Jugurthos expected.

"The law against bearing weapons in the city streets is not in abeyance," he said, as the gate shut behind them. "But—" as there was a growl from some of the caravaneers, "—under these circumstances, for this one time only, you can consider yourselves requested to assist the street guard in protecting Master Ergos." Aside to Tulip he added, "Get the damned armoury unlocked and arm the patrols. Tell them right off, there's a devil ruling the temple in the Lady's name. Tell them, they're sworn to protect the city and see the law's kept. The city's law, not the temple's. But any you decide you can't trust, don't arm." He named a few names. Tulip added several more. "And then, take a messenger's baton in case you're stopped and get to the apothecary's. Tell Hadidu I need him here. I need him to speak to the people."

"Are you serious?"

All or nothing. The last rush, the last leap to the far lip of the chasm, the sword-bridge falling away beneath him.

"Yes."

"Captain," said the old man. "Captain—what's your name?"

"Jugurthos," he said. "Barraya. Son of Senator Petrimos Barraya and Senator Elias."

Ergos was more than old enough to remember those names. He breathed out a long "Ahhh," and nodded, something understood. Stood a little straighter, took his great-niece's arm, rather than leaning on her. "Look, girl," he said. "Here's the true head of Family Barraya. He's no temple puppet. We're all right."

Or all dead together.

"We're going to carry your wife to the market," said Jugurthos. "The priest of Ilbialla—"

"*Priest?* A priest of Ilbialla? Are the gods returned?"

"No," said Jugurthos. "But that doesn't mean Marakand can't keep faith with them. The priest will come to give your wife a blessing for the road at Ilbialla's tomb." Not that the poor empty corpse was likely to have any ghost yet clinging to it. "Itulyan," he called back over his shoulder. "Get those copies made, *now*. And add at the end, *Come now to the Sunset Gate Market. Witness for yourselves. Hear what must be said, in the name of the true gods of Marakand.* I'll see to their sealing myself." With his mother's seal, which he'd managed to hold onto through everything.

Testimony, for some few of the gate and ward captains he was almost certain of, for particular senators and magistrates he thought, maybe, he could move. For certain elderly men and women, powerful in the

Families, who were not high in the temple's favour, who had lived quiet and retired long years now . . .

And then?

And then, what followed, followed.

Ilbialla and Gurhan and the true Lady, if there had ever been a true Lady, be with them all.

CHAPTER IV

Her thoughts were filled with voices, and all of them were hers. Zora, who was a temple dancer. Tu'usha, who was one of the seven devils of the stories of the north, who had once walked among the stars. The Lady, who was the goddess of the deep well of Marakand, betrayed by Tu'usha. Sien-Mor.

No, not Sien-Mor. Tu'usha had been bound as one with Sien-Mor, conjoined souls, but the wizard of the southern ocean was dead. She must be dead. She had burned. She-Sien-Mor was she-Zora, now.

But the thoughts yammered and piled upon her, a great tsunami to drown and crush and batter, and that was Sien-Mor's thought, she-Zora knew nothing of oceans, had never seen a lake, never even seen water flow in the dry river, the ravine that crooked like a bent arm to embrace Marakand. The most water she had ever known was in the temple baths. But in her mind, she saw a great wave, and she stood on a high hill and heard the gulls and the cries and—these thoughts that were hers and yet not hers—who was she who thought them, heard them? They drowned her.

Fool and coward girl!

She had fled the battle.

No. She had retreated. That was common sense. She was no blood-mad Northron berserker to stand to death, believing glory and songs better than the achievement of one's long aim. She had withdrawn from the suburb. She would return. And it would burn.

Not yet. No, not yet. The better part of her strength, the Lady's strength, her Red Masks, lay far away. She still drew on them, as all were one, one web of power, and she at its heart, sustained and sustaining, but they were not here. She must await their coming.

On her orders, the bells had rung from gate-tower to ward block-house, all over the city, the jangling peals of the all-in curfew, not briefly, as at sunset when the city gates were closed, but a long, unceasing peal, warning the folk to get themselves withindoors, to clear the streets or face arrest. Warning the captains of the city gates to close them, to seal the city against enemies within or without.

Both, maybe.

No warlord great enough to get his army past the Western Wall at the distant end of the pass had arisen in the Four Deserts in living memory; it was nearly twenty years since so much as a raider band had swept up to threaten the suburb, though the wall had now fallen mostly into ruin.

The Lady taxed the caravan road to repair it. The work had been ongoing for years.

The enemy at the city's gates now had not passed in by the Western or the Eastern Walls, except in the ordinary way of trade. They were caravaneers of the road, merchants' folk, even traitor folk of Marakand who had their homes and shops in the suburb. They were her enemies, Marakand's enemies. She was the Lady of Marakand. Her name was Zora.

Be calm. Breathe slowly. Let peace and stillness rise.

The white silk of scarves and surcoat flattened to her and streamed aside, stained dark. She stank. But she made a beautiful image, she knew, her slender figure straight and strong, her cascading dark hair come loose and blowing like a banner, the white silk rippling in the rising wind, and the blood against the white, the red-lacquered armour beneath, reminded those who might look up—huddled whispering clus-ters of priests, small mounds of yellow robe, from here—that she had fought for them, fought for their city. The long shadows of the westering sun framed her; she gleamed in the golden light of the dying day. Their goddess no longer hid, timid and shy, withdrawn in her well, speaking through a mad priestess. *I am my own mad priestess now.* They had seen how she rode ahead of them. She fought for Marakand. Marakand was hers to fight for.

Beneath her Zora could see the temple enclave, a depression below the level of the city like the footprint of a giant's horse, circled with cliff and wall, the gatehouse where the only entrance from the city plunged down a tunnel cut through the rock. To the north was the ravine, the dry riverbed; the temple wall there, ancient wall and buildings, was city wall. That was how the assassin who had slain the Voice of the Lady and doomed her, damned her, doomed and damned Zora, had found his way into the temple, through a forgotten and abandoned door high on the wall, where once had been a landing for boats. When there had been boats. When there had been a river. Some of her Red Masks had returned to her by that door, and they guarded it now, but that was not enough. The wizard and the bear-demon and the dog who was not a demon—but she did not want to think what he might be, what he must not be, could not be, not *him* not here not—of course he was not. Her brother would never so demean himself as to take the body of a dog—

Zora had no brother.

Hush, hush, hush. Be still.

—they might come that way. They would kill more Red Masks, if they did. So few were left to her. She would be starved of human wizardry if they attacked again. She had sent too many of her servants east with the captain of her Red Masks, her beautiful golden captain, whom she would make high king of Praitan in the Lady's name, once Praitan was restored to Marakand.

She could not risk the few who remained to her against the Grasslander wizard and her demon and the dog, not now. Not until her captain returned. She could not risk the loss of any more nodes in the web of her wizardry, which was not hers. Neither Zora, nor bodiless Tu'usha nor the Lady of Marakand were wizards as Sien-Mor had been. The wellsprings of human wizardry no longer lay within her, for all the wizard's knowledge she possessed. She had made the Red Masks to be not her wizards but her wizardry, to restore what was lost with Sien-Mor's death.

So. She must wait. She must hold here, until her captain returned. He was Red Mask, but he was a great wizard and swordsman. She would set him against the Grasslander, she would set him against the demon of the earth, the bear, she would set him even against the dog, whatever it truly was, and then she would have many Red Masks, the wizards of Praitan Over-Malagru, and the wealth of Praitan would be the seed of an empire, and Marakand would be strong, Marakand would be great, and it would be her fortress against what she knew gathered in the west.

She had only to hold, to wait.

Zora narrowed her eyes. Wait, until the wizard great enough to break even her spells—woven of human wizardry, strong with many silenced voices—rode the demon to her very gates? Wait till the—call him monster, spirit, creature of the mountains, call him anything but what he must not be, could not be, was not, surely was not—

—he is a devil and you I do not know his name.

—No. Never. *No.*

—wait till the dog came to try his strength against hers?

No. He was some creature of the mountain-goddess. No devil. Not possible.

Wizardry was humanity. Wizardry was of this world. Wizardry was not hers, not Zora's; the knowledge was dead Sien-Mor's, but the magic flowed from others.

But she did not need it. Not for what now lay in her mind. There was a cost, but it would not be paid by her, and she was beyond caring. If the earth itself lay dead and barren, soul seared—it was only a little scar.

If, for those who could read it, it was a sign that she was here, that she was—what she was—so be it. *He*—and he was not the dog was not he—he her brother Sien-Shava *I have no brother* knew already.

He would know, he must know, he would come, she had been fool to leave the well to take form to take flesh that might call him, flesh to flesh to blood to blood not his flesh not his blood not his never his Sien-Mor was dead—

Hush, hush, hush.

Yes.

She had learnt of the demon who had guarded her in her tomb, her prison of undying flame. She had learnt fire. Sien-Mor, in her dying, had known fire.

Fire would guard her, and fire, this fire, needed no wizardry.

She called fire. Fire answered.

In the streets bordering the temple wall in Greenmarket Ward, where the fodder-sellers came, and in Templefoot Ward, and the East Ward, and in the wilderness of the ravine along the temple's stretch of the city wall, fire was born. It was small, at first, a shimmer, a shiver in the air, a heat as of noontide sun. There were houses and shops backing against the temple's wall in all three wards, and in them, beams began to smoke, the first white smoke, reaching and coiling, of a log thrown on the fire. Householders who noticed ran for their water-jars, ran to private cisterns or public wells, but almost as one, roofbeams, floorbeams, cracked and spat, furnishings blackened and crisped, writhing. Dogs and cats fled into the streets. They were mostly small houses, narrow, yardless, stacked high, floor built on unsteady floor. Zora watched as if she walked among them. Porches, balconies, smoked and charred. Bedding smouldered, oil-jars burst into flame, meal and rice likewise, and householders fled, all-in curfew or no.

Then the whole was burning, plaster crumbling to dust, roofs falling, almost as one, almost silent, only a dull and distant rumble. No great scarlet flames striking high, no roar of furious air. A shimmer, a heat haze, and the small yellow-white flames, dancing on the ruins. It was their own fault they lost all, those wailing folk; each and every house had been built contrary to the city law, hard against her walls. Most folk had made it out. Most. Not all. Even Zora could not care, mesmerized by the dancing of her flames. She must not care. If she screamed and shrieked and wept—

The Lady did not scream. She was their goddess and their lives were hers, to spend as she needed.

The Lady wept. Did she? Her face was wet. Pointless. Tu'usha—she was Tu'usha, she must remember she was Tu'usha, true name, true self—laughed and opened her arms to the city.

"Come to me now, if you dare!" But who it might be she taunted, she did not know.

She left the roof, down the narrow stairs, the dark ones, down within the walls, to the maze of mundane rooms that backed the great central hall under the dome where the dancers danced the worship of the Lady, where the Voice in days now ended had conveyed the Lady's will from the high pulpit, hidden behind her silver mask, muttering and shrieking, hands writhing, her mind long ago broken.

Murdered, the Voice, by the assassin who was now captain of her Red Masks. *His fault, he had done this to her, Zora would have been gone out of the temple in a month more, free.* . . . No. *She is I am the Lady.* The death of the Voice had set her free, given her the spur to action, the sign that her time of passive hiding was past. The Lady had no need of a Voice. The Lady was incarnate now and spoke in her own voice. Zora's voice.

I am my own Voice. I am Voice. I am—

She had danced here. Zora had danced here. In the dance, there had been only Zora, and she had not danced to the Lady's glory, but for her own lost god Gurhan, and for herself.

She could dance for herself again. The swirling, circling patterns of the floor called her, woke the rhythms in her mind. She could. *Yes, dance.* She would. *Find the stillness within.* In dance, there was stillness. *In silence, hear.* In drumming, in the pad and scuff of bare feet, there was silence.

Zora shed her wraps, her boots, raked fingers through her hair, stretched.

There was no drummer but her own heart. No music, but memory brought it.

Yes . . .

Zora danced.

Red Masks held the doors, and the Lady of Marakand danced.

CHAPTER V

The lack of his sword nagged at Varro, like an itch that wouldn't be eased. Red Geir's sword, or so Holla-Sayan claimed that the devil Ulfhild Vartu had told him. It looked a kingly sword, that was certain, and old enough to have come over the sea with Red Geir. Cursed, Holla-Sayan also said, and told him to throw it away. They'd had a rare fight over it some months ago, and he had completely failed to knock Holla down, of course, but at least the Westgrasslander had left off nagging. Rocking the baby's cradle with a booted toe, Varro bounced daughter number three on his knee, singing, as his father had sung to him:

> *A white horse, a black horse, a red horse for thee,*
> *But mine is a grey horse, from over the sea.*
> *There's a moon on the towers and frost on the hill,*
> *And when the wind blows, I can smell the sea still.*

It was nonsense, and only Jasmel the eldest spoke any Northron, but the child shrieked and yelled, "Again, again, dada!"

> *Bread on the hearthstone,*
> *Butter in the churn,*
> *Honey in the beehive—*

The door to the shop opened with a bang, and Watcher shot up barking. Varro swung little Iris to the floor and put himself in the connecting doorway between kitchen and shop, thrusting the clattering bead curtain aside. He felt naked without the sword, and he wasn't obsessed with it, no matter what Holla said. Holla was more than a little prone to obsessions himself. When a man had a treasure, of course he didn't like leaving it behind, even locked in the boss's room at the caravanserai. Just like Talfan couldn't stand it long, when she had sent the girls and the priest's little boy away into hiding with allies among the Barraya family manors, back when the Lady first revealed herself and destroyed Hadidu's house, executing his brother-in-law, the partner of Master Kharduin, who ran one of the more celebrated eastern road gangs. They'd thought they were about to be arrested and dragged off to death themselves, his wife and Hadidu and probably some others Varro didn't know about. He'd arrived to find Talfan's house dark and locked and, after climbing over the yard wall and kicking in the shuttered kitchen window in a bit of a panic, had discovered his wife, a baby, and Master Hadidu living in a second cellar he hadn't even known existed.

But when several days went by and nobody came searching, and there was no rumour at all that anyone but Hadidu was under any suspicion, Talfan got word to her aunt, and the whole gang came creeping home, by some secret route over the wall in the night, as furtively as they'd left. Thank all the gods that were and ever had been. When a man came home after so long away, he wanted his family about him.

A girl—a pleasantly buxom girl—in a street guard's grey tunic slammed the door closed and turned to drop the bar, panting for breath. She clutched a messenger's white baton.

"Tulip!" Talfan said. "What's wrong?"

"Not sure," said Tulip, eyeing Varro. Appreciatively, he hoped, but she seemed more to be considering whether she should invent some intimate rash and send him back to the kitchen in male embarrassment.

"This is my husband, Varro, home from the road. Jugurthos knows him."

"Oh," said Tulip, visibly relaxing. "Right, then. Hadidu?"

"Upstairs with the girls, grinding herbs for me. What's—"

"The Lady," said Talfan. "Took a company of temple guard to the suburb. Red Masks. Started arresting wizards, or trying to. Someone started fighting back. *Killing* Red Masks. Some great wizard with demons and—" she shook her head, "maybe even the Blackdog of Lissavakail's out there."

"The Blackdog?" Varro raised his head sharply. "No. He wouldn't—" He clamped his teeth together on the words. The women didn't notice his interjection, too absorbed in their own excitement.

"The suburb's rising and the Lady *fled*, Talfan, back to the temple and ordered the gates of the city shut, even against her own temple guard, any that didn't make it back with her. People must have seen, Talfan, seen her fleeing from Riverbend Gate to the temple."

"We heard the bells."

The rhythmless clanging of the general alarm, Talfan meant. There had been a quick scurrying around the neighbourhood as people tried to find the cause, but it meant a general all-in curfew, and a patrol had come by, so everyone had retreated, to wait and breed their own rumours of Praitannec war and desert raiders.

"That won't keep it quiet for long, and that's not the worst of it. Or the best. I think Jugurthos is mad, but maybe he's inspired. I don't know. I knew who he was when I told him yes, that first night, I knew then what he dreamed, and I meant yes forever, not one night. I'm not running now. But Old Great Gods—he must be mad. We're all damned."

The street guard seemed as elated as she was fearful, though. Varro caught Iris as she tried to push past him, crying, "Auntie Tulip! Look! This is my dada!"

"Be a good girl and go get Uncle Hadi," Talfan said. "Varro, you were at Lissavakail."

He admitted as much, warily. He'd been juggling secrets longer than he cared to remember, a burden for a man well able to admit he loved a good story and that most of the pleasure was in the telling. But it was young Zavel, not he, who swaggered round the taverns with a nod and a wink and a dark hint about his friend. Varro didn't boast of the Blackdog, and he never told the gang why he seemed to save so little from his own personal trade of Northron goods, letting his friends think it was all flung away through high living when he got home to Marakand or lost by a spendthrift wife. Perhaps she was that. His earnings bought apprenticeships for young wizards in the Five Cities, weapons that were stockpiled—somewhere, he didn't know where. He'd have raged about his daughters being put as playthings on Talfan's board, except, well, he'd known she was mixed into the forbidden worship of the old gods when he'd married her. Part of the bargain. But he wanted to take daughter number one to the road with him this time. She was old enough, and Gaguush could use the hands. Get her out of it, at least. Show her a larger, saner world.

"The Blackdog," said his wife. "A demon servant of the goddess Attalissa—he really exists? He killed the Lake-Lord?"

"Um," he said. "I think—well—he's not a demon. Definitely not a demon." Not anything so safe and natural and belonging to the world as a demon, though just what he was, Varro couldn't guess. A mad spirit bound to a human host to serve the goddess Attalissa, except that, now, he wasn't. Bound to serve, that was. Mad, yes, and unfortunately bound to a host Varro did not think was all that human anymore, love him like a brother though he might.

"And they say the Lake-Lord was one of the seven devils of the north. A human priest like a Red Mask, even with his goddess's blessing on him, is nothing to that." Talfan's dark eyes were shining as if he'd brought her rubies. "The Blackdog killed the Lake-Lord. And now the goddess of the lake has sent him here? If we can rid ourselves of the Red Masks—"

"It was a bit more complicated, and it wasn't—" Varro began.

"But the Red Masks aren't priests; that's the truth that'll unravel all the lies—" cried the soldier.

"Tulip," said Hadidu, grave in the kitchen doorway, a lean, hollow-eyed man, his black beard already greying about the mouth, though he couldn't be any older than Varro, if that. Varro stepped aside for him.

Tulip launched into her tale—report—again.

Bare feet came pattering down the stairs.

"Mama—!"

"Not now, Jasmel."

"But, Mama—"

"Not now, Ermina."

"Mama, the temple's on fire *and* the suburb now. We can see it from the roof."

A general rush for the rooftop followed, Talfan pausing on the way to gather up the baby.

There was certainly a fiery glow to the northeast, though little haze of smoke. The smoke over the suburb also seemed mostly to have died away.

"Someone attacking the temple?" Tulip wondered aloud, but she seemed doubtful. "Jugurthos? No. He's waiting for you before he does anything, Hadidu."

"Hadidu can't—" Talfan began.

Tulip raised a hand. "No one's letting me finish. Hadidu, listen."

Necromancy, that was what she told them of. Wizards murdered and enslaved as Red Masks, and a wizard capable of putting the Lady, goddess or devil, to flight. A monstrous dog and a wizard riding a demon bear.

"Er," said Varro. "A bear? A northern bear, tawny-gold, not brown?"

"A golden bear, that's what people said."

"A woman?"

"The wizard's a woman."

Varro nodded. "And the Blackdog of Lissavakail?"

"That's what they're saying. You see what Jugurthos is thinking, Hadidu. The Lady is false; she's a necromancer, no goddess. A *devil*, maybe, an incarnate devil. Ju thinks he can *use* this. Now, before the Lady rallies, whoever or whatever she is. The suburb's ready to burn the city down to get at her, but if we can get them on our side, if we can raise the city for ourselves—Hassin at the Riverbend Gate will be with us—Ju has the testimony of the sandal-maker about his wife, proof of necromancy. He has the body. He thinks he can swing the other ward captains to our side and get the temple's lapdogs out of the senate or call up a new one from the old family elders or something . . ."

"We can't fight a devil," Hadidu said. *The gods are dead*, he had said bitterly, only this morning. And he had wanted Varro to find some merchant's company that would take him and his son south to the Five Cities, abandoning his goddess and the secrets he had been raised all his life to keep and serve.

"Lissavakail and Serakallash did fight a devil," said Varro slowly. "And they won." Was that hope, a little, like an uncoiling shoot of green, in Hadidu's dark eyes? "We need to find the Blackdog." Devils take all—devils, he was as mad as the rest of them. He should keep his mouth shut and drag his daughters off to the desert, with Talfan gagged on a camel till they'd gone too far to turn back. "I can. . . . Look, Talfan love, I've never told my friends your secrets, right? And I've never told you theirs."

"What secrets?" asked Talfan.

Sorry, Holla. "You know my friend Holla-Sayan? Great Gods, you know his daughter Pakdhala?"

"The one who married and stayed in Lissavakail last year."

"Her. Yes. Um. Pakdhala, ah, would be the goddess Attalissa of the Lissavakail. The lake, you know, not the town. Well, goddess of the town, too, of course." Babbling. He should shut up now.

Talfan blinked. "In my kitchen?"

"Yes."

"Playing with my girls?"

"Yes."

"So Holla-Sayan . . . but he's from the Western Grass."

"Well, yes. And he's the Blackdog regardless. I did tell you he was a bit mad," he added defensively.

"All caravaneers are a bit mad," she said. "You as much as any. Sweet Ilbialla, Varro! You brought the Blackdog to my house, a creature like that, in this city. The Red Masks can smell magic and you didn't think to tell me—"

"I didn't know! I didn't know, then, not till last summer. And he's not a wizard, he's—"

"We need to find him," said Tulip. "We need to find him now."

"And contact whoever's in charge of the uprising in the suburb," Talfan said.

"I doubt anybody is. It's just a mob, mad for revenge. Once they cool, maybe they'll hear sense." But Tulip sounded doubtful. "Maybe. Maybe we can find someone they'll listen to. Jugurthos thinks so." She eyed Varro, seemed to dismiss him. "Someone they respect. And the city's going to be in the same state, unless someone takes charge quickly."

"In that case we'd better make damned sure it's Hadidu," said Talfan.

"Hadidu?" Varro's involuntary protest meant no insult to the man, but Hadidu? Priest, all right, he could accept that, but . . . Hadidu ran a coffeehouse. He baked pastries. He didn't lead men.

"We need someone all the city can put their trust in," said Talfan. "Otherwise we're doomed. We'll die arguing, fighting, city against suburb, Family against Family, till the temple gets its nerve back and we're all in the cages, dying in the sun."

Maybe Varro had nodded a bit too vigorous agreement with the last. Talfan scowled at him.

"You're right in one thing, Talfan," Hadidu said. "We can't afford to have suburb set against city or caravaneers against Marakanders. Varro?" His voice dropped, becoming even quieter. "Can you find your friend?"

"The Blackdog's hard to miss," said Varro. "And Mikki—you did say a bear—he's, um, well, demon, yes. Half-demon. He's a half-blooded *verrbjarn*, and it'll be night by the time we can get out there. You just need to look for a seven-foot-tall, yellow-haired Northron. That'll be him. With a spooky sort of silver-blonde woman with eyes like ice and steel beside him, glowering at you. Find *her*, and that'll be the end of your Lady, I imagine." Though not the end of devils in their city. What did Vartu Kingsbane *want*, anyway?

He wasn't half so optimistic as he tried to sound. Holla was going to—Gaguush was going to kill him, getting Holla-Sayan into this.

On the other hand, Holla seemed to have managed most of it himself.

"Let's go, then," Hadidu said. "Talfan, get Shemal ready to travel. Send him to—to someone. I don't want to know who. Send your daughters. Get them all away again, over the wall to some manor on the southern road where we have friends, up to the mining towns, anywhere out of here, and *don't tell me*. Do it now, start now. We can't fight this war with hostages against us so readily to hand. And if the temple takes me, and you somehow survive—don't bring my son up to this. If the temple takes me, let it be over."

Her lips thinned, but she nodded. "Auntie can take them, like last time. I won't know where. The baby stays with me."

Hadidu didn't suggest Talfan go too. Varro didn't suggest that it was maybe his job to order his children's comings and goings and take thought for their protection. He just nodded, obedient as the rest.

"I'm going down to Ilbialla's tomb," Hadidu said. "Varro, find your friends. Jugurthos and I need to talk to them."

Varro slipped out the Sunset Gate into the eerily quiet dusk of the suburb, where bonfires burned at many intersections and people lurked, guarding against they hardly knew what, with the native Marakanders mostly barricaded in their houses. Not good. He asked wary questions and hunted the demon and the Blackdog down eventually, in Master Shenar's caravanserai, licking their wounds, figuratively speaking.

No sign of the devil Vartu.

Holla-Sayan was watching a Northron camel-leech putting stitches into Mikki's bare and impressively hairy chest. And the damned great Red Mask killing, bear-riding wizard turned out to be the absolute last person Varro would ever have thought to see slumped asleep against his friend's shoulder. *Ivah.* She'd bespelled and abducted Pakdhala to hand her over to the devil of Lissavakail, she'd had her *noekar*-woman kill Bikkim, and only Vartu's devilry had saved him, she'd—Holla-Sayan knocked him down without stirring from the bench where he sat, when Varro swung his fist to rearrange the Tamghati traitor's pretty little face.

"Bastard," he said mildly, picking himself up, keeping his distance, but Holla-Sayan didn't seem inclined to move farther, and the girl slept on, steadied by Holla-Sayan's arm about her.

Holla-Sayan said nothing in retort, which Varro figured was a bad sign. And he had that dangerous look, a fire behind his eyes that wasn't Varro's perception breaking out into poetry. Sliding into the mad dog's view of things, a view which was a bit simplistic, to put it mildly. Varro had his suspicions that the Blackdog's world broke down into *mine* and *enemy*. Best not to put yourself into the latter category. He settled down on the floor, arms wrapped around his knees, non-threatening as he could be.

"All right," he said. "Be that way."

Holla-Sayan rubbed his face, some sanity returning, maybe? "Leave her alone."

"Why?" There, a simple, mild question. That wasn't threatening, was it?

"Because she was carrying Nour."

"*Nour.*" Hadidu's brother-in-law. Caravaneer. Secret wizard, Varro now knew. Taken by the Lady when the coffeehouse burned, and therefore dead.

Not dead?

"Kharduin's bringing him back. We took him away up the cliffs, when the Lady came after him. He's—he'll live. I think. Maybe."

"He'll live," Mikki rumbled. The camel-leech sat back on her heels, shrugged at him.

"Best I can do. Sorry."

The demon's white skin, untouched by sun, had a sheen of sweat, but he hadn't flinched from the needle, only baring his teeth once or twice in a grimace of pain. He leaned back against the wall and sighed. "It'll do. I heal quickly. What did you want, Varro?"

It wasn't he who wanted anything, but Talfan and Hadidu, who wanted—who dreamed. Peaceful folk who'd never faced so much as a bandit raid, who'd never seen a battle, not even the one fought at their very gates this past day. And they were going to overthrow a goddess who was really a mad devil? He didn't want to be trying to bring up four girls alone, a widower on the road. Marakanders talked and talked. He wasn't sure they were good at much else. They needed—someone to show them what to do next.

"Holla-Sayan, really—did the Lady flee you? Really? Because you've started something and they're all going to die, my wife and her friends who've been waiting for some never-come day when they'll overthrow the Lady, unless you finish it."

"I didn't—"

"You did. The Lady's never left the city before. I don't think she's ever sent Red Masks beyond the city walls before, except for this expedition east to Praitan they're talking of. All this death and burning out there today, that was her looking for you, wasn't it?"

"She was looking for Ivah and Nour."

"Same thing. You're the one took them from her, ya?"

"You'd have left them to die?"

"What were you doing in the temple in the first place? No. Never mind. I don't care. But you began this, and you can't just skulk off to the deserts pretending you didn't and leave us to—"

"What *us?*"

"Talfan. My wife. She's, look, you know how Attalissa's temple went underground when Tamghat came? Same thing here. But they were all children. A couple of youths hardly men and a handful of children, hiding and keeping faith with their gods best they could. Waiting for the Old Great Gods alone knew what. And now they think it's come, the time. In you. They've seen that the Red Masks can be faced and killed, they've seen the Lady run, and they're going to follow through on it. But if you abandon them, they're all going to die. You did all that, out there—" Varro waved a hand towards the door, "—for *Ivah?* Then you can't leave decent folk to be murdered by the Lady for something you've done."

"I can't kill the Lady, if that's what you're asking."

"She fled you."

"She didn't need to."

"She obviously doesn't know that. Look, you know what they're thinking now, Talfan and Master Hadidu, the priest of Ilbialla? They're thinking that we—they—have the gods on their side. The Old Great Gods have given them a sign that their time has come."

"You're not serious! You can't tell them that."

"I don't need to. The great wizard—" his lip curled at Ivah, "—and her demons have proven it. You're a demon now, by the way."

Holla-Sayan just shut his eyes. The man looked done in. Well, he'd come through the thick of the past day's battle and been fighting Red Masks in the temple before that. And even Ivah—no, Varro did not, would not pity her. But she looked pathetic. She was wrapped in a too-large coat, snuggled into Holla-Sayan's side like a child to her parent, only a bit of face poking out, ragged-nailed hands clenched up tight on her lap. She looked aged and frail, the golden-brown of her skin grey-hued and lined, marked with dark scabs from earlier injury, wisps of her once-wealth of midnight hair now cropped and clinging.

The real demon watched him watching them, black eyes thoughtful. "Ivah is Ghatai's daughter," Mikki said softly. "Did you know?"

Tamghat's daughter? That shocked Varro. "It's no excuse," he protested. "She tried to murder my friend. She had her hearth-woman cut his throat."

"I know. But it is an explanation. Now she leaves her father behind and grows into something else."

"Does that make her a devil too?" Better to cut her throat now, while she slept helpless, in that case.

"I doubt it."

Holla-Sayan opened his eyes. Ah, damn his tongue for a fool's, Holla'd finally succeeded in getting barren Gaguush in a family way, right. That's all he needed, to be talking of unnatural halfbreeds and making the man fear she'd give birth to puppies. Varro eyed Mikki, whose father had been human, his mother a bear-demon. That . . . no, he didn't want to picture how that came about.

"What do you want?" Holla-Sayan asked.

"Go talk to Master Hadidu. He sent me to find you, to ask you to come to him. Talk to him, before you decide to pretend all this is nothing to do with you, all right?"

"And what's your place in it, Varro? You weren't out in the suburb today."

"I didn't know! They shut the gates, remember? I was in the city."
But that was what Talfan would be thinking of him, too, no matter that
he had been where he belonged, with her. People had fought the Lady,
and he hadn't been among them. "But I've been thinking, I have an
idea—I need to talk to some people."

And here came one of them, Master Kharduin, surely. Varro knew
of him by reputation. Wealthy in camels, trading in silks and spices and
drugs of Nabban, master of a gang that travelled hard and fast, taking
branches of the eastern road others did not dare. Possibly because he
was allied with the lawless folk that plagued the badlands. He was a
burly, black-haired man with the gleam of gold in his ears and a beard
that curled like a ram's fleece, blue-eyed and brown-skinned. An exile
of the eastern deserts, they said he was, a chieftain's warleader outlawed
from his tribe for some grave crime or betrayal that varied with the gos-
siper, but there were always such stories about anyone who drew the
interest of the road. Even a western road man like Varro had heard those
stories of Master Kharduin. Lots of speculation about the meaning of
the black scorpions tattooed on the insides of his wrists, which matched
those on the backs of his partner Nour's hands. No tribe's markings of
west or east. Some brotherhood of outlawry, some secret vow of death
to be fulfilled . . . probably the scorpions signified nothing more than
some personal bond or lovers' whimsy. Whatever Kharduin had been
or done—and maybe it was nothing more than leave his home for the
caravans and make a success of it—the caravaneers respected him and
the Marakanders likewise. If Varro could persuade him to Talfan's cause
and Talfan's gods . . .

Maybe he wouldn't have to do that much persuading. It was surely
Nour's cause, Nour's goddess, even more than Talfan's, given his close
kinship with Hadidu the priest, foster-brother and brother by marriage.
The pair of grim, dusty, silent men who came with Kharduin were carrying what Varro first thought was a bier of spears and blankets between

them. On it lay Nour, whom he had met once or twice at the coffee-house, though he hadn't known him for a wizard. The Marakander cara-vaneer looked dead, his face gaunt, grey, and hollow about the eyes, his lips cracked and scabbed, but he breathed.

Ivah woke as suddenly as if someone had called her name, stumbled to her feet and went to Nour with only a brief, vague look at Varro, as if she didn't even remember him.

"He's doing better," she said, like a prayer.

If that was better. . . . She lifted the blanket from over his chest, touched the hand of his linen-wrapped left arm. Scarlet blood seeped through the bandage. The camel-leech craned to look as well. "Much better," the Northron woman agreed. "That's clean. The swelling's down. I thought the skin of his fingers was going to burst when you first brought him in. Hah, I'll take a demon's blessing over surgeons, any day."

Mikki smiled faintly.

"Upstairs," Kharduin said, looking past Varro with little more interest than Ivah had spared him. "Get him to bed. If he wakes up, get some broth into him. Lord of Forests, would you . . . ?"

"I'll sit with him," Mikki said.

They all ended up climbing the stairs together, Holla making an unnecessary point of keeping himself between Varro and Ivah. Mikki was stark naked and nobody seemed to mind. The women politely didn't even look. Since someone had to do the decent thing, Varro ducked into the first open door he saw and snitched a blanket. Not even Kharduin's broad shoulders matched Mikki's; no one's coat or caftan was going to hide anything. Mikki took it with grave thanks and a wink, and twisted it around his hips as a kilt of sorts.

Varro gave Master Kharduin time to get his partner settled, to take a swallow of tea, before putting himself forward.

"Master Kharduin," he said. "You don't know me, but my wife's the apothecary Talfan, a good friend of Master Hadidu of the Doves, and of Captain Jugurthos of the Sunset Gate."

That got his attention, ya. Practically made him family, didn't it, since Kharduin and Nour weren't partners merely in business?

"You know what they're up to, those two, and Nour?"

A nod.

"You can guess what they're thinking, with what's gone on out in the suburb, Red Masks destroyed and the Lady fleeing and all. But what odds they let the moment slip? They're city folk, even the soldier. Talkers."

"Gods, Varro, and you're not?" Holla-Sayan muttered. "Your tongue's hinged in the middle."

"If we can take what's begun and push it further . . ."

"No," said Holla-Sayan. "I can't kill the Lady. Mikki can't kill the Lady. Moth is lost, the gods of the city are lost—"

"Hear him out," said Kharduin. He squatted by the bed, hands laced together, watching Varro's face. "It might not be your fight, Blackdog, but it's become most definitely mine."

Revenge, he understood. Varro took a breath, carefully didn't look at Holla-Sayan, who might believe himself when he said the Lady had no cause to fear him, but Varro didn't need to. She had run. What more proof did they need? And Holla wasn't a man to turn his back on his friends.

"So," he said. "Here we are, with the suburb and the Marakanders ready to start fighting one another, two stupid gangs quarrelling over whose camels drink first, and desert raiders sitting up the hill watching, right?"

Kharduin raised an eyebrow.

"We need to knock some heads together and remind them who the real enemy is."

"And?"

"And we've got a stronghold of the Lady's folk cutting us off from the road east. Do we want that?"

Kharduin grinned. "Ah. The thought had crossed my mind, actually. Think we can do it?"

Nour woke up briefly while he and Kharduin were talking over one another, ideas flying. That gave Varro a means to shut up Holla's objections and insults of his intelligence, by sending him to Talfan and Hadidu with the apparently-not-dying man's messages. Hadidu had asked to speak to the Blackdog, Hadidu was the priest of a lost goddess; Holla-Sayan was, looked at a certain way, the priest of Attalissa, so could he refuse, holy man to holy man? And Hadidu didn't even yet know his brother-in-law lived, reason enough for Holla to make haste with that news—which, admittedly, Varro should have sent by someone the moment he heard it. Privately, Varro thought that Hadidu, so intense, so, ya, gods-touched, could persuade Holla, if anyone could, that he was needed in Marakand. Was meant to be in Marakand, to serve this. The Old Great Gods had put him in the way of becoming the Blackdog for some purpose, surely, and why think it had ended with Lissavakail? He made the mistake of voicing that last aloud.

"Not in all the cold hells," Holla-Sayan snarled. "Don't you ever name the Old Great Gods so to me . . ." He rubbed a hand over his face, what had seemed real fury dying into confusion. But he shrugged and left with his message for Hadidu, making no more arguments.

Kharduin set out to round up a few respected gang-bosses and caravanserai-masters, and some leading Marakander men and women of the suburb as well. Rather him than Varro. Some of Kharduin's gang headed for the Gore to strip the collected Red Mask and temple-guard corpses, if they hadn't already been looted. Ivah had been put to bed by the camel-leech, who fussed over her as if she'd singlehandedly saved the city from all seven devils at once and flatly forbade Varro to conscript her for his scheme. Saved Varro having to say he'd as soon trust a real Red

Mask to watch his back. He would have liked to have had Mikki along, but the demon had rolled in his blanket by Nour's bed and gone to sleep while they still debated.

He'd said he would go help strip the corpses, which was going to be no pleasant task, especially the mess the Blackdog and a bear were likely to have made of the Red Masks—though at least they wouldn't have bled, from what he'd heard—but first Varro borrowed a pony from the caravanserai yard. He would ride out to Rasta's caravanserai at the far western edge of the suburb to collect Red Geir's sword. And to let the boss know her giant, bone-crushing black monster coward dog of a husband was still in the land of the living, since he'd noticed how Holla-Sayan had been avoiding any suggestion he carry *that* message himself. Gaguush would find a leash for her dog for certain after this, dragging them all into another gods' war.

Holla was going to owe him for the shouting he was about to endure in his stead, indeed he was.

CHAPTER VI

They drifted from the houses, warily, defiantly. Bonfires burned in the market square, heaped at the far corners, and it was street guard who tended them. Anyone venturing within would be putting themselves against the light. But street guard with lanterns on poles stood around the goddess Ilbialla's tomb, and a handful of people had climbed atop its barrel-vaulted roof. A woman with another lantern, they could see, an officer with ribbons on his helmet, four archers, kneeling at the corners. And a man they ought to know, all who lived in the streets about the Sunset Market square. So they came. A few had been told he would be there. They had whispered it to others, rumour spreading fast as feet could creep from house to house in the curfew-empty streets. *The priest of Ilbialla.* So they came.

Jugurthos had thought they would.

The tomb of the goddess had brooded over the place where once stairs had descended to the well of Ilbialla since Jugurthos was a boy. It had been built in a night, by Red Masks, the folk of the neighbourhood had said. The cave of Gurhan among the folded gullies and ridges of the Palace Hill, Gurhan's Hill, had been sealed as well. The frieze beneath the eaves of the tomb, like the wall sealing the cave, was carved with a long, flowing line of script that no scholar could decipher, though Nour had taken furtive copies as far as Nabban and the imperial wizards of Nabban, seeking aid. Since the two tombs were built, the gods had been silent. Those who had tried, in the first day, to break up the stonework had died, but it could be touched safely if you didn't intend harming it. Children played stalking games around the tomb. Beggars and singers sat in its shade. Dogs marked it.

It made a fine podium, if you did not forget you stood on a curving roof.

Hadidu had his eyes shut. Praying, maybe, to a goddess who could not hear, who at best slept beneath their feet, sealed in the prisoning tomb, or at worst was beyond hearing any prayers ever again. But maybe he only sought for words. His lips moved, silently. Jugurthos put a hand on his shoulder and found him trembling. He spared a moment for a prayer himself, to gods that could not hear and the Old Great Gods, who did not intervene in such minor affairs of life—death and what came after being their province. Let Hadidu not faint from sheer nervousness, let him not fumble his words and hem and haw, let him, at the very least, stammer out something moving and to the point, before he dried up altogether and Jugurthos was forced to take over and present the arguments of their hastily sketched harangue. It would be better coming from a chosen of the goddess of this ward, even Hadidu admitted that, but being born to the priesthood did not make one an orator, and Hadidu had always been so shy . . .

Talfan was down there, in the front row of the faces looking up. Arms folded under the baby sleeping in her sling, Great Gods, what risk. But her outlander husband hadn't yet returned from the suburb to gainsay her and was thoroughly under her thumb anyway, and who else had the right to order her home? Eyes wide, intense. Beside her was one of the magistrates for Clothmarket Ward, a scarf pulled up to hide much of his face. To the other side a pair of armed men, two of the four bodyguards a senator was permitted. The senator, Beni Sessihz, lurked in his enclosed chair, with his other two guards and the four burly chairmen standing close about. He'd been old when Jugurthos was young, no blame to him for staying put now. He walked only painfully, and that with two sticks. But he'd come, and moreover put himself in the front, from which it would be difficult to flee if they were—interrupted. A lesser Family of the Twenty, Sessihz, but Beni himself still commanded some respect among the elders of the Families. He had been a scholar of the law and a magistrate in his younger days, was a survivor of the earthquake collapse of the senate palace dome that had killed so many of his colleagues. He was likewise a survivor, in his way, of the purge of the so-called rebel senators, which had followed not long after. Jugurthos's parents, both so newly risen to senatorial status, young elders of their respective branches of the Family Barraya after the earthquake deaths of their parents, had been leaders among those who dared speak out against the temple's arbitrary assumption of unprecedented powers. They were arrested by the temple guard and Red Masks whose disbanding they had called for and were executed without trial. Locked in iron cages in the palace plaza below the senate palace and library, to die of thirst and sun.

The bones were still there. Not the ghosts. Furtive charity had set them all free to take the road to the Old Great Gods, over time, as the temple watch grew disinterested. All it took was a handful of dust.

Senator Beni Sessihz had survived by not being there for that vote. Many who feared to assent but could not bring themselves to openly sanction the temple's formation of an illegal private army had done likewise. Jugurthos had come, perhaps not to forgive, but to understand those who had done so, as he left childhood rage behind.

Beni had never stepped aside from his place as senior-most elder of the Sessihz Family or given up his rights in the senate to some younger relation. He had defiantly abstained from any vote on any temple-prompted matter, or slept through the votes, or missed them altogether. Falling into his dotage, it was said, and had been for thirty years, a frail old man, a place-holding ghost of the past. Jugurthos had never thought so. The old man had turned up hard on the heels of the messenger sent to his house with the sealed testimony of the sandal-maker. There were others in chairs as well, a handful, senators or magistrates or the elderly heads of great merchant branches of the Twenty Families, but they all kept back beyond the bonfires, in the mouths of lesser streets, and the Family emblems on the curtains or the wooden doors of their chairs were one and all covered. Sensible caution, perhaps. There might be others, even more sensible, or younger and fitter, who had come afoot and anonymous. He hoped there were.

Word of this could go straight to the temple, but how it would get in through the circling wall of unnatural fire his scouts had reported, Jugurthos didn't know. No doubt the Lady would have her ways.

He had posted lookouts at the five gateways into Sunset from other wards. If the temple came in force they were done for, but maybe the folk would have time to scatter innocently to their homes. There were few actual gates left between wards to close. Tulip had suggested barricading the gateways with carts, but that would only let them control the day's traffic, not prevent any rush of temple guard. No point, tonight. Tomorrow . . . gates could be improvised. Some of the warehouses had great doors that might almost do. *And then?* He shoved that thought away. Hold this ward. And take the next. And—find that wizard of the suburb and her demons, all hung upon that. A power to put the Lady to flight? Old Great Gods, Ilbialla and Gurhan, speed Varro's search. Could the spirits of the mountains really have come to their aid?

A patrol of guards emerged from a northern street, and folk swirled away, fading into shadows. Jugurthos put himself in front of Hadidu, tensed to shove him down. He saw spears, no bows, a helmet crested with ribbons, the tension of his own guards about one of the fires, confronting this. But then one stepped back and nodded, and the new patrol came on. Tulip moved as if she would drop the horn-paned candle-lantern on its pole away over the side of the tomb, to leave them in darkness.

"No, wait."

Only a five-man patrol, but the sixth, the officer, the short, stocky shape, Jugurthos knew, and then stepping deliberately into lantern-light, Hassin Xua of the Riverbend Gate pointed questioningly up at the roof of the tomb.

"Hah." Jugurthos went to catch his reaching hand and help him haul himself up. "Hassin, you're mad, coming here."

"I? You should have seen her, Jugurthos, smiling like she thought she scattered blessings with her gaze and soaked in the blood of folk of the suburb, all over her face like—like some barbarian war paint. That was no goddess. Is it true the Red Masks have been destroyed? Because if it isn't, we might as well cut our throats here and now and have—" He stopped, seeing what lay down to the other side of the tomb, the corpse, the old man sitting by it, the niece standing sharp and nervous over him, with the other folk of the suburb who had dared accompany the sandal-maker close about. The caravaneers were subdued and wary now, feeling themselves few and outnumbered for all they were armed, marked by their coats and braids as folk of the road. Such had beaten to death one of the magistrates of the suburb, in mindless vengeance for the Lady's attack. That word had come around, as the dusk fell. Hassin looked down at them, and his lips tightened.

"Master Hadidu of the Doves." Jugurthos drew his attention back. "Hadidu, Captain Hassin of the Riverbend Gate Fort."

Hadidu nodded. Hassin glanced over at the darkness on the eastern side of the square, the pit and rubble where the coffeehouse had stood. "Ah," he said. "Yes. I had a fondness for your almond cakes. Forgive me—there was a little boy. Is he . . . ?"

Hadidu's petrified look broke into a smile. "My son. He's safe." The smile died. "My brother, though, and my lodger . . ."

Hassin murmured his sympathy.

The Lady had made a mistake, allowing her temple guard to gossip of the outcome of their errand to the Doves. Not only the capture of two wizards, but the death in the fire of a priest of Ilbialla and his family. That, Jugurthos thought, was what had brought Hassin to him, not only horror at the Lady's deeds. The temple said there had been a priest of Ilbialla alive in secret, and then the city heard that for all the temple's efforts, the secret priest lived yet. Hassin was a native of Riverbend, which like Sunset had been Ilbialla's especial care. He would have been a young man on the day of the earthquake. Well old enough to remember his goddess and her priestess.

Yes, the word was out there, in the errant, twisting breeze of rumour. *Priest of Ilbialla . . . there was a priest of Ilbialla, still, all these years later.* And following that, tonight, like slow eddying in the depths of a pond, *There was a priest of Ilbialla, and he escaped. He lives. He calls us . . .*

Hadidu stirred. The market square was not filled, not nearly that, but the clusters of folk were numerous, and there were more than could be accounted for by the curious of the neighbourhood. Rumour spread, regardless of the curfew. Red Masks slain, the captain of Sunset brought proof. *Priest of Ilbialla, at the tomb of Ilbialla.* And, *There is a devil in the temple.*

"In the days of the first kings in the north," Hadidu said abruptly, and stopped, stepping into Tulip's light. His voice shook only a little as he began again, more loudly. He folded shaking hands into the sleeves of his caftan, which gave him a look of calm assurance Jugurthos knew he did not feel. "In the days of the first kings in the north, the songs say, there were seven wizards, wise and powerful. And there were seven devils, who had escaped from the cold hells where the Old Great Gods had sealed them after the last great war in the heavens. Bodiless, they roamed the earth. And being bodiless, creatures with no bond to it, they could not be sustained by it. They hungered to be of the stuff of the world, as the wizards hungered for knowledge and power, and so a bargain was struck between the seven and the seven, that the devils would join their souls to the wizards' souls and share the wizards' bodies, sharing knowledge, and unending life, and power. But the devils deceived the wizards and betrayed them, taking the wizards' souls into their own and devouring them, taking their bodies for their own, becoming as gods upon the earth. In the end they were defeated, as the tales tell us, by the valour of humanfolk and the strength of the gods and goddesses and demons of the earth, with the aid of the Old Great Gods of the distant heavens. The seven devils were defeated, yes, but not destroyed. They were bound in eternal imprisonment upon the earth, dead and not dead within their graves, and they were guarded by gods and goddesses and demons. But the tales also tell that some, at least, have escaped. One, for certain, we know. He drove the human incarnation of the goddess Attalissa from her lake, scattered her priestesses, made her temple his own, and ruled her land as a tyrant in the body of a Grasslander warlord, powerful almost as a god himself. But he was defeated. You've heard this story also. The folk of the road tell it. Attalissa returned, with her guardian Blackdog at her side. Her priestesses emerged from hiding, her folk rose up and threw off the yoke of Grasslander tyranny, and the devil was destroyed."

A listening silence.

"It was only a story of a distant land," Hadidu said. "Even though it was but last summer that Attalissa returned to her lake. Even when the Tamghati survivors came up the pass from the Four Deserts, fleeing the wrath of the mountains and the Red Desert, it was only a story, and the Voice of the Lady hired them to fight the temple's wars in Praitan. We have had peace with the tribesfolk Over-Malagru for long years now, and the temple hired this warband that had followed a devil to make war on them."

"The Praitans murdered the Voice!" someone called, shadow against a far fire.

"A conquered folk will use what weapons they can," Jugurthos retorted, as Hadidu hesitated. "They were conquered by the treacherous murder of a Praitannec queen by temple ambassadors and by terror of the Red Masks, but we're not here to talk about Praitan."

"Show us the dead Red Mask!" someone else shouted. "We're not here for a storyteller!"

Hadidu drew a long breath. He put Jugurthos's reassuring touch off and raised a hand. "You know me, many of you. Hadidu. The coffeehouse of the Doves, there, the ruin, was mine. And I am not here to tell you stories, save one. This is all one story, do you not see it yet? You know me, and some of you know me truly, a story you've buried in your hearts and kept secret, keeping faith with me. Keeping faith with my mother. Keeping faith with Ilbialla, who was goddess of our ancestors here, with her brother Gurhan of the Hill and sister the Lady of the well, in equal respect and equal love, time out of mind. I was the orphan the master of the Doves took to raise with his own children. The little cousin who was no cousin. My name was Esau, once. On the day the Lady's temple guard murdered the priestess of Ilbialla, my mother, and hacked my grandmother and my infant sister to pieces in the earthquake-ruins of our house, the master of the Doves saved me. You all, all you folk who live about the market square, all who knew or suspected and kept silent, saved me, so that I am here today to tell you, now is our time. Now we, who kept faith in the shadows and the silence, must save our city."

Jugurthos forced his attention back to the audience, drawn nearer by the passion of Hadidu's words. He watched for the incongruous movement against the light of the bonfires, the reach for bow or javelin or stone. Hard not to turn and stare at the priest, though, as rapt as they. If he didn't know Ilbialla to be sealed or dead within the tomb, he would have thought his friend god-touched, inspired, speaking, if not prophecy, then words of divinity nonetheless.

"Do I need to tell you of the evils done in the Lady's name, these three decades past? The murders, the folk slain in the streets by bullies and thugs in the uniform of a private army, no better than an invading barbarian horde, acknowledging no law of the people? The men and women and even children taken, who are never seen again? Marakand was a great city, famed for its library, for its scholars, its wisdom. Where are our wizards now? What folk slaughters its own divinely blessed, who should be there for its aid and comfort? The temple of the Lady, which used to feed the homeless and the hungry, became nothing more than an invading warband, led by a tyrant such as took Lissavakail in the mountains, oppressing the folk, killing those who spoke against it as the senators faithful in upholding the law of the city were killed, with a barbarity you wouldn't find even in Nabban. Was that the act of a goddess? Of a holy priesthood, a temple founded to care for the poor and the sick? Such charity was ever the true Lady's calling. And like a warband the false temple has robbed the folk for its own gain, its priests grown fat on your poverty, your taxes supporting its agents of your oppression, feeding an army, the temple guards, whose only real enemy is you, the folk. It has divided us from our neighbours, turned kin against kin, friend against friend—suburb against city—to stop us uniting against our oppressor, who is the *false* Lady of Marakand."

Movement, far closer than Jugurthos expected. He had seen no one crossing the square. He turned, crouched into the darkness, saw a man intercepted by a pair of guardsmen to stand, hands raised in a gesture denying threat. Caravaneer; he made out the silhouette of knee-length coat and braids. And a sabre at his side. He wasn't one of those who had come in with the sandal-maker; none of those had moved from the group on the other side of the tomb. No way any others should have been let armed through the city gate. No way anyone should have been let through the city gate at all.

"And we must unite. We must stand against this devil—for the rumours you have heard are true. The thing that calls itself the Lady is a devil, one of the seven of the north. We have a duty, not only to ourselves, to our parents, our dead, not only to our living, to our children, our future, not even a duty to our lost gods, but to all humanfolk, and to the gods of the high places and the goddesses of the waters and the demons of the wild. We have a duty, under the Old Great Gods, to stand against the devils and deny them the place they would take in this world."

Jugurthos dropped from the tomb and went to the detained man. The caravaneer had folded his arms now, head cocked a little to one side, listening, face expressionless, but it might be just the damned tattoos that made him look so dark and unreadable. His face was covered in them, temples and cheeks. A man of the deserts or the Western Grass.

"You Captain Jugurthos?" he asked in the desert dialect that was the common tongue of the western road and one of the two languages of the city, the other being a Nabbani dialect, not that real Nabbani of the far empire would admit it as such.

"Yes," Jugurthos answered warily. "You are—?"

"Holla-Sayan!" Talfan elbowed and ducked around a guardswoman, halted in confusion. Ah. Owls flaring wings, curling around the eyes, snakes writhing on his cheeks, those were Westgrasslander markings. This was the man she had thought she had known. The Blackdog. Talfan steadied the baby with a hand. "Oh. Holla-Sayan. Is Varro . . . ?"

"He's talking. Still."

"With whom?"

The caravaneer shrugged. "People. A magistrate—the one they didn't kill, some caravanserai owners, some caravan-masters and such. I've a message for Hadidu, from Nour."

"Nour!" Talfan silenced herself with a hand over her mouth, a hasty glance up at Hadidu, who spoke on unreacting to her shrill cry. Perhaps he had not made out the word.

". . . Not in vengeance, not in the blood-lust of a roused barbarian. We are Marakand. We must be true to Marakand. We are a civilized folk, a folk of law, and we have our law still, we have our senate, the senate of the three gods, we have our street guard—" Some dodging in from Captain Hassin, a murmured word. Hadidu nodded, not pausing. "We have, under the law, provision for a militia, when the city is threatened. It is threatened now, and not by Praitan. How many of you offered your names to the temple or the magistrates, swept away by the false Lady's charms or thoughts of Praitannec plunder? You were willing to fight for a lie. For the sake of the three true gods, hold yourselves ready to fight instead for the truth, for Marakand, and for your gods, lost though they may be."

"Nour!" Talfan hissed. "Alive?"

Jugurthos didn't have words. *Nour*, in defiance of all hope.

"That's Hadidu up there, is it?" Holla-Sayan asked, looking around the market square. "You won't take the temple with this few."

"We're not planning to," Talfan retorted. "Not *tonight*, anyway."

"You don't want to give her time to recover her balance. A speech isn't going to keep her behind her walls."

Jugurthos silenced them both with a lifted hand.

"I beg you, if you hear me with an honest heart, if you do nothing else, carry these words to the city. The folk must know. They must be warned of the cost of denying the truth. Will you have the city follow this devil, this slayer of our true gods, to destruction? Each one of you must choose, must stand for what you know is right before the gods and the Old Great Gods. The Red Masks are fearsome, yes. Pitiable, corrupted, and abused shells, victims of necromancy, their souls, we trust and pray, gone to the Old Great Gods. We still cannot fight the Red Masks, you and I, mortal as we are, but we have allies who can. The Lady's unfortunate slaves cannot infect you with the madness of their terror any longer. That is our greatest weapon, that is why we must act *now*, while the false Lady, the devil in the temple, is weakened by the loss of her greatest weapon, which was our fear.

"Marakand's gods are lost, maybe, or maybe dead, I don't deny it. But the Old Great Gods are over them, and you all, every one of you, will come at the end of your long road to stand before them. Will you have to confess then that you broke faith with memory of your gods, that you denied Ilbialla and Gurhan and the true Lady of the Deep Well, whatever dire fate has befallen her, to worship a damned and outcast devil? To give honour to a murderer, a child-killer, a necromancer who torments even the dead? If you do not now stand against her sin, now that you see it and know it for what it is, you make it your own. You will carry that guilt when you come at last before the Old Great Gods. It is better to die fighting for what is right before men and gods and Old Great Gods, than to live long, corrupting your soul by partaking of such wrong as this Lady has brought to Marakand."

Hadidu fell silent. Tulip took him by the arm, looking around. This was no time to show uncertainty. Jugurthos caught the edge of the tomb and swung himself up to the roof again.

"We can't fight her one by one," Hadidu shouted. His voice had gone hoarse. No, don't. Jugurthos wanted to say. Leave it right there. You have them. But Hadidu seized him by the shoulder. "In the old days, when the city was threatened, the senate would appoint a warden, a Warden of the City to rule over the three wall-wardens who command the guard, to rule over even the senate. The senate now is divided and broken. Though some may hold true to the old gods in their hearts, they sit under the Lady's thumb, they speak only what the priests tell them, and worst, they do it too often not even for fear, but for selfish gain. But the senate is meant to be only the voice of the Twenty Families to which we all, in greater or lesser degree, belong, the voice of folk, and the voice and the will of the folk must be greater than the Voice and the will of the Lady. In the name of Ilbialla and Gurhan, let the folk name a Warden of the City, to lead us through this time of darkness. Name Jugurthos Barraya, Captain of the Sunset Gate and heir of both Petrimos Barraya and Elias Barraya, to lead you."

They roared, like the blood in his ears. Hadidu ducked his head.

"Hadi—" Jugurthos's whisper was strangled. He had seen that somehow getting himself proclaimed Warden of the City was the only way to take the authority he would need, to stop it all being a few riots followed by victory for the temple in the city's uncoordinated confusion, but he had meant to get the other captains, or a majority of them, behind him first, to get some faction of the senate to name him so. Hadidu gave his shoulder a squeeze and turned him loose, shoved him half a step forward.

Jugurthos was suddenly entirely sympathetic to Hadidu's earlier shaking fear, now that all those eyes were seeing him. Stripping him naked, to fail and burn, sun and heat and flies and a rotting public death, taking them with him, carrying them all . . . which was what he had just forced Hadidu to, was it not?

He swallowed, took a steadier stance on the barrel-vaulted roof and raised a hand, commanding silence. They gave it.

"The Lady's fled to her temple," he told them, "but she isn't going to stay there. We *can* fight the Red Masks, with the help of our allies in the suburb, wizards and demons—"

"The suburb murdered Magistrate Tihma," muttered Hassin at his back. "Tried to burn my gates. If they'd gotten through . . ."

"We have someone getting them under control," Jugurthos muttered back and prayed—to whom?—that it was true, or would be by morning. Kharduin, for love of Nour if nothing else, wouldn't stand for the suburb warring on the city. He raised his voice again. "And we can certainly stand against the temple guard. Sunset Ward and Riverbend—" He paused, looking at Hassin.

"And Riverbend," Hassin affirmed.

"—will fight for the three gods, for Ilbialla of Sunset, for Gurhan of the Hill, for the true Lady of the Deep Well, captive though she may be or murdered by this devil. For our gods or for memory of them. For Marakand free under its ancient law, which was the expression of the will of the folk, for the good of the folk. No kings in Marakand, no warlords, no tyrants, whether they rule through the sword or the mask of a god. We can stand against the devil. We will. I, and Captain Hassin Xua, and Hadidu Esau, beloved chosen of Ilbialla. We don't fight alone. The suburb is in arms, a wizard chosen and blessed by the Old Great Gods has come from the wilderness, a great bear-demon of the wilds has heard the prayers of the lost gods, and the Blackdog of Lissavakail, who slew the devil of Lissavakail, has been sent, a goddess's gift to a goddess, Attalissa's gift to Ilbialla, to our aid." And if they had vanished by morning, the mysterious powers that had arisen to fight the Lady beyond the walls, still, they had been there, and that was gift enough. "You can join us, you can raise your friends and family to join us, or you can flee. You can even choose to fight for the devil who has slaughtered so many honest folk of Marakand, who's hiding coward in her stolen temple like a rat in a hole this very moment. You are a free people. None can compel you, if you withstand your own fear. But you have to choose. Now. Tonight. No one can hide any longer. We've been set free of that slavery at last, by the grace of the Old Great Gods and their blessed wizard. Come. All of you here, come. See, bear witness, here by the tomb of Ilbialla. The wife of Ergos the sandal-maker, taken by Red Masks thirty years since as a wizard for her coin-reading, taken for death in the deep well and her corpse enslaved by the devil necromancer. That's what you've feared all these years. That's what's ruled you. A devil, a necromancer, and a perverter of the dead. Come. See her. Pray for her. And make your choice."

They did come, a tentative few, then a surge. The murmur started. The old man's words. *A wizard. The Lady, murdering decent tradesfolk with her own hands. A devil. She was a devil. Enough. It's enough. It cannot go on, not now. The wizard has shown the way. Without the Red Masks, the temple is nothing. We can fight them, at last. Captain Jugurthos.* He heard his own name. *Barraya. Those Barrayas.* His father's name. *Petrimos. You remember. Petrimos. And Elias, too. They didn't bow down to the temple . . .*

"Warden of the City . . ."

"Warden Jugurthos . . ."

"The Barraya . . ."

"But the senate—?"

"Damn the senate!" a woman cried.

Something thumped, three times, drumming. A stick on the roof of a carrying-chair? An old voice creaked shrill. "Family Sessihz affirms it. Jugurthos Barraya shall be Warden of the City, till the Lady is defeated and the true gods and law restored." A fit of coughing, but someone had heard, and that shout was carried through them like a wind-wave through the barley, *The Sessihz for Jugurthos, the senate is here, the senate for Jugurthos*, which hardly followed from one old man's vote, if you could even call it that, in such a time, in such a place. The coughing ended in spluttering and another creaking gasp. "What does it matter? I might as well die grandly as choke to death in my bed. Fool boy. Fool boys, both of you. Do you have any plans to get yourselves and all these fools who follow you alive past the dawn?"

But there was another cry going around. "Senator Demrios of the Xua for the Warden. Senator Shiwasa of the Xua for the Warden, Family Xua for Jugurthos!"

Senator Beni laughed, and coughed, and choked, and flailed his curtains aside to lean out on the door, like some disturbed tortoise peering from its shell. His once-plump face fell in sallow folds, dry as parchment, looking like a touch would tear it, more a corpse than the Red Mask woman. "I'll bring the Family to heel, for what anyone ever listens to Sessihz. I'll see what other fools I can round up for you. I'm dying. What do I have to lose?"

Jugurthos bowed. Hadidu gave a solemn nod that somehow looked like a blessing. The old man cackled and let his curtains fall back. A scrawny arm, hand heavy with rings, appeared, waved the chairmen around, and the whole equipage turned to take its leave. "See you die at least as well as your parents, young fools."

"Oh, gods," said Hadidu.

Jugurthos wished that uppermost in his mind was not, now, the memory that though a Warden of the City had more or less absolute power for the duration of the crisis of his appointment, his or her handling of that crisis would be judged by the senate, afterwards. Wardens of the City had been exiled before now, if they were found, after the fact, to have been deficient in achievement or otherwise unsatisfactory in their handling of their powers. Or they had been arrested and executed, or assassinated, when disinclined to give them up again. Jugurthos shook his head and grinned. "I should live so long."

"What?" asked Hadidu. He croaked almost as badly as old Beni and leaned on Jugurthos now, muttering, "Gods, gods, Old Great Gods, don't you ever make me do that again, Ju. Don't."

Jugurthos gave him a hasty one-armed embrace. "You were—Ilbialla can't be dead, Hadi, she must be still aware, somehow, in her prison, reaching out to touch you. I've never heard words of such power—I'd strip the gate of every man and woman in my command and storm the temple this minute, if you told me to." All five patrols of them. They were all fools.

Hadidu sank down on his heels, head on his knees, arms wrapped close. "Don't be an idiot. Find me some water. I'm dry as the desert. And for Ilbialla's sake, tell them *something*, give these people some orders, before we have a mob like the mob of the suburb in here."

"We're all fools," said Hassin, which was so much Jugurthos's own thought. "There'll be no storming of the temple gates. We can't get through the fire around the temple, and there's no way we could hope to put it out; there's no fuel left for it, and it's still burning. I went to have a look at it myself, before I came here. Saw a body, or part of one. Some boy didn't make it out of a house in time. He'd fallen. Just his head and shoulders, an arm. The rest was inside the fire. Gone. So are the houses that were there, just stone rubble and what looks like puddles of glass, if stone could turn to glass. The—the rest of the boy was a bit of white, might have been bone, just a streak of ash fused to the stone. That's all. We're not getting in through that, unless your wizard of the suburb can work another miracle. If she exists and is on our side at all. But the Lady'll be able to come out whenever she's good and ready, you can count on that."

"So we need to be ready, when she does." Jugurthos raised both hands over his head, stilling the folk who surged and jostled around the tomb, the nearest folk reaching to touch Hadidu's feet, his hands where he crouched above them, petrified again, Jugurthos thought, at the faces, the gaping mouths, the frantic eager hands.

But he was not without plans. He had planned, since he was a boy. If some flaw in the Lady's hold appeared in *this* way, then *that*, and if *that*, then *this*. . . . Sudden revelations of devilry and necromancy had not been in all those hypothetical exercises of planning, the substitute for the active revenge he could not take for his murdered parents, but he had his road before him now. A few steps of it, at least. Run. And swiftly, before anyone noticed there was nothing beneath his feet.

Warden of the City. That was several steps in itself. At least, if anyone in authority outside this square chose to acknowledge that declaration of the mob.

In the silence compelled by his upraised hands, he spoke again. Shouted. Orders. But he'd already given them to his own people before they ever left the fort.

Patrol-firsts began calling up the guards he had assigned to barricade and hold each of the five ward gateways. Not even a full patrol, just a couple of bodies for each, as a disciplined seed for what must grow larger. They shouted, inviting the younger men, the younger unmarried women, the folk who had come out half already tensed for action. The Lady wanted a militia? He had a militia, right here. He just needed to put himself at the head of it.

Captain Hassin leaned from behind. "Send your men meant for the Riverbend gateways to strengthen your watch on the Spicemarket and the Clothmarket walls. We don't need to have a border between us. Riverbend's mine. I'll raise what force I can and hold it for you. If I can."

"Good. Go. We need to keep in close touch. Make sure you can trust your couriers."

"You make sure no one gets a knife in the priest's back, Warden. He's the one the Lady will want dead, even more than you." Hassin saluted and jumped down. Jugurthos nodded to Tulip, who followed Hassin off the tomb. In the darkness she left behind her by going with her lantern to keep an eye on the crowd pressing about Ergos, he and Hadidu slipped down unobserved.

Talfan, though, was watching for them. The Westgrasslander Holla-Sayan was still with her. He hardly seemed a demon, not that Jugurthos had ever heard of a demon in human form anyway. They were usually animals. This Holla-Sayan seemed only a man, younger than Jugurthos, filthy with dust and sweat and what Jugurthos now realized was drying blood, his coat black and stiff with it, too much to be his own.

"Master Hadidu." He gave Hadi a nod that was not quite a carava-neer's hasty bow. "I'm to tell you your brother-in-law Nour lives."

Hadidu swayed forward as if he would grab at the man, who raised an arm to fend him off, stepping back. "He escaped? How? Where is he?"

"With Kharduin. He's not well. He was imprisoned—you know Ivah?"

"Ivah's alive and with him? Thank the gods."

The Westgrasslander's mouth twisted wryly. "Or something. Yes."

It was a foul tale he told, of the slow death Nour and Ivah had been left to. Worse than execution by drowning in the well, or had that always been a lie?

"You should at least have brought Ivah with you," Talfan said. She seemed to have rapidly gotten over her brief unease with the man. Or whatever he was. "We never knew she was a wizard, and one of such power and skill to boot. We need her here. If the Lady tries to break out of the temple—"

The look Holla-Sayan gave her was not exactly friendly. "She's been beaten and starved, and then she dragged Nour half-dead with Red Masks behind her, walked a mile through rubble and thorns and blister-vine nearly naked, fought temple guard, fought Red Masks, and fought your doubly damned Lady for you, wizardry to wizardry. She is *sleeping*."

Talfan subsided.

He turned his attention back to Hadidu. "They're both safe enough for now with Kharduin. Both sleeping. I wish I were. Come to Shenar's caravanserai in the morning, if you can. I don't know about Ivah, but Nour's in no shape to be moved yet again. They had to carry him off up the cliffs to hide when the temple came."

"Yes," said Hadidu, and then, wearily, with a look at Jugurthos. "If I can. Tell him I will, if I can. I don't know what might be happening here. Tell him I'm safe, and Shemal, and all the rest of the household got away. He'll want to know."

A nod. "You think you can take the city. Have you seen the temple?"

"The fire?" Jugurthos asked. "Only from a distance." He hesitated. "Have you? And how did you get through the gate, armed? You weren't with the handful of outlanders I let pass." *What fool of mine decided that was licence for any outlander with a sword?*

There was *not* a spark of green fire in the man's glance at him and away, Jugurthos told himself, but the fine hairs of the back of his neck prickled, and he had to quash an impulse to take a step back. Talfan entirely failed to stifle her flinching, her hand protectively over the sleeping baby's head.

"I didn't come through the gate," Holla-Sayan said. "And no, I haven't been to the temple. But I can smell it. You won't put that fire out. Neither will Ivah. It's not natural, and it's not wizardry."

"What is it, then?" Talfan demanded. "It can't be any divine fire. She's no goddess. Everyone says, now, that she's a devil and—"

"Did it never occur to one damned soul in this damnable city to wonder, till now? A goddess ordering the murder of wizards?"

"You mean the wall of fire is devil's work," said Hadidu, bringing them back to the point. "And you don't think a wizard can break it."

"Yes."

Talfan protested, "But Ivah broke the spell on—"

"The seven devils of the north were wizards. The spell the Red Masks could summon to flatten everyone with terror was human wizardry, but that wall of flame is most definitely not, and I haven't any idea how to bring it down."

"Then we pen the Lady in and let her starve—let her temple-folk starve, until they desert her and it's the devil alone we have to deal with. Slay her. Somehow. It must be possible. I hear it's been done before. The Lake-Lord was a devil, one of the seven . . ." Jugurthos waited, but the man did not contradict that, "and he was slain."

"Not by me, whatever you've heard," the Westgrasslander said. Hesitated himself. "Talk to Mikki."

"Who's Mikki?"

"The bear. He's sleeping, too. But Varro and Kharduin are," he shook his head, "talking about taking over the Eastern Wall fortress. If you want to hold the city, you'll want that. Sitting here isn't a choice for you. The Lady's afraid, she's confused, taken by surprise. Unsure of herself. She won't stay that way. Time's only going to sap your strength, such as it is, and restore her nerve. Warden, is it?"

"Apparently."

"Want some advice?"

"You have much experience with this sort of thing?"

The man's face went still, reflective. "You wouldn't think so. But I remember. I think." A grin. "Varro's ideas are old and simple and born of tales. He set Kharduin's gang to collecting Red Mask and temple helmets and uniforms from the corpses we left out there, while Kharduin went to talk to the people they hope the suburb will listen to. If you want to stop *him*, do it now. If not—well, I think they may carry their plan through. Kharduin may be only a caravan-master, but he commands a lot of respect in the suburb. You're damning this folk to worse than anything the Lady's done yet if you back down and let her regain her footing, but you can't hold the city with a stronghold for the Lady sitting right next door. I doubt the Western Wall will hold long if the Eastern falls, but it's farther away. You don't need to worry about it for the next day at least. Any idea what the numbers are, at the Eastern Wall? I'm heading back out now."

Take the Eastern Wall and its gate, now? Before he even knew if any captain but Hassin would join him? Running on a slope of scree, and the stones beginning to run beneath his feet, sweeping him—

"What are they doing?" Talfan asked, and turned, clutching her baby closer.

Jugurthos looked to see what had drawn her attention. People were kneeling by the tomb, or touching it, heads bowed as if they prayed. A focus, Jugurthos thought. A rallying point, a reminder and a promise, they would—Old Great Gods alone knew how—free their gods and restore the city. He could make it that. He would. He needed some such symbol, to hold the folk as one.

There, what Talfan has seen: a stirring, swirling among the people about the tomb. Gleam of lantern-light on an upraised sledgehammer. Holla-Sayan's head snapped about, and he roared, "No!" but the stone-mason—Jugurthos knew those bulging shoulders, the man lived only a street over—brought the hammer swinging around at a cornerstone of the tomb.

Lightning seared his vision, and Jugurthos flung up a warding arm before his eyes. It had arced, not from the clear night sky but from the tomb itself. People cried out and scattered, but there was no second strike. Jugurthos ran, but there was nothing to do for the stonemason. He was manifestly dead, the cloth of caftan and shirt burnt away in a patch broad as a spread hand, and the skin beneath charred black and flaking in the lantern-light. The haft of the hammer, too, was charred, and the iron head lumpish and deformed.

"Gods have mercy," whispered Hadidu, catching up, falling to his knees at the dead man's side.

"The Lady is not here!" Jugurthos shouted. People were fleeing. They were going to be useless. At least his own guards stood their ground. "The spell is in the tomb. Attempt no violence against it, not yet. We'll free our gods, but not this way."

He heard the words even as he said them and thought, how, when even the scholars of Nabban had no answer? But the folk had to believe it.

Hadidu was praying, the old blessings for the road, invoking the three gods of Marakand and the Old Great Gods. Some folk, the older, who knew the words, joined in.

"Remember, there is a wizard in the suburb who has come to aid us, a wizard who has fought the Lady and put her to flight, who has stripped the Red Masks of their blessing of terror and shown us the truth of their torment. If our gods are to be freed, it is wizardry will do it." Please, Ilbialla and Gurhan and the Old Great Gods, that they still existed to be freed.

The rush away had checked. People grimly gathered again to the street guards who had been organizing them. The stonemason's men, stunned and silent, gathered him up. "His wife," one kept saying. Just that. "Who'll tell his wife?"

Was he going to lose them all? *Claim the ward*, he had said. Holla-Sayan was right. Take the city while he still had something to take it with. Don't give the passion Hadidu had kindled time to die. They waited, but it was already cooling, in sudden death before them, in the blazing reminder of the Lady's power.

He held up a hand, holding them a moment. "Forty at the Eastern Wall fort," he told Holla-Sayan in haste. "Maybe fifteen are street guard under Captain Orta Barraya, and he commands the four patrols of the suburb blockhouse too. Six or seven patrols of temple guard as well. The two don't mix well. Captain Orta aspires to be temple guard. I doubt he'll rush to join us; he's from Ashir the Right Hand's branch of the Family Barraya, not mine. Ashir's the chief of the Lady's priests," he added, since he didn't suppose the caravaneer had ever paid that much heed to the temple before. He raised his voice, shouting, pitching his voice to carry. "People of Ilbialla! People of Gurhan! The Lady strikes at us even here, but we can stand! We can, we will hold this ward for the gods, for Marakand free again. The wizard of the suburb, the Lady Ivah, leads her army of the suburb to take the Eastern Wall. Will you break faith with your true gods, when even the outlanders fight for them?"

The Westgrasslander made some noise that might have been a choking laugh, and then he was gone, a shadow, a darkness that twisted the night, and a black shape like a wolf bigger than any dog Jugurthos had ever seen was loping away.

Talfan abruptly sank to her knees. "In my kitchen," she said. "With my children. How could he? Varro is such a fool."

Holla-Sayan didn't head back to the suburb but went away through the city, through Riverbend and Greenmarket, into Templefoot, strangely named, as it stood above the temple, not below. The streets were empty, curfew kept here. He didn't even see any patrols. When he came where he could see the pale glow of unearthly fire he took man's shape again and walked even more warily. He touched the white pebble in its amulet-bag at his throat. A token of his god, such as nearly all wanderers carried, to remind themselves they were not godless and lost. Sayan had himself sworn Holla-Sayan was still his, after he became the Blackdog. And sworn so again, when he blessed Holla's marriage, though he knew, he could see the change—and Holla-Sayan himself confessed it because he would not lie to his god—what he had truly become, and of his own will, to save the girl he had loved as his daughter.

Which was a devil. The man he had been ought to have died under Attalissa's altar. The two of them, man and devil dying together, had done what they must to survive, to go on, to save not the goddess but the girl. The Blackdog spirit had in truth been a wounded and crippled devil, forgotten, overlooked by the Old Great Gods, soul-scarred and lost to itself in a war fought across the lands of the old empire of Tiypur. Not even the bards of the road remembered those stories; it had all been long before the devils' wars in the north that had made the seven such figures of fearful renown. A crippled and soul-wounded devil, but a devil nonetheless. Enslaved by Attalissa of the lake, bound to but not bonded with a human host. Free now, and whole as he could be, bonded one, not two, not they, not he and it. He might still think of the dog as something separate, sometimes, but it was no longer the truth.

He could smell the fire, as he had told Talfan and the Warden, not the clean water-on-stone scent of wizardry but something like fire and metal. It was more than scent. It was a feeling, a pressure, a twisting of the world from its nature, as wizardry was not. It was . . . a wrongness, like a wound.

There were plenty of people here, hiding in the houses, watching from shuttered windows. He only imagined he smelt their fear.

The fire—smelt him. Or something. It leaned, licked the street. Heat reached for him. He stepped back. True fire he might risk. Not this. And what could he do if he forced a way into the temple? Fight the Lady and die? Slink furtive through its half-ruined buildings again and find no more trace of Moth than he had before? Defeated? Dead? The demon said not, but that could be a lover's hope, not any demonic certainty. Holla-Sayan could not believe Vartu Kingsbane, so old and—and *whole*, had been overcome by that confused child he had fought in the suburb, vicious though the girl might be. But what, then? And what hope for any of them, if the Lady could defeat even Vartu?

He should go back to Master Rasta's caravanserai, go home to Gaguush. She would be worried and worse than worried, furious. It was last night now he had gone off into the restless dark. Seemed a month, at least.

Something knew he was there. Not Moth, but the Lady. He felt her attention fix on him, strangely dreamlike, remote, as if she hardly knew what she did.

You. What are you?

He didn't answer, made himself quiet and still.

You are not he.

What did he see of her? Not the fury of battle now, the baffled rage of a thwarted beast as the fight turned against her and her servants were broken one by one. Confusion. Doubt. A great weariness. Fear. They were not all one. It was as though he touched two souls. Or three? The third, in terror, slid away, deeper.

Where is he?

—What is he?

Listen.

He listened. Nothing spoke. The impression of her awareness faded from him. If he had not been alone, when he first began watching the temple, he was now.

What had he seen? What had the dog understood?

She was young. Now he understood. They had said the Lady never left the well, and then she had, in form like a young priestess. Too many minds. *In this bonding, this body, she is young.*

She didn't realize how old and strong she was; she didn't remember. That was why she had fled him. She feared he was—someone else. *You are not he.*

He flexed a hand. A reborn devil, confused and uncertain? She was a roiling disharmony, fractured, twisted, discordant in her soul. Souls. Perhaps she could not see very far out of her own confusion. He knew madness. He, a part of him, the part that still could not find its words, had been there. But he was whole, now. He was one.

The Lady did not feel whole. Not yet. But she would be, surely. Varro and his friends were right. They needed to take all the resources they could from her, before she realized her strength and regained her confidence. Even Tamghiz Ghatai had needed his warband to hold Lissavakail.

Or to hold himself human, to be a warlord, a ruler, and not a mad tyrant over abject or mindless slaves. Could Ghatai have slain every priestess of the temple and nested there among the ruins, greater than a god of the earth, awaiting Attalissa's return? Holla-Sayan rather thought so. Tamghiz Ghatai had been sane enough not to want to. Strange thing to respect a hated enemy for.

So the Lady was broken, insane, but she was still far the stronger, and he could not breach her walls. He did not think anything but the sword Lakkariss would sever her from this world, a thought that brought cold sweat out on his skin. Had Moth taken the black sword with her, when she disappeared into the temple? If that shard of the cold hells, obsidian, ice, tear in the world, whatever it might be, fell into the hands of the Lady . . .

No. Or that mad girl would have come after him with it before now.

While she still feared him, though, while she still hid, they could at least strip her city from her, steal the resources of her tyranny, leave her nothing but her own self, and buy time for . . . for what? Aid to come? From where? Were they to wait for Moth to return? With the sword she had warned him would be his own death, if ever he came to the notice of the Old Great Gods?

Wait for the gods to awaken? What could they do against a devil? One god, alone, might only be able to die, but there were at least two in Marakand. And him. And Mikki. And Ivah's wizardry, and other wizards furtive in the suburb and now owing Ivah so much. . . .

The spells on the tombs felt, smelt, only like human wizardry, though they were woven with another will, another strength, the devil's touch. Still, wizardry was the framework of it, and you didn't need to bind what had been destroyed. And Ivah had already destroyed one great work of the Lady's, taken one weapon from her. Maybe she could give them one against the false goddess, as well, in the gods of Marakand themselves. Maybe, even as symbol and hope alone, they might prove to be Marakand's strength.

He didn't think Varro was right. He had not brought this down upon the city by failing to leave Ivah and Nour to die, by inciting the Lady to attack the suburb in search of them. No. He, they, he and Ivah and Mikki between them, had done it by giving the faithful of the old gods a hollow hope, by luring them out of their patient, fruitless hiding. Which shouldn't make him responsible for their damnable rebellion.

Gaguush's argument, he was sure. It wasn't going to sound any less hollow when she made it. He was in this now, no walking away. All it would take was for the Lady to send a handful of her invulnerable Red Masks out, immune to weapons and wizardry even stripped of their miasma of terror, to strike down Hadidu and Jugurthos with the fire of their staves. The city would fall at her feet again, wizards would be taken again, murdered and enslaved as Red Masks, and a devil come out of hiding to grow stronger, sitting at the nexus of the trade of the world. She was already reaching east to Praitan. How far would she stretch? West to Lissavakail? Beyond? To the Sayanbarkash, his parents, his brothers? His god?

No. Lying quiet and waiting only served so long. Too long. Time the city fought, and it could not do that, if its leaders had every moment to fear a death they had no hope of defending against. That fear was what had kept it lying passive so many years already.

No turning away. He'd already come too far.

Holla-Sayan let the dog take him and loped away through the empty streets. If the fearful eyes behind the shutters saw—let them.

CHAPTER VII

Come the grey hour before dawn, Varro was at the Eastern Wall. He had half hoped for Holla-Sayan to appear to back him up, but no surprise he hadn't. He'd probably gone back to Shenar's to sleep, or if he was rash enough, to Gaguush at Rasta's. The man had looked dead on his feet. Still, he shouldn't need the Blackdog here, even though he and Kharduin had just a hundred or so men and women, and half of them Marakanders of the suburb, tradesmen and grooms and the like, people he wasn't sure he'd trust not to pick up a sword by the sharp end. At least there were a handful of real street guard, ordered to join the expedition by Magistrate Pazum, the surviving authority of the suburb. Kharduin had led the man to think he had an equal share in directing things, wily desert snake that he was. He'd practically offered the caravaneers as mercenaries for the three gods, and somehow, within a very short time, they were all talking that way, folk of the road and folk of city, that they were all folk of the suburb together, serving the priest of Ilbialla and the three true gods of Marakand as if there'd been no murder mere hours past, as if the blood of the suburb's other magistrate and her clerks didn't still stain the earth.

The only brief problem had been Magistrate Pazum's own son, who had at first seemed to think he was in command of the expedition against the Eastern Wall, though he'd shut up and had the wit to stay shut up when Kharduin gave him a long, slow, considering stare from his icy blue eyes and asked him, "Led many raids, have you, boy?" Probably he'd been put up to it by his father. Truth was, he'd seemed more relieved than anything to be shoved into one of the Red Mask uniforms and told to follow Varro and do as he was told.

The Eastern Wall was ancient work. It flowed, partially ruinous, from the cliffs and steep scree slopes that were the southern edge of the Malagru Mountains to cross the dry riverbed of the ravine with only narrow arches for the passage of the forgotten water, ending where lesser cliffs rose to the city. The road from the east passed through a gateway of massive square towers. The ravine here was not dry but a swampy bed of tall reeds, their feathery heads whispering together. Too much whispering behind him. Varro turned to glare back over his followers. A few carried torches or the candle-lanterns of the street guard swinging on tall poles. Behind the dozen or so Red Masks and an equal number of equally false temple guard, the latter mostly Marakanders whose short hair would not betray them, the remainder of the force, under Kharduin's command, hung back in the darkness.

The fortress of the Eastern Wall was very like the city gates, double towers flanking the gateway, but dwarfing the defences of the city proper as a bull did a calf. The long wall and the fort were mirror to the one at the Western Wall, through which he had passed on every trip he'd ever made to Marakand. There would be doorways into both towers within the tunnel under the arch, and along the road ran lower walls enclosing stables, kitchens, other outbuildings, probably disused and half ruinous if the Western Wall were anything to go by, and pens for the courier-ponies. And, of course, the back doors. They were not necessarily unlocked or undefended back doors, but, the odds were, neither would they withstand Northron axes, if it came to that.

Not that he had an axe. He'd kept his own sword. It wouldn't stand out. The Red Masks had been armed with a variety of blades and some had had Northron weapons. Murdered Northron wizards, or just whatever weapons the temple had acquired? Whose had been the swordsmanship of the dead—the Lady's or their own?

And why was he worrying? Varro hitched his cloak over the ragged tear that ran from the neck down towards the left breast of his armour—Mikki's work. He wasn't facing Red Masks here. They were Holla's problem.

He'd better not be facing Red Masks here. He should have taken a longer farewell of Talfan, not just gone blithely jaunting off like that on her errand to send the Blackdog to her. He didn't like the way Talfan looked at Hadidu now, so fondly possessive, as if the priest were some creation of her own. He didn't dislike the man at all. He still didn't have to like finding him living in his own house with his wife.

Silence fell, no whispering now, as they marched up alongside the low wall enclosing the backside of the fortress. He hesitated. They hadn't been certain. Unconvincing if they pounded for admittance on what might turn out to be a gate into a corral or something. Nothing that he could see in the dark through the wretched narrow eyeslits of the suffocating helmet showed which of the several solid wooden doors was the commonly used way into the fort. The moment's hesitation was hardly noticeable, he hoped. Surely they kept some sort of watch. He led his troop on, into the deeper darkness beneath the arch. At the far end of that long, cool tunnel between the towers, the gates themselves were faced with beaten bronze, never closed except when an enemy threatened the pass, but they were closed now.

Pointless, when your enemy was within rather than without, and you opened your doors to him. Which was what the garrison of the fort did now, even as he lifted a gloved hand to pound with his short white staff of office upon a door in the northern wall. Why the northern? He chose at random. It might just as easily have been the southern he chose.

Obviously they had been observed coming. The masked, triple-crested helmets of the Red Masks were distinctive, and in the torchlight the red glowed with sullen fire. His heart raced. If they were challenged—

A temple guardsman saluted, stepped back, and saluted next some Marakander woman in temple guard officer's ribbons who stood near Varro. "Lady be praised, you've come at last," he told her. "We were starting to think the courier must have deserted or been taken by the rebels."

Red Masks didn't, Varro supposed, wait for invitations. He shouldered forward and oh, Haukbyrgga, goddess of the lake in the high dale of his youth, be with him now, let the others follow. He cut off the motion to touch the stone snail-shell in the amulet-bag about his neck.

The others did follow, flowing after him, gratifyingly, menacingly silent.

"Tell them up above!" the temple man shouted over his shoulder. "The reinforcements are here."

Reinforcements for what? Another temple guard peered around a doorway and thudded off up some stairs. And where were the officers? This man was only a patrol-first, by the thin stripe on his hem.

The man bowed to a point halfway between Varro and the woman in lieutenant's ribbons. "The rebels still hold the southern tower. We don't know if Captain Orta lives or not."

"A hostage?" the supposed lieutenant asked, and glanced sideways at Varro. "Give me, ah, a full report. Guardsman."

"A prisoner, at any rate."

"Are you sure he's not allied with them? A rebel himself."

"No, he's just a fool."

Ya, temple and street guard were not known for their brotherly relations. What started it? What had they heard, to rise in rebellion? And how many? Holla had said there were only three patrols of street guard here, and thirty or forty temple guardsmen. Ask, ask. Varro would have kicked the woman in the ankle to prompt her, but she didn't need it.

"How many?" she asked.

"The whole damned lot of the street guard and a few of our own, too, and I'll deliver them to the foot of the Lady's pulpit myself once I get my hands on them. Orta's lieutenant's the traitor; she took them all off and had the doors barred before we realized what was up. We expected some help before now." The guardsman's look of baffled weariness began to tighten into a frown. Taking in, maybe, their unavoidably ragged and bloody appearance. Not-so-fresh from battle. They filled the small anteroom, the last rank still holding the door open, blocking it so with their bodies.

"You're not first company. I don't know you." The man's hand went to his sword, and he took a step backwards, frowning at the false officer.

This wasn't some great empire's army. There couldn't be more than a handful of captains and lieutenants in the entire temple force, known to all. The first impression of the uniforms had gotten them as far as it was going to. Varro raised a hand and swept it down. They all surged past him, through the opposite door and up the stairs, through into other doorways. The guardsman opened his mouth as shouts of alarm came from some inner room. The woman clipped him hard on the jaw with the hand clutching her guardsman's club. She gaped in astonishment when he actually dropped, looked at her fist, and grinned. "I wish my brother had seen that."

Varro left her behind, taking the stairs two at a time to catch up with the leading edge of the surge. A disorganized roar followed him from behind. "Ilbialla! The gods of Marakand! Ilbialla and Gurhan for Marakand! Death to the false Lady!" Accents of the road dominated.

Kharduin caught up with him at the top of the stairs, where Varro pulled off his helmet. The protection it offered was little use when he couldn't see what he was doing. He hurled it at a cluster of temple guardsmen impeding one another on yet another set of stairs, over the heads of some other Red Masks who were likewise shedding helmets.

No shields. Forcing stairs held against them without shields was going to be deadly. His men were already hesitating, faltering back. Varro shouted and seized a bench from along the wall, a long, unwieldy weight, but Kharduin caught the other side, and with it between them like a ram they ran for the stairs, their own folk pressing back to let them through, closing in to put their weight behind it. The temple guard fell and were run over or fled scrambling up.

"On your knees!" Kharduin roared, as they burst into a chamber filled with red tunics. Some were already coming towards them, weapons in hand, but others still clustered to a door in the far wall, which they had been driving another bench against, trying to force it open. Hah, the passage over the gate to the southern tower. "On your knees and ask mercy of your true gods!"

"Murderers! Devil-lovers!" someone else cried.

Some of the caravaneers below set up a yell and came boiling up in an incoherent clamour, pursued by—dear Haukbyrgga, Holla had said a mere thirty or so temple guard, hadn't he? No time to count, and these were scarred and scared and desperate, some at the back still lacing helmets or barefoot. They'd been sleeping. Varro damned himself for a fool. The yards out back. Barracks there. Of course. These were survivors of yesterday afternoon, cut off and abandoned when the Lady ordered the city gates closed. And a tide came *down* yet another flight of stairs, forcing back those of his own band who had started up. Lanterns had been dropped or gone out when their bearers flailed with them as weapons, and only a couple of the torches still burned, waved aloft, though one smouldered on the floor. They were packed too tightly into this room and another adjoining it, hardly room to swing. Those with the short stabbing swords did better, but in places it seemed mostly grappling, hand to desperate hand like a damned tavern brawl, fists and heads and boots and even teeth. In the dim and swirling nightmare light friend and foe looked one.

"Ilbialla's guardsmen, get down!" Kharduin roared. "Down on the floor, for your lives! Now! Down and out of the way, for the gods of Marakand!"

Some, obedient without thought, dropped; others hesitated. "Get down or lose your damned heads!" Varro roared, and then they understood, most of them, and not only dropped but crawled away between legs, seeking a safe corner. Now there were fewer rebels standing in the clothes of the dead, but gods and Old Great Gods, ya, those on their feet had room to use the longer swords and sabres favoured by the caravan mercenaries, and in the chaotic torchlit flare and shadow any guardsman's silhouette was enemy. Or had only its own slow wits to blame.

Made the fact they were outnumbered worse, of course, with so many of their allies ordered out of it.

Varro drove forward, the sweep and swing of the blade a dance. Cursed sword, hah. A damned excellent sword was what it was, and if the enemy faltered, confused by his Red Mask armour, so much the better.

"The Lady is dead!" he howled and watched a man's eyes widen, a hesitation, overcome as he tried to close in to stab, but Varro sliced the flesh of his arm away and trampled him down. Another voice, Kharduin's, took up the cry from the foot of the stairs to the uppermost storey. Others added theirs, made it the battle cry, and there were more temple guards huddled on the floor than they had brought with them, surely.

"Throw down your arms! The Lady is dead! The Red Masks are dead and the Blackdog comes for you!" Kharduin cried. "Death comes for the devils! Death for the false Lady!"

Varro had cut a clear way to the landing of the stairs from below, stood there with an undisguised Marakander and some grey-haired Nabbani man at his back, to hold it against any further push from below, but the handful of temple guard left down there, apparently as rear-guard—and hadn't Kharduin done that himself, or had the whole mob ignored him and pushed on up?—had dropped swords and staves and held out empty hands.

The Nabbani ducked around him and walked cautiously down, sword ready. "Sit," he told them. "Along the wall, there. Don't move." He kicked weapons out of reach, shouted without looking around, "A little help, down here?" A couple of the Marakander street guard, pale in their grey tunics, edged by Varro and clattered down. A third stood with him.

Movement in the corner of his eye. Varro turned just as a red-tunicked guardsman who'd been crouched on hands and knees by the wall rocked forward and stabbed through his ragged red cloak. He yelled and struck with all the force of his turning. The man's head lolled back, throat fountaining, and the knife, tangled in dirty silk, scraped shrieking on the armour beneath as the man fell away. The Marakander beside Varro, so slow to see, to move, now finally yelped and leapt back, wide-eyed and sprayed scarlet. "I didn't see," he stammered. "I didn't see him there, I—"

"Damn your eyes, watch them!" Varro snarled. More street guard pushed up around him, dragging another temple guardsman, terrified and stammering his innocence, to his feet.

"Take their weapons and lock them in the gaol for now," a woman shouted. "Sort them later. We'll find an oath they'll fear to break."

"Not me, damn it, I'm a weaver of the suburb, I'm for Gurhan," someone cried.

"All the warden's folk in temple uniform, the three gods' folk, get over here. Get someone to vouch for you." That was Kharduin. "And someone stamp that fire out."

Varro threaded a way through the throng to him, trying to wipe at least his gloved hand and hilt clean.

"And who in the cold hells are you?" a woman with a burgeoning black eye was demanding. Single wide black stripe on her hem; a lieutenant of something or other. Grey tunic. Street guard. Hadn't come with them from Magistrate Pazum.

"Kharduin," Kharduin said. "You're—Lieutenant Jing." Of course, an eastern road master, he'd know the officers of this fort. They'd have taken the tolls off him often enough. "Where's Captain Orta?"

"That fat—dead."

"How?"

"He fell."

"Fell where?"

"Onto the road."

Kharduin's expression said what Varro thought.

"Lady my witness, he did. He got away from us and was trying to get over here to the north tower on the roof in the dark."

"Pick another god," Kharduin said darkly, dismissing Orta.

"*Gurhan* be my witness." Her voice shook and her hand was tight on her sword's hilt. "Orta fell. It might have been the judgement of the gods."

Kharduin merely nodded. "Ally of Jugurthos, are you, Jing?"

"Jugurthos? Sunset Gate? No, not in particular. What's he got to do with it?" An assessing look over both of them. "That," and she poked at Varro's torn armour with her sword, "should have been fatal."

"It was," he said. "Or would have been, if the man hadn't been dead already, Great Gods help him find his road."

"True, then? They're walking dead, the Red Masks? Wizards. Dead slaves. I believe that. I saw. . . . And the Lady's the necromancer?"

"Who told you?" Varro demanded.

She scratched her chin, considered the pair of them.

"Kurman," she said. "Cousin of mine in the temple guard. He's the one over there stripped to his shirt, or what's left of it. We didn't have any spare grey for him. His idiot mother put him into the temple guard, but his heart was never in it, you know. We're from Silvergate Ward, Gurhan's folk from long back. Anyway, you, Northron, I don't know you, but *you're* Master Kharduin. I heard your Nour was taken for a wizard."

"He escaped," said Kharduin shortly. "He's alive. Did Hassin tell you there's a Warden of the City been proclaimed by the folk and the senate? Jugurthos Barraya."

By a few of the folk, anyway.

"*Him?* Warden of the City? The Lady really has lost control, then. No, but I haven't had any couriers from Captain Hassin in a while." She waved her few patrols away. "Give these a hand. They're on our side, outlanders notwithstanding."

"What was going on here?" Kharduin asked. "What started the fighting?"

"The temple guard showed up here fleeing the battle in the suburb. They put their heads together with Orta, and the bastard ordered us all to barracks. He was going to turn the place over to them. Kurman got me aside and told me what had gone on out there, folk butchered in their homes and the demons that came for the Red Masks. I'd have had trouble believing him, but he was so shaken he could hardly stand, and I've never seen the boy cry before. Anyway, we'd had a few caravans bolting out before the order to close the gates came, and Master Lu, the horse-dealer, he's an old friend, he told me what was going on up past the Gore before he fled, and what Kurman said meshed with that. Something's wrong in the city, and I wasn't going to be locked up unarmed by temple bully-boys with lies in their mouths. They'd already locked up three of ours, the ones that survived that Nabbani wizard or assassin or whatever she was, the day before the Voice of the Lady died. Because we let her escape, they said. As if we could have stopped her, after she beheaded a Red Mask! And she'd killed everyone on gate-duty. If that's the great wizard who's fighting the Lady for us, then I'm not sure there's much to choose between them."

But Holla-Sayan was still on the road with us, Varro thought, and even Ivah couldn't kill Red Masks; Holla said so.

"I—I don't think it was our wizard," Varro stammered in the face of the lieutenant's accusing glare. Defending Ivah, devils take him. No, not that, not when they were real and present in the city. Old Great Gods forgive him. Sneaking murder was more Ivah's style than bold assault, but he couldn't offer that in her defence. Kharduin was her devoted servant now, and she probably hadn't had to bespell him to it, though she was quite capable of that. "No," he said firmly. "It couldn't have been Ivah, the wizard of the suburb. She was—" what had Talfan said about her, "she was living in the city then, at the Doves, disguised as a scribe. She hadn't," and he was surprised the words didn't choke him, spinning legends for the traitorous bastard Tamghati, "revealed herself to the city yet."

"I hadn't heard anything about another wizard killing Red Masks either," said Kharduin, plainly fascinated. "Lady Ivah's full of grief for her friend Ghu. He showed her they could be killed, she said, but he died at the Doves—at least, he wasn't imprisoned with her and Nour, and no one's found a trace of him since. But this wizard you saw left the city before the Doves burned?"

"She was an old woman anyway, not a man," said Jing.

"Old, you're sure?" asked Varro. "Not just pale-haired? You might think sort of silvery-old, but really just a sort of autumn beech-leaves colour?" They didn't have beeches, here. Or any real autumn. "Maybe a really fair-haired Northron?"

"She was Nabbani."

Not Moth, then. Damnation. One wizard—one *devil* he wouldn't mind having turn up.

"And a swordmaster, what a swordmaster," Jing went on reflectively.

Varro shook his head. "We don't know anything about that. Pity she's gone, though. The more Red Mask killers we can find, the better."

"Not if they're going to kill three or four of my guards for every Red Mask," said Jing. "But you wanted to know how this fighting started. When they told Orta to arrest us too, we took the south tower and dragged Orta with us. That's all. I didn't really think it through. Stupid. I just didn't want to be locked up." That seemed to remind her. She shouted in the direction of the stairs to someone to "Let Young Ead and the others out. And so," Jing went on, turning back to Kharduin. "Master Kharduin. What are you doing here? Aside from the obvious."

"Taking the Eastern Wall for the Warden of the City, in the name of the senate and the true gods."

She snorted at "senate," rubbed her face. "Lady, that hurts. All right. You've taken it. Now what?"

He bowed, mockingly. "Captain Jing Xua, it's all yours."

"Thank you. Going to clean up your mess?"

Kharduin looked around. Bodies and blood. Not much sign of the quick and easy overrunning they had hoped for. No, this *had* been quick and easy, comparatively. Varro remembered Lissavakail.

"Will you look to our wounded and the dead? I don't think we can carry them all away."

"I don't think we can tell them apart," Jing muttered.

Varro had crouched by the woman who'd been so proud of knocking down that first temple guardsman. Dead. Some sword had found the damage in her stolen armour. The magistrate's boy bore only a cut cheek and a sombre look; he was leading an effort to carry the wounded down to beds in the barracks below.

"Tell them apart? No," said Kharduin. "You probably can't. That's the problem when a tribe fights itself." He turned away, scowling. "Lay the dead out decently somewhere, Jing, all of them. People may come seeking them. Varro, round up our lot, count heads, and go let Warden Jugurthos know we have the Eastern Wall."

Varro thought about protesting being conscripted as a mere errand-boy, considered the cold ice of Kharduin's eyes, and settled for a nod.

By the time he'd hauled the Red Mask armour off, Jing was pressing a sealed tablet on him for Captain Hassin, too.

Demoted to courier, was he? At least he'd be the one carrying news of the victory to Talfan. He plundered the horse-pen for the best of their ponies.

CHAPTER VIII

The scouts didn't see their enemies coming, didn't hear the two stalking them afoot until the first arrow whined from the hazels and took one of the three in the cheek. She'd aimed for the eye. Deyandara didn't swear, just nocked another arrow. It was not, after all, so very different from hunting deer. The man had fallen, but she didn't think the angle had been such that he could be counted dead and out of the action yet; it wouldn't have struck up into his brain. The other two scattered left and right, one making it to the horses, the other disappearing on his belly into the gorse that rolled down the hillside behind the campsite. The horses panicked suddenly, swinging haunches around, heads into the wind, ears back and eyes rolling, and the man who'd been about to mount had to spring away or be trampled. He turned, too, which gave Deyandara a brief clear shot between helm and the thick leather collar of his coat.

Dead, but now she'd lost the other from the corner of her eye, and in the dusk the first to fall had vanished as well. No, he was trying to keep out of sight, creeping down towards the stream and the horses, the arrow broken off. A second bit through the jerkin he wore, deep into his ribs, the leather little use at this range. He scraped frantically, then feebly at the earth, trying to pull himself onwards, before he stopped moving. Up the hillside, a man cried out. One of the horses broke free and bolted downstream.

Rustle and crack to her left. Wrong. There were only three. Arrow on the string, she swung to face into thickening shadow, deeper in the thicket of hazels that had let her creep so close along the bottom of the hill. Nothing moved. Slowly, she sank down on one knee, looking between the stems. Still no movement. And where was Lin? Lin didn't break twigs. She was uncannily silent in her stalking.

Deyandara heard the Marakander at the last moment, a new rustle that sent her leaping back as his sword thrust from beside her. She loosed the arrow, but with a bush between them it tore twigs, snagged, and tumbled harmless. The man dodged around, a Grasslander with matching scars on both cheeks, his sabre raised for a proper slash now. It caught on a branch; she had her knife, but he kicked at her as he wrenched his blade free. She fell, rolling away, slashed at his following legs and made him dance. Squirming to put another many-stemmed hazel between them again, she bounded to her feet and shouted for Lin, who had a sword, damn her, and was wizard besides. The Grasslander bared his teeth, circling. She kept moving, kept hazels between them, and there was Lin, running doubled over, weaving through the brush like a coursing hound. The man turned in time to see her before she cut him down.

No old woman should run so fast.

"Where were you?" Deyandara demanded, searching for the bow she had dropped, queasy with nerves now that it was all over. There, and not trampled, thank Andara.

"Up the hill."

"Doing what? You said you'd circle around."

"Circling."

"You took your time."

"I'm an old woman."

"Not so as anyone would notice."

"I was persuading a fool of a Praitannec scout that I wasn't a Marakander mercenary, if you must know."

"What?" That cry. "Andara prevent you didn't kill one of Marnoch's scouts!"

"No, he's still up there, and in one piece. Or," as there was a sudden slithering and crashing, "perhaps not. Down here, boy!" she called, raising her voice. "The Marakanders are dealt with, and Lady Deyandara wishes your escort to Lord Yvarr."

The scout was no boy but one of Marnoch's own huntsmen, balding and with a grey-grizzled beard. He came through the hazel thicket much more slowly than Lin had, spear levelled and a red welt rising on his cheekbone.

"My lady Deyandara!" He raised the spear and grinned. "It really is you."

She not only knew his face but remembered, after a moment's frantic thought, his name. "Faullen! Well met. This is Lady Lin, a wizard in the high king's—in my service."

"We introduced ourselves just now," said Lin gravely.

Faullen eyed her. "Wizard, eh? It's been a while since an old woman kicked me in the face. And I wasn't even trying to steal a kiss. I think you've loosened a tooth or two, as if I had any to spare."

Lin kissed her hand to him. "Next time, friend Faullen, listen when a lady whispers in your ear."

He grinned. "Next time, Lady Wizard, try whispering something more to the point than, 'Hush, I'm a friend.' A man believes that when he's stalking Marakanders, he deserves gutting. I take it you've dealt with all three of them, or our happy get-together would have been interrupted by now. Can I ask, Lady Deyandara . . ."

"I'm on my way to Lord Yvarr," said Deyandara.

"The Lord Seneschal is up at his own *dinaz*, four days ride, but Lord Marnoch's army is camped just a few miles northwest of here. He's been making a circle, to come at the royal *dinaz* and the Marakanders from the west."

"Even better," Lin answered for her.

"Yes," Deyandara said, with a quelling look at her. They had overshot, then; they had left the road almost at once after Marakand and struck out into the trackless hills, angling towards where Lin's nightly divination told her Marnoch would be. And for over a week, she'd had Lin telling her, *Remember you're their queen's rightful heir returning from a mission set you by their goddess, not a truant child slinking home.* Lin had better remember she was Deyandara's wizard, not her tutor or grandmother, to speak for her. "Can you take us to him?"

Faullen and Deyandara salvaged everything useful from the Marakander mercenaries, and Deyandara recovered her undamaged arrows, dividing the Marakanders' quivers with the hunter. By then the third horse had returned. Faullen caught it, saying that spare mounts were going to be useful. He left dealing with the dead to Deyandara, who pulled up a handful of muddy grassroots and dropped it on the one lying by the brook; she did the same for the man who had gone for the horses.

"Go to your road in peace," she said. "Don't stay here to trouble the decent folk whose rightful land this is."

Lin had remained within the hazel thicket, kneeling with a hand on the chest of the man she had killed. Praying, maybe, though she hadn't bothered to pray over others she had slain in their two previous encounters. The light murmur of her voice rose and fell, paused and rose again. By the time she rejoined them the dusk had thickened into night.

"They were on their way back to Ketsim with the news that Marnoch was near," she said.

"I knew that," said Faullen. "Why do you think I was looking for their camp? They wouldn't have lived past the dawn. I was about to leave to report back when someone started sticking them full of arrows." He clapped Deyandara on the shoulder. "You shouldn't take such risks, my lady, going in outnumbered like that."

Deyandara was on the verge of saying it was Lin's insistence, not her own, and that this was the third time they'd taken on greater numbers of Marakander scouts, when Lin's pinch on her arm silenced her. Yes, don't make childish excuses, pinning the blame elsewhere. "We thought they might be carrying word of where Yvarr's made his stronghold," she told him, picking the best of her reasons. "We couldn't let them betray that to Ketsim."

"You shouldn't risk yourself," he repeated. "I'll see you safe to Lord Marnoch, now. Do you bring word from your brother?"

"I've been in the south," she said briefly.

"Best you save the tale for Lord Marnoch," Lin added.

Faullen, reproved along with Deyandara, merely bowed.

Faullen had been doing his stalking on foot; riding one of the cap- tured mounts, he accompanied them over the gorse-covered hill and up a bend of the brook into the narrow valley where they had left their own horses, leading the way on between the hills again. Marnoch wasn't trying to conceal his presence yet; from a hilltop half a mile away they saw the fires—too few, surely, for an army—but they had been challenged by a patrol well before that. Faullen sent a boy from the patrol that met them riding ahead to "Tell the war-leader that Lady Deyandara's come back to us, with news from the south." Deyandara felt queasier at that than she ever did in the aftermath of attack. She'd told that meeting over in her mind so many times on the way from Marakand, and somehow it always ended up being only herself and Marnoch, alone, and the words came easily. Now they fled her. It would be a public meeting, of course it would. By now the entire folk would know Cattiga's bastard niece had fled the royal *dinaz* before it was abandoned to the enemy.

She should have believed Lin when the wizard said she would go with her if she ran away, and not haul her back to her brother by her ear. She didn't want to be here. She shouldn't be here. She had walked into a little room, a narrow, windowless room, thinking she could bear it, telling herself it was duty, and now they were closing the door and there was no key and her heart was racing, the reins slippery in sweating palms.

Marnoch rode out to meet them, in a shirt of ring-mail such as only a king could afford, at least among the Praitans, and very formal. Probably it was some treasure of the royal house, saved when they evacuated Dinaz Catairna. Her heart lurched at the sight of him. Him, most of all, she did not want to believe she was a girl—a woman—who would flee her duty. At least riding Ghu's white mare Deyandara felt larger, or taller, anyhow, and less foolish at being bowed to, though she would rather Marnoch's face had not been so set and blank in the torchlight, or his words so stiffly correct. Lin didn't help, keeping half a length back, equally expressionless. At least Lin could be counted on to always look regal, never a torn thread of her brocade from racing through the undergrowth, never a smudge of ash or moss or mud.

Even once Faullen, to his disappointment, had been dismissed, and a girl had taken their horses, another bringing hot towels and wooden bowls of watered wine, Marnoch remained cold and correct, ushering them into his lanthorn-lit tent and introducing the two lords, one lady, and one lord's heir who stood waiting. Only Gelyn, the chief bard's daughter, seemed glad to see Deyandara safe. The woman embraced her like a sister.

"We haven't known what to think, since you disappeared from the *dinaz* in the night, Lady Deyandara," Marnoch said. "It's good to see you safe at last. But why aren't you with the high king?" *Did you run away to him*, he meant, of course. *Are you returned as his servant?*

Deyandara drew a deep breath. *I only came to say I didn't mean to run away, but I can't be your queen, I can't live trapped in a hall with people about me every waking moment of the day. I need the hills and the wind, a horse and a dog and old songs. . . .* Now, if ever, she should speak queenly, but . . . how would the bard Yselly have had a princess tell it, in a tale?

Lin, at her shoulder and a pace back, arms folded, was more queenly than she could ever be, and more threatening than the armed lords about Marnoch, for all her grey hair and lined face, if only they knew it. She should live up to that escort, but the truth was, Lin mostly made her feel small and young and shabby.

"I did not abandon the Duina Catairna of my own will," Deyandara said, and heard her voice tremble. She clenched her hands on the hem of her jerkin and relaxed them again, carefully. "After we met, you and I and the Lord Seneschal and some of the lords, I went out to see to my pony, to be ready when the time came to leave the *dinaz*. We had been speaking of that—"

"Speaking of Ketsim's approaching army," muttered the youngest lord, Fairu, who had been there. "And you fled."

"I—" *Ignore him.* She almost heard the words, in Lin's voice. "Catairanach came to me, there in the stables."

Fairu sniffed. Lin shifted, ever so slightly, to look in his direction.

"She said—" Catairanach had said she would have no child of another god's land rule her folk, but repeating that would do no good now, "—the goddess told me to take a message for her, to an assassin of the Five Cities dwelling near Gold Harbour. She appointed him her champion to see her vengeance brought to the Voice of Marakand for the murder of blessed Cattiga and my cousin Gilru, and the treachery done against them in their hall. I wasn't permitted to tell you, Lord Marnoch, or to ask your aid in this, though Andara knows I would have wished to. The goddess's will surrounded me, overwhelmed me, and I simply— I went, like a goose drawn south in the autumn. I have no memory of leaving the *dinaz* or of how I avoided the advancing Marakanders. I came to myself again well away from the *dinaz*, knowing it besieged or abandoned behind me."

"Abandoned and burned," said Marnoch.

"They've quarried the south of the hill away and built a wall in stone atop your dyke," Lin interjected.

Another sniff. Lin simply rolled a hand in the air, sketching some sign, and held it up brimming with liquid light, as if to study Fairu's fluffy-moustached face more closely. The sceptical lord backed hastily away.

With an effort, Deyandara ignored the byplay. "I found the Leopard, as the goddess bade me, and accompanied him and his servant to Marakand, where I met Lady Lin, a wizard and my former tutor, who had come in search of me. She has sworn herself to my service rather than my brother's, to accompany me safely back to you."

Short, to the point, and every word true.

"The high king was at the ford of the Broasora, awaiting the last forces of the Galatan and the Duina Lellandi just over a week ago, Lord Marnoch," Lin added, rolling formal phrases grandly off her tongue, but then, she always did have an old-fashioned formality to her speech. "He may be on his way west, by now."

Marnoch's face had lightened as Deyandara spoke. "Deyandara, this is true?"

"If Lin says so. We came from Marakand."

"We did know he was at the ford, with a large army. We're not without wizards ourselves and at my father's *dinaz* we thought it safe for them to work. It's much more easily defended than Dinaz Catairna, being folded tight in the bare fells. Numbers can't come at it. We've seen a few scouting patrols; none have lived to return to Ketsim." A brief smile touched his face, reporting that. "To tell the truth, we expected to find Durandau at Dinaz Catairna by now, but there's been no word come up of that. We haven't dared work another divination since we set out, for fear of betraying ourselves to the Red Masks. It's true they smell magic. A soothsayer with my scouts disobeyed orders and cast the leaves to search for enemies out in the hills, when he was far too close to Dinaz Catairna. Red Masks came down on them not long after, and took him. Two of the scouts with him were slain and the third left for dead, which is how we know about it at all."

"The five of you are all that march to meet with Durandau?" Lin asked. "Do the rest of the lords of the *duina* follow?"

Marnoch's jaw tightened. "All who could or would join me have. The Lord Seneschal would have come, but someone has to stay apart from the fighting to keep order, or we'll have war behind as well as ahead of us."

"Costen and Hicca are already at feud," muttered Fairu, "and between them they've driven my folk out of their eastern grazing. Do we need that light, wizard?"

"And Hicca has entered into some kind of treaty with the Marakanders, we know that. Paying tribute, maybe, maybe even sending some of his bench-companions to Ketsim at Dinaz Catairna," said the older lord, Goran. The lands of the ridge of high hills between Dinaz Catairna and the caravan road were Goran's, the first to be overrun by the Marakanders.

"We can't fight the Marakanders, not with the Red Masks leading them and—we saw it first when they drove the rearguard from the burning *dinaz*—reducing everyone who comes near to a cowering child. We'd all heard those stories from Marakand, but I didn't believe it until I saw it. Felt it. They didn't bring that power against us in the hall. They didn't need to. And they still fight invulnerable, with their Lady's hand on them," Marnoch said. "The lords know it. Too many see it as a choice between death and saving their own folk."

"We've even tried fire-arrows!" burst out Dellan, daughter of Austellan. "They can't be killed. Small wonder if the lords would rather keep their folk home, but my father says, better to die true than live a forsworn bondsman of some city goddess. He's with the Lord Seneschal, my lady. You know he's blind, since the pox last autumn, or he'd be here with us, but—"

"And even if their own followers are as unmanned as we by whatever power gives them such fear, there's always more of them sweeping around the edges, killing warriors still too panicked by the Red Masks to resist," said Marnoch wearily, waving the young woman to silence. "I've seen men just wrap their hands over their heads and wait to be dropped dead like a clubbed rat. But if we can meet up with Durandau, if he has even half the warbands of the kings with him, maybe there'll be so many of us we can prevail and leave the Red Masks standing alone, without anyone to follow them. For our own honour and that of Catairanach, we shouldn't scatter and hide and wait for the high king to tell us it's safe to come out of our holes, or wait for the Marakanders to lure half the *duina* to them with promises of favours and wealth at their neighbours' expense. However few we are, we need to be there, with the high king, to remind him *we* are the Duina Catairna and he comes at our asking."

He took a breath. "But Deya—my lady—the goddess sent you from us? I had the wizards divine for you, once we were away. We thought it safe enough to call them back and have them to do so; Ketsim seemed to be settling in to rebuilding the *dinaz* with no urge to push farther north. They could learn nothing of where you had gone, or even if you were alive or dead. They began to think dead, and then one, I think it was Mag, said no, only very far away. We thought, if the last drawing of the wands was right and you did live somewhere that the wizards couldn't see, that you must have gone back to your brother in the Duina Andara. That's when the lords began to withdraw to their own valleys. Without you . . ."

"I didn't mean to leave you," Deyandara said, and her voice shook again. She steadied it, looked around at them all, chin up. "My lords, believe that. I knew my duty as blood-heir of Cattiga and Gilru. I didn't mean to abandon you. I had no choice." The lies came easily, because they were the right thing to say in a tale. She almost wished the fatal snake had bitten her instead of Yselly, in the long-vanished autumn. But Marnoch was smiling at her again.

"We could ask Catairanach, if she'd speak to any of us," muttered Lord Fairu. His *dinaz* lay in the east on the borders of the Duina Broasoran. If one of his neighbours was already allied with the Marakanders, he might have no way back to his own hall but through a victory at Dinaz Catairna. "No one's heard from her since the night we abandoned the *dinaz*."

"You've no call to doubt Lady Deyandara's word," Marnoch said. "No one saw her pass out of the gate. We'd feared some foul magic of the Red Masks abducting her." Or shielding her flight, if she were an agent of Marakand after all, no doubt. "If Catairanach's hand was over her, that accounts for the way she disappeared from the eyes of men and the divination of the wizards."

"Easy for her to claim that, when the goddess refuses to come even in dreams to the wizards or to the Lord Seneschal. Have the wizards test her words for truth, before we trust her," said Fairu. "But not here, so close to Dinaz Catairna and the Red Masks."

"There are those who will stand to defend Deyandara's honour." Marnoch set his hand to his sword's hilt. "If you mean to accuse your queen of treachery or even cowardice, Fairu, do so openly. She will not be insulted so, taken before the wizards for judgement as if she's a servant accused of theft."

"Indeed," Lin purred, without moving at all. "But you, Lord Marnoch, have duties as war-leader of the *duina*, at present. I will stand as the champion of the queen-presumptive."

"It is the truth and you can ask the wizards to try me, for all I care," Deyandara snapped. Lin put a hand on her shoulder, demanding silence.

"A champion who is wizard cannot bring wizardry into the circle of judgement against an opponent who is not," said Fairu. "Perhaps your foreign wizard doesn't realize that, Lady. And I'm certainly not going to fight an old woman."

Lin merely smiled, closing her hand on her light, which winked out. Fairu backed away a step.

"Catairanach will appear again when she judges we have need of her," the bard Gelyn said. "I, for one, have faith in my lady Deyandara and acknowledge her Cattiga's heir and successor. I speak for my father in this as well."

"I was willing to swear to Lady Deyandara as my queen at Dinaz Catairna the night the goddess sent her away," said Lady Senara, who was surely too old to be carrying a spear into battle, but who wore a sleeveless vest of leather and bronze scales nonetheless, her white hair braided tight around her head. "I still am."

Fairu, after a moment, bowed his head. "Since the war-chief and the bards place their trust in Lady Deyandara, I will do likewise. For now. Let her prove worthy of it."

"Thank you," Deyandara said, when it became clear everyone, even Lin, now waited for her to say something. It came out sounding dry and sarcastic and rather like what she thought Lin—or Ahjvar—might have said, not the gasp of relief she actually felt, not for the fact that Fairu accepted her, but that there would be no duel between champions. She had no fear of Lin failing to win any fight to blood or death in the circle, but it would be a devils' victory, apt to create more strife, raise accusations of unlawful wizardry, because how could a woman of Lin's age do what she did? Or was it wizardry, some spell preserving youth's strength and speed, and without it would her self-proclaimed champion creak and groan and stoop?

The tone bit. Fairu flushed but gave another, deeper, bow.

"Now," said Marnoch, and his smile, finally, was welcome, for her, her alone and not Catigga's heir, "your news, Deya?"

She left most of their tale for Lin to tell, of Marakander scouts evaded or ambushed.

"And you bring no word from the high king at all, Lady?" Fairu still sounded mistrustful.

The question was meant for Deyandara. Lin waited on her answer. "I wasn't going to come back to you on my brother's leash."

"We'll see the truth of that once we meet him, I suppose. And what about this assassin?" asked Fairu. "Do you mean the Voice is dead? Do the Marakanders at the *dinaz* know it yet?"

"I don't know," Deyandara had to admit. "She was alive when I left Marakand, but news couldn't have outrun us, anyhow." The Voice dead, or Ahjvar, and if Ahjvar, then likely Ghu as well. She had tried not to think of them at all since leaving the city behind; there was nothing she could do about them. That she had carried the goddess's command didn't make her responsible for Ahjvar having obeyed it. It was all very well for him to risk a horrible execution for himself, but to drag his servant into it . . . getting angry about that did her no good. She should have tried to command Ghu to come with her. He wouldn't have listened. He only saw Ahjvar.

"Does it make a difference?" Lord Goran asked. "If the Voice is dead, if she isn't—we still have to retake Dinaz Catairna and see Ketsim's head buried beneath the gate."

"It may make a difference to what the Marakanders do," the bard Gelyn observed. "Should we risk the wizards, my lady?"

After a moment and a glance at Lin, arms folded, silent and smiling tightly at her shoulder, Deyandara realized that question, as well, was meant for her.

"I don't—what do you think, Lord Marnoch, Lady Lin? Has anyone learnt how near the Red Masks have to be to find a wizard?"

"Pagel may have discovered it. He was the soothsayer of my household, who got his fellow scouts killed," said Fairu, with a dark look at Lin. "The third died later, did Marnoch say? Pagel knew he was forbidden to use magic, even the little divination he was capable of. Whatever powers the Red Masks have, they're strong, and it goes beyond spreading panic like a stench around. It was the Red Masks in a body who rode first into the storm that came about the *dinaz* in the morning as we abandoned it. I saw. I was with the rearguard, the last left to witness. But when they rode over the brook that's fed by Catairanach's spring the rainstorm ended. The waters calmed, the wind died, the fog burned away—and maybe the goddess with it, for all we can tell. And those of us who were left in the burning *dinaz* to try to get a true report of their numbers and what they might do next fled, mad and wild as our horses with terror. We shouldn't risk bringing that down on ourselves. Trying magic here might be like building a great beacon on a hilltop to signal where we are. They may already be sniffing us out."

"If a little light were going to draw them, they would have been on our heels days ago," Lin retorted. "I'm so dreadfully lazy about kindling fires with flint and steel. So frustratingly slow, when one has been riding all day and wants one's supper." A cheerful lie. Deyandara suppressed a smile. They had been living mostly on oatmeal soaked in cold water, raisins, and the leathery, sweet-salt smoked meat Lin had been carrying, not risking a fire made by whatever means. "Your unfortunate soothsayer must have been very close to the Red Masks when he made his ill-fated experiment. Divination is usually a fairly quiet undertaking, as it were. It makes few ripples on the surface of the world. That's why even the weakest in talent can eke out a living as soothsayers. Perhaps I could meet your wizards, Lord Marnoch?"

She didn't quite imply the other Catairnan wizards were mere soothsayers as well, though her tone walked close to it. Not even Fairu protested the insult; all Praitan knew the weakness of Catairnan magic.

Divination for the fate of the Voice had had to wait until morning. The wizards wanted daylight, but dawn came with mist filling the valley of the brook they followed. The tops of the willows broke the surface like islands in a pearly lake. Deyandara stifled a yawn with the back of her hand. A chance to wash in a basin of hot water, to wash her hair for the first time since the bathhouse in the suburb of Marakand, a night's sound sleep on soft blankets in a tent, and a large—and blessedly hot— breakfast had somehow brought home to her body all the weariness of the past weeks, months, of travelling. She could have slept the day around, but the warriors were breakfasting, the scouts and outriders spreading in a fan before them, her tent was already down, and the wizards were waiting. Her braids had been wound close around her head, held with many pins. Someone had provided a close-fitting helmet, one of the few women of the bench-companions a shirt of scales, heavy on her shoulders but not over-large. She would be much more comfortable in leather, like the huntsmen turned scouts, skulking in cover and shooting unseen. No sword; she hadn't the skill or the strength, but she had her bow and a new, long dagger. With Lin at her side she did not need a sword herself. Marnoch had set Faullen to be her groom, with Rozen, a young woman of the scouts, to be body-servant to her and Lin; both were guards as well and carried spears as they followed her, still in their scruffy leathers and green and brown plaids. Not much of a royal household, but she wasn't much of a queen and didn't command much of an army.

She wasn't queen yet, anyway. It needed more than blood, or even blood and choosing by the last queen; only the acclamation of the lords and the blessing of the goddess could make it true, and what happened when the goddess denied her before them all? Shame, dishonour . . . escape from the need to take on the duty she owed the aunt she had so briefly known?

"Lady." Mag, an older wizard-woman of Yvarr's household, greeted her and Lin both with a cheerful grin. Hallet, a brown-haired man from the western hills, distant cousin of Gelyn, bowed more formally, while the third wizard, his brother Haildroch, looked up from the small fire, kindled with two sticks, which he was puffing into life, feeding carefully with small twigs. Haildroch winked at her. The yellowish smoke smelt of pine needles. Beyond the lords their bench-companions and household folk crowded, and beyond them anyone else who had no other pressing task. Witnesses, she supposed. Lin stood at her back again, not, after all, taking part.

Deyandara had seen divination performed often enough in her brother's hall, either the simpler casting of the leaves on water or into fire, which one alone could do, or this greater ritual of the wands, which needed three. Hallet, who had the best voice, began without any warning to sing a prayer, swaying back and forth to the beat of Mag's drum. The onlookers fell into silence, or at least subsided to a distant whisper and mutter on the fringes. *Catairanach blesses the willow, roots in deep waters. Catairanach blesses the alder that burns hottest . . . the oak that crowns the heights, the elm of the straight grain . . . the Old Great Gods hold the world in their cupped hands. . . .* Haildroch passed the wands, long slim twigs from each of the eight trees of the sun, the eight trees of the moon, and stalks of the eight holy herbs, through the smoke three times. Some, the willow and alder, poplar and rose, yarrow, dock, and nettle, were new-cut, their green leaves unwithered. The smoke, instead of rising, began to pool about the three of them and their fire, like the mist in the valley bottom. It was the sort of airless, windless morning that promised a scorching day, but the smoke roiled and turned as if tugged by conflicting breezes. Someone coughed.

"Three questions," Haildroch said.

"Three answers," Mag responded, while Hallet still sang. It was no longer a prayer but one of the old chants that only the wizards and the bards preserved; the words had meaning for few even of them. There did always have to be three questions, or three faces to your question, and three wizards. Lin's Nabbani coin-throwing involved no prayer or ritual at all, only scraps of poetry that went with the configurations of the coins. She always seemed amused by the Praitannec method, even the simpler casting of the leaves, though she would play the drum for Launval the Younger and Elissa, when Durandau called for a soothsaying in the hall.

Blessed by the smoke, the twigs were arranged like a nosegay of flowers in Haildroch's hand.

"Is the Voice of the Lady of Marakand gone to the Old Great Gods?" he sang, weaving the words into Hallet's chant. He wandered the circle, stopped before Gelyn, who knew what she was to do. The bard closed her eyes and plucked a twig. Yew. Deyandara saw the dark needles and knew that one. Anyone would. She sighed with relief, even as Haildroch held the wand high and named it. Mag sang, "The Voice has passed through the darkness, the Voice has taken the road." Haildroch threw the yew twig on the fire.

Death, the simplest meaning of the yew, and that meant Ahjvar had succeeded; she could hope after all that he had escaped safely, as he presumably had so many times before, and that Ghu had found him and they were safe and out of Marakand. She also hoped Ahjvar had not beaten him for giving away the horses.

"Is there strength in our enemies yet, or do they falter in the loss of their great priestess?" Haildroch took his fistful of wands to Marnoch, who, a hand over his eyes, drew out two.

"The oak and the elder."

A stir, faces settling into grimness. Oak, at least, always represented strength and age and that which endures time itself. Not, in this context, a good foretelling for them.

"There is strength unbroken among our enemies," Mag sang. "Though the Voice is dead, there is new life, new strength, new will."

It was not a matter of merely knowing what each twig or stalk or leaf stood for. If it were so, every man could cast for his own fortune. It was the power that flowed through a wizard's blood, which ran ahead of thought and voice and flung back echoes of the eternal stars, the words that spilled from the wizard chosen to answer, all unknowing. Haildroch crossed the circle again. Deyandara felt herself blushing, all eyes on her. She should have known when he went to Marnoch in the second place, Marnoch who was war-leader and lord of them all for this time. No wizard had ever offered her the choosing in a wand-divination before;

they wouldn't, not in her brother's hall. Her curse, her ill-luck, couldn't be allowed to taint any wizards' working. But she was the great lady here and must be the third.

Haildroch hesitated. There, he would turn away, go to someone else. But he was only waiting for the wording of his question to come to him. "What strength is there then to oppose us in Dinaz Catairna?" he almost whispered. "What strength is there in Marakand? What power dares keep Catairanach's queen from her own?"

No friendly winking now, just dark, unfocused pupils. With the eyes of all the war-council on her, Deyandara froze. Lin kicked the back of her heel. She snatched jerkily at the twigs, forgetting to close or cover her eyes, gripping the wands in a sweating fist. Her palm stung and burned. She looked to see what she had chosen. Gorse. Nettle. Dry stalk of old thistle. Haildroch didn't take them from her but raised her hand by the wrist.

"Gorse," he cried. "Nettle. Thistle."

"Ever-blooming," Mag cried in answer. "The undying come to war. The poison burns in the heart of the well of Marakand and they will know grief and bear the punishment that must be theirs for they have slain my Voice my word my chosen one and brought me to this and they dare to rise against me they dare to slay my chosen my servants my own to send my own against me I see her now she dares to set herself against my will the land is mine this land is mine she will not you will not be their queen their god—" Mag's voice rose to a scream. "You will die again and die again and die again for we are dead and she is dead and the fire can burn even you as she burned—" The drum had fallen. Mag clawed at her own face, and Hallet, waking from his trance, flung himself to her, seizing her hands, shouting her name. Haildroch dropped Deyandara's arm. The spined wands fell, trampled as Lin pushed past her, sweeping a hand, hissing some word that sent a white fire flaring like lightning, making a circle, leaping from body to body all around the ring. Mag burned in it. Deyandara saw her own shaking hands outlined, the red rash of the nettle rising on her palm turned into a tracery of white like frost, Marnoch's dark hair silvered as if with age. The smoky fire roared up, consumed in a sheet of lightning. It settled into ash as the last smoke billowed skyward. Everyone fell back. Mag moaned and rocked herself in Hallet's arms but raised her face while people were still holding out their hands, touching face and hair, reassuring themselves they were whole, unharmed.

"What in the cold hells was that?" Mag demanded. Her voice squeaked like a child's. She wiped her scratched face on her sleeve, pushing herself up shakily by Hallet's shoulder.

"Protection," said Lin drily. "It would seem we have still the power behind the Red Masks to deal with." Her fingers dug into Deyandara's shoulder, gripping like claws.

"What power?" Haildroch asked.

"That," Lin said, "is what I am wondering, too."

"But Catairanach marches with us," Marnoch said, and seized a spear from Faullen standing near, brandished it high, shouting for silence, commanding the eye of all about. "Catairanach and the justice of the Old Great Gods go with us. You saw the sacred fire drive the enemy's will from our midst."

"And Lady Lin has slain Red Masks," Deyandara added. "Even if Ketsim's mercenaries still hold the *dinaz* with the red priests' aid, they're not invincible. I've seen them die."

"Oh, hush, child," said Lin, but she folded her arms and looked reassuringly foreign and dangerous as all nearby turned to stare. Deyandara flushed. "Well, you have. They need to know."

"One Red Mask. Once."

"That's more than anyone else can claim," said Marnoch. "Why didn't you tell us sooner, Lady Lin?"

"Because I'm an old woman and my lady's guardian, not some assassin or a Northron berserk for you to send to the fore."

Marnoch's eyes narrowed. "We can talk about that later, in a less public place, I think."

"And how did you do it?" demanded Hallet.

"I—" Lin waved hand. "It's not something I could teach you."

"Hallet," said Marnoch. "Not here."

"That wasn't any divine fire, that drove—whatever it was—from this drawing of the wands," Hallet persisted. "It was you, but what kind of spell—"

"I couldn't teach you," Lin repeated.

"And after that, better the folk believe the gods do march with us," muttered Haildroch. "As I'm sure Catairanach does, in spirit, at least, if she can't lend any practical aid. Marnoch . . ."

"I know." The war-leader took Hallet's arm. "Listen to Haildroch. Don't speak of this beyond the lords in council. Only those at the front saw what happened; let it be thought the goddess's work, for now, to give them heart. Look after Mag."

Mag was rubbing her temples as if with headache. The other two wizards swept her away, to find their horses and servants and make ready to set out. Marnoch spoke a few words to the lords and ladies, and they, too, scattered, to speak to their captains and their village-captains. In a very short time the company was on the move again, travelling in a single winding column, with pack-ponies in the rear, no wagons. The lords rode with their own mounted bench-companions, but over the course of the day each of the four tended to drift to Marnoch and away again. A council on the move.

It was Deyandara they discussed. She knew it. Whenever they stopped to rest the horses and let the stragglers catch up, the lords all came together with the wizards and Gelyn. Deyandara didn't feel comfortable joining them but kept a little apart with Lin and her shadowing scouts. When the purple dusk began to stretch long from the west and they made their camp—the last at which they would put up the tents or risk cook-fires—the bard came to summon her, bowing low.

They met in the open, and again, the bench-companions of the lords made a ring, and beyond . . . it seemed half the camp gathered, beyond. Deyandara's knees had gone watery. She knew what this was about, but when Lord Fairu stepped forward she thought for a moment she was wrong, and it was a challenge of her truth instead, till he dropped to his knees.

"Lady," he said. "Will you swear, in the name of Catairanach our goddess and Andara your god, and in the sight of the Old Great Gods above, that you are the bastard-born daughter of Palin, only brother to our queen Catigga, and that she so acknowledged you to be?"

Deyandara swallowed. Why did he have to be their spokesman?

Because he was the one who had challenged her word and impugned her honour. He was the one who had most need to demonstrate loyalty now.

"Yes," she said faintly. "So far as I know." Luckily that did not carry far. Marnoch's mouth twitched. But then he went down on his knees too, and so did Lady Senara, stiffly, and Lord Goran, and Dellan, with their bench-companions, the wizards and Gelyn, and on in a tide outwards. Only Lin did not kneel, but a queen's champion would not, in such a time.

"Then you are our queen," said Lady Senara, "by right of blood, by word of the late queen's will in her own voice, and by acclamation of the lords on behalf of the folk."

"And when the land is free again, we will ask you to call Catairanach on our behalf, that she may give you her blessing," finished Gelyn. It did not sound quite like the proper ritual for making a queen. Shorter than what she remembered of her brother's ritual of accession following their—his father's death, and the goddess should surely have been there. There was no heavy royal collar for the bard to place around her neck, either, no ancestral sword or spear to be laid across her hands.

She should have spoken before now. When Catairanach denied her blessing . . . but they needed her. Four lords and the seneschal's son to take back the *duina*? The tribe was already falling apart in ruin like an abandoned house. The high king wasn't coming to aid them as a lord should aid those who followed him; he would be coming, when he finally felt strong enough to be safe, as a greedy neighbour, to chase off the brigands and plunder what they had left, to claim the land and rob the stones to build his own outbuildings. No wonder their goddess had already given up.

It was the other way around, surely. The tribe fell apart because their goddess took no interest in seeing a new king or queen quickly named and blessed, to unite them against their enemy, and made no effort to fight the strange powers of the foreign goddess and her priests but pursued instead her own secret purposes of assassination and revenge. Catairanach left them sheep without a shepherd, straying lost on the hills.

But it wasn't over. Folk stirred and rose and began murmuring to one another, but as Gelyn paced towards her, carrying a folded dark cloth in both hands, her bard's ribbons fluttering behind, they fell silent again, craning to see.

"Lady," Gelyn said. "We've carried this with us, hoping by Catairanach's blessing to find you with the high king. It's not the collar of the kings of the *duina*, which is hidden safe against a happier time, but it is an heirloom of your house and a token of your accession. Wear it as a sign you are ours, that you will do us justice, and be the messenger of Catairanach to your folk."

After an awkward moment Deyandara remembered she should kneel, which she thought was right; at least, she remembered her brother kneeling, when the god Andara brought his father's collar to him. The bards stood for the gods, when there was need of a proxy. She went down with a thump and had an impression of braided gold and green-eyed animal heads, snarling, ears folded back, as Gelyn shook the torc free of the cloth, but she couldn't see it as the bard worked it on, pinching a little in the process, and cold. Cats, maybe? Heavy on her collarbones. Not so heavy as the great breast-covering collar of the kings would be. The cord and the amulet bag with the token of her own god's hill, the carved thornwood disc, was an odd thing to wear beneath a royal neck-ring.

Gelyn raised her by her hands and turned to the folk, raised her own hands high and they cheered, crying out for Catairanach's blessing, long life, victory, and death to the warlord of Marakand.

So she was queen, by the will of the lords of the Duina Catairna, or at least those of them who had not run to their own halls. Queen until the goddess refused her. At least she was not queen for the high king's convenience, which was what this ritual, and the royal heirloom, were really about. There remained only for Marnoch and the four lords and ladies to kiss her hands, and then to ride through the camp, with Marnoch and Lin at her side, Faullen and Rozen at her back, to show herself to the folk. Her folk, the warriors of her company. They knew her and they cheered her, but without Marnoch to lead the folk, they would all be scattered and hiding, waiting for their lords to fall to the Marakanders or to come to terms with Ketsim, one by one.

She was Marnoch's banner.

CHAPTER IX

Oats and barley and wheat were green in the crooked stone-fenced fields of the valley bottoms, where what earth there was, was sweet, as Marnoch's small band drew closer to Dinaz Catairna, but the scouts, trying to thread a way through the long ridges of the high, bare hills that would keep them from friendly as well as unfriendly eyes, reported seeing few folk on the tracks that ran from village to village. There ought to have been more sheep on the fells, and cattle and horses, too, on the lower hillsides. The few they did see wandered on their own, without humans or dogs to herd them. One village the scouts dared to approach in the early dawn they found deserted, and a great raucous flock of crows rose to circle from the village-centre chestnut, fading away like a scudding raincloud over the hills.

"New graves," they reported. "And what looks like a single grave-pit too, very new. A new hall where the threshing floor used to be, up on the rise above, with a paling around it, but the gate was open and the place empty, except for wandering fowl and swine. Graves there, too, a few new, and a pit again. Not the number of carts you'd expect, and the houses empty of things like baskets and tools. They've gone in good order."

The lords were still mulling over that, when another pair of scouts came to tell of traces, two weeks old or more, of beasts being driven away to the northwest, sheep and horses and maybe wagons.

"They're trying to escape the Marakanders" was Deyandara's suggestion, one made in desperate hope, maybe. "They rebelled, there were killings, maybe of the lords set over them, the survivors fled, and the folk are heading for the far hills."

"But to leave their sown fields is desperation," Gelyn said. "And, I'm sorry, my lady, but I don't think you can be right, not if there were no signs of violence."

Nothing beyond the graves, the scouts who had gone to the village said. No burning, no smashed storage jars, no slain dogs.

"But that wasn't all," said the elder of the two who had found the trail of the village's departure. "The tracks of sheep and horses, plenty of those."

"No cattle?" guessed Marnoch. "Catairanach prevent, not again. It's been three years."

"Cattle straying abandoned on the hills, my lord," said the scout. "Some look pretty bad, just lying there, not even switching the flies off. Snotty muzzles and running eyes. Dead cattle, too. I took a look, though from the carcasses alone it's hard to say what they died of. The crows have been busy."

"Cattle-murrain."

"I'd say so. And the folk've simply given up and gone."

"Last night I dreamt of empty houses," said the wizard Mag, low-voiced. "It won't be only their cattle. There's bad air here. It's taken their Marakander lord's household and half the village, so the rest have fled it."

A scout who had gone to the village wiped his arm over his face, as if to brush off some clinging taint.

Lin shook her head but said nothing aloud to contradict that verdict; they pressed on without lingering.

Bad air, Deyandara thought. It didn't look the place for that; the brook curving around the village ran swift and white over stones, plunging downwards between the green and purple hills. The fevers that came from living on swampy ground or by stagnant pools didn't make for a sudden filling of graves. It was the privilege of wizards, like bards, to speak in poetry, but this was no time to call one thing another.

"Plague, or the bloody pox?" she asked for Lin and Marnoch to hear.

"There's been no plague come along the eastern road in years, that I've heard of," said Marnoch. "The pox, maybe. It should have burnt itself out by now, though. I wouldn't think there were so many in any village this close to the *dinaz* who hadn't already survived it."

You didn't take the pox twice, even if you'd only had the milder eastern disease it was said had first come from the desert road. Marnoch's scattering of pitted scars were fainter than her own. He was safe, there was that, anyway.

Abandoned fields and families wandering as nomads, with only their sheep to support themselves. The folk, like the folk of all Praitan, were few, and settlements scattered. There'd be grazing they could take without fighting, but for anything other than what their flocks could give them, they'd have to fight, and it wouldn't be just the herd-raiding that was half a sport and so rarely led to deaths. There would be brigand-gangs laired in the folds of the high fells, come the autumn's cold rains. The queen and the leaders of the folk of these particular hills should be sending a warband to fetch the wanderers home to their planted fields, but she certainly couldn't spare any of her few lords and their compa-nies to deal with it now. All she could do was hope they didn't carry the murrain with them, taking a few apparently healthy cows or oxen along to drink from other village streams and leave dead on other village pastures.

Even if Durandau did succeed in driving the Marakanders out of Dinaz Catairna, the fighting would be far from over.

Marnoch's band did swing westward again, putting more distance between themselves and the chance of Marakanders riding in search of the vanished villagers. The scouts later the same day reported a small party coming from the west and the villages of the far hills, Grasslanders and desert folk guarding a string of camels; Marnoch sent Fairu's company to take them, since they couldn't be avoided. They lost one man themselves, killed most of the Marakander mercenaries, and brought two back captive. The woolly, two-humped camels, loaded with wool and woven cloth, beer and cheeses, were stripped of their harness and turned loose, most of the load abandoned, since the scouts knew nothing of handling such beasts, but they brought back the foodstuffs.

Deyandara was not witness to what went on with the prisoners that evening. Perhaps she should have been, but she thought of herself that night in the thunderstorm with the brigands, bound and helpless whatever they chose to do, knowing that a few punches to the face were the least of what she might expect. She couldn't bring herself to go to watch. Marnoch had certainly not wanted her there.

She did hear the woman scream.

Lin appeared at her side while she was grooming Cricket, singing an old, slow, sad song of lovers parted by war, while Rozen, with more enthusiasm than tunefulness and certainly more lusty cheer than suited the song or her lady's state of mind, joined in the burden.

"Lord Marnoch says they are to be killed, and will you come, my lady?"

She kept her eyes on a knot in Cricket's mane, teasing it free. "Do I have to?" Low-voiced, her back to Rozen. Faullen was taking advantage of the early halt to clean the mud-stains from Ghu's white mare, downstream in the brook of the valley bottom, but she had bench-companions of her own besides the pair of scouts, two warriors of each household of her five lords. They were never far away.

"No," Lin said.

"Should I?"

A hand under her chin, tilting her head up. No amusement, no mockery in the set of Lin's mouth, the corners of her eyes, which made her look almost a different woman, older and younger in one. "They're your enemies, executed in your name. Do you think you should?"

She dropped her gaze again. Nodded, shortly. The torc made the back of her neck ache. She handed the comb to Rozen and with a gesture borrowed from Lin, swept her warriors around her.

"What did they do to them?" she asked.

"You should ask, what we've learned. Or what they've done, in the months they've been taking such tribute from the villages."

"Marnoch will tell me that."

"This isn't Pirakul. I don't see your Marnoch skinning men alive, no matter what he wanted to know of them."

"I thought that was a Nabbani torture."

"Really? Huh. I wonder who they blame in Pirakul? Anyway, they were beaten. The woman's hand was put in the fire when they tried to tell us that they saw a large party of Red Masks and temple guard to the southwest, two days ago. A hundred riders or so. Marnoch thinks it true, that Marakand is sending more of its red priests to reinforce Ketsim against Durandau's coming. Goran thinks it a desperate lie to deceive us and set us fleeing." Lin added thoughtfully, "It was true, or both of these Marakanders believed it to be so. They couldn't agree how many were Red Masks. I wonder how many there ever were in Marakand?"

"What about the village we saw?" Deyandara asked. "What did they say about that?"

"They didn't know anything. Their own captain's assigned village is to the west; they were escorting tribute to Ketsim."

Deyandara frowned. "At least the Red Masks they saw—they say they saw—should pass south of us, if they haven't already. We should camp here another day to be sure of it. They shouldn't have any reason to turn up towards us. How near do they have to be to detect wizardry, do you think?"

"Do you want me to find out?" Lin chuckled. "They're likely at the *dinaz* by now. If my queen wishes, I'll try to find them, once these are dealt with."

These were a woman with long braids and a man with swirling lines tattooed in black on his forehead. The man's hands were bound behind him; the woman's were not, and one was swollen and red, blistered and seeping. She clutched her wrist with her good hand, and her eyes were glazed with pain, not seeing them. The man's nose and mouth bled, and his eyes were swelling shut.

Marnoch caught Deyandara's eye, so she went to his side, face set not to show anything, to him, to the prisoners, who probably could not see, to any of the lords who might yet doubt her fitness, or their warriors standing about. Which had held the woman's hand in the fire? She didn't want to know. It could have been Marnoch. It could have been any one of them. But any one of them, all of them, could die, if they rode unwitting into Ketsim's mercenaries out in force, or if they met the company of Red Masks. She thought of Cattiga again, astonished, bleeding, murdered, and Gilru running to his mother. She was able to look at them then.

"My lady," said Marnoch. "Lady Lin's told you what we learned of them?"

"Briefly, yes."

"Is there anything else, my lady?"

Should there be? She shook her head. "No."

Marnoch gave a sign to two of his household men. They killed the woman first, striking off her head where she knelt. The man struggled and was kicked down to his knees. Maybe they had been friends, lovers, kin. It took two blows of the axe to sever his head. Grooms dragged them to a shallow grave already dug. So swiftly it was over. So easily.

Lin had not even stayed to watch. She had walked a little away from them all and stood alone, under a leaning pine atop the ridge they followed, looking west. No, looking at something she held in the palm of a hand. Deyandara touched Marnoch's arm and started up that way, but of course, all her spearmen, eight men and two women, had to follow, spreading out around her, and his as well. Lin glanced over her shoulder and turned to them, looking down again. She held a disc of polished silver or a mirror of glass on silver, maybe, with a complex spiral pattern cut into it of cobweb-fine Nabbani characters. The reflections of clouds like wisps of fleece and the green boughs overhead seemed to hump and rise and twist away down the spiral as Lin angled it, becoming a stormy sky, leaden, copper-lit, with swirls of grey that could have been rain or smoke. She saw Deyandara craning to look and tucked it away inside the breast of her coat, leaning back against a shoulder-high cairn of piled stone beneath the tree. It marked the ridge as a holy place. Some god dwelt here, revered by the folk whose pastures these were, or had once been, who were nonetheless Catairanach's. There were always a few lesser gods and goddesses scattered across any god's *duina*. Lin treated the cairn as a piece of furniture.

"Devils take it, Lin! Don't scry for Red Masks, you'll bring them down on us! Remember that scout."

"I need to leave you for a little," Lin said. "Lord Marnoch, you'll keep her safe."

"Nobody is leaving," Marnoch said.

"Lady Deyandara did tell you I killed a Red Mask at Marakand, yes? You wanted to know how. I still can't tell you. But those Red Masks and guard from the temple have changed their course and are heading for the track up from the road. They're riding against Durandau now. The high king is just south of the *dinaz*, and no matter how small the troop, he has no way to fight Red Masks. I swore to protect Deyandara, though. Not your queen and not your tribe, not this land, but her. Since she is your queen now and the heart of your tribe, I do serve that, and by what I hear and what I see, I think I can probably serve her cause better . . . doing what has to be done now, than I would by standing among a crowd of perfectly able warriors all eager to lay down their lives for her."

"You're going back to Durandau?" Deyandara asked.

"No."

"You're not going to fight dozens of Red Masks on your own?"

"I don't know what I'm going to do. We don't know how many there are with Ketsim. We don't know how many more there may be in Marakand. It's Marakand that sends them. I'm going to the city."

"Tell me why," said Marnoch.

"What good does that do us?" Deyandara demanded. "You know something about them you haven't told us."

"I don't know."

"You guess."

"I might, but I hardly serve you well with guessing. I need to know."

"Needing and wanting aren't the same thing. You told me that."

Lin blinked. "Did I?"

"Yes. I forget why."

"Probably you were being foolish."

"Probably I was. Possibly you are."

"Deya, dear child, I am old enough to have survived any number of follies. I have vast experience of them. This, however, is need. I can only be in one place at once. I can defend you against Red Masks. I can't at the same time defend your brother, or the goddess of this land, or Marnoch, or his old father up north, or the folk. Remember what the wands told. The Voice is dead, but the power behind Marakand is ancient and unabated."

"Give us some space," Marnoch told his captain, and Deyandara nodded at hers, waved a hand, sending them all to a distance.

"There's something else coming out of Marakand?" Marnoch asked. "Something worse? Then say so. What did you see in the mirror?"

"I'm certain of nothing. I don't see why your stony hills and your sheep should interest anything that might have made its lair in Marakand. Those red priests are no priests and no servants of a goddess. They're a work of necromancy, I'm sure of it, and I begin to see . . . I'm not sure what. It's hidden from me. But there is a power—there are *powers* in the city that have no place there, and I think they are what send the Red Masks against you."

"What kind of powers? What about the Voice and the Lady? How do we fight them, then?"

"I'll know that when I know what, and why. That's why I must go to Marakand. Why am I arguing with you children?" Hands on hips, abandoning her propped and casual air, she might almost have stamped a petulant foot, if she had been sixty years younger. Mocking of her own irritation. "I mean to serve Deyandara in this, Lord Marnoch. Believe that, if nothing else. I will not betray her, and I *will* return to her."

"That's great loyalty, for a tutor."

Lin shrugged. "I swore."

"No," Deyandara said.

"I did. I remember it quite vividly."

"This isn't the time for playing the fool, Lin. You know perfectly well what I mean. You can't ride off back to the city. We need you here. I've seen you fight like a woman half your age—like a *man* half your age *and* twice your weight. I'm very certain my brother and even his wizards have no idea just how great a wizard you are. You're the only one with any chance against the Red Masks, unless you can teach Lord Launval the Younger and Lady Elissa to do what you do, or even Mag and the wizards we have here."

"I cannot."

"If we can kill enough of the Red Masks and capture Ketsim, we can demand Marakand's surrender. Or kill him and hope his followers break up and scatter. They're only fighting for money or some promise of plunder. They're not serving their own gods or kings. They shouldn't have much loyalty to Marakand. It's our only chance of defeating them. And if our folk see that the Red Masks can die, they'll rise up for us. If we go on as we are to join Durandau without you, we're doomed. Everyone in this army knows it. They all knew when they set out they had little chance of doing anything but dying honourably and—and horribly. The terror of the Red Masks will drive everyone mad, and the Marakander mercenaries will cut us to pieces while we cower. You're the only hope we have." She raised her voice over Lin's beginning protests, "And if you leave, half this company are going to decide you're a Marakander spy."

"There are a few Nabbani among Ketsim's folk," Marnoch pointed out. "You could be one of them, that's what'll be said."

"Colony folk," Lin said with disdain.

"I can't tell the difference," said Marnoch. "You've all got black hair."

"*You* have black hair, Lord Marnoch."

"They'll suspect you, Lin," Deyandara said, before that could get any more childish. "And from you they'll suspect me. We're going to be meeting Durandau before long." Please, Andara and Catairanach, that it was soon, and that her brother could hold out against the Red Masks till then, take the nearest *dinaz* as his stronghold and make a stand there. "Then there'll be people who know you, a whole court that knows you. Once we have Ketsim you can argue with Durandau for going after the masters of these Red Masks, and I'll argue for you, if you've found a way to overcome the Red Masks in Dinaz Catairna. If you can kill them with a sword, you can kill them with wizardry, surely, and more than one at a time. I know you can. That will give us a chance, a fair fight, and that's all we need. Then you can go to Marakand. But not now. We need all the wizards we have. Besides, Red Masks aren't the only danger. If Ketsim gets wind of us, he could cut us off from meeting up with Durandau even without Red Masks. We need you here."

Lin bit her lip, tapping her foot. She turned to look away again, to the west.

"Very well." She faced Deyandara again, frowning. "In that case, I want my supper."

"She's angry," Marnoch said, as they followed Lin back down to where the camp was spreading out, each company together, two in a valley bottom, three along the hillside opposite. "I'm sorry, Deya."

"You're right, though. We can't let her go. She's wrong, for once. On her own against Marakand!" When had Lin become the reckless one and she the voice of reason?

Marnoch had put his hand under her arm, as if she might find rough grass difficult going. Deyandara tucked it in against her side, dared to smile at him, and found her blush rising, but they drew carefully apart when Fairu rode towards them with some question about sending extra scouts to the east and down towards the *dinaz*.

Lin took nothing but beer at their cold and fireless supper, sitting apart, her mirror reflecting that other sky, tilting this way and that, as if she sought for some elusive vision, until Deyandara ordered her to put it away, for fear of drawing Red Masks. Sulking, she would have said, if Deyandara had behaved so.

Deyandara was dreaming she wandered through pelting sleet with lightning smashing the sky above her. She should get off the high ground, she knew, but she had to struggle to the crest of the steep ridge none the less, to look away, searching, whistling, calling. . . . Badger was lost, and Cricket straying. She was alone on the hills, and if she did not find them she would be alone forever. She carried her komuz in one hand, and the wet would warp and crack it. Its strings were already broken, flailing soundless in the wind. In her dream there was a god. Not Andara, but a god's voice nonetheless, deep with memory of earth and stone and the roots of trees.

Queen of this land, beware your goddess. Queen of this land, there will be famine, and war, and the sickness of the soul of the land seeps upwards. The folk will perish and the hills be herdless and the valleys untilled. The cold dark of the stars walks beneath the night and the dead ride the valleys in its service. The songs of the past are past and should not come again. You must make the next king, you must choose, you must fight, you must flee. Queen of this land, wake, wake, wake!

"Wake up, little bard," said Ghu, sitting cross-legged under a pine tree, with the lightning playing in its branches. Statues of dogs in polished grey stone sat either side of him, alert and guarding, and their eyes were jewels lit by fire. His own eyes were closed. Snow fell gently onto his black hair, but small flowers, the bluest blue she had ever seen, bloomed all about him in the grass, with tall, water-loving irises and sweet flag, which should not have been growing on a dry and stony hill. Sheets of rain ran over the grass, bending the long blades of the river-rushes, tearing twigs from the tree, tearing whole branches, and the thunder of their breaking woke her.

What had woken her was hooves. She scrambled groggily from the blankets as Rozen yelped and sat up, someone else treading on her.

"Marakanders in the camp." The voice was that of Shaugh, one of her bench-companions, a man formerly of Lord Goran's household. "My lady, quickly, arm yourself."

Rozen was already there, stumbling into her, fumbling to drag Deyandara's mail shirt over her head. "Hold still, my lady!" Deyandara groped for her boots, glad she'd slept more or less full clothed. She held still long enough for Rozen to cinch her belt tight, assured herself her dagger was easy to hand, but couldn't find her boots.

"Lin, make a light!"

Shaugh seized her by the shoulder. "My lady, to the horses, now."

"Lin? Where is she?"

"She's gone!" Deyandara heard Rozen moving around the dark tent, blundering into things. "There's no one else here. My lady, I swear she didn't go out past me, but she's gone!"

"No time," said Shaugh.

"Boots," Deyandara protested, and they were thrust at her. She got them on over bare feet, hopping as she was half dragged out the door, Rozen running at her side, spear in hand.

Grey twilight, harbinger of dawn. No small affray, a party of Marakanders stumbling upon their watch unawares. They had come up the valley of the brook, and if the alarm had been sounded at all, it had not given her people much warning. Most had slept in the open, and as she ran, Shaugh's hand still gripping her arm, a wave of riders on horses and camels swept in amongst them. Some, the heavier sleepers, were ridden down where they lay. The screams were sickening. Some ran for horses, but the picket-lines were a snorting, stamping frenzy of spooked beasts, as much danger to their masters as the enemy was; others ran to rally at their lords' tents.

A string of galloping horses turned out to be Faullen and most of her own bench-companions. There was Marnoch, fully armed and on foot.

"Deya!" He grabbed her, hustled her to the white mare, heaved her up. "Devils take it, why bring her a horse so easily seen? Ride for your brother, don't wait for stragglers. Go!" He slapped the mare's rump and leapt out of the way as the horse surged forward, the other riders, six, seven, a dozen, a score of them, including Lord Fairu, closing in around her. Deyandara found her stirrups. She had to hold the mare back to keep her from leaving the others behind. A quick glance behind. Rozen was running after Marnoch. Someone had broken out the banner of the royal house, Hyllanim's black bull, and pursued Marnoch with it to the slope of the hill below the pine. Men and women, on foot and ahorse, fell back on him. Order was emerging, archers, spearmen, lord's men, but the ground where they had camped was thick with enemies, not a lord's warband, maybe, but enough for a raiding party. If they'd met in open battle, not been taken unawares, they could have prevailed, but—Red Masks.

Where in the cold hells had Lin gone, tonight of all nights?

Two Red Masks, only two, but they swerved to ride hard after Deyandara's flying party. She saw the Marakanders close up into a tight body again—some of the shouting was orders—leaving their pursuit of men still chasing horses or running solitary to join larger groups, and then split like a flock of birds, like water meeting a stone, half to gather, waiting, planning, a threat to Marnoch, assessing the moment, half to ride hard after the Red Masks, after her. She looked away, as the Marakanders loosed a flight of arrows against Marnoch's company.

She and hers crested the long slope of the hill and pelted down, angling west, though who was choosing their route she couldn't say. The white mare, maybe. It certainly wasn't she. Her brother's army would be somewhere to the south and east, but they could hardly gallop all the way to him even if it didn't take them under the walls of Dinaz Catairna and Ketsim's nose. Lose themselves in the hills and valleys, find the regions of stone, of ravines and scarps and steep forest, hunters' land. They needed to abandon the horses, go furtive on foot.

"My lady!" Fairu had come in next to her, shouting, pointing. "We need to stop and switch horses, break up, while they can't see us. They'll follow the white. Those poplars!"

A quick glance at the poplars climbing a steep bank away to the left, a quick glance back. The Marakanders were already pouring down the hillside after them, desert-breds pulling ahead. She pointed back. Even if they could put the trees between their pursuers and themselves, there wouldn't be time to halt. Fairu looked behind, spurred his horse cruelly, crouched low, and the white mare surged ahead with him.

"You and me," he shouted. "Mag, I'm taking the queen's horse, you'll come with me." Mag, white-faced behind, nodded. The Red Masks might be lured to follow a wizard. A wizard, rashly working magic, might deliberately lure them, if their obsession overrode whatever orders they had. "Faullen, go with the queen, no matter what."

Slowly, she and Fairu lengthened their lead, leaving their companions to follow. Lord Fairu's bay was red-nostrilled and lathered; it was not going to have much left by the time they did reach the poplars. A horse squealed and screamed, and she looked back, though she shouldn't have, to see legs flailing, neck twisting, someone's mount down screaming with another atop it. One horse staggered up, riderless, limped a few yards, and then stood, head hanging. Its rider turned to face the onrushing Marakanders, spear braced. Some of the others checked briefly as if to go back to his aid, then came on, leaving the fallen. The other horse that had gone down still flailed, trying to rise and unable to. Its rider, Andara bless, Shaugh, lay half under it, unmoving. She saw the arrow then, standing from its ribs. It gave up the struggle and stretched itself on the grass, though its side still heaved. The Grasslanders and desert folk shot from the saddle. The man afoot fell and did not rise.

Fairu looked back as well. "No good," he said. "We're not going to have a chance to switch mounts. You might outrun them on your own. Lose yourself in the hills and get to the road and your brother."

He let his labouring beast drop back and turned. The white mare slowed, without a challenger at her side, and tried to turn as well. Deyandara set her straight again, kicked her to a new burst of speed. Behind her, there was shouting and the clash of blades.

She was only the banner. They shouldn't be dying for her. She wasn't any more use than one of the younger scouts, no more worth than any of those who only followed their lords because it was their duty. But she was the sign they defied Marakand, that they were still one folk and not a scattering of brigand-lords. She looked back again. Horses ran, riders lashing them. Those unhorsed, both her own and the mercenaries, ran, ignoring one another, or cowered like children fearing monsters, hands over their head.

The Red Masks rode straight and hard after her on long-legged desert horses. Deyandara felt the edge of the panic claw into her.

They shouldn't know her. They shouldn't care about her. She still couldn't believe Lin would have betrayed her. Lin might haul her back to her brother by her ear, though she hadn't, but not betray her life. The mare had the bit in her teeth and was going flat out, swerving away from the valley bottom towards clearer land, but steeper, too. Deyandara crouched lower, smaller, but no arrows came, only the pounding of hooves. "Andara, Andara, please, no, please—" over and over, all the prayer she could shape, mouth dry as sand. The mare suddenly decided safety lay in the shelter of the poplars after all. She veered, flinging Deyandara off-balance, and lifted, leaping like a deer over a summer-dry rivulet that came twisting down the slope, and with her last flash of sense Deya got her foot out of the one stirrup she still possessed, knowing herself falling, lost. She rolled, stunned, with the wind knocked out of her and a searing pain in her shoulder, heard the hooves fade and grow louder again, the mare fleeing, the Red Masks circling, trampling. Her breath came rapid and wheezing, and she couldn't move even to crawl, couldn't even open her eyes. Creak and thump, a rider dismounting. There would be the blow of the white staff, a moment of agony, burning, and she would be dead, or they would hack at her, like Gilru, but she wore armour. Her helmet was lost; they would crack open her skull. She heard herself whimpering, high and shrill like a blind puppy strayed too far from its mother's warm belly, and found that like the puppy she was crawling, blind, flat, and every reach of her left arm was as if their swords had thrust into her shoulder.

She was seized, struggling, screaming and crying, kicking and punching, eyes finally open and the red woollen tunic filling her vision as he clutched her by the throat, holding her off.

"Settle down, girl," said the other, "or it'll be the worse for you." The woman caught her arms, twisting them behind her.

Her knees gave way. She shrieked, because the fire in her shoulder was worse than anything, even the terror. Everything went red with the fire, or maybe it was that the Red Masks filled the world. Her crying was lost. Even her own panting breath was drowned by the hot wasp-buzzing that filled her ears, till that, too, was lost, and darkness claimed her. But she thought, as she slid away, *Red tunic, not armour. There was armour underneath. I punched it. Mail. Red Masks don't speak—and not the Praitan of the tributary lands.*

CHAPTER X

The winds were not so favourable this night as when Yeh-Lin Dotemon had made her last journey to the city. They came from the south, carrying memory of the sea, the airs of the lands beyond, the great trees and the blue hills. . . .

She had to use them anyway. Powers brooded over Marakand. Her mirror had shown her something there, warning, something to come, a rift in the world. The ice of the cold hells. All was still, waiting, poised, but the balance shifted. She could feel it, like muscles tensing to deal the great and fatal blow, something was set in motion, the first shiver far below that would wake the great wave. And the ice would reach for them, draw them in, hungry.

They were fools. They had all been fools, and they still were. Lin saw them, in her mind's eye, three powers of the distant fires, grappling over Marakand, tearing one another to pieces over—what? Rule of a little human city, the glory of mere human tyranny? To be a lord over the little lives? They had fallen so far, forgotten so much of what, and of why. Especially, perhaps, of why.

They were here, she would say to them—but they would not listen. *We are here. We are now. We have only here and only now. The ice is behind, the stars beyond our reach. Be here, be now, be in this world and use it with more honour. Be the careful guest in the hall, mindful of your lord and hosts, small and weak and swift-dying as they are.*

Be quiet, and patient, and walk gently.

She thought of the Eastern Wall three, almost four weeks ago now, and the soldiers who had died there, and shook her head at herself. Hypocrite. Well, she tried. At least the fools at the gate had started that fight. She did try. She held memory of the tree in her inmost heart, her tree, who had wrapped her into *her* heart and held her like the tender worm in the cocoon, and sang to her, long, long years, sang the life of her land and her folk, the goddess in the baobab with her roots in the deep aquifer under the hills.

She had learnt patience there. She thought she had. The patience, not of the spider—that she had always had, when she was Yeh-Lin, who had been serf and concubine, poisoner and wizard, mistress and mother and empress and exile—but the patience of roots in the earth, of the elephant crossing the dry plain, of the hills awaiting rain. Patience of the goddess who one day opened her heart and told the prisoner she held, *Go, fly free again.* The chains that bound her had long worn away, and she had been content to stay, to watch, as the baobab-river goddess watched, the folk of that land. But like a fledging, or a moth new-hatched, Yeh-Lin had crawled from the nest, her cocoon, to stretch stiff and clumsy wings and find life in them after all.

She still did not know quite why she was released to the world again. The Old Great Gods would not have wished it so.

Find out for yourself, the baobab river had told her. *Walk gently in the world. You hold it in your hands. The least child does.*

In her wanderings in the dawn-fresh world she had found Deyandara, prickly, angry, unlovable child. She had never done well at motherhood. She had found it no easier, and yet the child needed someone. Not her, really, but she was the only one who seemed willing to take an interest, until the bard Yselly. Better Yselly than her, she had thought, but since she had failed for all her careful trying to pluck that tangled curse fully from the girl—what a mess that was, and so strangely woven, through

life and death, and rooted in the land and the goddess of the land—
Yselly had fallen to it. Her fault? Maybe.

Now she had sworn to protect the girl. Sworn to what, she wasn't
sure. Sworn to eyes like the night between the unreachable stars and
a weight, a weight in the world she felt heavy even weighed against
herself, and yet held so lightly in a single hand.

Was that what she did, now? Did she act to protect Deyandara? This
gathering of powers in Marakand was a great danger; she did not lie to
herself in saying so. But a danger how, and to whom? And when?

To all the human world, maybe? Surely they knew better than
to be so. There was the wasteland of Tiypur to remind them, and the
blasted dead lands of the eastern shore of the Kinsai'aa. A danger to
Over-Malagru, which was Deyandara's land, they were that. This day,
this season?

Maybe not, but in the long run, they were a danger worse than the mercenaries and traitor lords arrayed against Marnoch's pitiful band, a danger
worse than that army, small though it was, anchored on invulnerable priests
that humans and human wizardry could not oppose, and if she did not do—
something, she had no idea what—who would? Who could?

Old Great Gods have mercy. She would die, probably, and ripped
from her body she would die a second death, rootless in a world that
could not sustain her.

It was necessary.

Or perhaps it was merely selfish curiosity. Running her neck into
trouble for a childish whim to poke things with a stick to find out what
would happen, to stir up trouble, to toss the stones and see where they
fell and watch the ripples spread.

That thought had the heaviness of truth, landing in the chest. Or
did she doubt and mistrust herself beyond reason?

The gibbous moon silvered the hillside and the god in the tree
watched her, wary but unthreatening.

Earth beneath her feet. Stars over her. Yeh-Lin sat, rested her hands on her knees, shut her eyes. She floated, between earth and sky, roots in the deep waters, branches in the clouds. Thought slowed, breath almost ceased. Slow, careful, she laid out the patterns in her mind with the rhythm of her breath, the pulse of the tree's ponderous tide, leaning to the sun. There was a power in Marakand she did not know. One she did, wounded and enraged and suffering. Could she help it?

No.

A third—she could not see the third. But there would be fire, and death, and the ice reached for them all.

In this time, in this place . . . the dead gathered, puppets of greed, of the desire to possess, to control, to break the world to a single will. The dead . . . ah. And so they did not bleed. Necromancy. Ghatai's game, that had been. She never had liked Tamghiz, vain and swaggering male arrogance made flesh.

Durandau brought the army of the kings combined to Dinaz Catairna—finally, after delaying and delaying at the ford of the Avain Praitanna, waiting for Lin and her promised return with Deyandara—but still he hesitated. Durandau the cautious. Rumours ran to him of disease, of death, and now, having given up hoping for his sister, he waited, drawn warily near, the jackal slinking to the wounded buffalo, for disease to do his work for him, against mercenary conquerors and Catairnan lords alike. Since Lady Lin had not, as promised, brought his lost sister to him, the Catairnans were without a blessed and sanctified ruler. Once the land was purged of the strong and quarrelsome who had taken the field . . . he had sons. And brothers. The land would need a king.

But the invulnerable dead massed against him, protected by a devil's shield, and Marakand's hand reached to take all Praitan, which he was too short-sighted to see.

Deyandara and her Marnoch needed the army of the kings. They needed Durandau.

The Red Masks would scatter his army and kill the kings, the spearhead and vanguard of Ketsim's army, the kings would die and the wizards fall and Praitan, weak and lordless, fail. The Five Cities would stretch the tributary lands north, the secretive forest kingdoms reach south, and whatever emerged victorious from the brewing conflict in Marakand roll eastwards.

That did not protect Deyandara, be she queen or wandering child.

Find the puppet-master. Wrench the Red Masks from his, her grasp, and the Grasslanders, grown overconfident and complacent, would fall to Praitan spear and sword easily enough. Even if it cost her—everything. She owed everything.

Yeh-Lin, Dotemon, the Dreamshaper, they named her, though that was mere Northron poetry, surfaced through the dreams, the chaos where all was one and all was possible, death and victory and despair, the girl robed in blue and white, Marnoch at her back, the girl lying naked in the arms of a hard-eyed Grasslander with the scars of Tamghiz Ghatai's long-dead cult on his cheeks, the girl dead in a burning tower, the girl, eyes shut, arms wrapped about a komuz, a dog resting its head on her feet . . . the girl at her brother's side, mouthing his words, and dead riding at Marnoch's side against a horde of Grasslanders, and the high king riding too late . . . the high king falling, spear-stricken, trampled beneath the hooves of riders in red, Durandau stabbed in the heart in his bed, in his tent in his camp, his guards dead, his champion Launval the Elder dead with never time to draw sword, Red Masks moving swiftly through the camp, singling out the kings and queens, the lords, the champions, the wizards, silent and sure as tigers, and a red-cloaked figure crouched over the king, a shadow shape lying on it, drinking the cool-flowing fire of fading life. . . . The girl, smiling, at a great harp in a king's hall, dog at her side again, the same dog, a dark-haired man in a carven chair . . . Yeh-Lin opened her eyes. She couldn't see the way. Maybe it was not her choosing that would make it.

But still she had to choose.

Deyandara needed the spears of the kings. The spears of the kings could not endure the Red Masks. Yeh-Lin could hunt them, could kill them one by one. But while she was killing one, another could be killing Deyandara, or Durandau, or the threesome of devils in Marakand might see her and ally against her, if they were allies and not already locked in some strife that would destroy the city and distract, perhaps not in time, whichever one it was who claimed the name and rights of the Lady.

Yeh-Lin sighed. She stood and stretched, and drew her sword, cut a new circle in the dust-dry turf. She began with the simplest of the sword-forms, turning slowly through the circle, drawing in the smallest and softest winds, the breeze that curled about the stems of the grass, the last shimmer of sun's heat held captive in the day-baked stone. She wove, her sword the weaver's, beating the layered strands into orderly flow. She drew down the upper airs, slower now, yet slower, for their resistance and their strength, their mindless will to their own course, was great, and they could not be severed from their stream, only borrowed. She wrapped her fabric of winds like scarves, Pirakuli draperies, flowing to sky and earth, horizon to horizon, the great contained in the small, the compass of her arm's reach. Then she cut the circle, to ride the winds again. Westward, to Marakand.

Riders of the wind. It was an old title of the imperial wizards of Nabban, though very few among them ever had the strength or the skill to master the art. Half the stories of dragons were only peasants looking up from their fields to see a wisp of cloud flying counter to the prevailing wind, leaving roiling chaos in its wake.

CHAPTER XI

Something woke him. Ghu listened, but there was only the wind in the gorse of this stony hillside, the distant murmur of the little stream in the valley bottom, an owl calling, like a warning, far away. He had been dreaming, not of Ahjvar, whose dreams he fell into all too often, nightmare that left him sitting, watchful, unsleeping, while at least the mare and the dogs got their rest, but of Lady Deyandara. In his dream, she slept, while some serpent banded black and orange crept near, and she had tossed and turned in nightmares of her own, unable to wake, while the thing coiled about her wrist, slithered up her arm, circled her neck, black tongue flicking over her face, her eyes, and lips. Wake, he had tried to tell her, but in his dream he couldn't be certain whether she heard; he only knew she sat, suddenly, and there was no snake, but she stared wide-eyed at or through him, and there was the scent of pine all about, and cool water, as the dream faded. He hoped she had come to no harm. Perhaps he had only woken because she did, or she had, or she would. Would, he thought. The snake had not yet come.

But then one of the dogs growled.

Ghu flung his blanket aside and stood, looking up at the sky. He was tired, bone-weary from riding bareback and often sitting at a trot, mile upon day, three weeks now, he thought, three weeks and some, by the moon, which kept track when he forgot to count the days that ran together.

It was not yet midnight. The stars were scattered with small, moon-silvered clouds, scudding shadows against the sky, and fog pooled in the valley. For a moment the wind, which had blown steadily from the south all day, growing stronger and stronger so that he wondered if some great storm might be beating on the cliffs over which he had lived with Ahj, skirled about, flattening grass into circles, rolling west. Jui, the silver-ash dog, barked and leapt at nothing, teeth snapping. Even his stolen mare, whose weariness must overreach his own, woke, shaking her mane and laying back her ears.

"No," Ghu said. Hardly knowing he did so, or how, he reached into the wind and gathered it, shaking it free from the knots that bound it, pulling it, combing it loose.

For a moment, they stood in buffeting storm. He flung an arm over his eyes against the dust, and the mare swung around, tail-to, head lowered. Jiot, the black and tan, crouched and snarled, and Jui put himself safely behind Ghu's knees.

He caught up his forage-knife laid close by the blanket as Deyandara's wizard landed, shaken from the wind, to stand before him, sword in hand.

Different, even by moonlight. Not an old woman, now. Black hair swinging to her hips, tangled and knotted by the wind, but beautiful, as a tiger was. Best appreciated from far away. Old eyes. Angry ones, holding their own light.

"You," she snarled. But after a moment she sheathed her sword. "How in the cold hells did you do that?"

Ghu blinked, shrugged, and spread his hands, though he did not lay aside his own blade.

"Don't play the idiot with me. I don't for a moment think you're the fool the girl takes you for. Nor nearly so young or innocent. What did you *do*?"

"I don't know. What have you done with the lady?"

"Deyandara? I left her queen of the Duina Catairna and with Lord Marnoch. He's the Catairnan war-leader. She's safe enough." The wizard didn't meet his eye.

"You said you'd protect her and take her to her brother."

"She didn't want to go to her brother. Her duty was elsewhere, she decided. *I* decided I could protect her best by ensuring her *duina* is safe. And nothing in this part of the world is safe, nothing, with a devil in Marakand. Three devils." She considered him. "You're not surprised. You knew there was a devil?"

"Not three, unless you count yourself."

"You see so well, do you?"

He shrugged again. "Neither goddess nor demon of the earth, nor human wizard. Now you give me the word, and it settles into place on you yourself. What else could you be, except a dragon? And I don't think you're a dragon."

Her eyes narrowed. "Have you ever met a dragon?"

"Yes." He considered. "One. Once. I think."

Her mouth opened and shut. "You think. You don't know."

"It might have been a dream. I have strange dreams." Deyandara with a snake about her throat.

She folded her arms. "I am one of the seven. My name is Yeh-Lin. I was your empress, once."

"Never," he said, "*my* empress." And she backed a step. He smiled, to hide his confusion. "I may be older than the little queen thinks, but not nearly so old as all that. Yeh-Lin was dowager and regent, never empress, in the songs of the market-singers, and she was driven to the west and into the tales of the north long ago. Though I've heard she came back, too, and then maybe she called herself empress, but she is not in the lists of the emperors sung at imperial funerals and the gods themselves fought her. Yeh-Lin the Beautiful. The devil Dotemon, yes?"

She seemed not so much to slump as to relax, gesturing with an open hand, letting something go. "Very well, if you refuse to be impressed, I shall stop trying to be impressive." She eyed him sidelong. Even by moonlight, he could see she was beautiful, her face unlined, now, lips full, her eyes dark, long-lashed.

"That won't work either."

She snorted. "So Deyandara says. I think she's mistaken. Shall I be an old woman again?"

He did laugh, then. "She's very young. I think her world is very simple. Yeh-Lin, you don't frighten me. Maybe you should, but you don't. You are very lovely, and I'd sooner make sweet eyes at a dragon. You were never a convincing old woman."

"Yes, I decided I could do without bringing back my aching knuckles and my bad knee. Once in a mortal lifetime was enough. I was an old woman when I drifted to the north."

"Fled, the stories say. What are you going to do, since there are three devils in the city? Will you join with one of them, bring allies to Deyandara?"

"Not likely. But if I can find the one who's made the Red Masks, I can destroy them, all at once, and Durandau and Marnoch between them can deal with Ketsim and make Deyandara's *duina* safe for her—if Durandau will let her rule it, but that's a separate problem. And what are you doing here? You went into the city to find your assassin. Did he kill the Voice?"

"Yes," he answered, because what did it matter? He could see her road, this devil-wizard, through the air, the winds she would gather, how she meant to drop like a thunderbolt upon the city, weaving a dance with her sword against the power that bound the Red Masks, thrusting herself into the heart of it, turning the chains that wove about them to fire, swift and sudden. Ahj—Ahj burning in the fire from the sky, every Red Mask, poor dead slave, burning, cleansing the empty, defiled bodies. That was what the devil intended, and Ahj burned in his nightmares, so many nights that he didn't even remember, didn't even wake, but he cried out, reaching . . .

"Move your hand, Nabbani man."

Ghu's hand was over hers on the grip of her sword. Jui and Jiot had come one to either side, silent, hackles rising. He could see her, see into her, how she was flesh and bone and liquid light, spun together. If she resisted him, if she fought . . . what was he but flesh and bone and a confused dream?

There was a red light behind her eyes, and he could feel the fires within her, but he only tightened his fingers. They were bone, flesh and bone, and if she wanted to fight him as anything else. . . . She jerked her hand away, leaving the sword standing.

"What *are* you?"

"Nothing," he said. "Only becoming. But he has no one else to defend him. I do name him mine, then. In this time, in this place. He will not burn again."

The devil was confused, distracted, demanding, "Who?" and though she had backed a step from her sword she still looked at him as a curiosity, a little creature hissing harmless defiance.

There was a pine on the mountain. There were willows with roots in the river's rich silt. She had been bound so before. Roots stretched, and for a moment Ghu saw her as bone, a skeleton standing before him, laced with veins of golden light, her veil of hair still silken lovely, white claws reaching for the sword, and then she crumpled into the earth, bone upon bone, and roots held her, under snow, under stream.

He fell to his knees and tried to breathe.

"Not yet," he whispered. "No."

The dogs came to him, wet noses, whimpering, pressing, licking their concern, because he hurt and he was afraid and he wept. He didn't remember why.

There was a sword standing in the earth, and the long silken tassel of it blew in the wind from the south. It was the east pulled him, dragged, to break his heart.

Ghu rolled up his blanket, made up his bundle again, whistled for the mare, who came willingly for all the hour of the night, lowering her head to the rope halter and single rein that was all the harness he had for her. She was a hill-pony cross, black with a kite-marked face, tall, but sturdy and hardy, and if she was still a bit on the bony side, she was strong and willing enough, and her unshod hooves were sound. She was looking glossier, maybe even fatter, than when Ghu had slipped her loose from a dealer's picket line in the night, a day's journey beyond the Eastern Wall, though for over three weeks she had fed on nothing but what the hills gave. He would ride on now, while it was cool and the wind was fresh. They could sleep through the heat of the afternoon.

CHAPTER XII

"Something's wrong."

Deyandara looked up wearily. Chieh, the Nabbani woman from Gold Harbour, was scowling across the valley to the rising hill crowned by Dinaz Catairna. Deyandara had been riding in such a pain-numbed daze she hadn't noticed when cresting the last ridge brought them within sight of it.

It was wrong, the way the very shape of the land had changed. As Lin—cold hells take her for a false and lying traitor—had reported, the south side of the hill had been quarried away into a cliff, and a stone wall topped the ramparts. A square stone tower of three storeys, its roof thatched—easy to set that alight with a fire-arrow—overlooked the wall at the south.

The Grasslander man, whose name sounded like Lug, tugged at Deyandara's reins, drawing her horse closer. Not the white mare but some stray from the battle they had captured in passing as they raced away. She had woken from her faint to find the two of them shoving and kneading at her dislocated shoulder. Screamed in agony and fainted again. Now it ached mind-numbingly and her left arm was useless, strapped to her chest. Chieh claimed her father had been a surgeon and she knew what she was doing, the arm would be fine given time and rest, but Deyandara didn't think she trusted that. And her right wrist was tied to her saddle, which meant she was going to pull that arm as well out of joint, at best, if the stupid horse shied at anything and she fell.

A day and a half they had ridden, and there had been no pursuit that Deyandara noticed, though they had dodged and twisted up and down the valleys. Neither had there been any sign of the rest of the Marakander mercenaries, either flying back to the *dinaz* in defeat or returning victorious with Marnoch's head on a spear. She ought to be glad of that, at any rate, but it had become hard to rise above the pain to feel anything except a sort of hopelessness.

She was Lord Ketsim's prize, and he was going to make himself king through her. Red Masks. That plan was a secret from the Red Masks. The Voice of Marakand and her temple certainly wouldn't want Ketsim setting up as king in his own right.

"The Voice is dead," she had said with satisfaction, but that was yesterday when rage still bubbled through the pain and exhaustion. "You don't have a paymaster in Marakand anymore."

Chieh had shrugged. "There's always a new high priestess," she had returned. "Anyway, if there's no paymaster in the city, all the more reason for the warlord to take the kingdom for himself, right? But I wouldn't believe that. If the temple meant to cut us off and abandon their plans for the Duina Catairna, they'd recall the Red Masks."

How had they dared imitate the Red Masks?

If anyone had even looked closely, Chieh had said, laughing, they'd have been done for. Painted imitations of the masked helmets, odds and ends of red changed into just before the battle—Ketsim's own folk had known nothing of any Red Masks riding with them, which had made their fear that much worse, a good joke on her own comrades, Chieh thought. Deyandara did not find it amusing. There was something shaming in knowing that it was her own belief, the belief of every man and woman there, that had so reduced them to senseless flight, Praitan and Marakander mercenary alike. Even the white mare had panicked, recognizing the look of what had so terrorized her at Marakand's Eastern Wall. All a ruse to capture her, because Ketsim had known that the rightful queen was with Marnoch and marching south to meet up with the high king.

She was reminded of how it had seemed she was sought in Marakand, and how it had seemed more likely it was Ahjvar, a Praitannec fighting man, who drew their attention, and she only as his companion. Heir to the *duina* or not, she didn't feel important enough that the Voice of Marakand should have been dreaming of her, but in Dinaz Catairna, someone certainly had been. Pagel, the soothsayer scout captured not long after Marnoch's band set out. The Red Masks, said Chieh, didn't after all kill but carried off all captive wizards to Marakand.

"Ketsim argued them out of taking Pagel, said he had better uses for him that served their Voice," Chieh said. "They don't say a thing, so no knowing what they thought, but they let him take the soothsayer. Not that he's worth much. It takes that liquor the Grasslanders brew up from some root or other to get anything useful out of him. I tried to teach him coin-throwing—my gran did a bit of that—but it was no use. This business of throwing leaves on smouldering coals to get a smoke, it seems to me you might as well play with the dregs of your tea, which my gran did too and admitted she always made it all up. Less coughing if you use tea, and you get a nice drink out of it. Pagel said the queen was with the rebel lords, 'Not the queen but the bride of the king, the mother of kings,' he said, which gave Ketsim ideas, if he didn't have them already. He's setting up trouble for himself, I think, with Marakand and his sons, but that's his look-out. Yours too," she had added, generously. "But there's years before your sons would be any threat to his. A lot can happen between now and then." She had eyed Deyandara speculatively. "You're going to need friends in the hall, as your folk say. I don't have much liking for Ketsim's sons."

Deyandara had managed a nod. She had learned enough sense, she hoped, not to throw away a weapon when one was offered to her.

She tried to make herself take an interest now. Information. She needed to know everything she could, if she were to have any chance of escape, or of survival.

Escape to what? Marnoch, Fairu, Gelyn . . . they were probably all dead behind her, and the oath Lin claimed she had made to Ghu was worth nothing.

But now Chieh said, "Something's wrong."

"What?"

Chieh gave her a look that suggested she was half-witted not to see it for herself.

"No banners at the gate." She spoke to the Grasslander man Lug, and when he nodded, urged her horse ahead, while he waited with Deyandara.

Deyandara shut her eyes for a while and imagined her brothers, all of them, at the head of an army, rushing over the crest of the long ridge to the south. She would fall weeping in Durandau's arms now, if he came for her. When she opened her eyes again the day seemed colder, grey despite the sun. Nothing moved except some sheep, straying shepherd-less along the slope below them.

That seemed wrong. Chieh appeared again, winding back between the snaking dykes that made the approach to the *dinaz* gate a trap for the attacker. She waved her arm in broad sweeps. Lug grunted—he mostly seemed to grunt, or maybe that was what the Grasslander tongue was meant to sound like—and put the horses into a trot down across the valley bottom, over the stream, and up to meet her.

They talked together anxiously in the speech of the western road. Lug drew out a little pouch on a thong about his neck and kissed it before hiding it away under his shirt again. In reaction, Deyandara's free hand went to her own amulet, the carved disc of thorn from Andara's hill, but her bonds wouldn't let her raise her hand so far.

"What is it?" she asked.

"Trouble," said Chieh. "Come on. Your lord needs you. Maybe it will make a difference."

She spoke to Lug again, and they rode forward together, with Deyandara in the middle. Voices carried, as they approached the gate itself, out of the muffling baffles of the dykes. Shouting. Grasslander.

She sat back hard, and the war-trained horse stopped, braced a moment against Lug's tugging, till he slapped it.

"What kind of trouble?" she demanded.

"You know what I said about Ketsim's sons? Son trouble." Chieh frowned. "We've only been gone a week, Lug and I. Everything was fine when we left, or my lord would never have sent us. He needs his tent guard about him, with this lot. Someone said there's fever in the *dinaz*, too."

Fever . . .

"What kind of fever?" she asked sharply, and Chieh, native Over-Malagru like herself, with a few faint silvered pock-marks on her cheeks, which were hardly noticeable, the eye distracted by some longer, ritualistic slashes, turned a sour smile on her.

"Your guess is as good as mine, at this point. Is it true there was a curse on this land before we ever came?"

"Yes," said Deyandara.

"That explains a lot. We should have gone west. I'm going to cut your hand free. You're going to smile nicely at Ketsim—he's the man on the steps—like a proper bride rescued from the rebels with her brother's blessing, and you're not going to bolt for the gate or shout at any Praitans you see or spit in his face, right? There's enough here still loyal to Ketsim to make mincemeat of you, and the rest will make mincemeat of you anyway, if you don't have our protection."

Deyandara, dry-mouthed, nodded. Chieh was as good as her word, and, Deyandara's wrist cut free, sheathed her knife and drew her sabre, shouting something as they emerged from between the gates.

From inside, Deyandara would not have recognized the place. The round, dry-stone walled houses with their thatched roofs were Praitan enough, but they were marshalled in rows, occupying only a small area of the scorched and weed-grown ground, and none had any wattle-fenced vegetable-garden or fruiting bushes about it; no hens scratched in the lanes, no children scampered about. Most of it, especially near the gate, was given over to paddocks for horses and camels. They rode down the central lane, turned sharply, and came to another open space where mounted riders on horses and camels milled about the foot of the tower she had seen rising above the walls. Banners—presumably the ones Chieh had missed at the gate—drooped from several spears, long scarves of brilliant orange.

Men and women turned at Chieh's shout, hostile faces, mostly Grasslanders, a few Nabbani or Praitan, a few Marakanders or tattooed desert folk.

One man stood alone in the doorway of the tower, with spearmen ranged below on the stone stairs. He folded his arms, smiled, and roared something. Deyandara clenched her teeth and swallowed. She didn't smile, but she didn't snatch for her reins to wheel the horse away, either. This wasn't the time. Not yet.

Ketsim—that must be he—had the look of a stout man who'd lost too much weight too quickly, his face sagging, maybe ageing him past his due. His cheeks were marked with parallel slashes that had left scars deep enough to stop his beard growing there, the same deliberate scars that marked Chieh's face, and Lug's. His hair and skin and eyes were all light brown like just-turned beech-leaves, but near his head his many long braids had turned white. He wore bears' teeth clattering in the ends of braids, a bright cloak of Praitannec plaid over a leather jerkin, and no shirt, so that his arms showed the same fleshiness-gone-slack as his face.

"He's saying that your coming is proof of the alliance with your brother, that the Marakanders are soft and priest-ruled and will never even challenge us." Chieh kept close at her side. Ketsim kept speaking,

against a low undertone of other voices. Deyandara wasn't the only one
there who didn't speak Grasslander, or the tongue of the western road,
or whatever this was. "And he says that now you've come, Catairanach
will bless him and bless the land and lift her curse from it, they don't
need to fear the fever. . . . Cold hells, I don't like the sound of that. Now
his eldest son—that's him there, with the beard dyed with henna—is
saying that the Praitans have always known the land was cursed, and the
Voice of Marakand knew it, and that's why the temple sent foreigners
to do the fighting for them, so the curse would fall on us rather than
Marakand, and they could reap the spoils after the land was barren of
folk—he's a fool, what's here worth fighting for? All Marakand's ever
wanted is an easy route to the iron of the forest kingdoms, and that trade
vanished east as soon as you surrendered to us. *They* won't be half so
easy a conquest. And look, that's a man of the Marakander temple guard
right beside him, smiling, he doesn't have any idea what's being said.
So Siman, that's my lord's son, now he's saying he's not keeping good
men and women here to die, now that the Red Masks have abandoned
Ketsim and gone to their Marakander captain—Old Great Gods, is that
what's set spark in the tinder? He and his brothers are going to fight for
the captain from the city, who isn't afraid to move against the king, but
then they'll go to Marakand and demand what's owing to them, and go
home to the Grass wealthy; they've had nothing but ill-luck since the
Lake-Lord died, and his father's a fool for thinking he could ever wear
those boots."

Now both men were shouting at once. Chieh took Deyandara's reins
and said something urgent to Lug, who nodded and forced his way ahead
of them. Deyandara was glad enough to have the mercenaries guarding
her; there was a lot of jeering at her and jostling of her horse, as if she
were somehow an agent of all this. The man from the temple guard gave
her an intense look. Scuffling fights broke out, but more closed up with
Chieh and Lug, though Praitan voices among even those said things like

"That's one in the eye for old Yvarr, thought he'd snagged her for his dog-loving son, didn't he?"

That snapped her out of her witless morass. She looked for those faces, committing them to memory, and she let them see her doing so. Traitors.

"Down," Chieh ordered, and Lug was there to grab her, bustle her up the steps with Chieh at her back, the horses left to others. Ketsim put out a hard arm and crushed her to his side, fingers digging in. He looked down at her, flushed and sweating, now she saw him close to, and grinned, saying something.

"Welcome to Dinaz Catairna, princess," said Chieh. She gave her lord a nod, stared, and her face seemed to lose its colour.

Camels cried, horses whinnied, men and women shouted, but it didn't turn into war then and there; they sorted into a rough order behind the orange banners and poured away through the lanes towards the gate, mocked and jeered at by others just as much as Deyandara had been. Ketsim's loyalists came swarming back then, cheering, brandishing spears, wheeling horses and camels as if they'd won some victory, driven the rebels away, though the son—sons—had taken the banners and by far the great numbers with them.

"That," said Chieh, her voice unsteady, "was Ketsim being deposed as warlord of the orange banners, and it's a title his fool sons are going to find he lost his claim to long ago, for all his bragging otherwise, if they ever make it past Marakand alive and ride beneath those rags on the Grass." Ketsim raised his voice again, a hand in the air, speaking. More cheering. "He says, what's a chieftain of the Grass compared to the king of a land rich in grazing and the tolls of the great trade roads, and brother by marriage to the high king Over-Malagru. He says, Durandau is marching to your wedding and this new captain it's said has come from Marakand is nothing but a soft-handed priest, and Durandau will bring you his head as a wedding gift." Then she laughed, a bit wildly.

"How long till you're a widow, my lady? You remember I've stood your friend in this, when you take back your land."

Deyandara swallowed hard and licked dry lips, still looking up into Ketsim's fevered face, with the first signs of the rash already burning in his skin. In a day or two he would be covered in stinking, pus-filled boils, if he were blessed by the Old Great Gods. He might live, if he survived for a fortnight, long enough for the scabs to come. If not, it would be the blood breaking free and weeping under his skin, flushing him black, with no blisters oozing to expel the poisons, and he would be dead within a week.

"A friend?" she said. "Maybe. See that you remember to be one, then." She tried to smile as the Leopard might have.

There was a strange, nightmare quality to the wedding feast, if that was what Ketsim thought it. Two long tables were arrayed down either side of the ground floor of the tower, with a third across the wall opposite the door, the high table for Ketsim, his bride, and the favoured lords of his tent guard, which included Chieh and Lug. Others of that guard, not feasting, stood armed behind him, and held once again the gates of the *dinaz*, but Chieh and Lug had served well and the celebration was in part theirs. They were chiefs of the queen's tent guard now, her bench-companions, she was given to understand. Queen, as Ketsim used it, did not mean ruler, but merely the king's lady. A new banner to replace his orange rags.

Deyandara, bathed under Chieh's watchful eye, her armour laid aside and fresh clothes found for her somewhere, strange loose embroidered shirt and baggy black trousers, her left arm in a clean linen sling bound across her ribs, ate bread and sipped water they brought from Catairanach's spring, offering it as though they thought it had some significance to do so, although the mercenaries and their Praitan traitors drank wine. The neck of her shirt was unlaced, the blue plaid shawl

Chieh had brought her pinned low on her breast with an admittedly fine brooch of gold and turquoise, Ketsim's orders again, to show the golden torc. Her hair was combed and her braids coiled around her head, like a married woman's, not a bride's loose cascade, and there were no flowers woven into it, but she didn't argue. The Praitans snickered at that. A widow might wear her hair so at a second marriage; it implied she was no maiden bride, and she blushed for that, ashamed that she could care, with what was to come. Chieh drank far too much. There was an empty place left between Ketsim and Deyandara at the high table, for the goddess, who did not, despite Deyandara's stilted praying at Ketsim's order, appear to bless them. Or to save her.

Ketsim told his people that Deyandara had come with her brother's blessing, that they were now allied with the high king of all Praitan against Marakand, that come morning Durandau would be marching from his camp a mere twenty miles to the southeast to join them; they would quash the rebel lords and drive his traitor sons from the land, with the blessing of Catairanach to strengthen them.

But his sons had ridden out to join some Marakander force in fighting her brother. Durandau wouldn't be coming, even if Ketsim, trusting in Chieh's and Lug's success, had sent some message announcing her capture and this mockery of a wedding. There were Red Masks, real ones, out there. Durandau, and Elissa and Lord Launval the Younger, any of her other brothers who had ridden with the high king, all would be killed by them. Deyandara blinked rapidly and swallowed to stop the tears spilling from her eyes. She wouldn't let Ketsim think she was weeping for fear of him. He brushed the back of his hand over his moustaches and looked over at her assessingly. The cheering seemed more due to the wine and a desire to believe than to any confidence in him. The Praitan lords murmured together, their eyes on Deyandara as well. A prize for the snatching, the moment the warlord's grasp faltered. They'd seen the fever and the rash on him as clearly as she had. Lug watched them, narrow-eyed, but staggered out from the hall halfway through the meal, greasy and sweating in the face. He had eaten little and drunk less. As Chieh's gaze followed him anxiously and Ketsim turned to make what was probably some coarse Grasslander joke about men who couldn't hold their wine, Deyandara leaned to watch him as well and slid the knife from Catairanach's place into her sling.

The pox, regardless of whether it would take the mild eastern or the dangerous southern course, began with an aching back and queasy stomach, Deyandara remembered that much, and then the swelling pimples in the mouth. Chieh watched Lug when he returned with a face like death but said nothing, refilling her cup and holding his hand under the table. Deyandara counted a dozen Grasslanders who seemed to be having trouble eating, choosing only the softest foods, picking at them, trying to hide the pain of chewing and swallowing. Others, like Ketsim, already showed a rash.

She was dining with the dead, she thought.

The drinking seemed set to go on and on. Ketsim's bench-companions, tent guard, or whatever they were called and the Catairnans seemed set on trying to outdo one another. Lug sat slumped on the bench with his eyes shut, not making even a pretence of drinking any longer. Chieh slipped away at some point, leaving Deyandara feeling naked and small. She was gone a long time, came back looking grim and sickened to slide in between Lug and Deyandara again, taking up her earthenware cup and draining it.

"What?" Deyandara was emboldened to ask.

The Five Cities woman turned bleak eyes on her. "The houses," she said. "They're full of the dying and the dead. Those damnable traitor sons of his rode off and left them lying." She murmured in Lug's ear; he shook his head, looked at Deyandara, shrugged, and left again, came back carrying another jug of wine, which he poured for the warlord with some jest and a desperate grin. Ketsim drained his cup, refilled it, and waved for the jug to be passed on. Servants, a couple of young Praitans who weren't folk of Dinaz Catairanach that Deyandara recognized, hurried to do so. When they tried to pour for Deyandara, who had long ago emptied her cup of water, Chieh put a hand over it and shook her head. "The lady's had enough, I think. She has a long night ahead of her and she doesn't want to sleep through it." Deyandara cringed under her wink at her lord.

Ketsim rose not long after that, which seemed a sign for all to rise, most stumbling out the door, some helping the servants drag the benches to the walls, where they seemed prepared to sleep, as the boards of the tables and the trestles were carried out of the tower. He took her by the hand and kissed it, then hauled her close and kissed her, while the hall whooped and cheered. He smelt of wine, but he didn't linger over the kiss, didn't open his mouth on hers. She had a hard job not to recoil anyhow, thinking of the blisters within his mouth bursting, oozing . . . she managed only to stand unbowed and wooden. He didn't seem to notice, took her hand again and tugged her away up the stairs. They were followed by raucous, singing Grasslanders, waving torches.

Andara help her, Andara save her, they didn't—they weren't—there were stories that the kings of Tiypur long ago had taken new-wed brides to their beds with witnesses, all the night, so that no one could deny the marriage had been consummated. Tiypur was in the west and so was the Great Grass. . . . She should have kicked her horse around and tried to flee so soon as Chieh cut her hand free. Her god Andara was far away, Ketsim beyond any justice of his, and Catairanach wouldn't care; Catairanach had rejected her, Lin abandoned her, her brother would— her brother would use Ketsim as her husband, if it suited him, and it might, to have a strong king in the west, bound to him, except that Ketsim would die, Ketsim was dying. She knew she couldn't take the pox again, no one had it more than once. . . . Her breath came in frantic pants and her ears rang; she was going to faint again.

They continued up the stairs through the second storey's single room, an armoury and dormitory, with pallets and rugs and quilts scattered among baskets of arrows and bundled spears. Lug dodged ahead of them, to push open a trapdoor. They climbed through it and up to the upper floor under the eaves, shedding most of their escort behind them. It still smelt of clean straw from the new thatch. Here the only light was a candle, carried by Chieh. Even Grasslanders wouldn't be such fools as to bring torches beneath thatch, she thought a bit drunkenly, and when Ketsim released her arm she huddled away to the nearest window and the cool night air. South. It looked south, where the waxing moon silvered the hills. Light bloomed around the room behind her, Chieh lighting more candles.

Ketsim spoke, sounding irritated. Chieh made some soothing reply and asked, "Do you want some help with your shirt, my lady? Your arm—"

"No," she snapped.

"You could find a good many worse husbands in the hall down below," Chieh retorted. "Or suffer your sister's fate, which is what Marakand wanted for you. Be grateful to him."

"Cattiga was my aunt," she muttered under her breath, but Lug spoke, Chieh answered, and the trapdoor dropped behind the two tent guard with a slam, leaving her alone with the warlord.

"Deyandara."

She had to look at him then. The bed was only a pallet on the floor with a strawtick on it, no grander than what his tent guard slept on below. He undid his belt, set boots and sabre aside, and sat, slowly and carefully, patting the blankets beside him.

"Come," Ketsim said. "Sit. Talk."

She shook her head. His brows lowered, lips turning down. A powerful man, a lord of a tribe, and he had this day lost that rule, seen his sons turn their backs on him. She shouldn't be a fool. If she had been going to die in a grand gesture of defiance, she should have done it while there was someone to see. She crossed the room to the bed, shaking a little, and sat where he indicated, shoulders hunched.

"Catairanach," he said. She waited. He waved a hand in what she realized was frustration. Almost she hoped he would shout for Chieh to come translate again. "Nabbani," he said.

Catairanach was Nabbani? He wanted her to call Chieh, his Nabbani bench-companion? Foolish. He wanted to know if she spoke Nabbani.

"Colony-Nabbani, yes. A little," she made haste to add, in case it would be useful not to understand, at some point.

He sighed. "Good, good." Smiled, carefully and deliberately. "How old?"

"How old—how old am I? Seventeen winters."

"Ah. Old enough."

She scowled. "How old are you?"

He laughed then and slapped her back. "Old enough, little girl. Don't worry. Deyandara is my fourth wife. They all happy till they die. Good husband, I."

"How did they die?"

He frowned. "Maca, first wife, she die . . ." He frowned. "Baby. Long time since. Both we very young. Better that baby die then, I think, than grow to be this son. I not so—so tired, I kill him, now, ride after. Too much trouble. Sons always trouble. Better to be king of quiet land with good daughters, I think. Lysen had sickness, very long, very bad. I cry long time, brother take clan, I go with warlord, leave sadness behind, great lord. Governor of Serakallash, I was. Serakallashi wife, Adva, died in fighting, little daughter killed too, rebels kill her. She only five, very little, very sweet. Very sad. Not there, I with my lord in mountains. He dies too."

"I'm not sorry for you," she muttered in Praitan. "They're all dead and it won't do you any good, marrying me. Catairanach says I'll never be queen."

"Yes, queen for Catairanach," he agreed, catching those few words. "We talk of Catairanach. She not come to bless. You call her and she refuse. You true Deyandara, not other girl?"

No humour in his look now. If she were some decoy, she could expect a short wedding night.

"Yes, I'm Deyandara. But—but Catairanach can't approve a wedding like this. She won't give her blessing for a wedding by force. Whatever you do on the Grass—"

"Hah, on the Grass your brother cut off—" he grinned and made a gesture that left her in no doubt what was to be cut off, "if he catch. Or you do," he added. "More likely you, eh, if you good Grasslander woman? But not little Praitan girls. Not Praitan kings. Weak folk, Praitans. Weak gods."

There was a knife in her sling. It probably wasn't very sharp.

"Catairanach," he said again and, his face serious, touched hers with his fingertips. She flinched away. "She curses us," he said, and touched his own face.

"The pox," she said.

"Yes. It comes, the burning. I feel it. Very sick. Very tired. They come from villages, they say, Praitans curse us, many die, but Chieh, others, they know it, they say the pox, from the sea, from the desert. Fevers in the *dinaz*, fevers in my hall. They start to die, my folk, this week, here. But I marry you, goddess blesses, land is good, happy wife, we live. Can be good king, was good lord of Serakallash. You see?"

She shook her head. "It won't work. Catairanach won't—" But if he didn't believe that, he didn't have any use for her. Beyond the obvious. She drew up her knees, made herself small, and felt she was back on that hillside in the rain, with the brigands—outlaws of the Duina Catairna, her own folk—debating her death at their fire. And no Ghu to come throwing stones at them and cut her free, no Ahjvar . . . her hand went to her throat, the animal heads of the torc and the spot between them his blade had pricked. No Marnoch, waiting, trusting she'd come back. She blinked furiously until the heat of tears faded. Ketsim was watching her. He looked old, older than he maybe was, and tired, as he said. He touched her face again, the dimpled scars of the eastern pox, which had been bad enough for her, down her throat.

"Little leopards," he said. "A kitten, I think. Soft claws." Down to circle her nipple with a thumb, cup her breast. She couldn't breathe. "Go to sleep, little Praitan kitten," he said. "Too tired, too sick, for a fourth wife tonight. If Deyandara's goddess has no blessing even now, we all die, I think. Deyandara too, if her king dies. No one else will have her. I say so. Lug knows to do it."

He fumbled with the blanket, eyelids sagging. After a moment she helped him, covering him like a child before she crept, quietly as she could, to the window.

How soundly did they sleep below? She sat, good arm hugging her knees, waiting. The singing had long died away; would they sleep, or did they keep a watch? If she could get to a horse—no, better to climb the wall. With one arm? Would Catairanach send a fog to hide her again, if she prayed, if she begged?

The trapdoor rose, carefully, without a creak or a thump, and Chieh appeared.

Deyandara raised a face embarrassingly tear-stained, wiped it on her sleeve, and glared defiance.

Chieh went to her lord, knelt and felt his forehead, shook her head and came to Deyandara.

"He'll sleep the night away, and probably the best thing for him. Barley-spirit in his wine. He's dying, isn't he? It is the bloody pox they've had here since the winter, isn't it?"

"Yes."

"Lug's taken the fever now," Chieh said, and sat down beside her. "We've been married twenty years."

Chieh didn't look old enough for that, but Deyandara didn't say so. Couldn't make herself say she was sorry, either, when the man had orders to kill her if Ketsim died.

"My father did inoculations," said Chieh. "You know about that? You take scabs from someone, best someone with the eastern pox, but even if it's the southern you can, and—"

"I've heard. People die. People who weren't sick, before."

"Not very often. Hardly at all. Just—once in a while. My brother did. The only one my father treated who ever did. So he stopped. And I had the southern pox, but not the bleeding strain, and I lived. But I remember watching him. I know how it's done. When they first talked of disease spreading, six weeks ago, it must have been, I said to Lug, I can fix you so you don't die of this. You'll be sick a bit, but you won't die. And he said, no bloody way was I sticking his leg with someone else's pus, and I didn't argue." She was silent a while. "Those bodies out in the houses—the living are rotting with the dead. You can't recognize faces. Friends. And the damned Praitans, the servants are sneaking away, and the ones that came over to Ketsim willingly, they're most of them as safe as you or I. They've had it, and still they're refusing to bury the dead. Saying they won't touch cursed bodies and they're not their dead. Treacherous bastards. They're waiting for us all to die so they can seize the *duina* themselves. There's ghosts out there, and the living, all weeping together."

"Go back to Lug," said Deyandara. "He needs you. I don't. I'm not going to leap out the window."

"You remember who your friends are," Chieh said. "You'll be a bone thrown among the dogs without me to look after you, once Ketsim goes to the road."

"Where's Pagel?" she asked. "The soothsayer. You said Ketsim kept him."

Chieh shrugged. "They're saying the Red Masks took him when

they went. He'd have been no use to you anyway; Ketsim was forcing so much of whatever that hellbrew was, into him, that he had the tremors and twitches like an old man. His wits weren't in any better shape. No great loss." She stood up. "I wouldn't betray my lord. He's been a good friend to me these long years, he'd have been no cruel husband to you, and many a girl's faced worse than an old man in her bed, but he's not got many days before the Old Great Gods call him and I've got to look to my future. So you remember, girl, you remember tonight. I was your friend."

"I do remember." She remembered Fairu, who didn't like her and had been going to switch horses to lead the supposed Red Masks after himself to save her, and Mag, who would have lured them with her wizardry, knowing it was her death, and Marnoch, most of all Marnoch. And Ghu, and Ahjvar. She touched the animal heads of the torc. Leopards. The pommel of Ahjvar's sword was a leopard's head. Chieh crept away again. After a while she tried the trapdoor, setting a candle quavering in the draft on the floor, but there was a bed made up right at the landing of the stairs below, where Chieh sat bathing Lug's face and chest with water in the light of another candle, singing softly in the Grasslander language, while he tossed and turned in his fever, so she lowered the trap softly as she could and went back to her window.

Maybe she slept, sitting there. She must have, because she grew stiff and her hips ached, and her shoulder. Water flowed around her, cool and clean. She wasn't surprised to see Catairanach standing by Ketsim's bed, mist eddying around her feet, water rippling the floor. The goddess turned, a shimmer of blue gown and brown hair that flowed down into the water, became the water, coiling around the room.

"You aren't meant for him," the goddess said. "I sent you for the Leopard. Where is he?"

"He went to Marakand to kill the Voice. You told him to."

"The Voice is dead. He should have come here."

"I'm not answerable for him," Deyandara snapped. She should have bitten her tongue. Her fear was worn out, nothing left. "I'm sorry, Catairanach."

"He will come," the goddess said. She looked down at the sleeping Grasslander. "He will. He must. I've seen it. You didn't give yourself to this one?"

Didn't she know? Deyandara felt her face heating. "'Giving' wasn't going to come into it. But no, he's ill, too ill, he said. He fell asleep. Where were you? Why did you let this happen? How could you abandon your folk this way?" The last came out almost a wail, and she muffled her sudden sob on her arm, because maybe it was a dream, and maybe it wasn't.

"I have abandoned no one," the goddess hissed, and for a moment she seemed to tower to the peak of the roof overhead. "Least of all you, last child of Hyllau, foreign-born though you are. The Lady of Marakand is great, and she hampers me in everything I reach to do, she and her wizard slaves. They sing and raise their foreign spells against me so that I barely have strength to leave my waters. She thinks she will come to set words against me in the end, if we do not retake our land, and my spring will be dry and I will be no more—but not yet. Not yet, and not ever, now that her army is fled, carrying hidden disease back to her city. Within her walls, her folk will burn in fevers and die bleeding and rotting in their beds. In Marakand's streets the pox will make itself a nest and never leave, and the yards will stand empty, the markets and the mines fall silent, the fields grow weeds, and it will be long before she has the strength or the gold or the men to think of conquest again. But this," a hand flicked dismissively at Ketsim, who moaned and twisted in his blankets, "this is not my doing. I only make the way easy for it, a little, as I can. This is his curse on the blood of Hyllau and through the kings of the land, the land. Our weakness. This is Catairlau's legacy. We can all be thankful for it at last."

She dwindled to a human woman again, squatted down, and put a hand on Ketsim's forehead, as Chieh had done. Whispered something, breathed on him. Not, Deyandara thought, any blessing of healing. She edged away as the goddess crossed, her pace slow as though she waded in water, to join her at the window. The stars were fading, the moon near setting.

"You don't yet know what it is to be a mother," Catairanach said at last.

There wasn't much answer she could make to that. She didn't know what it was to have a mother, either.

"It is sorrow. To see what you love taken from you by the world, battered and twisted, changed. I tried to keep her with me, within my heart, but a child cannot grow so. He had gone. He was a wanderer, and I knew it, I knew he would not stay, and he did not. I tried, so long, to keep her safe in my waters, years and long years, lives of men, but finally I had to give her out to the world, and the world, the folk, would not understand that she could not be like they were, that she was meant to be different. How could she not be? She was my child, and his. They came to me, again and again, to complain of her, but they would not believe when I told them she was only willful, a little selfish, and what child is not? She only needed them to love her and guide her, and she would have grown straight and true. They were too harsh, too jealous of her. And in the end she would not listen even to me, and so she set her feet on a mistaken path. She was betrayed by the one who should have stood faithful at her side, and he destroyed her."

"Lady Hyllau—the wife of King Cairangorm, was your daughter?" Deyandara asked stupidly. "Hyllau of the day of the three kings?"

"She wasn't meant for Cairangorm, but she was beautiful and she wanted to be the king's wife and the mother of kings. She was young and impatient. She didn't want to *wait*."

"To wait for what?"

"For Cairangorm to die," Catairanach answered, as if it was of little importance. "She shouldn't have accepted him, but she did, because he was king, and Catairlau wasn't. Since she did choose Cairangorm, she could have waited. He was old."

Hyllau wasn't meant for Cairangorm, and Deyandara not meant for Ketsim. She shivered. The water of the spring was icy, and the branches of the mountain ashes weaving together overhead looked like flexing claws. Ketsim moaned again and the tower room was back around her.

"That's—the bards don't say she was your daughter."

"Hyllanim her son didn't like them to sing those songs."

Deyandara looked at the goddess's profile, her golden-brown eyes, like pebbles under water in a brook of the peaty hills. If she had been Hyllanim's grandmother, and Hyllanim was her own great-grandfather . . . that was very far removed. She didn't feel any kinship to the goddess. It took more than descent to make family. "I'm sorry. But it was a long time ago, and now—now we're here, with Marakand still ruling us, no matter how ill Ketsim is, and the Red Masks are still out there somewhere, even if they've abandoned Ketsim. Marnoch may be dead—"

"He lives."

"Thank you. *Thank* you."

"You're not meant for him, either."

"I don't—"

"They've named you queen, but without my blessing. You wear the leopards of Cairangorm's house that Hyllanim rejected, but you are not queen of my folk and land, child of Andara's hills."

"I don't—"

"You are meant for the mother of a queen, the mother of a line of kings."

"Then I had better get out of here, hadn't I?" She wanted to go home, where her god was kind and thoughtful and—everything a father should have been, but which hers had not. This was like talking to her second brother's wife, who brought everything back to her gowns and her babies, in that order of importance, no matter what you said, as if she were deaf to any words but her own. "Maybe helping me walk out of here, as you took me out of the *dinaz* before, when Ketsim was coming to attack it, would get me out where I could find—your queen is going to need a father."

"She will have one. He carries her now, until the time comes he can give her to you to bear and bring into the world again. But he can't hear me. He's denied me, and he cannot hear, and I think—I cannot even see him, but I know he is near, very near. The Lady has him, but she can't have slain him. The world holds him. It will, it must, till Hyllau is born into it again."

"*What?* Catairanach, blessed lady, what do you mean?"

"He won't hear you. He won't hear me. But I think there is one he will hear. You will have to deal with that, afterwards, but it shouldn't be too difficult. You are so lovely, so like her . . . you can win him back. He wasn't meant for a lover of men. But the Nabbani spirit has already walked in your dreams. He still touches you. Perhaps he sees you, already. Perhaps he will come in time and bring Catairlau with him. If he doesn't—perhaps you will live long enough to bear a child, but you will be very unlovely to look upon, I fear. I don't think I can do for you what I did for him. So much of my heart went into him, to cradle her safe . . . I have made myself hollow." The goddess touched one cool finger to Deyandara's forehead, her sing-song voice sharpening. "The Nabbani spirit who rides with the Leopard. Call him to you. I will not have the mother of my darling die this way, not have Catairlau come back to you too late. She needs you. Call him."

"The Nabbani—you mean—you mean Ghu. You're talking about *Ahjvar?*"

"They are plotting treachery below. You don't want to burn as my Hyllau did, and I can do little here but touch your dreams. Red Masks sang silent words over the raising of the walls to keep me out. They brought me in with the water you drank, their little fragment of the marriage ritual." She laughed. "If Ketsim had drunk the water as he ought to have, he might have found ease from his suffering sooner. Pity they dug their own well down between the dykes."

The water rose into mist, filling the room, flowing from the windows like smoke, and then it was gone.

Deyandara sank down on her knees by the south window again, eyes shut, shivering and sick.

Through the north window, there was a sudden outbreak of shouting. Below, someone shrieked and was abruptly silent.

PART TWO

PART TWO

CHAPTER XIII

"**B**lackdog!"

Holla-Sayan rolled up to a knee, sabre in hand, uncertain, for a moment, of where he was. The days and nights began to run together in the past three, almost four weeks now, since the Lady retreated to her temple and raised her wall of undying fire. Outbreaks of fighting in the narrow streets, patrolling the walls of the temple-held wards, patrolling the ravine at least once most nights, alert for signs of a second foray out those forgotten doors in the abandoned buildings that formed part of the wall of the temple precinct along the dry riverbed. . . . Mikki was guarding Ivah at her work up at Gurhan's tomb, and they had no one else who could see in the dark, who could smell the Red Masks, or whom the Lady's enslaved dead would flee.

No one else who could stop them, at all.

He wasn't some godless mercenary to sell himself into this war. A caravan-mercenary, a caravaneer of the road, still rooted in the land of his birth, tied to his own folk and home, had no place here, save to defend what was his, his gang-boss's camels and what they were contracted to carry. But here he was, and he, or the men who had carried the Blackdog before him, had seen more warfare than ever the Warden commanding this city had, though maybe in worse causes, Attalissa having not always, in times past, been a peaceful goddess or a good neighbour. So somehow he had ended up carrying, it sometimes felt, half the weight of this fight, advice and planning, the forays into the temple-held wards where Jugurthos, the commander men would follow, could not be risked, and, too, when the Blackdog was not needed even more urgently elsewhere, guarding the priest Hadidu, in case the Red Masks came.

They might.

They had, though not for Hadidu, when the temple first tried to retake the Eastern Wall. Only a handful, they lacked the spell-gifted, unmanning terror that reduced even the bravest to cowering, whimpering, beaten children, but they were deadly enough without that, invulnerable themselves, capable of killing with a single blow of their short white staves. Captain Jing Xua of the Eastern Wall had died so, the side of her face seared to bone as if she had been struck by lightning, trying to hold the gate till aid arrived in answer to her bells. Holla-Sayan had come, too late for her, and he had destroyed three of the Red Masks who had been methodically butchering the street guard and caravaneers there. He had torn the long-dead bodies from the Lady's control, letting the wretched rags of soul that were all that remained fade way. One Red Mask had fled east, probably to cross the ravine and reenter the city by the Fleshmarket Gate, which the temple had still held, then. Holla had been too busy rallying the remnants of the garrison, fighting a near-overwhelming rush of temple guard through the spell-blasted doors of the towers, to follow.

Since then, they woke and slept with the fear of Red Masks, though the Lady had not sent them out again, even in the second assault on the Eastern Wall. That had mostly involved conscripted men of East and Greenmarket Wards, who had turned on their temple-guard leaders and defected. But no matter how mad she was, she had to realize that Red Masks sent against Hadidu or Ivah could undo all that Jugurthos and his senate had gained. Sooner or later, they would come.

The Lady awaited reinforcements, the company of Red Masks she had sent Over-Malagru against the Praitans, that was the word they had from temple-guard defectors. A great army of Praitannec tribal warriors led by Red Masks was coming . . . but the loyalists were going to call back the old gods, and their demons could destroy the Red Masks, and the Lady was mad and killed her own. And there was food in the loyalist wards. Despite the talk of a Praitannec army, men slipped away to them, every day. Families came over the walls in the night.

How many Red Masks in the temple, Jugurthos wanted to know, but there was never a certain answer. A handful, no more. Dozens, waiting in the Dome of the Well, but the loyalists could send their demons, they no longer needed to fear, and why hadn't the demons come to lay siege to the temple itself . . .

Only Red Masks could part the curtain of fire, when guard patrols passed in and out, and there were always Red Masks at the temple gate-house, they said. No temple defector had seen more than three or four at a time, but they all agreed the Lady kept them by her in the Hall of the Dome, and rumours that could not be confirmed, but which had their source in temple agents, Jugurthos was certain, said that there was a large company of Red Masks yet, fifty, a hundred—had there ever been more than that, and how many had been sent Over-Malagru?—waiting in the cavern of the Lady's well, for the day of the great attack from Praitan. And the greatest of the Red Masks, a slayer of demons, the will of the goddess incarnate, was coming from the east.

There had been a few Red Masks in the Fleshmarket, cutting a way towards the Warden's rooftop command post this day past. But men and women of the street guard had put themselves before them, and an untutored, wizard-born Marakander girl at the Warden's side had warned Nour by some pre-arranged spell; Nour, with Hadidu and Holla and Captain Hassin at the Riverbend Gate, had sent the Blackdog. He had been in time. Jugurthos said the Red Masks had turned in their tracks and fled the moment he hurtled over the rough and ready wall blocking the gateway from temple-held Greenmarket, scattering the temple guard there. That didn't make Holla-Sayan think the Lady had even fifty more hidden waiting in the temple. The Red Masks were all murdered wizards, and she had tried to take the suburb when she first emerged from the temple, in order to arrest and sacrifice the very few wizards there. Not a resource she could easily replenish, once they met their second, final, death. He had stayed in the Fleshmarket to guard Jugurthos, and fought, merely another sword among them, when the Warden finally went down to demand the surrender of the last cluster of Fleshmarket temple guard.

He had been called again not long before midnight, sentries claiming shadows on the wall, but there had been nothing at all when he came to the patrol on the Greenmarket border.

For too long a moment Holla-Sayan thought it was that summons again, that he had not yet gone to them. He was in—Spicemarket block-house, and the night had grown swelteringly hot, the air ripe even on the roof, rising from the narrow stairwell. Too many sweating bodies lying close in too small a space, twoscore militia recruits packed into a tower meant to house a few patrols of street guard.

Nour, still frail and so easily tired—he had had a foot on the road to the Old Great Gods, not so long since—gripped his shoulder and whispered again, "Holla-Sayan . . ." The Marakander wizard crouched beside him, and the priest was stirring on his rug.

In the corner of the parapet, a lone watchman turned, yawned, hand over his mouth. "Sir . . . ?"

Nour gestured to the north, and the militiaman turned back, taking up his bow, alert now, the scent of his anxiety strong, but obviously seeing nothing, peering down, this way and that, over the jumbled roof-tops of the covered marketplace of the traders in spices and dyestuffs and dried fruit. Valleys of shadow and moonlight.

Holla-Sayan smelt their nearness. Old, dry death and a tang like hot metal. Jugurthos insisted that Hadidu not sleep two nights in the same place, for what safety that might give against human spies, if not against a devil's divination, though Ivah had worked some warding against that, she hoped. They had begun to think it was only the human they had to fear, after all.

"There's something . . . cold. Near." Nour was no fearful man, but his voice cracked. Memory of the spell of unnatural terror Ivah had stripped from them was enough, for those who had faced Red Masks before, and Nour's fate had nearly been to join them. That fear was memory burnt into gut and marrow, not something the rational mind could easily overrule. But maybe, too, it was what had woken Nour before him, that whisper of wrongness in the world.

Silence below. Hadidu joined them, a weighted cudgel swinging in his hand, face grim. Nour took up his spear and stepped in front of his kinsman as Holla moved to the open trapdoor over the stairs.

Still and silent, only the sound of breathing sleepers.

"Stay here." Holla-Sayan started down, paused at the bottom to wake the woman nearest the stairs. She mumbled groggily. "Up," he whispered. "Wake the others. Quietly. There's danger. Be ready." She cringed from his touch but squeezed the ankle of the man nearest her, crawled to his side to whisper.

No armour, not even the leather and leg-wrappings of the street guards, just their everyday tunics or caftans. Their spears were no weapon for fighting in the confines of the blockhouse. He hoped they remembered that, before they skewered one another. Maybe he should have left them sleeping, for all the good wakefulness would do them against Red Masks, but that went against the grain, to leave them facing death utterly unaware.

"You, you, you," he heard behind as he went cautiously down to the ground floor. "To the roof, guard the priest and do what Master Nour tells you."

Silence here as well, but some were waking at the pad and shuffle of bare feet on the floor above. One door to the street, one to the roofed passageways of the Spicemarket. A sentry should be outside each, and a lamp burning within. Both lamps were extinguished, and recently. Scent of soot and hot olive oil and wizardry. Nothing inside yet that should not be, and the men did not see him in the dark.

The Marakanders feared him as much as they welcomed him. City folk knew little of demons, lacked country people's ease with the spirits of the wild, which is what they mostly thought him. He'd tried, even in—especially in—the fighting to stay human, when he could, because to kill with spear and sabre, no matter that he was faster, stronger, did less harm to the trust of these green soldiers. This company had been in the Fleshmarket, though; they'd seen him come through a patrol of temple-allied citizens no better-armed than themselves, when the Red Masks had been closing in on Jugurthos. They'd seen what he left behind.

The dog rose in him, a breath from being. His will; they were one now, and yet, there was still that fury waiting within that he did not want to call by his own name. He set a hand to the latch of the door. There was a freshly dead man beyond it, the sentry. Blood and urine.

A shout from above had him turning back, the soldiers waking noisily, just as the door flew inwards, torn from its hinges, careening off his shoulder, knocking him aside. He caught himself from falling outright and wheeled around. His blade jarred and slid on the lacquered scales of the Red Mask's armour, and without thinking he caught the deadly descending staff barehanded and jerked it away, small light-nings spitting, wrapping his arm, searing skin, as he smashed the thing under the jaw with his sabre's hilt, hard enough to snap the head back. He felt the devil's threads tear, the fragments of soul unfurling, begin-ning to drift up like mist from a lake in the dawn, so he wrenched, he couldn't have said how, at what was left holding it to the Lady in the temple and tore it from her, let it go, and flung the lifeless weight at the men hanging back behind, with the body of the sentry tumbled before them. Not in uniform, but they carried the short swords of the temple guard. Another Red Mask presence out there somewhere, but the priest of Ilbialla was on the roof, where men yelled and something thudded heavy on the floor, while living bodies crowded the stairs, shouting that the temple was attacking over the market roofs.

"Bar the door," he snarled, and he sheathed his sabre and leapt for the stairs, letting the dog free. The old bone-cracking pain of the change was almost forgotten. He was smoke and dark fire holding, held in, blood and bone, and the Marakanders flung themselves out of his way, breaking the railing, to flee him.

Not so large as the dog could be, only the big herd-guardian of the mountains, but weight enough to bowl over the fool who wasn't fast enough getting aside as he leapt the bleeding body of the woman he'd sent up to Hadidu, prone at the top of the stairs.

No Red Mask on the roof but a seething knot of blood and fear and anger, bodies down writhing underfoot, bodies trampling them, shoving, locked together with knife and sword or bare hands. Hadidu stood alone in a corner, club hefted ready and a man motionless at his feet. Nour was between him and the general brawl, the only real fighter they had, beset, shieldless, unarmoured, and with a weak left arm. Holla-Sayan hauled Nour's foremost opponent down, tore the shoulder and cracked the bone, left the temple man coiled and screaming, abandoned the other to Nour and plunged into the mass of them for the one who'd been shouting something about taking the wizard alive.

When next Holla saw him, Nour had Hadidu by the arm, heading for the stairs, though they broke apart, Hadidu beating aside a spear-thrust with his club as Nour circled and cut that man down.

Stairs, no. Red Mask down there now, no words to warn them. Smashing wood, shrieking below. Nour kicked the trap shut instead.

Holla-Sayan bore down the temple leader, flung him aside, and circled the scattering human herd, temple and militia alike. Hard to make any difference between them. Not his folk; he barely knew the scent of any of them, the ones who'd slept below. All reeked equally of fear. Some still wore the black rag about the arm that was the militia's only badge, but they weren't too careful about that in barracks. Two who must be temple made a rush for the parapet and the rope and iron hook by which they'd come up, checked and fell back, one right to his knees, cowering.

Red Mask. It came over the parapet, swinging itself up with an acrobat's grace, landing crouched and flicking in the same movement a knife. Nour, for all the bright moon sinking in the west, could not have seen more than the dark moving shadow and the flash of metal, but he knocked Hadidu flat, shielding his body with his own, and the knife flew harmless, lost in the night, as Holla took the Red Mask by the throat. Grown great, he snapped her neck and flung it, her, she had been, barely out of girlhood, into the temple guardsmen, who shrieked and fled as if even empty the corpse was death. Some scrambled and jumped the ten feet to the roof below; the emboldened loyalists flung down the hooks or hauled up the ropes, half a dozen of them, yelling triumph, and hadn't they thought of that when the first wave swarmed up? But maybe there'd been only Hadidu and Nour and the archer, then.

Someone had cut the archer's throat.

"He was temple," Nour said, as he and Hadidu picked themselves up, seeing Holla by the dead man. "Turned to shoot Hadi when the first ropes grappled on. When did he have time to send word we were here? He had a confederate, someone who slipped away down below. Must have. We need to get to Sunset, and Ju's guards." Lower voiced, a glance around. "I don't trust any of this lot. I don't dare."

A man screamed. The militiamen were killing their few prisoners, throwing the bodies over to the market roof below. Holla didn't interfere, hackles bristling, watching the trapdoor. Couldn't find the will to shift, to answer Nour. It was down there, the third Red Mask, the last, hesitating. Did it have the will to hesitate, or was that the Lady's uncertainty, weighing risk and gain?

Certainty. He would destroy it, and she needed them. They were more to her than soldiers mortal men could not kill, they were . . . he almost had her thought there, her hunger, her need for them. They were the web of her strength, they were . . . too few. Her awareness rode the one below, but now she drew back into herself like a snail to its shell, flinching from the Blackdog's touch.

The Red Mask turned back, retreating.

Holla-Sayan forced himself into the man's form, lurched unbalanced a moment, heaved the trap up and went through, sabre drawn. The living crowded away to corners in all too rational fear, no spells needed. The dead, who had tried to stop it reaching their city's last priest, were a barrier at the foot of the stairs. The Red Mask, staff in one hand, a sword in the other, was already running. He overtook it on the lower stairs, and left it an empty husk.

"Look to your wounded, wait for orders from the ward captain," Nour told the patrol-firsts of the survivors, following him down, those who had fought on the rooftop following, and Hadidu gave the dead a hasty blessing before they headed into the night, refusing any escort.

"Talfan's for the rest of the night," Nour said, short of breath and gasping. "At least no one there will sell Hadi to the temple. We can't trust the militia. The ward captains are taking anyone who offers to join, without anyone even to vouch for them."

"Sunset Gate," countered Holla-Sayan. More defensible.

"No. They heard me say Sunset, in there. Anyway, Talfan's is closer and Hadidu's hurt."

The priest was limping. "Bruised," he protested. "It's nothing. Next time you get the urge to fling yourself at me, check to make sure there's a cushion or two handy first, why don't you? You all right, Nour?"

"More or less." But the caravan wizard was slow, feet dragging, breathing heavily. Hadidu without comment put an arm around him, and Nour leaned on his shoulder.

"Blackdog?"

"Fine."

Someone, Nour, he thought, smelt of fresh blood, some new injury on top of his slow recovery from torment in the temple and a wound turned septic, but Talfan would see to that. And Master Kharduin, when he found Nour had been fighting, would haul him back out to the caravanserai and put him to bed for another week, given half a chance.

"You go on," Holla said. "I'm heading back to make sure nothing else has come out of the temple. Where will you be in the morning?" It very nearly was morning.

"Meeting with the senate at the Barraya mansion," Hadidu said.

Talking. The senate of the three gods, they called it, to distinguish it from the remnants of the old senate under arrest in the Family Feizi mansion in Silvergate. But of their talk came resolve, of a sort, and authority, more than what Jugurthos had seized in that first night. There were senators of the suburb now, two of them, Marakander-born caravanserai masters. Out of talk came law, old law, to uphold the Warden of the City, to give shape to the militia, to ensure no one profited unduly by any shortages, to try murders and looting and show the folk that the new order meant justice.

"You don't need to be there," Hadidu said, stopping Holla-Sayan with a hand on his arm. "Jugurthos called the senate, but he didn't say I was coming. Get some rest, once you're sure that was it for the Red Masks loose in the city tonight. When did you last have any proper sleep?"

Holla-Sayan shook his head.

"I'll speak to the senate and then go up to Ivah and Mikki after," said Hadidu. "They won't come again so soon. That's always been her way, these last weeks. She attacks and then pulls back to lick her wounds and nothing stirs for a few days, until she recovers her nerve. I'll be safe enough for tomorrow. All right?"

"Maybe," Holla said. "See you do go to Mikki, then." Because the senate, once Hadidu was with them, would want to keep him, talking and talking, arguing this, that, and the other. It was what Marakanders did. And then they would be burying the dead of yesterday's battle in the Fleshmarket, out along the city wall among the tombs of the Families, and Hadidu would be wanted to pray over them, and Talfan would want him sitting in on whatever she and Jugurthos were planning, the taking of Greenmarket, probably, and always there was the question of how to take the temple itself, and they would want him to tell them yet again he had no way through that fire . . . Hadidu would go yet again to sit in prayer, meditation, dreaming trance, whatever it was, by Ilbialla's tomb, seeking some sign she knew her folk kept faith, some sign Ivah's spell might begin to work . . . praying for the possessed girl who was the Lady?

Maybe he only sat in hopeless waiting because he was not a fighting man, and what else was there for a priest whose goddess was lost to him to do?

"I'll go up to the hill as soon as I can."

"Do."

He flowed again into the dog and turned away, heading for the temple wards to hunt, to search by scent and senses he could not name for any trace of further Red Mask excursions. A handful, a company. The Lady was afraid. A handful, he thought, as if he had the knowledge straight from her mind, a hazy dream of what she held secret. A handful to be hoarded, coin too precious to spend except for great gain. She had meant to sacrifice one, in the blockhouse, to give the other two time to kill Hadidu and take Nour, to shatter the fragile faith of the city in its old gods. A nervous gamble that failed. Possibly she would not try again, after that and the Fleshmarket. Not till the ones she had sent Over-Malagru returned, and what then? Jugurthos talked of alliance with Stone Desert chieftains, but the caravan-masters were not so keen on giving those tribes any authority over the road, which they were demanding in return for their aid. And that was still no strength against Red Masks, or to break the barrier of fire about the temple.

What in all the cold hells had become of Moth?

Holla-Sayan spared the porter a nod at the open gates of Master Rasta's caravanserai between the two dusty incense cedars. Rasta's was small, brick-built and unplastered, and the roof over the gate was missing tiles. It was at the far end of the suburb, the last caravanserai to the west, nothing but dusty road dropping away between the rocky walls of the pass beyond, until the Western Wall. The well was deep, though, and had never failed yet, and old Rasta got on with Gaguush, which not everyone could claim. Home, when they came to Marakand and unless Rasta had too large another caravan in. The open yard within was mostly empty, except for a girl sweeping dung, watched by a cat perched on the sunny well-coping. The bays under the arcades should have been filled with Gaguush's camels, but only a dozen or so dozed, hobbled and chewing their cuds in the shade. Red Sihdy regarded him with mild interest, groaned, which might have been a greeting, and closed her long-lashed eyes. Mules strange to him clustered farther along, switching tails and flicking ears against the flies.

"Mistress Gaguush is upstairs," the sweeper said, before he could ask anything so stupid as, "Uh, where did my gang go?"

Stairs rose right and left from within the gateway, under a patterned brickwork vaulting. Gaguush had the first room along for herself and the most precious goods, Northron amber and sea-ivory work, ambergris and bales of sable-pelts, in the chaos still unsold, despite a Xua merchant's interest. The bulkier goods were usually in locked bays below, but had those doors stood open? He rather thought they had. Maybe she'd found a buyer for the Westgrass weaving and sumac-tanned leathers.

A dark Salt Desert girl opened Gaguush's door to his knock, curly hair escaping her braids. She dropped her eyes shyly, didn't quite bow. Her tattoos were swirls of green that hinted of animal forms, but he didn't recognize the god they belonged to. The folk of the southern hills of the Salt Desert were few and rumoured to be mad and short-lived, if not outright stunted in mind, from a lifetime breathing the bitter dust. This girl was a runaway from something, too young to have taken the road otherwise, and definitely she had all her wits about her. Tamarisk, that was the name by which Gaguush had introduced her, one of several new hires, a couple of days ago . . . no, it had been last week. A good archer, knew camels, and claimed to be good with babies.

"Tamarisk, gods bless. Is Gaguush . . . ?"

She nodded and slipped by, pattering away down the stairs. In the gang a week, and she already had the "sandstorm coming" attitude down pat.

"Camels?" he asked, perhaps inanely. The chests and bags and bales of goods were largely gone, the bed an untidy heap of bedding with another cat—Rasta was fond of cats—watching slit-eyed from the midst of it.

Gaguush didn't look up. She sat cross-legged at a counting table, surrounded by baskets of scrolls, sheaves of loose papers, and old, greying tally-sticks, an ink-brush in her hand and a sheet of paper on a writing desk on her lap.

She could write? He hadn't known. She had a smear of ink on her cheek, almost lost amid her black and red tattoos. She slid two counters deliberately, made a mark, stuck the brush behind her ear, and only then looked up, arms folded.

"There you are."

"Where is everyone?"

"You know, I haven't seen you in a week."

"I didn't realize it was so long. I—"

"Bashra damn you, you could at least send me word to let me know you're still alive! Varro came this morning to tell me there was fighting again, yesterday. Why do I have to hear from Varro?"

"It wasn't much. I wasn't involved, really. We took Fleshmarket Ward."

"*We*," she muttered. He ignored that.

"They need me."

She scowled at him. "I'm sure they do. Nobody else can kill the damned corpses."

"Mikki."

"Oh, Mikki, fine, yes, I'm sure the demon's a big help. Varro says he never leaves the god's hill."

"Why are you getting all your news from Varro?"

"Because nobody else is telling me a damned thing! I haven't seen you in a week! Varro's left, did you know, did he tell you that? He's left, and yet I see more of him than I do of you."

He frowned. "Left for where?"

"Left the gang, left me. For good. Going to settle down and be a proper Marakander householder, apparently. The apothecary's finally twisted his arm, or he's decided if he doesn't stay with her he's going to lose her, I don't know. Anyway, Varro says they've got the demon guarding Ivah day and night, because they think the Red Masks are going to come after the damned Tamghati wizard before she can free their gods. So Mikki's no help, is he? There's just you to guard their priest and watch the walls. And how many miles of wall around the area the temple holds?"

"Less, now, than there was. Since we've taken Fleshmarket."

She didn't smile.

"Two, maybe." And he had been around it how many times, since the attack on Hadidu? Around, and quartering the temple wards, finding no trace of Red Masks, though temple guard were thick on the streets. Then he had been carrying messages from Jugurthos to the Greenmarket captain, preparing for that ward's uprising, and Hadidu was still with the senate, still promising to go up to Ivah and Mikki. . . . When he had walked blindly into temple guard in Greenmarket and had to fight his way clear, he'd had enough. Sleep. He'd craved sight and scent of Gaguush like a hunger, just to know she was real, and safe, and there.

"Two miles they could break out over, and only you to stop them? Are you mad? What right do these rebels have to ask that of you?"

They didn't ask. Nobody asked. He just—there was no one else.

Holla-Sayan wanted out of this city. He wanted the road, and the great vault of the sky and the far horizon, the wind untrammelled and smelling of earth and stone baking in the sun. Space, and the silence that was broken only by creak of harness, tinny clink of bells, the slow padding pulse of the camels' cushioned feet on the dusty earth, and the long-drawn cry of a distant hawk. He wanted Gaguush and the dry hills and sky. The words piled up unspoken, because she would only shout that he had a strange way of showing it.

She shoved counting-table and lap-desk aside and crossed the room to him, folding her arms again, lips thin.

"How long does this last?" she asked. "When is it going to be over? Six bloody years I had of you never really there, with the monster inside you, and now that Attalissa's back where she belongs and you're the one in charge, you claim, someone else has got a collar on you. So. For how long?"

"Until . . . I don't know," he said hazily. "They need to free their gods . . ."

"Damn you, anyway, Holla-Sayan." Gaguush put her arms around him, hauled him close. "Look at you. When did you last sleep?"

"Last night?" he protested. Admitted, "An hour or two."

"You've got shadows under your eyes so badly I'd think someone had blacked them for you, if I didn't know better."

He leaned on her, eyes shut. She smelt of roses. And camels, of course. And was trying to kiss him. Her lips were soft, not angry at all.

"Bed," she said.

"I—"

"Shut up. Bed. Sleep. You're useless. I might as well be a doorpost, if all you're going to do is lean on me. I duck, you'll fall over. I mean, here's your lawful wedded wife trying her damnedest to seduce you and you're practically snoring. If a simple kiss is that much effort . . ."

He protested. He'd only come to let her know he was all right; he had to get back, to guard Hadidu. She found his mouth again but then dropped the bar of the door behind him and started shoving him across the room.

"Bed. You're going to sleep, and if your damned priest himself comes looking for you he can sit outside and whistle."

Outside on the stairs with Tamarisk. Hadidu might enjoy a few hours with none of his own folk able to find him, come to that. Which reminded him . . . "Where is everyone?"

"Everyone who?"

"The camels are gone."

"Oh, you noticed?" Gaguush was hauling his coat off, unbuckling his belt. He tried to protest that, got shoved onto the bed—the cat leapt away and spat at him—while she pulled off his boots. "There's a war going on. The temple, the senate, I don't know who may decide next they want camels, or what might come and burn this end of the suburb. I scrounged up a load for a short haul, mostly barley for Serakallash, since their granaries are so empty still, after Tamghat, and it's been a poor summer there. We'll get a good price even given what I had to pay to get it. I sent the gang under Django. Kapuzeh and Thekla went with him, and the new hires, what did you think I wanted them for? Not to sit around the caravanserai doing nothing on my charity. Tihmrose has gone to her brother's mill up over the pass, says he wants her help with all their sister's kids and he'll need a fighter to protect what's his, if things get worse than they are, and Judeh's got the same idea, more or less; his mother and sister are both widows in Silvergate Ward, so he's gone home to them."

"Zavel?"

"Varro says he's hanging around in the city, picking up a living somehow. He's run into him a couple of times, bought him a meal once, which is more than I'd have done. I haven't seen the boy for weeks. Not since the day before the battle in the suburb, when he showed up drunk and begging. I hate to say it of Asmin-Luya's son, but he's no great loss. I wasn't going to take him on again anyhow. He's had too many second chances."

Varro hadn't mentioned that to him, and he'd been half expecting, all this time, that the boy's body would turn up somewhere, slain in the fighting. Of course, he hadn't asked, till now. He was too tired to even feel particularly relieved.

"Holla-Sayan, go to sleep."

That was easy. When Gaguush lay down with him, he pulled her close, arm over her, but really had no urge for more. Sleep, feeling her warmth.

"Holla . . ."

He grunted. Her hand was winding its way inside his shirt, and he was going to annoy her by simply not responding to that, but she only let it rest there, covering old scars.

"I bought the caravanserai."

"Urm."

"Stay awake just a moment longer. This is important."

He forced his eyes open, found her leaning up on an elbow over him. Beautiful, long, slanted eyes, smudged black with kohl.

"Caravanserai?"

"From Rasta. Half of it, anyway, with an understanding to buy him out entire when he decides he's had enough of it. Partners, for now."

"You—"

"We can't take a baby on the road. Not for a year or two, anyway, and I can't make another trip pregnant. It's too dangerous. Talfan says that at my age I'm mad to think of it. I'm starting to—to listen. I won't risk this child of ours. I won't. So. I was thinking . . . and Master Rasta's been talking about how old and tired he is for years now, and he's got no heir, no kinsfolk at all. He wanted a partner."

"How?"

"Holla, I'm old and plain and bad-tempered. Haven't you noticed that everyone says you married me for my money?"

"You're beautiful. They're joking."

"You don't deny 'bad-tempered.' You never do, *I've* noticed." She kissed him. "Y'know, you are so damned oblivious at times. It's not all in camels. I've been putting it into various things for years, with the Barrayas and Xuas"—the banking families that invested so much with the eastern road and the ships of the Five Cities—"Well, I pulled it back, some of it, middle of a revolt or not. That's all."

"All right," he mumbled.

"Holla!" A thumb jabbed his ribs.

"I'm awake!"

"You're not. Are you—do you mind?"

He blinked and tried to look alert, tried to get his thoughts into some rational vein. Saying, Great Gods, no, let's run away to the Western Grass where there's space and quiet and the gods leave their folk to think for themselves, was about the worst thing he could think of to say. Gaguush in a sod-roofed house, with a wealth measured in sheep and horses and blue cattle . . . not very likely.

How many head of cattle in the worth of a caravanserai?

"You're going to run a caravanserai?"

"With Rasta, yes, I am. You can take the caravan out, if you ever get free of the priest and his senate. Later on, maybe I'll hire someone and we can both go, teach our brat the road. But it's wise. I think it's wise.

We have to settle somewhere for the baby, and since you're so deep into Marakand's affairs—"

"Gaguush, there's a civil war going on. There's a devil in the city. The gods are lost—"

"Then fix it! That's what you're trying to do, isn't it? Fix it, because our baby's going to be born here and it's her gods—"

"His gods."

"Oh, you know that, do you? Fine, we won't name him Pakdhala, then. *His* gods you'd better save, *his* city you'd better set straight, because this is a mess, and you've got seven months before he's born into it."

"Oh."

"Oh," she mocked, and lay down again, tight against him. After a moment she asked, quietly, "It will be all right, won't it? The Lady must know she's beaten, or she wouldn't be hiding. She's afraid. She'll run, or you'll finish her once and for all, when she comes out of the temple again. You and Mikki and that damned Ivah, who's turned out to be so great a wizard. The three of you together can kill her."

The gods of the earth and the greatest wizards of the time hadn't been able to destroy the seven devils of the north, if the tales were true, only bind them in a deathlike sleep, and that was with the help of the Old Great Gods.

The Lady wasn't afraid. She couldn't be. She was waiting. He didn't know for what. Allies, if the rumours her agents leaked were to be believed. Jugurthos said the Praitans, even under a high king, never held together for long. Too quarrelsome a folk, cattle-thieves who couldn't trust their own kin. Or she was preparing some new attack, something that would make the Red Masks inconsequential. She hadn't really done anything yet that frightened him as Tamghat—Tamghiz Ghatai—had. If he hadn't smelt her, felt her and known her by the shape of her soul, the weight of her on the world, he would have thought her nothing more than some powerful wizard turned necromancer. Except for what she had done to defend the temple, the fire on the walls. That was no wizard's work, and that, he and Mikki and Ivah between them, could not find a way to defeat. He didn't know what she was, who she was, really.

Something pretending to be smaller and weaker than it was, a strategy with some aim he couldn't imagine.

He slid a hand down over Gaguush's belly, no more rounded than ever, but he could feel the life that pulsed there, something separate, something that was not Gaguush, such a small and fragile ember, so easy to extinguish. All human life seemed that way. "You should have gone with Django," he said. "Serakallash would be safer." He didn't suggest Lissavakail. Didn't, when it came down to it, want his son born Attalissa's.

"At least here, I can stay in bed half the morning and have Tamarisk bring me ginger tea till I stop throwing up. Since you aren't around to do it."

"Sorry."

"Go to sleep, Holla."

But he had her shirt untied.

"I thought you were too tired even to stand up."

"You keep talking. You're keeping me awake. Anyhow, I'm not standing up."

"Oh? Something is."

Eventually, he did sleep, lightly and uneasily; even then awareness of the fire on the temple walls never left him, like a ringing in the ears on the very edge of hearing, that nevertheless won't fade. In his dreams, he still seemed to be prowling the temple's boundaries, walking again through Greenmarket and Templefoot and East Wards, with a band of ash, and of adobe and mud brick and even stone gone to glassy rubble along the wall that topped the sunken temple grounds. How the fire had reached such a kiln-heat without damaging either the temple wall behind or the houses across the streets, nobody could explain. By day the fire still burned pale, without fuel, casting a heat-shimmer high into the air, and at night it was a curtain that rippled the colour of an autumn moon seen through desert dust. The narrow streets that followed the temple's walls were still passable, barely, if you kept to the far side. Most houses along the other sides of those streets and lanes had been abandoned now. No one knew, or trusted, that the wall of fire would not suddenly flare up in greater strength. Along the outer wall, where the temple boundary formed part of the city's defences, the woods of the ravine, which had been a river so long ago it was hardly remembered even in song, were burnt in an ashy strip. There would be no return of green, not in the spring rains, not next year or ten or fifty years hence, no thistle, no bitter cliff-rose, not even the shiny veil of blister-vine. It was dead as the eastern shore of the Kinsai-av along the cataracts, which folk said, untruly, was the scarring of a wizards' war. It hadn't been wizards did that. The dog remembered . . .

No. No. No, he did not.

Not his war, not his folk, not his gods. But Gaguush wanted now to make this city their home. He wasn't asleep but drifting between sleep and waking, restless, half lying over her as if to shield her from some attack. She muttered, "Holla, it's too hot and you're too heavy to use me as a pillow," shoving him over so she could escape. "I'm going down. You sleep. If anyone comes, I'll tell them I haven't seen you."

"Don't."

"Not unless they convince me the Lady's coming out of the temple." Her hand stroked around his ear, down his jaw, a finger tracing over his lips. "Now go back to sleep. A few hours, at least. I'll cook you some supper, too, before you go back."

Thekla cooked. Gaguush did not. But he hadn't known she could read and write, either. He smiled, words too much effort, and watched through eyes half-closed as she dressed again, muttering, Gaguush-like, as she hunted for odds and ends of clothing lost under the bed.

After that, sleep did take him, engulfing him like deep water.

CHAPTER XIV

It was all falling apart, and Zora didn't understand, the fool girl didn't understand what she could do about it. Nearly a month, she had been besieged in the temple. No, not besieged. Her citadel. Where else should she await her champion? He would meet the Praitannec high king soon. Now. Today. And Praitan would be hers. Then he would return. She would bring him back to her, and the priest who had gone to be her voice would stay behind to speak her will as the Voiceless Red Masks could not; the armies of Praitan would follow the Red Masks. She might allow Ketsim to live; his Grasslanders, certainly, would follow her king-to-be. Grasslanders always followed a victor.

—*It has all gone wrong.*

So she was not besieged. She held her hand above her next move, that was all. Pointless to throw away resources she did not need to spend yet. Pointless, dangerous, to send her Red Masks out needlessly into the city, for the demon and the Blackdog to kill. Working through the Red Masks, she had long since rebuilt the spell of the divine terror. It had been no difficult thing at all to do so, a matter of a few days, and she did not think the wretched Grasslander wizard would find it so easy to tear apart, this time, when it came to the test. But not yet. Not here, yet. No, she did not reveal it by sending them out against the city. Only to be her eyes, she sent them, not to fight. She could not lose any more. Every death weakened her, leached wizardry away, she had none left but theirs, and she feared now her enemies knew it. But when the time came to send the Red Masks out openly again . . . the yellow-eyed wizard would be dead. Or of their number. She had not quite decided. Or perhaps she should even invite her to . . . but the folk could not love a Lady so hard, so worn by war. Besides, the Grasslander wizard would not be so easily seduced as the innocent dancer Zora had been.

Don't think of that. *I am the Lady.*

The sowing of the fields, the summer days. These were the dances of hope and trust in the Lady's kindness. Zora was on her third cycle through the pairing, and the santur-player had just brushed his mallets over the wrong strings, sounding a jarring discord. He would not play in the temple again; she would turn him out, priest or no. The Lady was dishonoured by such imperfection. Sweat trickled down her face, between her breasts, made her limbs slick, as she circled under the bright patch of daylight beneath the shattered eye of the dome, the blue glass flown to shards in her anger—anger, not fear—when Vartu came seeking her. Her feet were so light on the patterned floor. In the dance, there was quiet, the deep, restful quiet of the mind, where truth could rise and understanding blossom.

Silent Red Masks stood along the walls, stood at every door, watching. Awaiting her will.

—*It is a lie. The devils lie. The caravans brought the songs of the Northrons, the songs of the Grasslanders. I heard my father sing them. The devils use. The devils devour. They have their own ends, and the wizards were deceived as I was deceived.*

No. *She* could see, yes, how it was, she, Tu'usha, was wiser than the girl. There were lies told against her, stories in the streets. Vartu had spread them, Ulfhild the skald had scattered the seed before Zora trapped her, or let her be trapped, and she had not seen. She had her ears on the streets now, her folk who loved her still, her priests, her loyal temple guard, who could walk abroad openly in the wards that still held true to their faith, Templefoot, Greenmarket, East Ward, and

Fleshmarket . . . but Fleshmarket had fallen, and now its gateway into Greenmarket was barricaded and guarded against her folk. She had priests and loyal guard who dared the rebel wards; they were too trusting, those rebel street guard and the untrained militias, when a man or a woman said they had business, or family, and they let them cross over the walls, roof to roof or through the houses that straddled broken wall. As well, there were doors, more than one, in the ravine wall. Oh, it was so easy to send a man out, to bring word in, and supplies. They thought they caged her, but they did not see she sat in a citadel, watching them strut, kings of their little dunghill, while she sharpened her axe.

— *This is not the city I would have made. The folk are afraid.*

The priest should have died. The wizard should have been hers.

— *Hadidu lives yet. Nour lives. Red Masks sacrificed in vain.* No satisfaction in that, no, she did not feel it was only the girl's memory it was anger she felt, yes.

It did not matter. Her champion would come, with his Red Masks and the Grasslander mercenaries turned to follow a true leader, and her Praitannec army, out of the east. They would sweep up the road from the Eastern Wall and teach the suburb it was Marakand's, and the city would learn to obey their Lady's word, yes, and to bow their rebel heads. The wizard of the Great Grass, the mistress of demons, would not be made Red Mask, no, she would be hung in a cage over the temple gate, bound impotent, and left to die over many days; the Lady would grant her water, but no food, and so her suffering would be lengthened, yes, and she would know her sin in rebelling against the Lady of Marakand. The Warden of the City would join her. The traitors of the senate would die, all the senators would die, those who defied her and those who cowered in hiding, who had let the rebels take their name from them, they would all die together, slowly, publicly, and this time there would be no forgiveness, no pretence that the Twenty Families had any say in the rule of Marakand.

The city would understand its error. Soon.

—I understand my error. I can't say I was deceived. Because I knew. I was threatened, I was afraid, and I fell. Better I had died, better I had lived possessed as Lilace the Voice lived, and kept my soul. Papa would have been strong. That Grasslander woman would never have given herself away to this. I have sinned, worse than a harlot, selling my soul to keep my body. Gurhan knows it. He sees. He weeps for me.

Gurhan is lost and will never wake. He sees nothing. Folly to think otherwise.

The folk of the city . . . so fickle.

They had loved her, adored her, only a few weeks before, and within days, mere days of that no it was hours by nightfall they had arisen in hatred of her they had turned against her they had betrayed their love—

—Because I killed folk in the suburb. Not even outlanders, caravan mercenaries, foreign merchants. I killed Marakander folk. Not wizards, not rebels. They made me angry and I killed them and the people saw and they know I am mad.

Vartu had done that, forced her to it. Vartu was *his* spy, sent to find her, to tear down her walls, to leave her naked to the stars where he would see her—

—Why didn't the stupid girl kill her brother, back when . . . the days are so clear in my mind, the canoe dancing up the long breast of the ocean and sliding to the dark valleys, and rising again against the sky, and the distant islands are only circling birds and a roughening of the smooth horizon of the sea. I remember—I don't want to remember. Not my memory. I would have killed him. I know myself now, weak, foolish, I'm a stupid child trapped beyond my understanding, but even as a child I would have known such a wrongness should die, and that there would be no sin in a knife in the dark. Why did a devil, a power even the gods of the earth fear, how did she-Tu'usha fall into this mad and broken mind of Sien-Mor's and not sweep it all away, burn her clean and rule her?

Was am I she so weak?

Because we are one and Sien-Mor is dead she burned he burnt her the fire ate her bones.

—*Then why am I are we mad?*

She shut her thoughts to the whisper, which was not hers, she had no doubts of herself. She was safe, safe behind walls, safe behind the barrier of the divine fire, even the Blackdog of the mountains, whoever he was had been what was he—could not pierce that veil to come at her, and if she parted it, so briefly, to let her true and chosen folk in or out of the temple on her business, that parting was always watched. The Red Masks would not let any enemy in. The Red Masks were true.

The Red Masks were too few. She could not replace them without sending them out to capture the wizards of the suburb, who had either fled to the road or joined the rebels, and if she did send them hunting wizards, they would be destroyed by the Blackdog, and her strength weakened. She could not afford that. Their interwoven wizardry was her strength.

Zora danced. The Red Masks watched. Every day, she had done so, since she sealed the temple walls behind her undying fires. The priests gathered in secret corners, out of sight, out of mind, they thought, and whispered. Temple guard sent out on patrol of her faithful wards did not all return. Deserters. Traitors.

Vartu's lies grew and grew, even though Ulfhild Vartu was lost, gone, trapped, forgotten. Storytellers retold them. The Lady sent temple guard to kill the storytellers, the street-singers, but now they were guarded by the folk themselves, the rebels, and knowing the temple sought them only made more gather to hear them.

The streets said that Red Masks had burned down a house in Sunset Ward, where a hidden priest of Ilbialla had still lived and served his people, but the priest and his child had escaped, though his wife had perished. Proof they told lies against her. Hadidu's wife Beccan had been long dead. Zora had not killed her, kind, sharp Beccan, who had let her help make pastries in the kitchen of the Doves. They sang hymns in praise of Ilbialla again, Ilbialla, goddess of the well in Sunset Ward, goddess whose care had been Sunset and Riverbend. A kindly goddess. A humble goddess, who did not take from her folk. Like Gurhan on the hill, who had dug out earthquake victims with his own hands. Where had the Lady been, that night? Where had her priests been?

The Red Mask priests were no priests, the city said, and the old order of the yellow priests grew fat on taxes and tithes and tolls meant for the public good of the city. The rebels whispered everywhere. The folk listened. It was because they were hungry. There was still food, if you had money. She must remember to issue a ration from the temple granary. They had said it was empty, but that would be a lie. Her faithful wards would praise the Lady for it. The mountain villages sent nothing, had sent nothing even when she had held the Fleshmarket gate. The rebels had warned them, threatened them, they feared demons, or they were traitors, defiant of Marakand, they were—and the manors of the south road and the southern foothills, and the poor, proud, free villages of the Malagru were all denied her.

The Voice was dead. The Lady had ridden in procession through the city after thirty years of hiding. They had adored her, worshipped her, but it had been devil's magic. They were deceived. They knew it. "I knew it at the time," each one said of himself alone, "but everyone else . . ."

She must remember there were those who held true. She must not be ungrateful. A goddess was not. The faithful senators were besieged in the Family Feizi mansion in Silvergate Ward, while the Families appointed traitors and false senators, men and women her Voice had long ago ordered disinherited from their Families, to their new senate, which perched like a flock of sparrows on the palace steps, pretending it listened to the spokesmen of the guilds and the folk of the wards. They had even named five senators of the suburb, which was not a part of the law of Marakand they claimed to embody. But her senate, the faithful remnant—they did nothing but send furtive messages, asking for temple guard to destroy their enemies.

Useless. They would die in the cages with the rest.

Liars and traitors and fools. She would burn the city and give it to her folk of Over-Malagru, settle them there, true folk, and turn the survivors of the city out to learn to till the fields. She would—

If she shut her eyes, she might be back dancing with the Voice in the pulpit and the secret honouring of Gurhan in her mind.

—*Help me. Find me. Save me.*

She was become the goddess of the city. She danced to her own glory.

—*Do you hear me? This voice, my Voice, not your own?*

The sharp, water-on-stones music swirled and leapt, carrying her with it, then settled into its final coiling round, slower, softer, repeating, stretched out, ceased, and she held the final pose, head flung back, daylight red against closed eyelids. She could hear the man's breathing. He was old. The afternoon was hot. He had always been kind to the young dancers. If his hands shook, that was mortal frailty and to be pitied. She should, in turn, be kind. To turn him out into this besieged ward, out of the temple that had been his home since before the earthquake, would be cruelty unbefitting the Lady of Marakand.

"That's enough," she said. "Thank you." She found a smile for him, watched, with satisfaction, the answering smile, grateful, awed, devoted. Yes, he was hers. She should treasure him. He served for love.

Zora wrapped a white woollen shawl over herself against the sudden chill of sweating skin, and because her silk robe clung, sticky, too revealing even before the old priest, certainly too revealing for the bowing younger man in the entryway, in the darkness between the pillars. A lieutenant of the temple guard. Ashir had come that morning with a plan, a plea, and she had said—had said yes, yes? She had. She remembered. He had interrupted her meditations on the failure to hold the Fleshmarket Gate, the treachery of the street-guard captain there, her failure to take Nour, her morning dancing, she had forbidden them the hall, she dwelt there alone, and priestesses brought her water and cracked wheat, and that was all she took, not even oil to the wheat, or mountain butter, because she must be pure, she must be clean, she must be holy as she waited . . .

She had told Ashir, yes, because he was so humble, so grovelling, so devout. He grieved for his wife Rahel, strange though that was, as if despite their long years of estrangement and enmity he had lost a part of himself when the Red Masks threw her down the stairs to the well, and he grieved for his idea of the Lady, and in his fear he must serve her, must prove himself the most faithful, the most necessary.

And perhaps he could do what she did not dare risk Red Masks to do, and bring her the Grasslander wizard, against whom Nour was nothing, a weak child.

Besides, the Grasslander was a danger.

The rebels nipped and gnawed at the bindings on the gods. They had no understanding, the demons of the earth knew nothing of such things, and the merely human wizards, even this wizard, with her magic that jumbled Grasslander and Nabbani practices, could not see, could not know. The Voice had ordered the books to be burnt, any that might hint, and besides she Tu'usha had set words of her own, words Sien-Mor alone could never have commanded, words the Red Masks would burn if they dared to speak, had they the will and the tongue to do so, into the bindings. The merely human could do nothing. But their nipping and gnawing irritated her, and the wizard who led them might make herself a queen over Marakand, a warlord of the Grass. She must be stopped. Most of all, she must be stopped, because she spoke of Gurhan the god of the Hill, and his name on her tongue was wrong. He was her god, Zora's god, hers, he should have been hers, she should be the one to praise and plead, and she should have found wizards who could nip and gnaw at her the spells, she should have known the gods were not dead, she should have Papa should have they should have tried they should have found this wizard called the demons of the earth to Marakand sought foreign gods and powers asked them not sent the girl the child to the temple alone and scared and spying for dead men who would never hear her words for a dead cause for—it should have been Zora, there on the Palace Hill, adored by the folk, their freedom, their warrior and wizard their champion who showed the true face of the Red Masks and the madness of the Voice and the Lady's lies to the folk, it should have been she at Hadidu's side, she in whose words Nour placed his trust, she the priest of Gurhan serving her god not an outlander a mercenary . . .

She wanted the Grasslander wizard dead. She wanted that mirror of may-be might-have-been dead. She wanted no wizardry set against her Red Masks, when her beautiful champion rode home. He might, of all of them, kill a demon, yes, at his side she would ride against the demons herself, she could be warrior, she had been. She would not be afraid, with him at her side, the girl's fear would not take her, swamp her, make her forget she was Tu'usha, who had fought the allied chieftains of the Great Grass at her brother's side, who had duelled the chief of the Blue Banners and his wizards—

"What is it?" she demanded of the guardsman, and he bowed yet again. He was not in his red tunic but dressed like a caravaneer in dusty, baggy trousers, high soft boots, and a striped coat with square pockets and a hood. He looked quite convincingly a man of the road, save for his short hair and shaven chin and the smooth, clean nails. But the hood would hide his lack of braids, nobody would look at his nails, and some of the caravaneers were shaved at the baths so soon as they came to a town. Who was he? Surey, yes, junior lieutenant of the second company. The officers changed so often, lately. She did not bother to remember their names. But Surey, she should remember. He was Ashir's favourite, his errand-runner, his own right hand, of late. When had that happened? She should not allow her priests to form their own factions, to suborn her guard. She should send Surey back to his captain and his company. But tomorrow. Ashir might yet need him tonight.

"The Revered Right Hand wanted me to tell you he has chosen his men and is ready, if the Lady would allow him through the fire."

"Is it so late?" She looked past him, and yes, the light was swimming amber and golden, the shadows long and blue. Evening. She swayed, rocked back on her heels. She must drink a little water. The body had its needs. Time passed, and the body measured it, pacing the days.

She shivered. Horses. Horses, hooves on the hard-baked hills. The sky was blue, and small clouds piled over the horizon and faded again, tinged with fire, and the sun burned smoky orange with dust. The hills shimmered. Red cloaks blazed.

Today. This day, she was suddenly certain, and the black pillars and the cracked plaster and waiting clerk faded to hazy dream around her. This day her champion would meet the high king of Praitan, and destroy him, and take the seven kingdoms for the glory of the Lady. This day or—night, night was in his thoughts, its thoughts, the ghost that rode him a hungry yearning, no, no, she would not must not—let it be so. Let the little work of death sate itself, and they would fear—he was her captain, a champion of Praitan, a king's sword in the manner of Over-Malagru, leave him to his business, if he would fight at night, she would let him, and in the dawn she would call him back, the priest who dreamed, Revered Arhu, would dream for her and speak for her, and the armies would come, riding hard, they would come to find her waiting, and the city would see them, a black tide rising up the pass, and—

Today. Tonight. Yes. That was it, why she would allow Ashir's plan, which was meant for his own glory, to ensure his own importance, his own essential place, in the eyes of the temple. She would begin to prepare against her champion's return in triumph. It would be at least three five-days before he could return, with Praitan left submissive behind, hers, its very gods knowing themselves subject to Marakand—of course it could not be made orderly so quickly, but Arhu her dreaming priest was there to speak for her, and she wanted her captain home her king her father of emperors home. Him, *him* she did not think the demons could destroy. She would set the wizardry in him free, set free the ghost that so hungered for the energy of life, give it a new host, a child—not her child, no, never, not—

—You're mad! Can't you see yourself?

The guardsman Surey was staring, trying not to. He watched her hands. She glanced down, blinking hard to drive the hills and the sky from vision, saw them knotted, twisting, writhing like snakes, like the hands of mad Lilace the Voice of the Lady. She stilled them, tucked them together, wrapped her shawl, pinched her lips together. Had she spoken, had she whispered, had she shaped words? No, she smiled, charming, kindly, benevolent goddess that she was, she murmured blessings on this faithful soldier, whose heart raced terrified in her presence.

"Tonight," she said. "I have decided. Tonight Ashir may try his plan."

"Yes, great Lady. He's ready. He's at the gate, and the first company of the guard is ready to force the blocked gateway to the Fleshmarket Ward, with the second standing in reserve. They only await your word. And the parting of the fire."

That wasn't reproof, was it? She knew perfectly well she had told Ashir he might try his plan, without Red Masks, because Red Masks would only draw the Blackdog and the demon to him.

They were fighting in Fleshmarket Ward. She was the goddess of the city. She heard . . . the Lady heard their dying.

No. That was past. Fleshmarket had fallen. Her thoughts ran ahead. It had fallen to the rebels yesterday, but she would retake it before nightfall. She heard the deaths to come. Yes.

The soldier watched her hands again, fluttering, butterfly hands, Lilace's mad hands, pleading, plucking, trying to tear a way free through empty air. He would die.

What was she thinking? A faithful guardsman, conscientious and devout. She was no murderer.

"Go," she said, and waved him ahead of her. She must watch them leaving, to bless them. It was what a goddess would do.

The first and the second companies of the temple guard were lovely in their armour, coloured warm by the falling light. How could any stand against them? They would give the Fleshmarket back to her, and the Drovers' Gate, and the southern foothills would be hers again, and she would bring fat sheep and cattle into the market, and her faithful folk would feast. She sent five Red Masks to the first company, a patrol, to stand about the captain. They would go before him, clearing his way through the barricades. They would go to purge the traitor garrison from the Fleshmarket gate. By the time the Blackdog could come, or the demon, they should be finished and returned safe within her fire, with no need to reveal the restoration of their holy terror, even yesterday, even last night she had resisted revealing that, but their presence would lure the Blackdog and the demon, yes, both, because the rebels would not dare to lose the Fleshmarket, to allow her a city gate again.

Ashir himself was dressed as a man of the city, with a caftan over armour, which made him bulky and strange, and a turban wrapped thick to protect his bald head. The turban was saffron-yellow, as if he needed to remind himself he was yet the Lady's priest. Twenty temple guard went with him, all in the clothes of the street, or caravaneer's coats.

Twenty men, though two were women. She did not like to see the women fighting. It was not right, her brother said. . . . They lacked strength, they lacked nerve, as she did—no. They had their patrol-firsts to follow, all men. She should not listen to the whispers he was *not* her brother he owned *nothing* of her and Sien-Mor poor Sien-Mor was dead, only a ghost in her mind, a memory haunting her mind, a pattern of thought was not a ghost not a soul was dead yes.

Twenty men. Twenty-one. Ashir had his caravan guard, the young Grasslander Zavel, who spoke like a man of the Red Desert, though he had no tattoos. The man wanted a place, money. Faithful Lieutenant Surey had brought him to Ashir, and to the Lady.

Zavel had proven himself. He told them of the Grasslander wizard, whose name was Ivah. A servant of the devil Ghatai. Who was dead. Servant of who else? He did not know. He insisted on his story, believed it even when the Lady herself questioned him, so maybe it was true: the rebel's great wizard was a murderer, a servant of Tamghat the Lake-Lord, a coward who had fled her lord's fall. Zavel drank too much and spent the money he earned of the temple on drink and the keeping of a girl and her family in a ruin of a house two streets from the temple, yet he was eyes and ears in Templefoot Ward and went over the walls to the rebel-held city and the suburb, listening and asking questions, and because he was of the road, not the city, he heard what the city did not hear and understood what the city did not understand.

The plan had been his, not Ashir's. The Right Hand thought the Lady did not know this. Zora knew Zavel's plan was not made for love of her. It was revenge, it was spite—she did not care. The caravaneer wanted the Grasslander wizard to suffer and die. So did the Lady. It would be so, and he could bring her to him, because he was a friend, he was trusted, he called the Blackdog by name. They were like brothers, he said, which was a lie in his mind that he wanted to be the truth, and yet it had some seed of truth in it. He believed that the Grasslander wizard had bespelled them all. The Lady would kill her, and set them free, and he would be honoured among his friends. Or if they died, then among the servants of the temple he would have honour. He had both thoughts.

He stared at her, worse than the guardsman. He might have been handsome, if he had not been so sweat-greasy and red-eyed, and he was only a little older than she.

Zora ignored him. He was a mercenary who betrayed his friends. He was beneath the Lady's notice. Let him strive hard to please her, to win her approving nod. But she smiled at Ashir.

"My faithful Right Hand," she said. "The Lady blesses you and those who go with you. Bring me the Tamghati wizard Ivah, and kill Hadidu the priest of Ilbialla, if he is there."

She would not be soft, not be weak, not the girl thinking of the men who had been kindly young uncles to her. Hadidu had made himself her enemy. She was strong. She could stand alone.

Ashir bowed. He was afraid.

"My lady," he said. That was all. He could hardly keep the tremor of his fear from being heard by all.

"Go," she said. "I will part the fire."

They went up the tunnel cut through the cliff-face, rising from the dell to the gatehouse. The Red Masks led, and two Red Masks stood as sentries in the darkness beneath the vaulted passage of the gatehouse itself. She let those that followed them feel the heat of the fire, gave them time to consider the shimmering, watery lemon light that slanted through the cracks of the gates, as the Red Masks unbarred and pulled them inwards, and for a moment they looked out through a curtain of pale fire. Then like that curtain it drew back, and they marched out. Ashir scuttled, as if he feared to feel flames licking at his heels. The flames rushed back, and the gates were barred again.

So. It was done. Ashir would bring her Ivah; he had a gag and fetters charmed against wizardry which should hold even her, she who had escaped from the temple cells. Or Ashir would die and in death and failure prove himself faithful, and she would appoint a new Right Hand, a priest or priestess who would owe all to her and have no confused thoughts that there had been a better time, before. Foolish of Ashir, who was old and stiff and puffed, to lead them himself, but the glory must be his, she understood that. And if he failed, this way he would not have to face her. They both understood that, he and she together. Zora smiled to herself and tucked her hands into her sleeves.

She would eat now. Perhaps she would allow herself some lettuce, with the boiled wheat. She would sleep a little, lying in the centre of the swirling mosaic beneath the dome. And then she would dance again. Her mind was never so clear these days as when she danced.

Zora did eat, swallowing each bite carefully. She had no hunger, but it was important to eat. Her mind was troubled, and after the priestess who served her, now that Rahel was no more, had left her, bowing low in silence, she paced in the scented garden planted by the Beholder of the Face behind her house, meditating, as evening fell and the shadows of her fires shimmered like water in sunlight. Then she brought one more Red Mask from his station, and sent him out into the gathering night, to pass unseen, wrapped in spells of concealment, to Gurhan's Hill. Ashir might, after all, fail, and there were voices, whispering, in her mind when she danced in the Hall of the Dome, clear-headed then or not. She did not think they were her own. The dreaming gods stirred, as if they heard a faint, distant scratching at their walls.

She did not want anyone scratching at those walls.

CHAPTER XV

Ivah sat back on her heels, scowling at the deeply incised lines, curling and twisting, that were cut into the stones sealing the half-buried mouth of Gurhan's cave, scrubbing her fingers clean on the hem of her coat. Thirty years of travellers and furtive scholars trying to translate it, Nour carrying copies away to imperial wizards of Nabban, and despite that nobody even knew the language, or could say more than that the script looked kin to something Pirakuli, except for certain words, which curled and coiled quite differently, like thorny vines.

Those were not a human language or human runes, Mikki said, and told her she could not and would not translate them. But if she could decipher the rest . . .

Gurhan's Hill was wormholed with tunnels, the long wearing of water or ancient mining, who could say, but Mikki, who had explored them, said none led to Gurhan's cave or hid the god himself.

Ivah wrote in charcoal where the inscription differed from that on Ilbialla's tomb. She could find that way the syllables of the god's and the goddess's names, word-endings that might show masculine and feminine, maybe, trace from the probable names sounds that occurred elsewhere, but that was nothing other furtive scholars had not already done. Nothing the men and women consulted by Nour had not already done. It was not what Hadidu hoped or what Jugurthos and the loyalist senate expected from her, their great saviour wizard, defier of the Lady. She had

245

taken it further, though. She felt as if she might understand, almost, the shape of the thing. It was a song half-heard, a shape obscured in fog. If she trusted, reached . . . maybe it would come clear. Maybe. Hope was all they had.

Ivah turned back to the semicircle of ground chalk she had poured out, arching to enclose the mouth of the cave and all the poplar-grown landslip that half hid it. With charcoal, she copied the names that must be those of the gods onto flat rocks set at certain points within. She wished she had the matching third, which would be the Lady, she was certain. Unless that goddess had been truly killed, when the devil came to take her place, it would be well to free her with the rest. Other characters, Nabbani, and Grasslander star-symbols, she had written in sulphur and cinnabar, the latter not easy to come by in this city where wizardry was banned.

Salt, too, she had used to draw at certain points, and she rolled and braided strips of the inner bark of the poplars over the hill, making knotted patterns, swaying and singing, sinking herself into a trance where the patterns would rise to her fingers and eye, without the conscious mind labouring. Some days she did nothing but sit, and listen, and wait.

Her father had taught her so. She had never been an apt pupil, her mind never still when he told her sit, be silent, listen to your own pulse and hear the stars, but his drugs had set her mind dizzy and jittering and made her sick. It was better to sing, softly, as he had sometimes sung to her when she was a little child and still more delight than disappointment, or as her mother had sung, lullabies, mostly. And as they faded she could hear the stars.

Or something.

She rather thought it was the poet's mind, the prophet's, the well in the marrow from which the words rose, and nothing to do with the Grasslander myths of the constellations. But it didn't matter. What mattered, now, was that she could find this place that had always eluded her under her father's eye, and out of it the knotted cat's cradles rose, to shape channels of will and power that would, maybe, take even the necromancer devil by surprise. A hairsbreadth crack, that was all she wanted. The clawhold of a fingernail in the granite-flawless prison of the devil's entombment of the gods. Give her that, and she would give Marakand its gods again.

Arrogant, oh, arrogant, and foolish, but it was not pride that drove her. Urgency, need, the righting of a wrongness in the world and maybe even more than that, the thing made because it could be made well, she saw it, felt it . . .

Sometimes she heard a whisper. It might have been the voice of a god. Nour came sometimes to watch her, still careful in his movements, but already getting back some of the flesh the long fever had eaten from him. He rode a courier pony, generally, with Guthrun, his gang's camel-leech, or Kharduin himself, a fussing mother hen of a guardian to harry him back to the Sunset Gate fort. Senators came to pray, to their god, for their god, for her, and Mikki would emerge from the sun-dappled shadows of the trees then to watch, to make sure no fool crossed her lines of chalk or harassed her with stupid questions or stupider demands. Other wizards came, caravaneers or travellers, and looked, and offered tentative suggestions, to all of which she nodded, looking thoughtful, waiting for them to leave. She would have taken any suggestion that actually settled aptly into her own mind, but they all jarred, and she only wanted the helpful strangers to be silent and go away. Sometimes she felt poised to fly and felt it would all fail and crash about her, wings, feathers, wind, tearing to shreds, a fancy, dream-born, a construct that had no waking strength or integrity.

Sometimes she thought she had been fettered all her life by her own fear of not being good enough, her own knowledge she could never be good enough, and to break those chains had taken the intent to sacrifice herself. She felt . . . larger. And very small and prone to fail.

She wished Ulfhild would return.

Ivah finished the last pattern she would set that day and ate with Mikki, spiced mutton and cabbage rolled in bread brought by a young street guard, a great platter of such fare, with apologies that Hadidu could not join them. He was meeting with Jugurthos and the senior guildsmen of the Fleshmarket Ward at the Barraya mansion. She could have gone to the camp amid the palace ruins, or the library, or to so many senatorial houses that would have been open to her, but she couldn't stand the noise, the talk, the questions, and the tension of hope. And retreating, with the rest of the—whatever they were, the leaders of the rebellion, the lords of the city, Hadidu and Captain, now Warden and Senator Jugurthos Barraya, and Nour, to the apothecary's house or the Sunset Ward Gate was not an option. Varro had been shaken—literally, she suspected—into a promise to leave her alone. That was all Holla-Sayan had wrung out of him. They kept clear of one another. It was enough, though it distressed Hadidu for her to be so hated, and he seemed to find it hard to believe Holla's gang might have cause to do so, though she told him so herself. She didn't care, so long as the gang did leave her to herself; that was grace sufficient. But she didn't want to be among the folk who saw her as their saviour, either, their champion and beloved of their gods. She wanted, needed, only silence and peace. She felt as though the wrong word, the wrong voice, the yammering of the uneducated, the ignorant, even the well-intentioned and scholarly, would jar everything loose and she would never find the threads again, the words . . .

Mikki understood silence. The moon, well into its third quarter, had risen, and as blue twilight fell it was silver already high among the branches overhead. Bats cut across it. Messengers to the Palace of the Moon, in Nabbani symbolism. It was said they carried prayers and wishes to Mother Nabban, but she dwelt in the great river of the land, so where the moon came into it. . . . *That's the sort of question your father asks,* her mother would have said, or maybe had, some time long ago. *But only of other folks' gods, not his own precious stars.*

"Do demons pray?" she asked Mikki. She would not go back to look at her work. That was her rule. Let it sit, let it wait. Evening was a time of second-guessing, of failing confidence and faltering will. Evening was the time to rest.

Street guard, the most trusted men from Jugurthos's Sunset Gate garrison, came up the trampled path, three patrols of them, fifteen men and woman with lanthorns on poles and spear and sword, who would watch until dawn, to forestall any furtive destruction. The entire Palace Hill was guarded and patrolled along all the streets that bounded it, but they took no chances with this spell. The senior patrol-first bowed to her. She gave the woman, Belmyn, a shallower bow in return and a grateful smile that she didn't chatter, that her guards were so careful, setting lights to mark a perimeter about the half—no, now it was a two-thirds-finished spell, so that no careless foot would mar it.

Let the morning bring renewed nerve.

"Pray?" Mikki repeated. "No. Not really. Good evening, Belmyn."

The guardswoman saluted Mikki less formally, with a nod and a crooked-toothed smile, one of the few able to take him as a man and not something bordering on godhead. He rose and padded away, not far, just out of sight, for modesty's sake. The line between day and night was crossed, somewhere beyond the hill's crest. He came back tying the sash of a caftan that strained across his shoulders, the hem barely halfway down his calf. Why did Mikki have to bother about taking his clothes off, she had dared ask him once. Holla-Sayan didn't, and didn't have to wander about muttering to himself as to where he'd left his axe, either.

Mikki had retorted, as he had when she had first remarked on his speaking, that Holla-Sayan was a monster who defied the world, whereas he was a natural beast, and where *had* he left his axe?

His moon-skinned pallor looked more unhealthy, less natural than it had, with his un-Northron black eyes hollow and shadowed. Marakand was nothing to him. She should be nothing to him. The demon wanted to be away searching for Moth, tearing the temple apart stone by stone, if need be, if only he could get through the fire.

"I'd call her back to you if I could," she said awkwardly, abruptly, as she followed him away, up the ridge and down its other slope, to the ruins where the priests of Gurhan had once lived, where she had a bed in a mostly-roofed goatshed, watched over by a horse's skull. He slept in a lean-to of brush under a tree, or, more often, sat or walked along the dyke of fern-grown stones, looking at the sky and murmuring Northron that had a different sound to it than what she had heard in At-Landi where the ships came down the river from the kingdoms of the north. So he didn't pray. Maybe he talked to his absent mistress. Maybe he recited poetry, to keep despair at bay.

She did not think she had been sleeping long when someone came shouting from the path to the menagerie, scrambling heavily up the dyke, breaking and trampling and gasping. Ivah was on her feet with her borrowed sabre in hand and a silver light like a second moon rising over the compound to light up her enemies before she recognized the voice as that of Varro.

The recognition did not set her at ease.

"Ivah!" he shouted. "Is Holla-Sayan here? Red Masks in the Fleshmarket again."

"I haven't seen him since this morning." He'd probably dropped senseless in a gutter from exhaustion. They wouldn't leave him alone, and most of the fools flinching at imagined red-veiled shadows, night and day, had never actually met a Red Mask. If they had—she could sympathize with the flinching. The memory of the terror settled into her gut, and she sweated, sick and cold, with fear of them breaking out of Fleshmarket, coming here, for her, to drag her before the Lady again. And she had faced them twice and survived. Knowing that the cowering terror they brought was a spell and was destroyed did not help. They were still invulnerable to all but Mikki and the Blackdog.

Varro bent over, gasping for breath. He must have run all the way from his wife's house in Clothmarket Ward. "The captain of the gate sent a runner to say she saw them coming, but there's been no word since and nobody knows where Holla's gone. Hadidu sent him away to rest, he says. Jugurthos sent to our house searching for him. Is the demon here, then?"

Mikki was beside him, light on his feet and little more noisy than a cat. "How many?"

"Great Gods alone know. Nobody seems to want to wait around to count. If we had some way of stopping them, some spell—"

"You all decided that since she hasn't shown any inclination to send them out against us in numbers, maybe setting these gods free was a bit more important," Ivah snapped "Remember?"

"Maybe it would be, if you ever actually managed to do it, but—"

Mikki growled, human shape notwithstanding. "Enough. And put out the light."

Ivah let it die and set a spark to the wick of a candle-lantern instead, a smaller, tamer light and one that, sitting on a stone at the shed door, would not be a beacon over this valley.

"I'll go," Mikki said. "Heading for the other wall and the drovers' gate?"

"Don't know." Varro still gasped. "Can you fight, like that? At night?"

Mikki gave him a somewhat sardonic look, axe over his shoulder. "I'm also a Selarskerry sea-raider, remember, valley man? Depends how many there are. Want to come help?"

"Talfan . . ." Varro straightened up, rolled his shoulders, and caught his breath at last. "Talfan said you'd go, if Holla wasn't here. I'll guard the wizard." He shrugged, tapped the hilt of his sword, which was old in style and ornate, still showing traces of gilt, not a caravan guard's weapon. "Unless the Red Masks come. Then she'll be on her own and you won't see the dust of me. She's not worth dying for." A sour smile at Ivah, who swallowed her reply and only nodded.

"Jugurthos is sending the militia of three wards in. If you can just clear the Red Masks out, they can hold it. The Red Masks will probably run when they see you coming, anyway," Varro added hopefully.

Mikki growled again, more disconcerting when he looked human than by daylight.

"Mikki, what if she's sent something after Holla-Sayan—if she's captured him—can you call him?" Ivah asked. The Blackdog had spoken to her mind, after all. Mikki might be able to do the same.

"He's not close by and I don't know him all that well. You'll be all right with Varro." In bear's form, he might have given her a reassuring nudge with his nose. Now he just grinned, showing those over-long eye-teeth.

"It isn't that . . ." Did even Mikki forget Holla-Sayan was a man, monster or not? It was Gaguush's right to worry about him, not Ivah's, but Gaguush wasn't here. If *she* were the Lady, it would be the Blackdog she struck against, not the human rebels whose shield he had become. But the Lady didn't seem so rational. Ivah let go a long breath. "Take care. The Old Great Gods go with you."

Mikki squeezed her shoulder as he passed, barefoot, unarmoured . . . Great Gods forgive, maybe Varro was right and she should be fighting Red Masks.

No. Mikki could fight a few Red Masks, if they did not come at him in a mass. What Ivah did, here, no one else could do. They needed their gods, and they needed them before the Lady could work some attack against the Blackdog, before a Red Mask finally got past Holla to assassinate Hadidu, who, well-meaning fool, had sent him away. But if the Lady had taken Holla-Sayan, if Mikki failed to come back . . . that was the bleak mind of the night talking.

Mikki vanished before she could talk herself into going with him. He would head into the city by the narrow path of steep stairs that ran east down the hill, buried in leaf-mould and overgrown, under a broken ceremonial arch and into Silvergate Ward. Varro, after a long look at her, said grudgingly, "You'd better go back to sleep."

"I couldn't." Not with Varro, who wanted nothing better than to cut her throat, looming over her on the dyke. After a moment she asked, "Tea?"

"All right." He didn't sound very gracious, but she didn't ask that of him. She made a small fire, sheltered in the hut where it would not blind his watch, pared away shavings from the brick of smoky tea into the kettle as it came to a boil. Sugar, butter, salt, camel's milk, flour, rice, stale shredded bread—caravaneers would drink, or eat, their tea with almost anything in it. He was going to have to drink his black and bitter.

Varro did thank her, gruffly, when she brought him the bowl, so she took her own a bit farther along the dyke, rather than retreating all the way back to the stuffiness of the shed. Once or twice he stirred, as if he would speak, but each time settled again into watching silence.

She heard the man coming up the path as soon as Varro did, a clumsy trampling, puffing, sandals slapping, and yet obviously trying for stealth. Not one of the street guard, who would have hailed them. Varro drew his sword and sank down with soundless care, so that he was kneeling on the ridge of tumbled wall. Ivah crawled a little higher up, sabre naked in hand. Not one man but two, the other silent. They both slowed, and the man in the lead whispered, "It's along here, I think. It's been a long time since I visited the priests of Gurhan, after all. Is—" He raised his voice. "Is anyone there? In the name of the three gods, is anyone there?"

Varro, she thought, waved at her. He was right, they shouldn't both betray their positions, but why did she have to be the one to speak?

Because no one came creeping here in the night looking for Varro, right.

"Stay where you are," she ordered. "Who are you?"

"Ashir," the man in the lead said. "The Right Hand of the Lady. Is that, um, Lady Ivah, the wizard?"

"Mistress Ivah," she said tartly, but her heart sounded loud in her ears. "Have you come to feed more Red Masks to the demon?" He wouldn't be chatting if there were Red Masks with him, unless he was meant to be a distraction. Where in the cold *hells* had Holla-Sayan gotten to?

"I came to—to talk."

"You lie. I said to stay where you are!"

He had begun to sidle towards her voice. She sketched a hasty character and sent light to hover over him. A pouchy, lined face flinched from the glare, though it was not so bright. The second man was younger and stood like a fighting man. A caravaneer? Not too likely, despite his coat.

"I did! I was sent to capture you, I admit, but I've ordered the rest of the men to wait down below the hill while I scout the way, and you can—if you'll hear me out, you can send your own guards to take them."

"I can do that anyway," she said, half an eye on Varro's stealthy creeping along the dyke to get behind them. "What did you say you were, the Right Hand? The first of her priests then, aren't you? Who's the other one?"

"No one. Only my guard."

"So what does a priest of the Lady want to talk about?" And how had he known to look for her here, and by name?

"They say you're working to free the gods."

"Who says?"

"We have our informants," he said haughtily. "Is it true? Can you do it?" And then in a rush, "Mistress, this false Lady is mad and growing madder. None of us are safe. She murdered my wife, she murdered the Mistress of the Dance with her own hand, when she first possessed the girl, for all I know it was she who had the Voice murdered too. We're not safe in the temple! She's shut herself up in the Hall of the Dome to dance, and she hardly does anything else, day and night, but dance and mutter to herself, and tell us to wait, when the dead king comes from Praitan we'll take back the city and she'll be empress Over-Malagru. If you can bring back the old gods, the true Lady, then there are those of us in the temple willing to acknowledge your senate as the true one."

"Generous of you," said Varro, and when the guard whirled around, a knife in his hand, the Northron clipped him on the jaw with the hilt of his sword. He grunted and fell; Varro kicked the knife away. Ashir backed from him, hands raised open, empty.

"I doubt the Lady—assuming there is still or ever was a true Lady—will really want a nest of priests who followed a usurper so willing and devoted," Varro almost purred. "I think you've seen which way the wind's blowing and just want to save your own hide, priest Ashir."

Ashir said nothing to that. Ivah went down to join Varro, sabre in hand. Ashir looked her over and couldn't, for all his evident fear, quite hide his disdain. Remembered her cowering before his goddess in the temple, maybe. Not his idea of a fearsome enemy? No, not his idea of a wizard who could threaten his Lady. Well, she was used to being a disappointment.

"I didn't come to trade words with mercenaries," the priest said, resolutely ignoring Varro. "I came to make a bargain. If you can free my true goddess and promise to allow her her true place in Marakand, I can lead the priests of the temple to you."

Ivah shrugged. "The Northron here's a better Marakander than I am, and whatever you think you can offer, it's neither of us you should be offering it to. It's the priest of Ilbialla and the Warden of the City who'll want to speak to you. Or not."

"I came to make a bargain with you, wizard."

"I'm nobody. A servant. I don't make bargains."

"Thirty years," said Varro abruptly. "We both know there were priests disappeared in the temple, Right Hand, for protesting the Lady's new decrees, after the earthquake. For protesting massacres in the streets, children, babies, murdered." His passion was honest, too, not put on for rhetorical effect. Hadidu had had an infant sister . . . Ivah had heard a little about that, one night, from Nour. "Did you speak then?" Varro demanded. "If your true goddess does come back, you'd better meet her with your face in the dust."

Ashir pinched his lips shut and refused to look at the Northron.

"We can—" No, they couldn't take the priest and his guardsman to the street guard over the ridge by Gurhan's cave; they'd found out about Ivah and where she stayed, which few knew; they might know about the spell being slowly cast there. Their true mission might be to destroy it and set back the work by days, or they might at least take the opportunity if it were offered. She and Varro would have to take them to the library themselves, and hand them over to the street guard stationed there, who could lock them up in some cellar room and send for Warden Jugurthos. She began to say so to Varro, speaking halting Northron, but his eyes narrowed, and he yelled what she only after understood—

"Down!" And he struck her with his shoulder and his whole weight behind it, sending her staggering sideways, leapt past her swinging his sword now two-handed, stumbling. Someone cried out in pain, a shape reeling back on the edge of the light, someone who had come creeping while they spoke. She sent the light high, flaring bright to rival the declining moon, and followed it, springing over Varro, foot just touching his bloody sword, the spear . . .

Zavel, and she had never given him a thought since that day in the suburb. His face was ghastly, grinning, gaping with pain, and he threatened her with a Marakander guardsman's short stabbing sword, but he swept it like a sabre, flailing almost blindly, panting. Rags flapped from his coat, and he hugged his body tight with his left arm, falling backwards. "Traitor priests! Tamghati whore! You've bespelled them all!" he was shrieking when Ivah sliced half through his neck.

Nothing moved behind him. No other shadows stirred. She watched, listened, trying to breathe silently, mouth open, and still there was nothing, except the terrible gurgling behind and a whimpering that was Ashir, so she turned back to Varro, who had fallen on his side, with the spear meant for her in his chest.

He breathed still, after a fashion, and his eyes were open. She knelt down by him and felt the wound. Hot, wet. His coat was already sodden, and the spear deeply embedded, the length of its head at least. She knew she wouldn't get it out without doing worse damage. She knew it wouldn't make any difference. She spread her hand, with the shaft between thumb and fingers, and felt the urgent pumping blood. Bubbling. He was drowning. Her light had died, all her will gone from it, and the night was dark, the moon dropping behind the hill or lost in the trees, but she thought he was trying to find her face. She could feel his fear.

"Varro . . ." She didn't think even a wizard trained as a surgeon could do anything for a spear in the lungs. Moth, maybe. Who was lost. Mikki . . . but a god, a demon, they could only work with what the world gave them. His breath panted and choked, blood and air spluttering together. He was afraid, and cold. It was dark, and none of his friends were here.

She didn't dare set down her sabre. Where had the priest and his guardsman gone?

"Can I help?" Unknown voice.

"No," she said, and with a forefinger drew light again, *the sun steps forth from the palace gates*, the dawn, hope, new beginnings . . . useless here but for its light. This was small and near and golden. Varro's eyes were very wide and didn't follow it, as if they already saw some other landscape, the long grey road to the distant heavens. The guard, a bruise already coming up on his chin, crouched warily by her. Ashir stood a safe distance back, fist to his mouth. She felt dimly surprised they hadn't bolted.

"Not my orders," Ashir babbled. "Zavel was supposed to wait with the guards, he had no business following us up here."

"He brought you here. He told you I was here." Because Zavel had found Varro, somewhere, and gone on about Holla-Sayan being with Ivah, and hitting him, and Varro had told him . . . something. Enough. Justifying Holla's having hit him, not having killed her, oh, she could almost hear his voice, how it must have gone, Varro speaking when he shouldn't have, thinking to defend his friend's honour. Varro's hand twitched, so she took her blood-slick hand from his chest and held his, still not setting down her sabre, still watching the shadows. She should say something to him. She should pray. Her fault. He had a family. She wasn't worth his death. Even if she could free the gods, who weren't his gods or hers, she in herself was not worth his death. If she freed the gods and saved all Marakand, she was not worth his death, because he had daughters and he loved them.

She began to sing; any fumbling words she spoke would be wrong. It was a Northron lullaby her father had sung to her, old, he'd told her. Maybe something he'd sung to his other children, long ago in the Hravningasland, when he was Ulfhild's husband, before the devils escaped the cold hells.

> *A silver moon on the tower walls,*
> *And the surf white on the sand,*
> *He rides a grey horse over sleeping hills.*
> *Listen child, do you hear the sea?*

A song that went with some forgotten tale, ancient and slow and sad. With a forefinger, in Varro's own blood, Nabbani hexagrams and Northron wizardry, she wrote, *Night mist fills the valleys, the mountains float as islands.* Which meant, peace, stillness, welcome dreams, and the easing of pain. She sang all seven verses, though Varro's choking struggle to breathe ended in the fourth of them.

She was not one who saw ghosts easily. If Varro had last words for his wife, it should not be she who carried them, anyway.

"Holla-Sayan will come," she said aloud, still in Northron, because the Marakanders did not need to understand. "Or Mikki. Wait for them." She still held his hand. She made herself let it go, closed his eyes, and stood.

Two prisoners and only she to deal with them. Ivah was not in a mood to deal with prisoners. Enemies dead, yes, not prisoners, who were an annoyance and a bother and, these two, without any use whatsoever.

She would not be her father. Though she did not think this Lady would have held long against her father, if he had ever decided he wanted Marakand for his own. She must not grow into him.

Ashir had gone over to Zavel, a sprawl of arms and legs and lolling head for which she felt no emotion at all. Varro's stroke, which had struck arm and ribs both, and deeply, would have killed him anyway. Her blow had merely hastened him on his way. The priest was chanting a prayer over him, a blessing of the Lady for the road, swaying from side to side and making sweeping ritual gestures.

"Don't!" she snarled. "Leave him—" But Ashir in his last bowing sweep of the arms crouched and scraped the dirt of the track and opened his hands over Zavel's empty face, scattering earth with the final words of his prayer. Freeing him to seek his road, conveniently beyond reach of even a seer's questioning. She seized the old man by the collar of his caftan and jerked him away, back towards—but the guardsman had vanished.

She and Mikki should have had a patrol of guards here with them, as Jugurthos had wanted, and now, now she felt like weeping. She forced the priest to a tree and tied him there with the sash of his own caftan, gagging him as well with his headscarf. His eyes were terrified. If the guard came back—she had to risk it. In all likelihood he had fled to bring the rest of his comrades.

"I'm sorry," she told Varro. "Old Great Gods bless you and make your way easy, Varro. I'm sorry. I'll be back."

With her light very small, not much more than a butter-lamp's glow to stop her tripping or putting an eye out on some stabbing broken twig, Ivah set off straight up the ridge opposite, to drop down on the valley of Gurhan's cave from above, and the nearest allies.

She had not reached the height of the ridge when she heard the gagged priest scream. He might have worked the scarf loose; she had carefully not been so brutal as she felt inclined to be, but that had not been a cry for help. Terror, and unless Holla had returned, what was on this mountain to terrify him? She began to run, an arm before her face to shield it, torn between brightening her light and extinguishing it altogether, but ended up scrambling nearly on all fours, using both hands to catch at limbs and trunks to pull herself along, stealth forgotten, crashing through interwoven, snaring branches, sweating, cold, heart pounding, gasping for breath and whimpering—

Red Mask. There was a Red Mask behind her, and the holy terror of the Lady clutched her. It should not, could not, she had destroyed it. It was restored and she must destroy it again, but she could not, she could not, she could not think. She ran like a mad animal, her will unanswering. She led it straight to her spell at Gurhan's cave, but she could not stop her flight; she would crest the ridge and crash flailing, stumbling, whimpering down through the poplars, down into the narrow valley where Belmyn and her patrol guarded the god's cave and the drawing of the spell, scattering her careful painting of powders and salt and ash, the coiled and knotted cat's-cradles . . . and the Lady would kill her and make her a Red Mask and know all she knew and—

Ivah caught a tree and swung herself around it, put her back to it, fists clenched, eyes closed for a moment's space, trying to slow her breathing, master her galloping heart. She had destroyed the Lady's spell of terror once, she could—it was a new spell, she knew that, she could feel it. There was Grasslander work woven into it, defying her, designed to catch and hold her magic and hers alone—but she had done it once. It could be broken again.

If she had time.

Like a child in nightmare, she was crying out, calling for her father, her mother, for Mikki, for Ghu, for Holla-Sayan, but there was nobody to come to her, there never had been, and the Red Mask came through the trees breaking branches and thrusting down saplings, armoured, with murky light leaking from his armour and white fire sizzling on his short staff.

"St-st-stupid juggler's tricks!" she screamed. "You are dead!" But the words meant nothing when she said them; she didn't have Ghu's power. Her teeth chattered, and with the tree against her back she drew her sabre and thrust it into the earth before her, began weaving a cat's-cradle with strands of braided bark and yarn out of her pockets, a three-pointed thing between her shaking hands and the sabre's hilt. And thoughts came suddenly pouring as if she had opened her mind to a river. Not burning, not binding. Give it to earth, let earth take it, set it free to seek the stars, a pattern that echoed and altered, that opened the gate, that loosed the knotted weaving. Let there be mercy. The ideas came from nowhere, the shape, the form. She could almost see—no, it escaped her and her web faltered, she held a loop hooked over a thumb with no idea, no instinct of where it should go, and the thing, which had hesitated, feeling . . . something, came on.

Her breath sobbed in her throat. *Holla-Sayan!* she cried, but the words weren't there; all she could do was gasp and choke as Varro had.

The Red Mask crumpled as if it were a child's doll flung to the floor, its light fading.

Ivah fell to her knees as well, unable to stand any longer, and the cat's-cradle, loosed, was nothing but a tangle, snarling her hands. She had lost her light when the panic took her, and now she was blind in the darkness. The only sound was her own rasping breath.

She stayed there, head on her knees, trying to breathe deeply, slowly, waiting for the breathless racing of her heart to subside. She was still there, coiled small, trying to find the will to rise and climb the last of the hill and make the long descent to where Belmyn and her guards kept the spell safe before Gurhan's cave, when the dawn-greying world was lit with a flash of brilliant white and the sound of a thunderbolt ripping the air. Deafened, unthinking, she flung herself forward, arms over her head, as whole trees came crashing down. A branch struck the back of her skull and there was silence.

CHAPTER XVI

Two days had passed since he met the flying devil, but Ghu tried not to think of her. He did not think she would be held for long, not a devil of the cold hells, whom it had taken the Old Great Gods to bind in a lasting grave, and even then, clearly, that had not been enough—but perhaps she had been a dream altogether. Perhaps she had not, and he thought, a wizard with the heart of a dragon, a tiger, she would forget her plan to destroy the victims of necromancy and come in wrath after the one who had defied her. Better, maybe, that she did, rather than that Ahjvar should burn.

If he were not dead.

Yesterday he had made a camp and rested the mare, hunted to feed himself and the dogs and slept through the noon and afternoon heat, riding on into the night again. This day he had let her take only a short noon rest, pressed with urgency, unable to settle. Jui and Jiot had watched hopefully as he took out the sling he had made, but he had only wandered, collecting suitable stones, and the cock-pheasant which had gone bursting into the sky from almost beneath his feet had been allowed to fly.

The dogs had settled for digging out mouse-nests, but they watched him now as he walked, the mare plodding wearily like a third dog a few yards away, snatching a mouthful of grass now and then, flicking her tail at the flies. The sun was setting. He ought to find water, if only a damp spot where he could make a scrape, and camp. Hunt, or cook the bread-root he had dug the day before the night he met the devil. He wasn't Ahj, to push himself to death to prove a point. It was dangerous to fall into dreams, where the world went soft and thin, where *then* and *now*, *there* and *here* ran together. Where he could think the very real devil he had met was a dream.

But he was close, he knew it. They had fallen behind—well, he had fallen behind, the first day; he had not thought it wise to venture back through the Eastern Wall to the suburb to steal a horse, and he had been a day on the road afoot before he found one he fancied and a man he didn't mind injuring with the loss of a beast. He would have taken a mount of greater speed and less calm wisdom, if one had offered, but the proverb that beggars could not be choosers went for thieves as well, at least when the road had not obliged him with a dealer in a better class of stock, before he left it for the empty places. He had caught up again, he thought, crossing the hills. The Red Masks had followed the road until they came to the commonly used track that angled north to Dinaz Catairna. Sometimes he saw them, dreaming, maybe, or hovering half between sleep and dream. Dead men, dead women, not sleeping, lying unseeing under the turning stars, while the horses, hard-used and making worse time because of it, after so many days on the road, slept and found relief from their nightmare days. They knew what they carried, unhappy creatures. There were living men with them, and they slept some distance off, with watches set, and fires that burned all through the night, and when it rained, as it had, a night or two, they huddled under their capes and kept silent, afraid.

They saw that the Red Masks did not eat. Their growing fear was a cloud.

Sometimes he thought he dreamed the Lady reached for the Red Masks, and there was music, high and silvery, voices like glass and crystal, that only they could hear. Or maybe they sang themselves, voiceless.

And Ahj among them.

He was close. Maybe tomorrow, he would come up with them. And then?

He had no plan.

He didn't realize how close, till he saw Jui sink to a crouch in the blowing grass of the hilltop as he walked up himself, incautious.

Ghu dropped flat. The horse, after a mildly startled look, lowered her head and began to graze in earnest, nothing there to startle anyone, a lone horse wandering, and she was below the skyline anyway. Jiot slunk to his side.

Across a boggy valley bottom, green and with pools of standing water between thickets of sweetgale and islets of scrub willow, a slow stream twisting through, rose a long ridge like a wave, facing him. The northern height of it had been made a camp, and it was defended with banks of new-heaped earth at which people still laboured, spears of sharpened willow set at angles facing outward. Banners were flying with embroidered symbols of trees and stars and knotted shapes he didn't know how to name. The hill dipped to the south and rose again, and on the southern and lower, flatter crest of it, about half a mile from the north, spilling down and out of sight to the east, was a moving cloud of mounted folk, horsemen and cameleers, and spearmen and archers afoot, with many different banners. Praitans, he thought, and Grasslanders under orange banners, and there were men of Marakand in red capes, tight together on the crest of the hill, and a priest in yellow sitting on a horse with his hands raised in prayer or blessing. And the Red Masks he had followed all this way, but there were more than thirty gathered here now.

The Praitans on the northern hill worked frantically, and a skirl of Grasslander horsemen charged them, riding in to shoot and wheel away, yelping like dogs. Arrows answered, and he thought some had fallen on both sides, but the Red Masks did nothing, and the Marakander camp—but it was half Praitan—drew in on itself, more coming up from the east and spilling down the west to settle along the edge of the bog, kindling fires. Taunting, not attack. Pickets went out from the Marakanders, scattering southwards, and others disappearing over the ridge, back the way they had come. They must believe some other force might come up to join with the high king.

Why not attack while the Praitannec army was hurried and harried, scrambling to raise some defences? The Praitans looked to have the Marakanders and their allied Praitans and mercenaries outnumbered. Save for the undying Red Masks and the terror they could bring, and perhaps—almost certainly, more Marakander allies out of sight, along the eastern side of the ridge.

So why not attack the Praitans now?

He saw men about the Red Masks, saw the sharp gesture of a hand, denial, the wave of bowing heads, the withdrawal from what had to be at best an unsettling and intimidating presence, the silence. Ah, the Marakander allies were asking the same question, and the Red Masks refused.

They were waiting for nightfall. Ahjvar—*she*—was waiting for nightfall.

He wondered if Deyandara were there, among the lords who tried to raise some obstacle against mounted attack, knowing, as they must know, that it would be futile when the Red Masks rode against them and its defenders fled. There were dead lying, he saw now, the length of the ridge, humans and horses. They had been pursued to that point and then . . . then the Marakanders chose to wait.

Because the Praitans, pursued too closely, might scatter and leave victory uncertain, disappear into their hills against another day?

But the Praitans, unwisely, had turned to face them.

Because they were cornered. The swamp curved north beyond the head of the ridge. They had been in a rout, hunted and herded in panic, and now they had a respite and faint hope, which would be denied.

Was that Ahjvar's humour? Ghu was afraid it might be, or not Ahjvar's but the other's.

The swamp fell into darkness. There was a goddess in the stream that meandered through it, and her presence gathered, drifted into the Praitannec camp. A little goddess, no power to oppose Marakand, but mist rose, cloaking the hill. Jui growled.

"Jui," Ghu called softly, a murmur only a dog would hear. "Jiot. With me."

He left the horse to her rest, a good journeying pony, but she had no speed and would only panic, brought where the scent was all of blood and death and fear. When she raised her head, still chewing, and took a step after him he whispered, "No," and willed her wandering far from violent and ruthless men, sweet grass and coming in time to some master who would hold her dear. She flicked an ear and turned away, drifting south. Ghu angled down the hill, towards where the swamp had seemed narrower, less spattered with ponds and open water, save for the stream. He was among the tussocks of the rising ground, barefoot and wet nearly to the waist, but not making too much noise, he thought, when there came a thunder of drums, brief and shocking, and then a great roaring. But the Red Masks had already gone before; he had felt the wrongness of them pass down from the southern height as he waded the brook. The mist, which had been climbing the ridge, rolled back like a racing ebb-tide.

Fire roared up in the trenches before the rough earthworks. Horses and camels and riders fell under a storm of arrows. He chose his target carefully, a Grasslander coming from his right, spear brandished high, and felt the stone fly true. The man was dead in the instant, struck in the temple below the rim of his helmet. The horse slowed and swerved aside from the dragging corpse. Ghu ran, caught the bridle as it shied, mounted and leaned to haul the body loose, with a silent blessing for the soul, lost and afraid and not even quite knowing it was dead, yet.

He was sorry. He thought, this is what I fall to. Murder for a horse. And I told Ahj I would not learn to kill from him.

It was a good Grasslander horse. Jui barked once, overexcited, then was silent. He turned the horse downslope, riding along the edge of the marshy ground. Someone shot at them, at Jui's pale coat, but the dog ran down and into the edge of the mist, and Jiot was shadow in the night. He reined back to a trot, the horse stirred by the rush above, the shouts and neighing, some charge of the Praitans out through the gap in their fires, but it was not a well-led sortie. There was screaming within, and he felt the terror of the Red Masks swelling.

The spell of terror was not so certain and solid a thing as it had been, weak and—discordant. It faltered and surged; some did find mastery of themselves and stand against it, but that only meant they died fighting, because no matter how skilled a warrior might be, the Red Masks went armoured in spells that shed blows. He had seen it.

"Ahjvar!" he shouted, which was pointless. He set another stone into the pouch of the sling, a second in hand, ready, dropped a man senseless who sat a fretting camel watching the steep westward slope of the besieged camp, and then the woman with the horse beside him, both living, stunned, and as the third man, a Marakander guardsman, turned to see, raising a horn to his lips to signal, Jiot surged past and leapt at his throat.

Ghu had not intended that. The man shrieked and flailed at the dog and fell off his horse, which bolted, kicking him in the leg but missing Jiot. Jui ran to join in, and he whistled them both back, sharp and urgent. They obeyed. The man, still shouting, crawled towards the bodies of his stunned companions. Since he was shouting, Ghu could at least trust he hadn't yet taught his dogs to kill, though Jiot seemed a little too willing to get into the spirit of the night.

"No," he told him. "With me." But he had what he wanted, an open way to thread through the angled stakes, and no mercenaries to think him one of their own, leading them in. He swung down to lead the horse, keeping its bulk and shadow between himself and any watching archers above, ducking under its neck as he snaked back and forth, almost to the fires.

The trench was continuous, and it burned without any fuel. Some wizardry fed it. He shut his eyes a moment. Heat. Heat to his left. There was wood, a bonfire. To his right, some distance, another. Between—it was only the illusion of fire. The horse smelt smoke, saw flame, and fought his grip. Jui grinned. Jiot tilted his head to one side, panting. They saw. They understood. Fire that wasn't. The world had become so much more *interesting*, since they began to follow him. They were young enough to think so still.

The horse was a problem, but he might want its height within. He flung his headscarf over its eyes, murmuring endearments, and led it at a trot to the ditch, which was not steep enough to throw it at that speed, though it plunged and scrambled clumsily. Partially grassed— it was an old earthwork, hastily refortified, that must be why the army of the kings had made for this place. A *dinaz* long-abandoned? He pulled the scarf free and swung himself up again as they mounted the dyke beyond and bolted down. Someone saw him and shouted, and he dropped to cling to the horse's side, putting it between himself and the Praitan, but shouted, too, "A friend! Where's the Lady Deyandara?" The name had at least had the virtue of confusing them. A moment's confusion was enough, and he was lost in the dark, cantering, trusting there were no more stakes set, or trenches, and hearing the clash and ring of swords away to his right again. Dark figures rose and fell against the fires, atop the mounds, but the light was sinking and then went out. A wizard had died.

Word floated, thin in the night.

". . . the king, get the king away . . . Durandau . . ."

He rode to the Red Masks and jerked the nearest from the saddle.

He didn't need the knife; an open-handed blow was enough, seeing the thing, the twisted remnants of it, driving it free, speaking a word of peace over it, and rest, and safe journeying on the road if it could find its way. He did not think she could, this broken remnant of a woman's soul. Peaceful dissolution into the earth's long breathing, that was all he could offer or she could hope, had she anything left in herself capable of hope. The husk fell away empty, and he caught the descending blow of a staff in his left hand, twisted it, pulling the man, a boy he had been, hardly yet growing a beard and so afraid, fleeing through the streets from guards sent by his own cousins, and all he had done was play with the coins, he knew no spells to raise against his enemies . . . he was freed and gone, and a woman afoot, white-faced, panting, with a rod of braided woods in hand, shouted, "The king, go with the king!" at him, trusting he was some ally, however unexpected, but he was not here to save her king. Her, yes, as she raised an arm that shook against Red Masks also afoot—the Praitans had been killing their horses, and they clambered over bulky bodies, living horses stumbled and were hampered, a barrier as effective as the shallow trenches—she was here before him, so he would save her, but he did not see any kings.

Or Ahjvar.

He had to touch them. Ghu circled through, and here the footing was made uncertain by more than fallen horses, here they had stood, a tight knot of Praitans who had not run, who had nerved themselves to endure the panic, who had stood, and there were banners, trampled, and the corpses of men and women, and many were scorched. He pulled down three more Red Masks. They pressed in against him, ignoring the wizard, who staggered with weariness. He reached through their tame lightning and shed it as if he were stone. He was stone, he thought, and they pressed against him because they knew it; they wanted a final death, they came to him eager as a blind puppy seeks its dam's teat, driven thoughtless to her heat and scent, the one overriding urge. "Go to your king," he called to the wizard, and, "Is Deyandara here? Take her away!"

"Deyandara?" she said, in shock. "No!" But she caught the bridle of the horse of a fallen Red Mask and fled away into the night, over the north and down towards the swamp.

There. A lone Red Mask, afoot, and though it carried a sword, it stabbed a man with its dagger and dragged him close as he died, and dropped the body, went after another, hacking it two-handed, kneeling over it, hand on its bleeding wounds. Then it ran towards a knot of milling warriors afoot, Praitan fighting Praitan.

It was not Ahjvar, but the other, the hag, the cursed ghost who rode him, and not killing once, but again and again, feeding without falling away, growing stronger. Would even daylight drive her back now?

A Red Mask had Ghu by the foot. His horse squealed and reared, eyes rolling white, came down and bucked, another clutching breast-strap and saddle-skirt as if it would clamber up. He struck right and left and gave them what they sought; they were not even bringing weapons against him now, desperate. He could feel their desperation, as if they knew . . .

All the Red Masks were bound together. He wheeled the horse free of them and rode for the shadow that had killed another man and sent the enemies, king's men and traitors, flying as one band. Jui and Jiot had kept back from the Red Masks, but now they closed in with him again, snarling at a Praitan who for a moment turned his way, spear lowered. She thought better of it and ran.

"Ahjvar!" he called, and there was no check in the thing, no reaction at all. In the darkness there was a second shadow, a hint in the tail of the eye, a woman's long hair, trailing smoke, cracked skin edged in flame. "*Hyllau!*"

She, it, Ahjvar's body, the Red Mask's crested helmet, spun to face him, sword raised. He rode as if to ride it down and turned the horse aside at the last moment, feet free of the stirrups, flung himself onto Ahjvar's body, striking the sword-arm up, bearing him down. He ripped the helmet free, laying the blade of his forage-knife across the throat above the hauberk's collar, the crooked knife easy to the task, resting there.

Behind him dogs snarled. One yelped, and was silent. There was a thud, something heavy hitting the earth. He did not look around.

"I will kill him," he gasped, and the body that tensed to heave him off was still. "I will. And I can. The death he's been seeking, I can give him that. Rather than let you have him, I will kill him, and set him free, and leave you lost and wailing in the world, houseless and fading and forgotten as his corpse rots around you."

She moved against the blade, and a dark line opened, black in the bright moonlight. He didn't change the pressure on the knife, didn't raise it even the slightest, wrist locked, but a sob choked him. For a moment he didn't think Ahjvar's heart was beating, and maybe the devil had killed him after all and there was nothing left but Hyllau's madness. The body beneath him was hot, as if it burned. But under his other hand the chest moved. Still breathing. Slowly. The blood welled to the rhythm of a pulse.

Hyllau hissed. The eyes focused on him and the lips worked, as if she might speak. A hand clawed upwards, but he held the knife steady, unblinking, and the blood dripped down into the trampled grass. The eyes lost their focus, staring blind into the night, and she sank away. Ghu gasped, another sob, shaken, and maybe raised the blade a hair's breadth, but if Hyllau had retreated, it was still a Red Mask controlled by the Lady he had beneath him. The hand moved for the sword it had lost when he bore Hyllau down.

"No," he said. "Ahjvar . . ."

He couldn't see the cocoon of spells, but he knew they were there, a spider's silken shroud, wrapped and woven tight, smothering, and if the souls of the other Red Masks had been torn to threads to weave their own chains, Ahj's, he thought, could not be, because Catairanach's curse bound him whole and entire to continue unbroken in the world, to be the womb, the cyst of Hyllau's waiting, with all the strength of her land forged adamant-hard in rage and grief. Ghu reached into the devil's shroud and ripped, the blade of the forage knife honed to the edge of the mountain's wind, capable of sheering stone. For a moment he hung in dark water, saw fire twisted and caught in ice. He cut the devil's bonds away and dragged Ahjvar free of them, into moonlight and night.

Nothing seemed to change, except that Ahjvar's hand found his sword and clenched on it. Then the eyes shut and he tried to roll away. Ghu moved to let him go. Ahjvar was breathing, now, as if he had been running. Or drowning. Thrust himself up on his arms, coughing, choking. Warily, because startling Ahj when he had a sword in his hand was a bad idea, Ghu put a hand between his shoulders, spread flat, just enough pressure to let the man know he was there, as he would walking behind a horse.

"Ghu?"

"I'm here."

"Good." Ahjvar went down flat again, head cradled on an arm. "Damn all gods an' Old Great Gods too. Headache."

"I know."

Nothing more. Ghu looked around, drawing a knee up to rise. They were in the middle of a battlefield, but battle had shifted aside—because there were Red Masks here, waiting, watching, a double handful of them, half mounted and half afoot and two lying empty that he had not slain.

And Jui, and Jiot. Silent, standing like sentinels, hackles bristling, guarding him.

A dog, a half-grown stray from the city streets, could not do what wizards could not, and tear a ruined soul from the devil's grip. Jiot looked round at him, stirred the base of his up-curled tail, hesitant, checking. Had he done right this time?

Ghu crawled to them, a hand on both. "Don't run so far ahead of me," he said. "Don't . . ." But he had taken them to follow him; already they saw his road, and that he could not turn back, not now; he'd gone too far this night and unwitting drawn them with him. Should he ask them to stay behind? "Good dogs," he said weakly.

One Red Mask backed away and turned its horse to ride after easier prey, obeying its Lady's will, that it should kill kings and wizards and take this land for Marakand. But the others still wavered, not even able to shape a thought, a hope, but still . . . waiting.

Ahjvar came crawling to him, used his shoulder to heave himself up, stood swaying, legs braced. "Where in the cold hells are we?" he asked, and added, "Get back. These things don't die. Necromancy . . ." Then he fell again. Ghu caught the sword so that he at least did not fall on his own blade.

"Drowned," Ahjvar said vaguely from the ground. "I was drowning. Her face kept changing—Ghu!"

Down by the swamp, where the flow of the battle had shifted, people shouted and shrieked and died.

"Go," he told the dogs. Just that, and they went, racing, grim and eager.

"Collecting dogs now? Cheaper than horses," Ahjvar said. "The moon's wrong." He tried to haul himself up again, using Ghu as a prop.

Ghu pushed him off. "Stay out of the way." Ahj was weak as an invalid and clumsy as a drunkard.

There were too many. He felt the fear radiating from them, stronger now, as if something knew there was opposition it had not expected. He could almost hear the high, silver singing, a voice of ice and garrotter's wire.

"Ahj," he said, as these Red Masks, his Red Masks, still watched him. But a stir ran through them. They would not wait for long. "You were Red Mask. Do you remember?"

Silence.

"Ahjvar?"

"No." But he added, "She's singing. I can hear her. They can hear her. It's in their minds, they're singing. The Lady's words."

"You've been inside it. Ahj, can you see it? Can you break it? I can only set them free one by one, and even the dogs . . . it will only take one arrow to kill me or them, still, and there are so many of the Red Masks. She shields them from spells and weapons, but you've been inside. Are you—can you even understand me?" he cried, because Ahjvar was bowed over his knees, and the Lady had wrenched some of the watching Red Masks back to her will. He had to keep them from Ahj, who couldn't move to defend himself.

But Ahjvar dragged his sword from Ghu's hand, muttering, "That's not a bloody shield, don't use it like one," and added, "Good," as Ghu kicked a Red Mask off and it did not move again.

Something mastered them, turned them, and they all fled into the night, to where, he feared, they could do more harm at less risk.

"Where are we?" Ahjvar asked.

"Praitan. The Duina Catairna. A hill by a swamp."

Ahjvar swore. "Who are we fighting?"

"You and I? Mostly everyone," Ghu said, because without the Red Masks making them an island to be avoided, they probably would be. Even short of full, the moon was bright enough that staying still would not hide them. "I look like one of Ketsim's mercenaries, and you—"

"*She's* been out."

"Yes."

"Someone's tried to cut my throat."

"Yes. Sorry. I didn't want to, but she wouldn't—she didn't kill only once, she kept hunting."

"Would you have?"

"Yes, Ahj."

Hand on his shoulder.

"How many?"

"I don't know. But I think it was she who was commanding the army here, not you. She waited for dark, and you're not such a fool as to start a battle in the dark. Half the dead have probably been slain by their own friends."

"How many?" And he didn't mean friend and foe mistaken in the night.

"Many, I think," Ghu said gently. "Maybe," he added, "at least, they were not all Praitans."

"Not on the road here, they weren't," Ahjvar said grimly. "I remember, a little. The soldiers were afraid. What Praitans are here?"

"The high king—Duina Andara, Duina Broasora. Others. I don't know all the banners."

"How many Red Masks?"

"You had thirty when I followed you from Marakand. But there are more."

"If you'd cut my throat, Ghu—could you have killed me?"

"You would have died, Ahj."

"Would I." It was said carefully, not a question.

"I'm sorry." He didn't mean for what might have happened, either, and Ahjvar knew it. Not for what he might have done, but for what he had not done, in all the years of nights Ahj would have welcomed it. But he could not have, then. He could not.

"You know you can't let her loose with wizardry, Ghu. You know that."

"I know, Ahj."

"Promise me you won't."

"I won't."

"Then break that seal, before we make this a kingless land. I can hear. I remember the shape of the Lady's spell, and it's only human wizardry, no matter how many wizards are woven into it, working it, no godhead to it at all. All I need to do is break it from within, and she didn't make it dreaming anyone could. Her defences all look outwards."

"She was never a goddess." But he used teeth and his left hand to pull at the knots of his purse, never leaving aside his knife, letting Ahj, barely able to stand, guard him, while he felt around for the clay seal that Deyandara had thought a blessing-piece, what seemed so long ago. Catairanach's token.

"I saw a goddess in the well," Ahjvar said.

"Maybe she showed you a lie." Ghu knelt again, with the clay disc in his hand, found a flattish stone for an anvil, and with the handle of his knife pounded the seal to dust. Nothing spectacular followed. At the first shattering there was, maybe, the fresh scent of water, a moment. That was all. He swept the dust into his hand, but, since Ahjvar had turned away, simply wiped it into the grass. A knot of fighting came their way, Praitans forcing Praitans back, and impossible to know which had come with the high king or which were the traitors. They saw the dark shape of Ahjvar, the Red Mask's long cloak, black though it was in the moonlight, and all fled.

Mist crept up the hillside. Ahj had a handful of stems, was muttering over them.

"Don't need the damned weeds," he said, looking up. "Not really. Enough to know they should be here. Make me a circle and keep it clear." But he began laying out whatever it was he had found anyway, starting at the east, so Ghu cut a circle in the turf around him, no more than drawing a line with his knife blade, but the light of the moon, low in the west, found it, and it glowed a spider-silk thread.

The mist stopped at the line and followed it.

Let me help you.

"You can freeze in the cold hells for all I care."

"Ahj!" But there had been no help for Ahjvar when he sought it, from any of the gods or goddess of Praitan, had there?

And what was I to do against Catairanach, whom the folk of this land had given care of this land? the little goddess asked. *Here, in this, I can help. If you will allow it, king of the* duina.

"We need three," Ahjvar almost snarled. "I didn't want to have to count the damned hag anyway."

Which was yes. She took no form at first, beyond the mist, but though the ridge had no god, she was the brook that spread through the swamp, and she rose in shimmers of mist and moonlight, a shape that might be birdlike, a heron, maybe, or a crane. Ghu reached a hand and drew her in, and dew silvered them, mist-wrapped. He stood ready against anything human or Red Mask that rushed them, but the Red Masks were scattered, and the humans moved away from the eerily shimmering patch of light. There were drums again, but he didn't know what they might signal. Horns distant to the north.

"Poplar," Ahj said, at the east, ignoring it all. "And gorse," at the south. "Yew." That was west, but the hill had been all grass and small flowering things. It was only knotted grass that he flung down at each point. He drove his sword in at the north, after a glance at the stars, and hung a crooked wreath of twisted weeds on the crossguard. "And we three, who are water and stone and blood." Ghu shivered at that, but Ahjvar was half singing now and, Ghu thought, hardly heard his own tongue as the words flowed through him. "Through fire, through water, and the third is the fire and the water of the blood you have stilled, the hearts you have taken, the minds and the souls and the bodies you have profaned. These are the words you have made and I unmake them. You took me into your song and showed me the way of it, and I find my place in it again and stand there with a whole heart and a soul unbound, unbroken. The barred hall is unbarred from within, the gates flung open by those who stand within, the great citadel laid open by the least soldier who stands within. The chains you have laid about them with their own souls are unmade by we three together, strand by strand

and link by link, word by word by note we unmake your making and lay
it bare to the moon and the wind and the witnessing stars. Let it be ash,
and let it be sand, and let it be dust flung to the four corners of the earth
and the high stars their home on the cleansing wind."

He sang, then, words Ghu didn't know, but they sounded of the sea
and the sea-folk who built no ships but came sometimes from the south
in the long outrigger canoes. He didn't suppose Ahjvar knew what he
sang, either, only that it was the shape of the binding of the Red Masks
that the Lady had left in his mind, and he wove grass as he sang, where
a spell with more time to consider its making might have used twigs.
In his woven grass, he set the wizards' alphabet of the trees against the
wizards' words of the sea, and the virtue went out of the Lady's words
and the shape of the binding frayed and loosened. The lingering silver
song of the Lady faltered and failed, because it was woven of the Red
Masks' own wizardry on a framework already grown brittle, frail, the
power behind it weak and dying. Ghu felt as if Ahjvar set his back
against him, braced to face some great battering, and the little goddess
of the brook wrapped wings of mist about them, all her will and her
grief at the wrongness of the necromancy pouring through into Ahjvar's
will against the Lady.

His voice grew softer, slower, lower, and the words faded. The last
twist of sweet-scented bedstraw and wiry grass fell from his fingers and
was caught by the wind, carried out of the circle. He swayed, but Ghu
caught him before he could fall.

"Done?" he asked, when Ahjvar stood leaning on him, unspeaking,
for so long he wondered if he had fainted. Or if it would be Hyllau who
raised her head.

"Better be. Let her out."

"Who—?" Ah, the goddess, who coiled now about their feet, a
snake of moonlit mist. He cut the circle he had made with his knife
again, brushed it away as if flinging back a curtain.

Help him, the goddess whispered, for Ghu alone, he thought, as her presence faded down to the waters. *But take him away, out of this land. We will not have him here.*

Ahjvar was on his knees again, shivering.

"Come on," Ghu said. "Let's go."

"Where?" Ahj managed at last, a hoarse whisper. "Great Gods, Ghu, where?"

"Anywhere," he said. "Away from here. If there are no Red Masks, let the Praitans win their own war. Come. But first we get you out of that red." Though pausing to strip him of the Lady's livery while battle still rolled about them—if it did, it had all gone silent, the only cries far in the distance now, except for the moans of some wounded man closer at hand. Another voice spoke, though, Grasslander, and the moaning was stilled. He got the dirty red silk off Ahjvar, anyway, and the shirt of scales, and led him like a blind man down towards the west. They almost stumbled on a body, a tall man with his hair in desert braids and a spear-thrust in the great vein of his thigh, with all the ground about him soaked, but he was tall, and not yet stiff, so Ghu hauled off his dark coat, trying to keep it out of the bloody puddle, though the hem ended up sticky with it, and made Ahj put it on, to stop his shivering as much as to change the look of him. Ahjvar seemed content to lean on him, too exhausted to walk. If he let him down, the man would sleep where he lay.

Screaming. A man running, screaming, the Marakander western road tongue and bastard Nabbani of the eastern jumbled together, "Dead, dead, they are dead, he has come, he will not have me, I am not his not his not she he cannot how can he—the Lady has failed and they are dead but he was mine how could they all how could he see—we will all die and the city be empty, the Lady's chosen the blessed are dead—"

The priest might not have even seen them. He ran and screamed like he was mad, and the skirts of his pale robe were stained dark. There was nothing in his hand but a guardsman's cudgel, but Ahj thought it attack, and that woke him so that he shoved Ghu back and stepped to the side of the priest's path, taking his head as he went.

Ahjvar's hands were still shaking as he cleaned his sword on the grass, and Ghu had to tug him up again as he knelt, staring at the ground, at the hilt of his sword, at nothing. He talked Ahj on as he would a frightened horse, till the dogs, whom he had almost forgotten, came racing up. Jiot limped, little slowed, and Jui whined and thrust his head against Ghu.

"*Brave* dogs," he told them. "Good dogs, such good dogs," but he didn't have a hand to spare, keeping Ahjvar from falling. They didn't seem to mind, closing in, one at either side, content.

They came on a Red Mask, fallen, and the clothes and armour were hugged in close, nothing but bones within, withered and dry, and the roots of the grass and the bulrushes were reaching, crawling, pulling. It sank, slowly, taken into the earth. Ahjvar retched and swerved away.

He wanted a horse, and there was a horse, his horse that he had ridden against the Praitan camp, he was certain, with the mist coiling about it, caressing and soothing, and another stray by its side.

"Thank you," he told the goddess.

He had to shake Ahjvar to get him to look around, to see the horses and make for them, and guide his foot to the stirrup, he shuddered so badly.

"Coffee," Ahj muttered at one point, through clenched teeth. "Head hurts. Coffee."

"Hush," Ghu said. "You're frightening the horse." But Ahjvar always frightened new horses, a little. They smelt his poisoned second soul.

Ghu walked, leading both horses, the dogs ahead now, following a trail of mist and fox-light. The moon was sinking low in the west. It would set before dawn and leave them in darkness for the last hours of the night. They should find a safe place where Ahjvar could sleep, and ride again with the dawn, away from here. The goddess did not speak, but they crossed the swamp no more than fetlock deep and found a hard-bottomed ford through the brook. He turned northerly, for no good reason that he knew.

Deyandara had not been with the kings here.

He thought he heard his name in the wind, a whisper, in the little bard's voice.

A curse of ill-luck on the royal blood of the Duina Catairna. Ill luck and ill-chancing, in every choice. He hadn't wanted her to come with them to the city, hadn't wanted her following Ahjvar, but her inherited curse was on her no matter whom she followed, and there had been death, always, shadowing her, since she came into their affairs.

"Ahjvar," he said. "The Dinaz Catairna. Where is it?"

Ahjvar looked around, as if he might see some hall of ninety years ago on a nearby hill, but he had only been looking at the shape of the horizon, the hills against the sky. He pointed, west and north.

"Is it far?"

A shake of the head answered.

"How far?"

"Leave it to the kings," Ahjvar said, his words slow and slurred.

"No," Ghu said, slow himself, words rising unconsidered. He could hear her . . . feel the racing of her heart, as if he held her, her breath sobbing, choking, wheezing, and stilled. The dead weight of her. Not yet. But how far, how far, and these horses, too, were weary. "No. Not the kings. Fire, and treachery. They plan to burn the little bard."

CHAPTER XVII

I n Zora's dreams, there was a steep green mountain, wrapped in mist about its feet, so that the white peak floated as an island in a pearly sea, and the moon was a silver canoe riding above it, a sickle for a harvest of souls. Bats, swallows, she couldn't in the dream say which, even though it was night and swallows did not fly by night, swooped and soared before her, disappearing into the silver haze. A river coiled about the mountain like a nesting dragon, black and nacreous, breathing out the fog, whispering to the reeds and the willows along its banks. *He is mine and I will take him home . . .*

Zora could not sleep, after that. Stupid human dreams, meaningless memories of some Nabbani scene on a lacquered tabletop, dead Rahel's taste. She slept on cushions in an alcove at the back of the Hall of the Dome, curtained in white silk, when she did sleep. Priestesses had laid out fresh robes and linens for her. Was that a hint? She did not have time to waste in the bathhouse. The soul was all, the body nothing, the body only served to house the soul and give it an anchor in the living world. They should not have dared approach so close. She should have heard them. The body betrayed her, the girl betrayed her, weak and mortal, tossing in meaningless dreams. Dance disciplined the body; she carried over that knowledge from what the girl had been. Through dance she wove herself into the pattern of the stars, anchored herself in the light of the universe, yes, remembered, yes, that the world was greater than this little place and patience was the foundation of her victory.

She danced alone, with a tambourine. The Red Masks watched, spaced about the walls, guarding. He would come, her captain. *He* might come, her brother. She had defeated Vartu, though. Surely she need fear no other. She was grown great, greater than Sien-Mor had ever dared to think herself, being the sum of such great wizardry. Many small stones made a great weight and a great wall, better than a single boulder.

In Praitan there was battle. The kings had gathered, and her captain of Red Masks had penned them and held his hand, held his hand, till the night came and the death in him woke, finding its strength and its pleasure, death in the darkness. Let them then fight by night, she had thought, by moonlight, folly though it was, and they had, and they did yet. In Fleshmarket Ward it had gone badly, but it was Ashir who had thought they should try to take the drovers' gate under cover of night, to give cover for his capture of the loyalists' chief wizard, to distract any guarding her. The sacrifice, the Red Masks sent to the Fleshmarket, had done their work and lured the Grasslander wizard's guardians from her, they must have done. The demon had gone to the Fleshmarket. The traitor garrison of the gate had fled into the streets, abandoned their tower, and fled beyond the walls, and the demon had come to kill, and had killed, yes, two of her Red Masks, which she had not intended, and two had fled, because she did not will that they should stand and die, and the demon hunted them.

Only the demon?

They were not aware of the dog. It had not come. Only the demon in his night-form, the Northron giant with the axe. And now the rebels knew she had rebuilt the blessing of the Lady, and that they must fear fear itself again, the spearhead of every attack, cleaving a way for the temple guard. Should she have listened to Ashir, had she been lured into betraying her hand too soon? The fifth Red Mask, sent after Ashir, still stalked carefully in the wake of the Right Hand's stealth. If Ashir could succeed in his plan, well and good.

—*No. I shouldn't have listened, shouldn't have sent them out from the temple, should keep all quiet within the temple and wait and wait, yes, I must wait, not fight them, wait, let the outlander wizard work—*

No.

Her temple guard with Ashir had found a way between rebel pickets, found a shelter, a house among the trees, only an old man there and a toothless bear sleeping like a dog with its head on the threshold, and they had killed both, because there was a demon bear in the city, they all knew it, and this was a bear as well. A stupid and pointless little vengeance. Ashir and Surey had gone on alone, and then the caravaneer, which was not Ashir's plan as he had presented it, but she had her Red Mask follow only distantly, because she was patient. She would give Ashir his chance. She would be fair.

—*Call them back.*

But they were too many, too scattered, her Red Masks, her will. A third died in Templefoot Ward, almost at her very gate, and—and—they had been dying in Praitan. All was weak and confused and hard to know, but they slipped from her—

—*No, it doesn't matter. They must die. They are already dead. I don't hear them. I don't feel them. Let Praitan go. The dance. The dance is all. The glory of the Lady, we beg her, mercy, forgiveness, help us, help me, help me, help me . . .*

She had lost Red Masks there, how? And in the glory of her champion and the distasteful hunger of the ghost that rode him, and the confused hunting of the demon, she had not realized how her strength ebbed, because as it ebbed it was more difficult to be certain, to know, to feel all points at once, to hold all in one gathered hand. Her wizardry, hive-united, was weakened, terribly weakened. What power walked in Praitan to tear Red Masks from her?

And the voices distracted her.

What voices?

Why had she decided to dance?

Her body was grown so feeble, skeleton thin. How had that come about?

There were priests in Pirakul who starved themselves to hear their gods.

Something—a wind of ice, a current cold and deadly, eagle, snake-head-pike, a fire like moon on snow—lashed into her heart. The rhythm faltered and the tambourine drooped in Zora's hand. She had not felt it coming. Her champion, her captain—she reached for him, felt an edge of cold iron cut between them, and he was gone, dragged from her grasp, and it hurt, it hurt, the tearing of the chains that wove through them all, because he was not dead as the others were dead. He was not rags and broken threads to leave dry and drifting strands she could knot up again, not a gap to be patched up but a great bleeding tear in her wizardry, and it hurt, Great Gods, it hurt. She screamed, falling to her knees, flinging will to seize him back, to bind him again. The city shook with her rage. She flung her fury out to destroy, but something stood between them, earth of the earth, stone and water, denying her, and wrath rebounded on the city, sought, like lightning, to earth itself in her. The air flashed and burned about her, but she held up her arms against it and was unharmed.

Would she be the Lady? *This* was godhead.

—*What have you done? What have you woken? Call it back, beg it to come back, to hear us*—

But it was gone before she could gather wit or power to fling against it again, and the assassin was gone. His god had taken him. That had been no small power of a spring in Praitan. How had she been so deceived as to think—

"Revered Lady, what is it?"

Plaster fell, as it had fallen before in her anger, when the stained-glass eye of the dome was shattered. Now the wall hangings had crumbled to ash and the pulpit was ruin. Her Red Masks stood unmoved, unharmed, as she was unharmed.

A fool priest stood with temple guard about him, hesitant in the porch. Zora whirled from the dance and faced him, straight and stern, tambourine held like a shield.

"I pray," she said. "I battle my enemies. Didn't I forbid any intrusion into my holiness?"

"Forgive me," he said, bowing, gesturing the soldiers, also bowing, back, out of the ruin. The roof groaned. "I—I thought I heard a cry. I feared—I'm sorry."

There were words in the night. Praitannec words.

. . . *water and stone and blood* . . .

What did he do? *Wizard of Praitan, what do you do?*

"No!" she screamed. "What do you do?" She began to sing, to strengthen the bonds, the weaving between her remaining Red Masks, her wizards, her wizardry, to knot it more firmly to herself, to the shell and the shadow that had been Sien-Mor, the ghosts of her bones, the memory in the soul, the only framework and anchor she had for human wizardry. There was no power in her own words, in her own body's blood and bone, but she was the channel for the Red Masks' magic, and voiceless, they could sing the spell, weave of her words her greatest work. Even her brother Sien-Shava had not framed anything so beautiful, so strong, so delicate, so intricate in its bindings. It coursed through them renewed, the ones who slew among the gathered kings of Praitan, the ones who stood about the walls, swaying with her rhythm, her beating heart, the one who crept shadowed through the alleys of Templefoot Ward with the barefoot demon stalking him, the one who hastened, Ashir the traitor dead behind him, to bring her the Grasslander who must not free the gods, who must after all be made Red Mask, soon, now, a power she must use, must have now, and now—

. . . *let it be ash, and let it be sand, and let it be dust* . . .

The assassin of Praitan, her dead king stolen from her, turned her own words against her. He pulled down the roof-beams of her hall from within, and stood unbroken, and scattered the palm-leaves of the thatch, and the stars poured in, and it all burned away . . .

"Dead," her priest Arhu cried, distant among the army. She had put a small power of the Voice on him, a power of knowing and speaking, and now his mind broke and he ran among the dead and cried the words that choked her mind: *Dead, they are dead, he has come, he will not have me, I am not his not his not she he cannot how can he—the Lady has failed and they are dead but he was mine how could they all how could he see—we will all die and the city be empty, the Lady's chosen the blessed are dead—*

Wizardry poured from her hands and was lost as if she grasped water. She was . . . they were . . .

Zora was laughing, on her knees in the centre of the mosaic where the dance had brought her, laughing and laughing as she wept, because she was a devil bound in human flesh, and she had no wizardry, and the Red Masks were falling, empty husks, crumpled heaps of soulless bone, and the staring priest with his temple guard fled her and shut the doors, shut her into darkness. She and the true Lady who still endured had won, their miracle had come all unlooked-for, where they only thought to buy time and hope for the rebel's wizard and the imprisoned gods; nothing now would stop the wizard freeing Gurhan whose priestess Zora should have been.

The stones of the dome shifted and groaned again, while plaster rained down around her. In the west, the moon had set, and the night was cold and empty.

CHAPTER XVIII

Ghu seemed to know where he was going. So did Ahjvar. The fool high king had gotten himself trapped by the Orsamoss, or maybe he had meant to meet his allies there, those horns in the distance. . . . The long ridge was a good defensible height, if only you came to it first and seized the length of it. The royal *dinaz* was where it had always been. His earliest memories were of riding these hills. The world kept slipping away from him, though, and he would surface, heart pounding, gasping, thinking he drowned, that he was being pulled again beneath the surface of the well, or that the hag was rising, but it was only exhaustion. Shouldn't sleep, couldn't sleep, on a trotting horse. His body felt strange and slow, heavy, and his mind seemed to run too slowly as well. But that was being half asleep. Half starved and half asleep. He remembered, now, what it was like. He had stopped eating once. Hadn't helped, of course. The gibbous moon slid down towards the west.

He jerked awake again. The moon touched the horizon, setting a silver halo on a few towering clouds. Those dogs were running ahead, disappearing over a hilltop. They followed, and he knew that long slope and the sudden height ahead, and the little unfailing brook that snaked along the valley bottom, Catairanach's waters, but the hilltop flickered and flared in scarlet.

Straight took them to the steepest face of the hill, the goddess's spring and no break in the wall, not in his day, at least. He put the weary

289

horse to a gallop, the Old Great Gods alone knew what had already been asked of it this night, and surged ahead of Ghu onto the old track, still there where he expected it, firm and sure underfoot, circling around to the west and the twisting causeway that rose to the gate.

It wasn't a mere house that was burning; it was the whole damned *dinaz*. It lit the sky.

The gates were shut. No time for the slow rituals of wizardry. Ghu swung his horse alongside, stood in the saddle with the horse still sidling about, caught the top of the gate and pulled himself over.

Someone yelled. It didn't sound like Ghu.

Ahjvar heard the great bar grinding, and then a leaf of the gate swung outwards. He took both horses through; they hopped and flinched at the blond man who lay there with his throat cut. Ghu said nothing but reclaimed his horse.

Penned horses, and camels too, were bunched together, jostling and afraid, but safe enough for now. It was the houses, far too few and set in untidy rows, and hummocky dark shapes he realized a moment later were collapsed tents, which burned. The roofs of many had already fallen in and the walls were failing. Save for the noises of the animals, it was strangely silent at this end of the enclosure. Not, he thought, because the place had been abandoned. Because the screaming was over. He knew the meaty smell of roasting human flesh. What in the cold hells had been happening? Beyond a massacre. There were a few bodies out in the wide and weedy lanes, but not many. He could hope the folk had all been dead before the fires, but somehow, somehow he doubted. There was a terrible air to the place, not the physical reek but a battering on other senses, a screaming that was felt, not heard. Somewhere a dog wailed. Ghu was white-lipped and looking—small, and young, the boy who'd sat on his garden wall in the rain, remote and dazed, as if he fled inside himself. The grey-and-white dog tipped its head back and howled. The black-and-tan joined in. Ahjvar reached over to put a hand on his shoulder, to pull him back, because if he lost Ghu . . . he was shaking, he knew it. Fire. Not fire, Old Great Gods have mercy, not fire. After a moment Ghu shook his head, blinking, tilted his head to press his cheek against the back of Ahjvar's hand.

"All right," Ghu said. "I'm here. Go. Jui, Jiot—enough."

He was manifestly not all right, pale and cold to the touch.

The dogs were silent. There was noise enough to the south. They rode to it in the growing grey light, going warily, alert for ambush, but Ghu suddenly slipped down from his horse to turn over a body lying in the lane. The man had been clubbed, the forehead stove in. Ahjvar circled to return, seeing Ghu sit back on his heels, hand on the corpse's chest. He looked down on a mottled black face. Not charred, which was his first thought.

"The bleeding pox," he said. "Ghu, get away. You didn't touch him—" But of course he had, and still was. "You've had the eastern pox, haven't you?" Please. The man had no scars.

Ghu shook his head. "I don't get sick." He rose, throwing a handful of dirt from the lane onto the body, and caught his horse again, clumsy and seeming half blind, Ghu who always moved with quiet, compact purpose. "They were all ill, in the houses. All of them, and left behind, when their comrades rode out to the battle. Dying. Murdered. Burnt alive. It was their Praitan allies, the folk of the lords who had gone over to Ketsim, who set the fires. Their souls are gone to the road to the Old Great Gods, those that burned, but Ahj, Ahj, their memory is still here, in this earth, in this ash. Do you—Great Gods have mercy, I hear it, still. This place will never be clean again."

"Up," Ahjvar ordered, when it seemed Ghu had lost himself, forgotten what had brought them here and even the horse he leaned on. Ghu looked up at him, vague and lost. "Deyandara," Ahjvar said, and that brought him back. "Where is she? If it was one of these houses—" they were too late. His horse shied at another body, a woman with a face that looked like a boiling pot, a broken spear standing in her ribs. The girl wouldn't have ordered this, but she wouldn't, he thought, have the strength to resist someone ordering it in her name. And it was an effective way of taking back control of the *dinaz*. But the pox would have done it for them, anyway.

"Tower," Ghu said faintly, and mounting again, took the lead at a careful canter, leaving Ahjvar to follow, the horse too tired to make more than a halfhearted token of resistance when Ghu veered sharply between two still-burning ruins, into blinding, choking smoke, and the heat reached for him—No. He didn't dare shut his eyes; he knew damn well what fire he'd find himself in then. Ghu had disappeared. He caught up, bursting out of the smoke into a churned area like a stableyard.

The square stone tower, built up against the *dinaz* wall, was under attack—Praitans, and defending the doorway, a pair of Grasslanders. No, the Grasslanders were trying to force a way out, and the thatched roof was ablaze. They cut down the foremost of the men penning them, forced their way down a few of the steep stone steps, more behind them, Grasslanders and some woman of the west, a handful, half dressed, mostly barefoot. Fire glared red through the doorway. Thatch, on a stronghold. Fools in haste. And no Deyandara among the attackers. Ghu had said, burning, so she would be inside. Prisoner or ally? He ought to be asking himself why the girl was his responsibility, but that was pointless. The Red Mask's helmet might have come in useful for clearing a way.

"Keep out of it," he said, drawing his sword. No time to assemble slow wizardry. They'd scatter from the horse and by the time they realized he was only one—he just had to keep going, to make it onto the stairs without being pulled down and hurt too badly to keep moving. And then deal with the defenders, who would see another Praitan coming at them. There was fire beyond them. Surely nobody was alive.

"Ahj!" Ghu called, and led off again, so he followed, with the dogs. The Praitans rushed the steps again, as he passed, forcing those trying to escape back. The Grasslanders retreated, slipping, falling, back towards the doorway. One down, two, wounded or dead didn't matter; once they fell they had no chance of rising. There were more within, shadows in smoke, and another woman fell, the last up. It didn't take more than one or two bleeding out their life on the stairs to make them slick and treacherous. Those within thrust the door to. They'd rather burn than fall to Praitannec spears? They'd never been touched by fire yet.

"Here, get back to the gate!" someone shouted, running after him. "If you're thinking you can get in for that blasted neck-ring, any man drags that from the ashes and doesn't hand it over to the king'll be—" His face went wide-mouthed with shock as it sank in he faced a stranger.

"What king?" Ahjvar demanded, but the man was already turning to run the other way, shouting, "Help, here! The high king's men are in the *dinaz*!"

Ahjvar rode him down with hardly a thought and circled back to Ghu. "They've named one of their own king." Ghu nodded at a window overhead. Narrow, and the shutters were closed, but—maybe. "Fine for an acrobat. You make sure the blessed horse stands still."

Ghu nodded and grabbed his bridle, so before he had time to think it through overmuch Ahjvar climbed onto the saddle. The horse shifted its weight about unhappily, ears back. Ghu murmured nonsense to it, and he caught the lintel, pulled himself up as the horse swung right around and away, and kicked. The shutters burst inwards, and he ended up crouching on the sill.

He squirmed through and narrowly avoided getting himself hung up with his sword, came down awkwardly onto what turned out to be a stone stairway rising along the wall, half-seen through rising smoke. The benches and tables were overturned in a heap, burning, as if someone had made a bonfire of them. Above him on the stairs a beam from the second floor had dropped, and above that was all flame. No one could be alive on the second floor, none on the upper floor beneath the roof, if there even was a floor there any longer. Ghu followed him, landing lithe and silent as a cat.

Fire roared above, and the burning meat reek was stronger than out in the *dinaz*. He swayed, deafened by the roar, and crouched down, but the smoke was thick, being sucked towards the window now. There were voices. Figures moving, down on the floor, he saw as the flames dropped and rose again, but there was another wall of fire beyond, between them and the door. If those who had shut themselves in rather than die on the stairs still stood beyond that, he couldn't see them. But then smoke hid them all, and he hadn't seen anything but dim shapes to know if the fool girl was among them.

Voices. A voice. Shouting at him. Calling.

Cairangorm the king was dead. He had fallen at the top of the stone stairs that led from the hall up to his private chambers in the loft. He had fallen, and he was dead. It was a sad end for a proud old man who had survived so many raids, so many skirmishes along the caravan road, fallen drunk, and right to the bottom of his new stone stairs in the grand new hall he had built to please his wife. But Lord Talwesach who was his wizard said, poison, and that changed everything.

There was stone beneath his fingers. He felt it. There was smoke in his lungs, and his eyes ran acrid tears, but he could not die; his curse sealed him to life and even burned, he would live and heal, in time, and he could leap over that fire from this place on the stairs and the girl was beyond it, he heard her calling on her god Andara and on Ghu, of all people, and he could not move, he shook so. He could not even release his grip on the edge of the stairway to stand.

Poison, Catairlau said flatly, but not in the wine. He cast the leaves in the hall fire to prove the truth himself, being a wizard, and one who would probably have been summoned to Duina Lellandi to serve the high queen there, had he not been his father's sole adult heir and his champion besides. His hands had not shaken then.

Poison. Not in the wine, which Hyllau had likewise drunk, but in the water, in the cup, the king's own cup, in which wine and water had been mixed. No, it wasn't like the king to drink to drunkenness, but Hyllau never mixed her wine. Lord Talwesach, knocking his hand aside when in fey mood he would have touched the water to his own tongue to test it, tried it with rose for truth and yew for death, and so proved it poisoned. They broke jug and cup and carried the shards to the hall fire below to burn clean. Had Cairangorm gone out to summon help, feeling unwell, or had his body been tumbled down the stairs to explain his death? His ghost had not lingered, and that was strange, when not even the simplest of rituals had been given him yet to free his soul, not a prayer or a pinch of earth, or salt in the mouth, which was a rite of the eastern deserts spread along the road of Over-Malagru. Catairlau called him, summoned him, writing a circle about the bier on which his body lay with the alphabet of trees, which was bordering on necromancy and sin against the Old Great Gods, but nothing woke in King Cairangorm to speak his murderer's name.

The hall might need that proof, but he did not. He went to the lady's bower beside the king's hall, where in her grief she had withdrawn, alone, saying she would see none but the new king. Even her son and his nurse were ordered away.

He couldn't stand. He could crawl. He could feel his way, blind in the smoke. She caught his hand, and her fingers were like claws. She pulled him forward, arms locked behind his neck, and he fell onto her.

Catairlau was his father's champion as well as his heir and his wizard, and if it was not quite justice, with no accusation made before the hall and the goddess and no proof laid before the king's councillors, it was not quite murder, either. He had been king-presumptive scant hours when he went into the bower of the king's wife Hyllau with his sword drawn.

She was in her bed, waiting for him. She must have seen her death in his face; he saw hers change as she leaned up on an elbow, naked and welcoming, her hair unbound and combed in a curling cascade down one shoulder, not quite hiding one breast, her sly, sweet smile stretching to an ugly grimace.

"He was old!" she shouted at him, as if that were a shield.

It was all her defence. But she was mad. He had always known it. But he forgot why she was accounted the third wizard of the king's hall, with himself and old Talwesach, though her wizardry was not theirs. A child who could not be bothered with tutors, who ran ahead of them and thought she had nothing to learn, and was never any use but when she stood with them in a drawing of the wands, because she had no structure, no discipline, knew few spells and saw no need, but spilled petty spite in ill-wishing when slighted. In her tantrums small lightnings crackled on her nails and she would laugh and say, "There, don't make me cross. You see what happens. I can't help the way I am." But underneath it all had lain a great dark reservoir, which only leaked and spat in the small seeping spring of her tempers, and now she was afraid, as she had never been afraid, and her rage had never been so great, either. Insulted, thwarted, rejected. She cowered down into the deep feather mattress as he reached for her hair to drag her out where he could kill her cleanly, without hacking and chasing, and the bed erupted in fire. She shrieked and clutched at him.

Her fingers were claws and she pulled him down, and then she laughed in his face and cried, exultantly, "But he's dead. We could have ruled together now, it could have been your time. I'll see you dead instead, if you're such a fool. My mother will come for me, you'll see, before you burn. I'll be the king's mother if not a king's wife. I don't need you."

Her hair was already burning, shrivelling, and she screamed and screamed, but he couldn't break free of her. The linens burned, and the feathers, and they stank worse than hair. Catairanach wailed and screamed at him for leading her daughter into this place. He had killed her darling, led her into this step by step, poor Hyllau, who should have been protected and understood . . . but he was burning, and she was already black and crumbling beneath him. The goddess had him in the spring beneath the mountain ash, in the waters beneath the stone, and Hyllau was a little child, and an infant, small and curled and beating tiny fists, but she smiled the same sly, sweet smile and opened knowing pebble-brown eyes at him, and she was a spark of light and he swallowed her, with Catairanach's hand on his lips.

"Ahjvar!"

There were ashes, hot, and charred posts, and stones, and he was ash and flaking, blistered skin. He crawled away blind, seeking water, cold water, where he could die and drown. His hand found the hilt of his sword. After a while he *used one hand to close the other around it, and used it as a prop to stand. His baked eyes could see, hazed and dull. There were shadows moving, but they darted and swooped like swallows, too swift to be known as folk of the hall. Their voices were high and chittering and far away. They didn't see him, either. That was because he was a ghost. Catairlau the king was dead. He heard them say so. Hyllanim the king saw him, ever-solemn infant, and clung more tightly to his nurse's shirt, watching. He walked out where there should have been a wall, and fell down the steep hillside that was almost cliff, and found the water, which did not ease the burning. Flesh wept into the water, and the spring ran fouled. Catairanach sang over him, but her songs were for Hyllau. He wove his own words into her song, only half aware he did so, dreaming, nightmares, caught in the fire. Hatred of Hyllau, cursing her lust for the shell of kingship, her greed and ambition and childishness, his own besotted folly, which had been as selfish, as blind, and it was only later he knew he had cursed what they had made between them too, the child who was not his father's son, and all who came after him, and as the king was the heart of the* duina, *all his folk.*

He didn't remember what came after, not for a long time. There were stories of a creature in the night, which came to the dinaz *and dragged men out to slaughter. When he did find himself again, he sought the wild places and tried to keep away from men, but Hyllau was with him in the long nights, and there was always the fire. It would be right, if he burned. If she burnt him again, calling him, holding him, long enough, this time, hot enough, even he could die—*

"Ahj!"

Not Hyllau's arms, fingers clawed into his back. Ghu's, locked about his chest, holding him back as he crouched with one hand on the edge of the stairs and one reaching into nothingness, blistering, fire below him. Ghu was coughing, his body shaking, wheezing; Ghu couldn't drag him back, but he wouldn't let go, let him go into the fire, not like that, into Hyllau's arms, which still reached for him. Ahjvar flung himself back so violently they both struck the wall behind, holding onto Ghu like he was a log in a drowning sea.

"You're here, Ahjvar. Not there," Ghu said. "Never there." But every word was a bone-shaking cough that rattled the both of them, face against his chest. "Deyandara. Down—"

"Get out." Damn Deyandara. He shouldn't have led Ghu into this. He shoved him back towards the window. "Out." He could hear the goddess of the spring, calling his name, exultant and afraid, and Hyllau, feel her fingers like grappling hooks, digging in—

"Ahjvar," Ghu said, and grabbed him again by the shoulders, resisting being forced to the window. "You're Ahjvar. Not Catairlau. I didn't take you from the devil in the well to give you to the fire. Don't listen to them."

"All right," he said, to make Ghu let go, but he still heard them, Catairanach screaming, *Damned fool, cursed and cursed again, she is yours. Forget the outlander halfling, let him burn. Do you want her to die here? She's the last of my children, the last, the last, the last of Hyllau's children, and you leave her to burn, worse than Hyllau who never meant you to die, you know she didn't, she couldn't have, she loved you. It was you who held her in the fire when I could have saved her body and soul. Be cursed again. You'll never come to the Old Great Gods' road, you'll burn in the night forever—*

"Don't listen," Ghu said, and his lips brushed Ahjvar's like a blessing before he let him go and went out the window. Ahjvar saw him drop and stumble away, falling on his knees, head down, coughing and coughing, and a pair of the Praitannec traitors closing in, spears levelled. Ghu, crouched and bowed and shaken with coughing as he was, had his hand to the handle of that great wicked knife at the small of his back and the dogs were slinking up, so Ahjvar turned away and stood, breathing smoke. Shaking, still. *I can't walk into fire*, he had said. *I can't, I can't, I've tried*, and Great Gods have mercy, he could not take that step and he was going to fall, down into the hungry flames and Hyllau's open mouth. So he leapt.

CHAPTER XIX

The trap door slammed open. Chieh and Lug and a handful of others burst upwards. Deyandara put her back to the wall, her hand on the knife hidden in her sling, but they hardly spared her a glance. Lug, flushed and sweating, and another couple of big men knelt down on the door, holding it closed against some battering from below. Chieh dragged at Ketsim, who groaned heavily and struck out at her, fumbling, half-falling from the bed. They were all shouting in Grasslander, at one another, at whoever was below, Deyandara couldn't tell.

"Marnoch!" she shouted, and that did draw Chieh's attention. The woman left Ketsim and crossed the room in three long strides to hit her.

"Not your bloody allies," she snarled. "This lot want you as dead as us. That weasel-faced eastern lord's named himself king."

Lord Fairu had said a pair of eastern lords had driven his folk from their land, and one was allied with the Marakanders. . . . There had been a Praitan at the feast she might have described as weasel-faced, if she'd been in any mind to describe him at all. "Hicca?" she asked.

"Him. Treacherous bastard." Chieh leaned to peer out the window. "He's laid his plans quickly, on top of Siman's betrayal. I wonder if he knew in advance? Starts to make me think the tales are true and the whole *duina* is cursed and damned, and anyone who tries to rule it. Nothing's gone right for us since Ketsim took the Voice of Marakand's gold. Do you smell smoke? They'd taken oath to Ketsim! They spread out quiet among us, they were sleeping all among us, but tonight they weren't. They must have had some signal. They all started killing at once, stabbing people in their sleep, all in the dark and unarmed."

"You trusted a traitor," said Deyandara. "What do you expect?"

Chieh shot her a dirty look and crossed to the opposite window, let out a yell. Deyandara and the Grasslanders all crowded to her. The houses and tents of the *dinaz* were burning. People screamed, and dark shapes ran between them, but they weren't making any effort to drag anyone to safety that she could see. Deyandara licked her lips. "You said they'd left the sick and the dying behind."

Chieh turned away, calling Ketsim, who rolled unsteadily to his feet and joined them, taking a possessive hold on the elbow of Deyandara's still-aching arm. She clenched her teeth on a moan and kept her hand on the hilt of her hidden knife. If he ordered her killed, at least she wouldn't die alone.

The battering at the trap door had ended. So had the noises of murder below. The Grasslanders put their heads together, debating.

They were foxes, run into their den by the dogs, and only one way out. That never ended well for the fox. Call Ghu, Catairanach had said, but she had been dreaming. He had been there for her twice, though, out of the hopeless darkness.

"Ghu," she whispered. She had felt so safe, sitting by him on that roof in the suburb of Marakand. "Ghu, Andara, help me. Please." Andara, Ghu, Old Great Gods . . . Durandau, Marnoch, someone would come, someone surely must come seeking her. They were burning the *dinaz*; this tower was thatched like any humble hut, and the sparks would spread, and the lower floors were held against them. . . .

The night stretched on long into nightmare after that. Hicca's bard came and tried to make some bargain with them. Chieh was translator, none of the Grasslanders having learnt Praitan, nor possessing more than their lord's halting trade-Nabbani. Ketsim, sitting holding his head, growled and snarled and refused every offer, though Chieh began to try making bargains on her own terms for her lord and her husband and friends to be left to live or die in peace. Ketsim's wits weren't so addled by fever or grain-spirit that he didn't notice, though, and that led to far too long a quarrel between them, which Deyandara couldn't follow, while Hicca's people shouted insults below. She went to sit by the south window, leaning her head against the wall, eyes shut, imagining Marnoch riding to the gate, her brothers, all of them, at his side, the river of horsemen pouring in among the burning houses, riding to the tower, and Marnoch at their head . . . Ghu's hand finding hers in the candlelit darkness and whispering for silence, slipping away through walls that somehow weren't there, and the rain beat down around them, lightning lit the tower, and Ahjvar set his sword against her throat. *Kill her*, Hicca said, *and she's the last of them, the last of Hyllanim's line. The last of the curse on the Duina Catairna. A new age, a new king, and the* duina *renewed.* She jerked awake. They were opening the trap door, torchlight flooding up, drowning the feeble candles.

"Girl!" Chieh hauled her to her feet. "Let's go."

"We're going?" she asked hazily. "No!"

"We're going," said Chieh. "You're staying. Hicca wants you after all, you and the gold about your neck."

"No!" She wrenched her arm away.

"Or kill her yourselves and throw her down to us," someone called up, and laughed.

"You get her only once we're out the gate," Chieh shouted angrily, and grabbed again for Deyandara. Ketsim's hand came down on her arm; Ketsim's sweat-slick face leaned in close, his breath foul with the disease.

"No," he said. Chieh let her go and took a step away. "She kill you, before another man take you, but she is not buy my life with my little wife." And then a torrent of furious Grasslander that had Chieh bowing, white-faced. In that distraction, Hicca's followers tried to force their way up, and one of the Grasslanders was killed before they got the trap door closed again.

Was the night growing thinner? More shouting, more battering, and Chieh refused to look at her, keeping close to Lug's side, while Ketsim clutched her hand. Then silence below.

More low-voiced Grasslander discussion.

"Maybe they go for axes," Ketsim translated for her, as if that should be a comfort. "But if I, I Hicca, not wanting queen, not wanting Grasslander lord, I set fire."

"Barbarians," muttered Chieh. "My lord—" And more in Grasslander. Ketsim seemed to agree with whatever she proposed, this time. "We're going to rush them," she told Deyandara. "We put you in the middle, we get out, we get whatever mounts are closest, and we head south to the road. Can you ride a camel?"

"No!"

"Siman probably took all the camels. Do you have a knife?"

Deyandara shook her head, hoping she hadn't hesitated too long.

"Useless. All those drunks at the table, and you didn't manage to hide yourself a knife?" The woman thrust a sheathed dagger at her, and Ketsim let her go to take it, nodding approval.

"Good," he said. "You kill Hicca for me, little kitten, little wife." He laughed and ruffled her hair; Chieh laughed with him. Even Lug smiled, though his face was drawn tight and he kept swallowing, as if his stomach fought him. Another of the Grasslanders already showed a face rising in blisters; she leaned on the wall, stroking the point of her spear with a whetstone.

Deyandara smiled. So now she had two knives. And her smile felt as false as their laughter, because what good would it do? It was the Catairnan curse on her still, that she should end up here with her own folk bargaining for her death and her only defenders her enemies.

A man at the window looking out over the *dinaz* spoke intensely.

Deyandara went to look. Marnoch—of course not. Praitans, yes, archers, and they were shooting fire-arrows at the tower, while the roofs of the houses fell in behind them. Tendrils of smoke began coiling down through the thatch, new and summer-dry.

A nod from Ketsim, and one of the men pulled up the door. The blistered spearwoman went down in a rush, Lug close behind her, and shouted, one word.

"Fire," said Chieh, and Ketsim seized Deyandara, hauled her down with them, into the sleeping-chamber of the bench-companions, which looked more like a yard where the fall butchering had taken place, blood pooled on the floor, bodies still in their sodden blankets, bodies sprawled ugly and ungainly on the floor. She squeaked and jumped back from something underfoot, saw it was a hand. No arm. Just a hand. Straw, rubbish, bedding, broken spear-shafts, arrows, bows, were heaped in the corners, already ablaze, flames reaching for the rafters of the upper floor, and there was a fire set under the stairs down which they had run. It smelt of pitch.

"The bastards were setting this while they were still talking to us," Chieh said. "And they've taken every bit of armour, not left so much as a shield. I told my lord only a fool trusted a Praitan."

One of the bodies moaned, and the sick woman started to it but was ordered back by Ketsim. They weren't going to carry the wounded. A moment's pause, while Lug threw up, and then they went down the stone stairs to the hall in the same order. This time they were opposed before they ever got off the stairs, and the woman went over the side, no railing. Lug made it a little farther, bearing down one Praitan with his rush, but someone with an axe cut his leg half away, and he went to the floor on his face and was hacked to death there, with Chieh screaming after him, her sabre sweeping Ketsim's way clear, Deyandara dragged stumbling in his wake.

A bonfire of furniture burned in the centre of the hall where they had feasted, and its flames reached to the ceiling. The door was held against them, shouting, jeering Praitans. They called *her* the traitor and a whore of Marakand. Ketsim put himself between her and a thrown spear, not for her own sake, but because he let no one take what was his, she knew, but still, he did it. She caught him as he staggered back against her. No armour, she thought dazedly, surely he remembered he had no armour, and then, unable to hold up his weight, she went down to the floor, kneeling, with the Grasslander lord slumped against her. At least he was a good thick body against a second spear, which followed.

In a song he would have had some last words for her, and she too, would no doubt have forgiven him his rough wooing, but he just muttered and groaned, and she didn't know if he died then, or later, but she stayed holding him until most of the mercenaries had forced the hall clear of Praitans and gotten so far as the door. The pitch-fuelled fire on the floor under the upper stairs burnt through about then, and a burning beam came down onto the stone stairs. More burning timbers fell, their supports gone. The stairs were cut off and so was the door, but Chieh and one of the men had rushed back for her as they fell, or for Ketsim, not knowing if he were dead or wounded, and now there were the three of them huddled together and the smoke making a blind hell of it, smoke roiling and red-lit, and the heat growing. The door was in the direction Ketsim was facing, but Chieh had moved him, dragged and turned him, shouting his name, and Deyandara found only fire, crawling that way. When she stood the very air was hot and choked her. The floor was cooler, safer. She could still breathe, though she coughed, and wherever the smoke parted, there were flames. Chieh ran against her, fell, and clutched her.

"Door?" she rasped.

Deyandara shook her head.

"Ketsim's dead."

"I know."

"You weren't worth it."

"This isn't my fault!"

"Bloody Praitan wasn't worth it. Cheating Marakand. What is it with you barbarian tribesmen, always wanting to be kings?"

"I don't."

"Lug's dead." Chieh was crying, and her tears were dark. She was hard to see, though they crouched face to face. Someone else was coughing, the third man, but he stopped.

"Going to find Lug," Chieh said, and shoved her away.

Deyandara clutched after her. Lug had been killed on the stairs. She had seen him lying at the foot of them, they'd had to leap his body, and there was fire between them, now. But Chieh vanished into smoke and didn't return. She crawled until she found a wall, felt over it, but didn't remember any open windows in the hall, remembered, somewhere, wooden shutters, but not where, and didn't feel any. It was hotter in both directions she turned, and she couldn't stand. She curled up small with her good arm around her knees, Chieh's useless knife long lost, and tried to breathe through her shirt and shawl. It hurt.

It wasn't Ghu who found her after all, but Ahjvar. She wouldn't have cared if it were Ketsim himself who heaved her up in his arms and mashed her face into his chest, but Ketsim was dead, of course, and Ghu wouldn't let Ahjvar hurt her, so everything was all right, and it was a good enough dream to die to. She'd rather it had been Marnoch, though. The flames roared and the heat seared her.

In a dream she wouldn't have cut her lips on her teeth, banging her face on his collarbone as he leapt and landed rolling, and dropped her at the bottom of the outside stairs.

She wasn't dead. She couldn't breathe—she could, but it hurt, and she couldn't stop coughing, but she wasn't dead. Yet.

There were dead Grasslanders, dead Praitans, living men and women in the dawn, weapons bare. She got to hands and knees and sat back on her haunches like a dog, still gasping. The air was sharp and winter-cold in her throat. A white-and-grey dog came gliding in beside her, licking her face. Its fur went black and smudged as it brushed against her. She ducked away from the dog, even her head wobbling, and tried to make her swimming eyes see Ahjvar, standing above her on the first step. He was black with smoke, even his hair dulled with soot, his coat scorched, and the skin of his hands was red and swelling against the gold bracelets on his wrists. Leopards, she thought. Like his sword. Little leopards. Leopards of the old royal line, before Hyllanim changed his emblem to the bull. Her eyes ran with tears. The Praitans just stood. Not that many of them, not so many as she had seen in the night, but it had been supposed to be all over, hadn't it? Ketsim and Cattiga's heir, dying together in the fire, the southern pox wiping the land clean of invaders, the valleys a prize for whoever could hold them, and what could a goddess do but bless the victor? In Hicca's place she'd have sent her men off to round up straying horses, and anything else of value that could be salvaged, before they abandoned this cursed place. Now they wouldn't have to rake through the ashes for the gold about her neck. She wondered, if she simply twisted it off and threw it, would they fight over it like hungry dogs for a scrap of meat? Worth a try. Ahjvar couldn't fight them all.

"Which one of you claims the kingship of the *duina*?" Ahjvar asked. His voice was little more than a whisper, but the silence was such that they heard. It resounded in her ears like a challenge, though there was no circle cut, there were no bards to witness. Her breath caught when she tried to tell him, "Hicca," and the dog was there, breathing out warmth, still trying to clean her face, so that her gasping breathed in moist dog-breath, and she found the next breath easier. The dog grinned.

She didn't have to be heard. Hicca stood forward, with gold about his own neck. "And why does a," his lip curled, "godless and drug-crazed mercenary have any right to ask? Ketsim's man. Traitor to your folk."

"I wish I were godless," Ahjvar said, and sounded as though he meant it. She could see why Hicca said drug-crazed; when she looked up, ducking the dog again, she saw how bright his eyes were, pupils too dark, large against the blue. He swayed where he stood, and it wasn't her own feeble shaking that made it seem so. "I wish the world were godless. But it isn't, and here we are, traitor to your queen's heir, traitor to the men who kept their faith and fought in their queen's memory, for the whole of the folk and the land, forsworn traitor to the invader whose boots you rushed to lick. Crow, come late to the field when even the ravens are done their feasting, to feed on the rotten scraps they disdain. You burnt the sick and the dying alive in their beds."

"I defeated Ketsim. The high king will uphold my claim against whatever's left of Marnoch and Yvarr the Seneschal. They've got no queen to follow, and you won't live to sell her back to her brother. This is my victory. If the Duina Catairna has a king this morning, it's me."

Ahjvar laughed, which brought on a fit of coughing. He smothered it on his sleeve, and there was blood. "There is only one king of the *duina* standing in this place, before cursed Catairanach and the Old Great Gods. He is not you."

He came past Deyandara, down the steps, and if Hicca had time or wit to raise his sword Deyandara didn't see it. His head fell, body crumpling after. "Out!" Ahjvar roared, as with a yell the spearman at Hicca's shoulder thrust at him. She didn't see all that followed, but two more of Hicca's men were on the ground, and Ahj hadn't given back so much as a step. "Get out, run, before the curse on the *duina* takes you all for this night's work. Traitors and murderers!"

They closed in about him in a rush, but there was a fog coiling about their feet, flowing around the corner of the burning tower, through the lanes between the smouldering ruins, ankle-high, knee-high, like rising water, cold as the waters from the depths of the earth were cold, and the air blew morning-cool, fresh and clean, for all the rising smoke. The dog sat back, head tilted to one side. Deyandara got to her feet, finding she could, as if the warmth of the dog had given her new strength.

The men about Ahjvar fell back, leaving him alone, chest heaving and wounded, but still on his feet. A woman walked up the lane behind with the fog running to twist about her like welcoming cats. Catairanach, dressed in the long blue and white gown of a queen, with the dawn sparking in her hair as if she wore a net of spiderweb and dew, or diamonds. Those of Hicca's folk who had never seen her in the hall at some blessing or judgement would nonetheless know godhead when it stood among them.

The goddess looked around them, at the men and the few women, nodded to Ahjvar, and turned her back, gazing out over the ruins of the *duina*.

"Enemies," she said, and her voice was like it had always been in Deyandara's dreams, but real, with earth and water in it. "My enemies, but—" As Hicca's people drew themselves up a little, "—I defend as I must, with the land and the powers of the land, and this epidemic was not *my* curse on them, but their own misfortune, in coming so vulnerable to a land where the pox was running. What king kills his enemies so, helpless in their beds? You did not even have the mercy to kill them outright, but left them to burn. What king demands murder of his folk and puts that burden on their souls? There is only one king left to the Duina Catairna, and he is Catairlau, Cairangorm's son, returned out of fire, through death and long years, to make my *duina* great again. If you think you can kill him, with my hand over him and my blessing on him, you are welcome to try. But touch the Lady Deyandara at your peril."

Somehow, such attention did not make Deyandara feel safer. She found the dog's head under her hand, thrusting upward as if to give her heart. Something moved in the mist behind the goddess. Ghu, another dog at his feet, leading three stocky horses. He waited there, fading in and out of vision, Catairanach's fog folding about him like a cloak. He looked very weary and sad, and he had a dark cut on his face.

"You don't notice any contradiction in your lovely words?" Ahjvar said, his own broken by another fit of coughing. He spat, and his spittle was ashy black. "Every name you give, every curse you speak—"

The goddess held up a hand, silencing him.

"Go," she said to Hicca's folk. "Go back to your own valleys, your hills, unblessed, denied. Go lordless and unforgiven, and take this word to your fellows, too, who have set out to raid the hills for Hicca's gain. Sleep in torment, seeing the faces of these enemies you have so dishonourably slain. Hear their cries in the night. And in a year and a day, if you live so long, come back to stand before your king, and ask his forgiveness in my name. Now go."

Her face was terrible. She lifted a hand towards the gate, and they went, running.

"Every curse you speak fell on me long ago," Ahjvar said. "Go away." He swayed so, Deyandara went to him without thinking to put her arm about his waist. He was terribly heavy when he leaned against her.

The goddess smiled at them, kindly, as if she were some queen and they her lords, standing before her to ask—but Deya couldn't have let Ahjvar fall. He braced himself on her shoulder. But Ahjvar's defiance gave her heart. And rage.

"You said you couldn't come into the *dinaz*," she accused, and was startled to hear her own voice ring loud, clear and unchoking. "You could have come any time, you could have sent Hicca's folk away before they set fire to it all. They died—they were my enemies and yours, but Ketsim died putting himself between me and Hicca's spearmen. Chieh came back into the fire for me, even though she'd been willing to hand me over to Hicca to be killed, before. You could have come any time."

"No," said Catairanach, cold and reproving. Deyandara cringed under the look she gave, but Ahjvar's arm went about her, so that they propped one another up. The goddess dismissed her but smiled on Ahjvar. "But you invoked me, Catairlau, you alone could do so, so old in this place, which was yours before these walls were ever built. You called me within the Lady's ban."

"Cursed you, I thought."

"Love me or hate me, I'm still your goddess, and you called on me. Did you know the high king, the Andaran, has defeated the Marakander army, the Grasslanders who came before and the new force that rode from the west only now?"

"I know. I was there."

"He will come here, with the kings and the queens of the tribes," Catairanach went on. "No doubt he thinks to set someone of his own blood over a kingless land, one of his brothers, perhaps. You will deny him. You will ask him for his sister's hand, and he will not deny you."

Ahjvar's grip on Deyandara tightened—reassuringly, she realized, and she took a deep breath.

"No," he said.

The goddess drifted closer, hardly seeming to move. Her hand rose to touch Ahjvar's face, and he flinched back, dragging Deyandara with him. The dog growled.

"Will you live with Hyllau still?" Catairanach asked. "Carry her in this twisted, perverted state? You've made her what she is. I never intended that."

"You made what you didn't understand," he said. "You've twisted the world against nature. You've denied her the road she should have taken long ago. You've created a creature cut off from the strength of the earth and the Old Great Gods both. What did you expect? She finds what sustenance she can, all you've left her able to touch. And she was twisted to begin with."

"She must be reborn, her soul clean and renewed. She will live again."

"I would sooner kill the girl myself, here and now, than see her made mother to that soul, and by me," Ahjvar said levelly. "I told you to go. If you say I called you . . . then I can send you. Go. I deny this place to you, these walls, this child of Hyllanim. *Out.*"

"Some night will come when you do not wake at all," the goddess snarled. "Do you want that for yourself, or for my daughter? You loved her once."

But she was fading as the mist sank. Deyandara was shaking, her knees weak, and when Ahjvar folded to the ground he pulled her down with him. The dog whined and nuzzled at both of them. Ghu was there, taking Ahjvar's weight so Deyandara could free her arm and sit aside, head on her knees, weeping, she couldn't have said why. Relief and exhaustion and terror combined. The white-and-grey dog thrust its nose in under her face, and the brown-and-black growled at the last of the fog.

"Come, Ahj. Up. We should go." Burning straw floated down around them like the first snowflakes of a winter storm. The tower creaked and groaned in a rising wind.

Ahjvar said nothing, but he levered himself up by Ghu's shoulder, and the horses were there.

"New horses," he said, after a moment, while Ghu, like the shield-bearer Ahjvar had called him so long ago, took his sword from him, and cleaned it, and gave it back, and, shoving him towards the horse perhaps more brother-like than as a respectful shield-bearer would, held his stirrup.

"Stealing horses is very easy, once you get started. The last were too tired. These are fresh. I think they were the traitor lord's. I've opened the gates of the pens, so the rest can find their own way out. Nothing living should stay in this place, I think, though the ghosts are all gone. Come, Ahj," as if he cajoled a cranky, overtired child, "before the roof-beams fall."

Ahjvar looked dreadful, now Deyandara saw him in full daylight, grey and gaunt and blistered with burns, wounds crusting and sticky, binding his coat to him.

But when Ahjvar was in the saddle with the reins in hand, Ghu took a moment to embrace Deyandara before he boosted her up.

CHAPTER XX

Holla-Sayan woke out of deep sleep and lay wondering where he was, and why. A bed, his bed, he supposed, since the arm before his face was his own, and the sprawl of black braids over it belonged to Gaguush. If they didn't, he really was in trouble. The room was dark, and there had been tremors of the earth in his dreams. He'd slept the afternoon away.

All hells, no, not unless Rasta had spun his caravanserai on its axis. The faintest of grey showed through the piercings of the carved window screen, and the round-arched window under the eaves faced the east. He rolled from the bed and began dressing. Gaguush had tidied up at some point. Clean linens, a shirt that couldn't stand up on its own, and the leather jerkin he hadn't been wearing last time he went to the city. She woke and rolled over to watch him.

"I did try to wake you," she mumbled, yawning, forestalling whatever he had been about to say, which might have been shouting, and probably unjust. "I cooked you supper. I said I would. I shook you, and you groaned and rolled over. Then you growled at me and went back to sleep. So Tamarisk and Rasta and I ate it."

For a moment they were eye to eye, nose to nose, as he groped for his boots, set under the bed.

"Really growled," she said, eyes wide, lacking his night vision, and very solemn. "I suppose I'm lucky you didn't bite."

He kissed her, since she was so close, her false solemnity curling

into a smile, and she made him take his time over it. When he resumed
dressing she grinned at him. "It's the truth."

"You should have thumped me."

"If you were that tired, you needed to sleep. They would have sent
if they needed you."

"If they needed me, they wouldn't have had time to send. Anyway,
nobody knows where I am."

"Then you should have told them before you came out here."

"I wasn't planning to stay so long." And he didn't bloody well
belong to them.

"Insulting. Is it still night? It is. Eat some breakfast anyway."

"Did you leave me anything?"

"Of my lovely fowl stewed with prunes and saffron? To sit overnight
in this heat? No, we did not. But Rasta's cook makes very good fried
bread, better than Thekla's, though I won't tell her that, and I wrapped
some up for you, because I thought you'd likely be waking by midnight
and in a tearing hurry."

"You're beautiful and I love you."

"Tell me that when you aren't dressed and running out the door."
Gaguush pulled on drawers and a caftan, handed him his coat, and locked
the door behind them both as they went out to the gallery. No one else
was stirring, except a cat sitting on the railing. They went down the stairs
and cut across the dark yard. It felt like trespassing, to push uninvited into
Master Rasta's own kitchen, but Gaguush seemed comfortably at home,
humming as she turned a cat off the low table, finding her way by feel to a
cupboard, sniffing until she found a stack of flat, oil-fried slabs wrapped in
a cloth, scented with garlic and cumin. Holla didn't remember when he'd
last eaten, and cold and greasy as the bread was, he tore off chunks like, as
Gaguush helpfully said, a starving dog. She had taken the clay cover off
the hearth in the gallery before the kitchen and was feeding last night's
carefully conserved embers with dung-cakes.

"Tea?" she suggested. "It won't take long."

"I shouldn't." But he sat with his back to a pillar and watched her fill the kettle at the water jar.

She hadn't put on a shirt, and the caftan fell loose. There was enough light for her to catch him looking. She put a hand over her face, then cinched her sash tighter. "Idiot."

"What?"

"Smirking like that. What is it about breasts, anyway, that are so damned fascinating? Udders, that's all they are. Udders and teats."

Actually, he had been picturing her making tea so, with a black-haired toddler clinging to the skirts of her coat. Coat, not caftan. On the road, of course, which they wouldn't be, not with a toddler.

"Now what?" she asked, sounding exasperated. "I liked it better when you were so obviously having indecent thoughts."

"I need to find Mikki." Sudden urgency clawed at him. He stood up. "No tea."

He felt the brickwork shake beneath his feet. There was the sound of thunder, not so distant. Camels heaved to theirs, groaning complaint, and the cat shot past, disappearing up the nearer stairs.

"No clouds," said Gaguush, peering skyward. "Bashra grant it's not another big quake, just when I've sunk everything in a heap of mud bricks and stone."

If he'd had hackles then they'd have been bristling. Holla-Sayan barely held himself human, felt the change of form shivering, crackling under his skin. Not thunder. Not an earthquake. He started for the gate, but Gaguush caught his sleeve and said, "Up," so they ran to the upper gallery and then took the narrower stairs on the far side to the roof, which was cluttered with drying racks and Rasta's private garden of scented herbs in pots, to which favoured patrons were invited to drink wine and watch the moon rise.

Dust piled high into the sky over Gurhan's sacred hill, a sandstorm haze obscuring half the city, and the first edge of the rising sun burning livid scarlet through it.

Others were following: Master Rasta and the servants of his small household, Tamarisk, a handful of mountain folk who must have come with the mules from the mining villages, all bleary with sleep and babbling.

"If there's going to be another, I want my camels out in the open. Tamarisk!"

The master of the muleteers had had the same thought, and in the jostling for the stairs, Gaguush let the mountain men push ahead and turned back to take Holla-Sayan's arm. "Don't," she said, "jump off the roof, not with all this lot watching."

"What?" She was hard to hear, very small, very far away. Something gathered itself, heavy, like the feeling of impending thunder over the Stone Desert, the air heavy, pressing. Yellow-white light flared over the city, near the Sunset Gate, he thought, and there was thunder, but it was not sound, not storm, not the cracking of the earth but the world itself, maybe, that cried out. He staggered under the weight of it, leaning on the parapet of the roof. Gaguush seized him by the shoulders. For a moment he could not remember to breathe, and the world was strange, heavy and broken, meaningless lumps and jagged streaks of matter that had no order, no sense, and he was lost in it, nameless. Gaguush put a hand on his cheek, and he gasped, finding sense there, pattern, in her eyes, her touch, the world re-forming itself, plaster of the parapet smooth and cold under his fingers again, real. But her hand shook.

"Your eyes are burning," she said. "Go, if you have to. But come back, Holla-Sayan. You promised me. You're mine. For all my life."

Words had fled him. Too far, too alien, lost in the sound that was not a sound, dying slowly, and dust like smoke rising, broken stone, stone burning, and the cry of a god. He turned his face into her hand, kissed her palm, and went over the side of the caravanserai, straight down, landing on all fours, then fast as a horse could run, for the temple.

CHAPTER XXI

Hadidu woke with a cry, and Nour, who had just been drifting on the edge of waking, bolted up from the gate-captain's bed they were sharing, Jugurthos and Tulip having decamped to a sleeping-mat in the office and records-room so that anything coming after Hadidu would have to get by them first. They'd broken Hadi's promise to go up to Mikki, but they knew and trusted the men and women of the Sunset Gate, and besides, who knew they were here beyond those who'd been in the watch-room as they came in?

The room was lit white for a moment, and thunder crashed about them, but there was no sudden rumble of rain off the mountains beating on lower roofs below, only Hadidu like a child wakened from nightmare crying, "No! No!"

Ilbialla. In the blindness after the flash Nour saw her as he remembered her from childhood, as he remembered Hadidu's parents, the cobbler and his priestess wife: vaguely, and yet vivid in outline, important, essential. Ilbialla standing before him, in the form of a woman younger now than he would have thought her then, a plain and pleasant woman with her hair loose over her shoulders and a caftan that somehow rippled and seemed still deep water, touched by breath beneath the sky, blue and dark. It wasn't him she came for. She reached for Hadidu, and kneeling up on the bed he seized her hands, but they faded from his grip.

"Esau!" she cried. "Esau . . ." And there was nothing but Hadidu bowed over his knees, weeping.

Nour scrambled over to haul Hadidu to himself, as if he had been little Shemal, safe away in hiding outside the city. No need to ask. He needed to be of no family consecrated to the goddess to feel that loss, as if the earth beneath his feet had been torn away and he was falling. Being wizard was enough.

Hadidu, without a word, pulled away from him and flung back the shutters, letting in the murky dawn.

"She's dead, Nour," he said, turning back, methodically fastening his sandals, pulling on a caftan and tying the belt with hands that shook. "We've taken the city and won *nothing*." Nour found boots and coat and sabre, feeling old, and slow, and stunned, but his nerves woke when the latch of the door jumped. Tulip froze before the sabre's edge.

"Ju says, stay here till he sends back to let you know it's safe," the adjutant said. "We don't know what—"

Nour got out of the way, and Hadidu thrust her aside, striding out.

"Yes, that's what I said you'd do," the adjutant muttered. "Nour, I have to stay here. Don't let him go alone."

"No," he said, agreeing, and had to break into a run to catch his brother-in-law up. Still weak, he was out of breath by the time they reached the market square.

Nothing. No folk. The warehouses here, the houses along the market, gone. Impossible to tell even where the burnt ruin of the Doves had been. Broken timbers, drifted stone and brick, plumes of smoke where some kitchen or courtyard cookfire had already been kindled in anticipation of the day and now burnt debris. No living thing, not man or woman, child or dog, or cat or fowl, crawled over the rubble. A branchless stalk might have been the persimmon tree that had shaded the baker's stable. Their ally, though he had called them names and shaken fists when they were boys, climbing his persimmon tree and heedlessly bending the too-weak branches. The market square was pitted, thrown up in waves of mud and cobbles, and Ilbialla's tomb was gone.

They had prayed for that.

Jugurthos was there ahead of them, armed and stubble-chinned, looking like another sleepless night. He left off urgent converse with a courier-rider and caught Hadidu by the arm.

"Don't. The ground's hot."

Hadidu pulled free and continued on, as if deaf and blind to him. Nour perforce followed. The air shimmered over the ground. He would not have put a hand to the stones, but it seemed safe enough for shod feet. Jugurthos muttered and caught up with him.

"What was it?"

"A thunderbolt, an eruption of the earth, and earthquake and lightning together, how should I know? You're the damned wizard. There weren't many witnesses, and most can't agree what they saw. If it's over, we need to search those ruins. There might be survivors." But Jugurthos sounded doubtful. "Hadidu!"

Hadidu had dropped from sight, down the steps, the descent to Ilbialla's well. Nour kicked aside, then picked up a fragment of the tomb's carving. It carried the script no one could read, the word Ivah said must be Ilbialla's name, but the word was incomplete.

The water was low, murky. Nour remembered the place as always cool, damp, sweet with the scent of moss and water, and householders chattering as they came for water or to make some prayer, the garlands of flowers they would lay about the moss-grown grey block of stone they called the seat of the goddess, though she would more often be found, if you were not seeking her in need for some private word, sitting on the low wall surrounding the well in the evenings, while her priestess told the old stories and the folk of the ward gathered to listen.

It smelt stagnant, now, like a fouled cistern, as if underground the water no longer flowed clean.

Hadidu dropped to his knees there, where the water and the last step met, and dipped his hands. If he prayed, his prayer was silent. And brief. He rose abruptly and came back to them, sweeping them up the steps with a jerk of his head, his face set.

More than Jugurthos's street guards had ventured out onto the hot wasteland, now, and the folk of neighbouring streets were already at work shifting stone, crying out at a discovery amid this ruin and that, but they brought out nothing but bodies, most burnt beyond recognition, or they turned up naked bones.

"Ilbialla is dead," Hadidu said, and that set up a wailing among those gathering, though for many—but Nour was cynical as Talfan—it was an empty ritual of grief. They hadn't known her, grieved for her these thirty years, loved her. But they might grieve for loss of the hope they had had.

"Ilbialla is dead, but Marakand needs to keep her memory alive," Hadidu said, and they fell silent to listen. Nour hoped they didn't hear how Hadi's voice shook. Jugurthos glanced around and nodded at his guards, trying to hold more of the gathering folk of the ward back, and they parted to let them through. "We need to remember, how Ilbialla wanted us to live . . ."

It was good preaching, though there was no hope behind it; Nour knew his friend, close as a brother, in his bleak and defeated moods, when there was no purpose to going on except that not to do so was to break faith, and without that, what had all those folk up and down the marketside—so many dead now, who had gone to bed last night in hope—risked their lives all these years to shield him for? The false Lady still ruled in the temple, and an enemy who could slay the very gods could not be starved to surrender, which had been the hope of Jugurthos and the senate.

In the end Hadidu, sounding calm and practical, sent the folk to be directed by the street guard in the search for survivors and for bodies for burial. He tried to slip away, but he needed to be engulfed by Jugurthos's own guards to free him from the press of people wanting blessing and reassurance. Nour linked arms. He felt—strange, wounded, and dreaming, himself, but Hadidu looked chilled and grey, like a man pulled from drowning.

Lightning flared over Templefoot Ward, and the ground shuddered beneath them. Hadidu clutched Nour's arm. He hardly felt it. Something . . .

They retreated to the Sunset Gate fort again, for what safety that could offer—none, against the Lady—and watched the play of lightning, or whatever it might be, that lit up the dusty air. The Hall of the Dome had fallen. That wasn't all.

"There's no light," Nour said, realizing it, late, slow, and stupid. "No fire on the walls themselves. In this haze, we'd see the glow of it. The temple's unwarded."

Jugurthos gave him a long look, nodded once, something decided, but if Nour had been consulted, he didn't know for a moment on what. The Warden of the City headed down, snapping out names. Couriers. Orders to captains. Companies of militia, the wall-wardens . . .

Ah. Ilbialla was dead, but something had come upon the Lady, and *now* they were going for the temple. Too late.

CHAPTER XXII

Cursing. Northron cursing, worse than anything she'd ever heard from her father's *noekar*, damning the Lady and all devils and their unlikely ancestors, and she was choking. Ivah moaned, rolled over, difficult because—because she was being dragged backwards down a steep hillside, over stones and broken branches, by the hood of her coat. Nausea overwhelmed her and she threw up. Mikki's nose pressed to the back of her neck, cold and easing the pain a little. Her head throbbed as if she were being beaten with a hammer.

"Up," he rumbled. "Please, Ivah, up, if you can."

She wiped her mouth on a fistful of leaves and tried to obey, shaking, hands and knees first and then an arm over his shoulders. The morning light was thin and dim, barely dawn.

"What—" she croaked, and looked back, up the slope. Broken and tattered branches, but higher, near the crest, the trees were blasted flat, stripped of leaves, lying like grain swept by the sickle, all aligned.

"There's nothing we can do. Come down to the priest's hut. Your head's bleeding."

She touched the back of her head gingerly, found a swollen lump, and nearly squealed at the pain of it. Sticky fingers, but no great flow. She let go of the demon and started back up the hill. They had only come a few yards from where she had fallen.

"You can't help," he repeated, but he followed, thrusting his head under her hand when she groped for a supporting trunk and missed. The air was harsh and stinging with dust, wind swirling every which way, barely settling from whatever had done this. She had only been knocked out for a few moments. There was Mikki's axe and a caftan ripped to rags at the seams. He'd been upon her when the dawn took him. There the cloak and armour of the Red Mask, there her sabre, on the edge of the flattened trees.

"I slew three Red Masks in Fleshmarket," he said, low-voiced. "And sent some temple guard running, those that got away from me. I think the captain of the drovers' gate and all her guards are scattered, but the temple didn't hold it yet either, when I left. The company Jugurthos sent was in there when I left, but it was hard for them to tell who was who in the dark. I hunted a fourth Red Mask through into Templefoot, and he was nearly to the gates when he was suddenly an old corpse, and the earth of the lane began to take him. But that whole attack was meant to be a distraction, nothing more, I think, to lure me and the Blackdog away while the Lady slew you or took you. It was you she feared, not us, you and your spell to free the gods. I should have thought at the time and stayed put to protect you. I'm no war-leader, Ivah. I followed a captain when I sailed with my raider cousins, and now I leave the long thinking to Moth. Jugurthos would have known better than to leave you. Varro's dead."

"I know." She leaned on him a moment, catching her breath. "Zavel brought priests and temple guard."

"Zavel," he said, and then, unhappily, "Red Geir's sword. It draws betrayal, witting or unwitting, treachery or ill-luck. Someone should have thrown it down a well."

"The guardsmen that came with Ashir—are they—"

"I found them sneaking along the path from the menagerie when I was coming back to you. They're dead."

"All of them?"

"*Ya.* I think so. Covered in the blood of the old man and his poor old bear. They were too stupid to run. They thought I was one man, and easy." She nodded, which made her retch. "A priest, the Right Hand, tried to betray the temple. Zavel killed Varro. I killed him."

"There's a dead priest tied to a tree, down there."

"I tied him while I went to warn Belmyn the temple was here, but the Red Mask came. I heard him die. You didn't see the other one? The other priest or soldier or whatever he was? Dressed like a caravaneer?"

"No." He let her scramble after all up the last few yards, over the fallen trees. The view down into the next narrow wrinkle of the hill was eerily open, the bare-stripped trunks of the trees slanting uphill. Partway down the trees ended, and there was only a shifting greyness. Ash, she realized, stirring in the morning breeze. Just ash, and stone, earth baked hard and the stone fired glossy. Her eyes fixed on a white stone that was a skull, half buried in ash. The little stream that flowed from a spring across and up the valley still found a way down, bare and naked to the sky rather than fern-shrouded and secret. Steam hung over it. Ivah found she was on her knees.

"The library's still standing," Mikki said. "Hadidu and Nour would have been at the gate, if not out in the suburb with Kharduin. They should—they must be safe. Nothing you can do here. Come back down to the priests' steading now."

But then he flung his head up, teeth bared, and a heavy paw slammed her flat. He crouched above her as away over the city the sky lit white, like sheet-lightning over the desert. A breath later the deafening thunderclap struck them, and a wind. Ash swirled and rose from the valley, stinging against the skin.

"Great Gods have mercy," Ivah heard herself saying. "Old Great Gods have mercy. Mikki, that was—"

"Not wizard's work," he said, and his teeth dragged at her hood. "Up. That was over Sunset Ward."

"Nour—"

"Nothing you can do." Muffled, through clenched teeth and cloth, pulling her. "Come."

"Let me go, I can stand." But she shook, and tears were streaking her face. "Where?"

"You—Gurhan's cave. She's already attacked here. What need strike again? And if she does it'll be some shelter. Come!" He was ahead of her, angling down the naked hillside. She caught his urgency, tried to run, slithered into him, and went on clutching the thick fur of his shoulders, down to where ash swirled up about their feet, and he picked his way, keeping to the ash, twisting and leaping to avoid the bare baked earth. Heat beat up from it as from the sands of the Black Desert in the noon sun. No trace of her spell. There was a sword, twisted, melted, and hardening again, and a spearhead, no shaft. A helmet filled with ash, and another skull. Dead for nothing. Guarding nothing. Much of the devil's spell carved into the wall sealing the cave was still intact, but a hole was broken, gaping dark, and with Mikki shoving to hasten her she climbed over the old mound of landslide rubble and crouched on the edge of the blackness.

"Go."

"What about you?"

"Something I have to do. Go. Stay there till—till night, I don't know. Then get out of the city, unless—just get out." He pressed his muzzle to her cheek, warm breath and bristles, a kiss, she realized. "Save yourself. I don't know that this city can be saved, if I can't find Moth—just go."

"How can you find Moth? You couldn't before."

"One thing I haven't tried, and it may be the worst thing I could possibly do. Don't wait for me. I doubt I'll be coming back. Go, once night comes." He hesitated. "And get Holla's wife and take her with you, to the deserts. They may be safe, for a time, if I—if—if I'm about to put a weapon to war on the heavens within reach of a crazed devil."

"Gaguush will cut me down as soon as look at me."

"Be persuasive. Get Holla-Sayan's child away from Marakand, if you have to bespell the woman or hit her over the head to do it." Another bear's kiss, and then a shove that sent her sliding with a yelp down a long slope of rubble, into the darkness.

CHAPTER XXIII

N *o. No no no nonono it must not be it cannot be they must come he will come and he will see I've left the well and he will see me now he sees me now. Without Praitan without the east without my captain my king my commander of armies I cannot stand I cannot hold the pass will lie open to him I cannot we Marakand traitor Marakand he has ensnared them to his will already he is here he must be here he works in shadows he has done this she has done this traitor cuckoo child she leads me aside you lured me from the well you stayed my hand when I should have been strong your whispering goddess your dreaming god betrays your gods betray your city my city my safe castle.*

The dome groaned and grated above her. Zora rose slowly to her feet.

Do you think I did not see not hear how you whispered together how you danced?

The temple. She did not need it any longer. She could use it no longer. She could be goddess no longer. She had been lured out of her safe hidden place within the well, within the shell of the Lady of Marakand and the mask of the Voice of the Lady, seduced by the dancing girl's desire to rebuild and renew. Seduced by her own desire to be flesh again, and walk the world, and no longer to lie a cocooned grub, to act and not lie passive—but that had been her error. She was no empress, no Yeh-Lin or Tamghiz to rule, to take command into her own hands; her brother

had always said so and he was wise where she was a child. She was no
Ulfhild or Heuslar, to look at the land and her king's desires and say, to
achieve them we move here, strike there and this falls in some distant
place and that one must then move. She did not play chess or fox-and-
raven or the game of the white stones on the board of the living world,
she did not see the threads that led one thing to the next when the minds
and hearts of men were the pieces she moved. She did not understand,
and she had lost, and she had no wizardry left, because even the last frail
wisp of Sien-Mor on which she had anchored the first wizard to be Red
Mask must have been torn away.

The gods dared make league against her. Their priests called the
mountain out of the east to destroy her servants, her Red Masks, and the
demons of the north, and the mountains, and she had done all that she
had done to save their city, to save them, blind they could not see the
light she brought the hope the fire that would bar the pass against the
fire in the west and the sword came out of the forgotten night—

The gods watched her. She felt their awareness gathering, because
her spell had been weakened, had been damaged, cracked. It would hold,
yes, it would hold against mere human wizardry, it must, but they woke,
and they watched, they saw or they dreamed, they knew, Ilbialla and
Gurhan waking from sleep, their will reaching and with the dawn there
would be the Grasslander wizard crouched on her knees muttering as if
mad, Grasslander words Nabbani words her hands stained with blood
with the red dust the poison with ash barring her face and salt on her
tongue she whispered and she chanted and she wrote the name of Ilbialla
in the script of the Old Great Gods. How could she know she see she
hear she looked up into Zora's eyes. She had seen one so, chanting with
the bear's blood on his brow. Tamghiz. This wizard was his. She should
have known from the bear, by the bear she should have known him his
totem his worship his eyes so sly and mocking in the wizard-woman's
face and in her vision the woman licked her lips and tasted ash and wrote

again unseeing unknowing leagued with Ulfhild against her come as harbingers of her fall she was nothing without her brother she knew—

You think so? You and your gods? You think Tu'usha is so weak?

Zora spread her arms like a falcon at the height of its climb and shrieked, swept them down, tearing the veil of the worlds, flinging heart and soul against the wizard her enemy the tool of her enemies the god of the hill of the city which must stand fortress against the west, but the wizard was not there was only vision only what may might have been would in the dawn be—

—No! And she screamed aloud with Zora's voice, "No, Gurhan, no!" But it was done, and in the valley of Gurhan's cave it was as if the sky fell. The men and women there died in the instant, souls flung to the Great Gods' road in fire, and she drank the light that lit the sky through even the eye of the dome, spread to it as a flower to the sun, and felt the fire wake within her. But the girl Zora fell to her knees and struggled for her will, and she had to fight the both of them, the girl and the goddess, fight herself in their horror, rocking, clawing at her arms, her face, screaming at them, *If not mine then whose, then whose, traitor, I am Gurhan's given named to him at my birth I am the Lady I am Marakand and she you will not you must not I we will burn will drown the sword is ice is night is an ending coming hear me help me hold me give me strength only a little a little longer*, and a hand grasped hers, held it, Papa's hand cool and free of the fever Gurhan's hand sun-warm stone strong the Lady's hand old and knotted and withered, tenacious as old roots, they all held a part of her and Ilbialla stood behind Gurhan and reached to her—

Her enemies gathered. *Smoke and scarlet fires twisting into a pillar. Sword like a splinter of stone, spinning frost across the stars.* She had seen that before, when she dreamed in the well. A black smoke shot with lightning that flew with a hurricane's speed, and her Voice had known them when she cried, *Death is walking the road of death of dreams of walking death is sleep is ice is death*, and they did not see she fought to save them blind they were and in their blindness served the end of all things and when all was at stake there was no room for pity for mercy for remembering the little gods and the little souls did they not see—

Plaster. Mortar. Stones, raining on her.

Not yet no not yet not now, wait he comes I come I will keep you safe hold you against the world only wait and I will be with you. Her voice, the Lady's, they had been the one and she did not know whose these thoughts were. The god of the hill called to the girl within her and she longed for his promises, the dead demon who had guarded her and been her friend in the fire when all was peace . . . he would come. He promised. And meanwhile, she would be safe within her wall of flame.

Zora crawled for the door, as the dome came down in thunder.

Where?

Voices cried, clamoured. She stood atop a hill of fallen stone, gaping pits about her, tilted blocks, dust yellowing the air, clogging nose, itching on her skin, her eyes weeping with it. Hill of stone, she at its height just touched by the dawn's first light. Ruin of the Hall of the Dome. She looked about. Priests. Temple guard. Servants. All huddled distant, as far as they could be and yet still gawk at her ruin. Fear was on them, horror, terror. No reverence, no. No adoration. What did they see but a madwoman in a ragged gown, hair in knots, face bleeding, hands stained, and the blood all caked with dust? And they were trapped with her within the temple, where their own choices had brought them, their own fault; they had loved her and they betrayed her, they had nothing to bewail now.

Godless Marakand. It had betrayed her. Zora betrayed herself.

"You abandoned your gods for me," she said conversationally, but they were too far away to hear, most of them. "You did. So they will die. You could have been strong. You could have been a fortress and held the pass of the Malagru, you could have been an empire, but you were too weak too useless you could not even be led be driven where you should have gone you only cowered and crept and your weakness betrayed me."

My weakness betrayed me I was too weak too wandering too lost in mad Sien-Mor she betrayed me she made me weak she makes all fail. They betrayed me to her.

And now the night comes.

Again she gathered herself. "Do you think I need *pretend* to be a god?" she cried to the staring priests. "No gods in Marakand. Only the Lady and the Lady, I am the Lady. If you are not mine, then whose?" She flung lightning to clear them from her sight, swept courtyards and the narrow passages between the buildings with the sheeting fire. Few had time even to scream, as bones burst and flesh became ash, and the gardens turned to baked clay.

And then she struck again, with all her will and all her strength, dropping fire like a shooting star to obliterate tomb and well and goddess and all, in the market where Ilbialla stirred in nightmare dreams and reached to cry out to her priest.

No more hiding.

No more gods.

She was Tu'usha the Lady of Marakand, and she did not know why she wept.

CHAPTER XXIV

U p the ravine of the dry river beneath the city walls was fastest, for the dog. Holla-Sayan had not forgotten the fires that ringed the temple. He went up the crumbling cliff and over the roofs of the houses there, down into Greenmarket Ward. There were no folk, despite the fear of earthquake, in the streets near the temple. Hiding indoors to await events; he doubted any were still abed. A drift of ash and brick and discoloured stone followed the temple wall itself, houses that had been. The fire flared and crackled as he passed, rising higher, heat stretching tendrils to take him. No illusion, and not wizardry, either. Into Templefoot Ward. A cloud of dust hung over the temple itself, and it was a moment before he noticed what he did not see, the absence of the high Hall of the Dome. Time to find out if he could walk through this devil's fire, he supposed. Somewhere along here there should be enough rubble he could leap to the top of the wall. If he survived so far—he smelt the bear before he saw Mikki, in the shadow of an abandoned coffeehouse across from the temple gates, and loped up to him.

"Knew you'd come here," Mikki rumbled. "Take that." A paw knocked something slithering over cobbles to his feet, and he jumped back before it could touch him. Lakkariss. Damned and damning sword, he'd thought it lost with Moth. And he did not want it lying at his feet.

What has she done? Where's Ivah?

"Ivah's safe, for now. Varro's dead. Something cut the Red Masks free of her, not Moth, and the devil's tried to destroy the gods," said Mikki, and Holla-Sayan listened, watching the fire, while the demon told him of the night's happenings. At some point he shifted to man's shape and, doomed and damned devil he was, took up the sword. The weight was only what he might have expected of a long Northron blade, but the cracked leather scabbard was cool under his hand. And the leather itself tooth-marked.

Varro. He felt as if he'd been struck a blow, but there was no time, no place for grief. Or guilt. He should have been there to fight in the Fleshmarket in Mikki's place. And all those daughters fatherless. Sayan, Attalissa forgive.

His fault beyond that. Moth had told him to get Red Geir's sword off Varro, who had picked it up on the battlefield at Lissavakail, some Northron tale of a curse. He had told Varro so, but the Northron had laughed, and a man couldn't go stealing his friend's sword—

"I can't use that," he said of Lakkariss. He could feel it now, growing, not exactly heavier, but as if it knew his hand and pulled him to it. "I'm not strong enough."

"Not to fight the devil," Mikki said. "I know what Moth says of you, and she's not trying to be insulting, usually, just saying what's true. Maimed and soul-scarred and weak. But strong enough to take the sword, yes, you are, Blackdog. You'd better be, or it will take you. It's nothing to me. Just an edge. It only lives for her. But in your hands it should remember it's ice—and that's fire, and I can guess which is stronger of those two. Lakkariss." He growled. "You think I don't know what it is? A weapon forged by the Old Great Gods, hah. Maybe. Out of what? Bloody devils, the pair of you, keeping secrets. The damned sword wants to take Moth, doesn't it? So it can bloody well find her. But if you and I are such fools as to let that mad devil get a weapon that can cut a way into the cold hells—we will be justly damned by all the gods of the earth and the Old Great Gods as well. But Moth's in there. Somewhere. And she *can* fight this devil. She just—she needs to want to."

Holla-Sayan, reluctantly, slung the baldric over his shoulder and drew the sword. The tapering blade was obsidian. Maybe. It drank the light. Ice that might cut steel. It seemed to fill the world, as if he fell into it, and vision grew stained with copper light: black ice, black stone, fires prisoned deep within, and in the white sky the moons bled into towering clouds. Mikki was gone to shadows, as of movement under trees, and the scent of forest earth. Then the blade grew into a crack in the world, a fracture into darkness. Mikki nudged him and his other hand found the amulet bag and the stone of Sayan's barkash. He had told the child-goddess there was magic in it, that first day. *So we always know our home, and our gods know us.* It was only a reminder, now, that he knew his home and the promise his god had made him. No power in that, not against Lakkariss, which cared nothing for gods of the earth, but it was good to remember. He made himself see only the glossy surface, and the edge, and hoarfrost forming on it. So. He would set the ice of the cold hells against the devil's fire.

Frost painted ferns on the blade; they smoked away and grew again, but banners of fog began to coil about him as he walked into the heat. The flames leaned away, as if Lakkariss were a wind blowing against them, and they turned from yellow-white to scarlet, twisted and hissed. The shadows grew strange, light falling from every direction, disorienting, as the fire closed about him, Mikki keeping close at his left side, and the sky grew copper stained, but a greenish flame streaked his hands, and there was a sound like water rising in his ears, words in it, but he could not hear. He set the point of Lakkariss to the cobbles of the gateway at his feet, there, where the line of fire ran blinding white, rooted in the stone and shivered, cold. For a moment he seemed to be the sword, to know what it was to be ice. The air hissed, and a slick of ice ran before him up the gilded wood of the carven gates. The whole line of fire died, hissing, steaming, like a torch plunged into water, all along the temple wall.

"Hah," Mikki said.

Rather more than what he had intended. Someone was bound to notice that.

He was no damned wizard, to blast the gates out of his path, but knocking did not seem likely to gain them admittance. Barred or locked? Mikki reared back and smashed his shoulder against them, once and again, and the second time they lurched inward. Without needing to discuss it, they shoved them wide. Holla-Sayan was dizzy, pulled off balance, vision still filled with a wash of copper light and hearing with a howling, empty wind. He went cautiously down the dark slope of the tunnel with Mikki at his side, but nothing came to oppose him, not so much as a trembling priest. Lakkariss was easy in his hand, but the air was very cold. It smoked like a river in a winter's dawn, and the fog wrapped tendrils around his arm.

The remnants of two Red Masks lay one to either side of the end of the passageway, dirty red robes, swords, staves of some pale wood, as threatening as any cowherd's stick and no more.

He could smell the devil: old sweat, unwashed skin, illness, metal and stone. And stone-dust over all. Timbers burnt, several buildings had fallen and were burning from whatever kitchen fires or lamps had been lit within. No one gathered to fight the flames. There were folk about, he could smell them, but they hid. Shadows scurried in the corners of his eyes, pale, ghostlike things, but they were living folk. Nothing, to Lakkariss. Ephemeral creatures of a lesser world. The great Hall of the Dome, where once when he was new to Marakand he had gone to see the pretty young dancers in a public worship, was a pile of rubble. The court-yards, as they followed paths that way, were littered with bodies, mostly ash and bone, as if fire had rained down from the sky on a gathered crowd.

A white-robed figure moved atop the rubble, swaying, twisting, feet light and sure on the shifting stones that grated and tumbled clattering beneath her.

A column of light and smoke, nacreous shimmer against the rising sun. She saw him, too, and stood in her dance as if frozen.

The air was very cold.

"Mikki . . ." He couldn't look away. *Moth went into the well, looking for the true Lady.*

I've been to the well. I found Ivah and Nour. You were there.

I can—not smell—just—far away. In the well. Within the Lady. Thought slowed, alien. The dog had no words of its own.

It wasn't he the devil watched. It was the sword.

You'll have to go, Mikki. Call her somehow. Make her hear. Take Lakkariss. You need—

No! He could feel himself falling, feel the sword's edge, piercing, to sever soul from soul, the blade turned against him in his own hand and the false Lady's fingers closing the leather-wrapped grip. *Take it out of that one's reach.*

The dust-heavy air was coppery-sullen and lit with streaks of silver light, blurs and swirls. There was ice, and the wind howled, pulling him. Pressure on his wrist, and the world was gold again, and grey with stone, white plastered walls and blowing ash. He was on his knees, and Mikki had taken his wrist in his jaws.

I see what you mean, yes.

Did she—

She, nothing. You were starting to, ah, dissolve, I suppose, into a sort of cloud of light and smoke? Very dark. Like a slow thunderstorm. Wonder what that says about the state of your souls? Hold onto me and sheathe the damned thing, then.

The demon let him go, and grounded, forehead pressed against the bear's flank, Holla-Sayan shoved Lakkariss home, hauled the baldric off again. Frost shook away from his hand, sparkling.

"I envy your hands now, bloody unnatural beast that you are," Mikki said. "Give it here."

He wrapped the belt about the scabbard, watching the devil over Mikki's humped shoulder. She still stood. No fire gathered about her, no indrawing of power prickled along his spine. Hands hidden. She didn't know what they did.

Run, he said, and went over Mikki's back as the bear snatched the sword. The dog was faster, and making for the devil, weaving through courtyards and over ruined garden walls, up the mountain of rubble.

She swung to face him, arms raised, and lightning washed over him, but he flung it aside as if he'd raised an arm. Maybe he had no body, maybe he was light, smoke, the fire of another world, and maybe she was a column of light and liquid flame, but she smelt like an ill and unwashed woman. His teeth met in her shoulder and as he struck he flipped and threw her.

She landed on her feet with a sword in her hand, came down on him silent, teeth bared in pain or ecstasy, and then she was beside him, where she had not been, and he had not seen her move. Her sword was real enough and so was the slash in his flank. He rolled away and came up on two feet, sabre in hand, circling, drawing her so her back was to the Dome of the Well. He could hold her off longer so, maybe. Maybe. If she would be drawn to fight sword to sword and play him a little while, before she struck to kill.

CHAPTER XXV

They rode only a couple of miles from the *dinaz* before Ghu called a halt. Ahjvar was falling asleep and jerking awake with coughing. Deyandara couldn't understand why she wasn't in as bad a state, or worse, but the time when the air seemed to freeze her lungs slipped like water through her mind, past and away, nightmare memory, no more. She eyed the pale dog, running ahead. A demon, maybe? It seemed to belong to Ghu. And Catairanach had called him a spirit, not a man. He seemed like a man when he embraced her, all smoke and old stale sweat and horses, needing a bath as badly as the rest of them. And how had she been able to smell him at all? More proof the dog—it had to have been the dog—was something more than what it seemed. Ghu's face had left a smear of blood on hers. A spirit should be—she didn't know what. Shaped of air and light, the servant of some god or goddess of the earth, sent—what, out of Nabban to follow a cursed and undying assassin? To rescue, three times and hopefully she would not need rescuing a fourth, an unregarded Praitannec princess? The gods of Nabban should have greater cares.

But there were halfling gods in the world, the songs said, human children of gods or goddesses, wizards, some of them, or seers, or ordinary men and women who spoke truth and saw more of the shape of things, and grew into wisdom that shared, a little, in their divine parent's nature. What Hyllau should have been.

341

Ghu led them in under the eaves of a walnut grove, a royal woods, it had been. There was a spring there, godless, no more than a trickle, running away between green mints and bulrushes, but he went to it as if he had known it was there. Ahjvar drank with his face in the water, drank as if he had not seen water in a month, and rolled over among the roots with his arm over his face and his sword flung yards away. He said something to Ghu in the true Nabbani she couldn't follow, and Ghu answered with what seemed reluctance. Something about waking up, she thought. She drank almost as greedily and moved down the channel to the next small pool to wash herself. Ghu came and prodded her shoulder, then took her arm from the sling and cut the immobilizing bandages off. It hurt, but it felt better that way, too.

"Don't use it much for a while," he cautioned.

"Yes. Ghu—" She couldn't ask him about the dog. She knew it had breathed into her; she had felt it, felt her lungs eased, but it sounded so strange to say it. *Did you know your dog was a demon, or something?* "Are you a physician, too?" That sounded like it was a joke, like she was making fun of him, when he'd said he was a slave and a groom.

He laughed. "No. But I've fallen off a lot of horses."

"You?"

"How do you think I learnt not to fall off of horses? Go to sleep, lady. I'll watch."

"You look not as bad as Ahjvar, and that's all. You should rest, too."

"Later."

"Wake me up after a little. I can at least keep watch."

"You can keep watch. No 'at least.' But later. Sleep now. Not," he added, "too close to Ahjvar." His eyes grew solemn, tired. Sad. He was years older than her, she thought. Strange. She couldn't think he was a boy at all now, even when she tried to see under the smoke and the blood and the grey weariness. She nodded and lay down where the ground was dry and the sound of the running water a comfort. The black-and-tan dog, she saw, had gone to lie by Ahjvar, head on its paws, eyes closed but still alert. Guarding, or guarding against.

The pale dog curled into a ball, tail over its nose, but it opened half an eye to watch her a moment, and shut it again. It looked as though it were winking.

Deyandara woke with a jerk at noise, the sudden roaring of the wind in the leaves as if a great river rushed by, creak of branches bending, both dogs barking and the horses whinnying. She was on her feet before she was fully awake, the small knife she had stolen in the hall in her hand, for what good it would do. Ahjvar was on his feet, his sword drawn. Ghu stood by a little fire and a pair of steaming pots with a dog to either side, but his arms were folded. He looked skywards. Leaves, twigs, tore and spun. There was cloud lit by streaks of fire, white like lightning, red like blood and glowing coals, pouring down before him. And then a woman, standing legs braced, hands on hips, her hair, long and black, still rising and twisting with the wind.

"*You!*" she hissed. "You *buried* me."

"Yes," said Ghu, and caught Ahjvar as he would have put himself between Ghu and the woman. Wizard. Lin.

"Lin!" Deyandara said, and then, uncertain. "Your hair—"

"Yes, yes, really, child, you need to learn to see what matters. You should have said, long ago, 'You're not half so old as you look.' Which would have been more perceptive and less true. And why aren't you with Marnoch?"

"You left me. You crept away in the night. Ketsim's men attacked—" She could hear the tears starting in her voice and shut her lips, furious.

"I was on my way to Marakand, to find the master of the Red Masks."

"The Red Masks," Ghu said softly, "are free and gone. You gave your word to protect Deyandara."

He hardly ever used her name. Ahjvar had shifted off to the side, where he had more room to move. As if he were Ghu's spearman. Lin hardly seemed to notice him.

"I would have done so. The Red Masks are—were—the keystone of the Marakander occupation. Without them, do you think any rabble of Grasslanders and city thief-takers could hold a *duina* of Praitan?" But Lin's anger seemed to have evaporated with the cloud and died with the wind. She sighed, giving him a long, long look, after which she glanced aside at Ahjvar at last, frowning. Then turned to Deyandara, not with her usual amused, superior smile, but solemn, and put her hands together, bowing.

"I'm sorry, my lady," she said. "I judged my duty badly. I'm grateful there were others on hand able to save you from my—impulse." To Ghu she bowed even lower. "I am not," she said, "become so wise or so patient as I had thought, it seems." She looked again at Ahjvar, her frown deepening, and said something to Ghu in Imperial Nabbani.

Ahjvar made some retort, and Ghu smiled. Lin looked a little abashed and gave Ahjvar a brief bow before walking away, with an again-imperious jerk of her chin at Ghu.

He followed. What man wouldn't, Deyandara thought. But he touched Ahjvar's hand as he passed.

"I made coffee," he said. "There's soup. Eat. My lady, see he does."

Ahjvar scowled after them and looked as if he would follow. The dogs did, hackles bristling. But then he sighed and sank down on his heels by the fire. "Deya, what is she?"

"A wizard," Deyandara answered. "My tutor. But that—" she pointed vaguely skyward, through the leaves. "You saw? That wasn't wizardry. Was it?"

"Stories," he said. "The emperor's wizards of Nabban could tame the winds. Maybe. But I'd never heard they turned themselves to smoke and lightning."

The coffee was boiling over in froth, and he just sat, head hanging, so Deyandara wrapped the end of her sooty shawl around the handle of the pot and took it off the fire. The other pot was soup, or at least, what looked like chunks of breadroot, famine food, boiling with some very small joints of meat. Squirrel? Two squirrels? It was cooked, whatever it was, and hot, and since Ghu and Lin were having what looked like an intense conversation away among the trees, she rummaged in his bundle and found not only a very old-looking scroll-case but a carved wooden cup for the coffee, a wooden bowl, and horn spoon. She served out about half the soup and gave it to Ahjvar, who seemed only interested in the coffee, wrapping his hands around it, eyes closed, but he did look less grey after he had drunk it. The burns on his arms and face were already healing. He ate when she told him to, throwing the bones of whatever small beast it had been into the fire, and his hands stopped shaking. He didn't look at her but at the flames.

She had to speak. She couldn't ride on with him, not knowing.

"Catairanach said . . . but I didn't believe her. She said—is she mad?"

"Not mad," he said slowly. "I don't think mad. That thing in Marakand is mad. Catairanach is merely obsessed, on one point alone, past reason. And that is the root of evil. I think." He opened his eyes and looked at her, really looked at her, thoughtful, not annoyed, or disdainful, or seeing her some burden he had to deal with. "I wonder if Hyllau poisoned her, too, fed that all-consuming instinct of a mother for the protection of an infant child, made it grow into that obsession? Catairanach has not acted as a goddess for the whole of her folk since, oh, my grandmother's day, I think, given the stories I've heard. Maybe longer. The hag used to boast she'd been lifetimes in the womb of the goddess, before she ever was born into the world."

"Catairanach said you were—she wants you to marry me, and she says you're my—if it's true, that's—wrong." Deyandara blushed and poked a few sticks into the fire. It was a small fire, mostly old twigs, and they burnt up quickly.

"I'm your grandfather's grandfather. Or possibly your great-grandfather's uncle."

"Don't you know?"

"Does it matter?"

"You could do a divination. Draw wands. You're a wizard, if you're—him."

"What difference would knowing make? Hyllanim was a baby, always about underfoot." He grinned. "He had an honest wizard for guardian and regent, who did well enough by him. He was as good a king as he could be in a bad time, and his fratricidal children didn't quite destroy the *duina* between them." He was still watching her. "You want to ask? But you know the story of the day of the three kings, little bard."

"I'm not a bard."

"I know."

"You didn't poison your father."

"I've poisoned people. I make my living at killing."

"You didn't poison your father."

"I was sleeping with my father's wife," Ahjvar said. "Before he married her, and after. I had no intention of marrying her myself. I was young and stupid and besotted, but not quite stupid enough for that, even then. It was easier, because she had no intention of marrying me. I wasn't king yet, you see. So she married my father, who was. And Hyllanim was born, and I doubt even Catairanach knew who his father was. The hag certainly didn't. I suspect he was mine. The curse, my curse, struck so strongly on his line and his land, when it was half myself I cursed. But that was later. After a couple of years Hyllau was more than a little weary of being wife to an old man who hadn't quite managed to see through her but who certainly had more wits about him than she liked in a husband and kept her firmly in her place as his pretty young bride, and not the power over the *duina* she thought she should be. So she decided it was better to be a young widow, and bride of a younger king more easily led by his—more easily ruled in bed. She poisoned the old man one night.

"I loved my father," Ahjvar said softly. His voice had grown softer, slower, and the Nabbani words she never noticed, because even in the high king's hall everyone spoke that way, were dropping out. "And we had done nothing but fight, since Hyllau came to the *dinaz*. She poisoned him. So I went to kill her. She had been born with far too much of a goddess's power of will over the world. Most gods have more sense than to let so much of what they are pass to a mortal child. She—we burned. I don't know if she meant us both to die together, when she saw I had come to kill her, or if she thought, being what she was, she could survive it. In the dawn I was still alive, in the ashes. Catairanach bound Hyllau's ghost into me, and it kills to keep itself alive. And that is why I have nightmares and why you're not safe sleeping in the same room with me. You do look like her. Somewhat."

He carefully poured the dregs of the coffee into his cup, carefully wrapped both hands around it. They were shaking again. She was glad he had added the "somewhat." But she couldn't think what she could say, as he drank the coffee. She wanted to put a hand on him and tell him it was all right, but what was? He flung the grounds hissing on the fire.

"Deya, do you want to be queen of the *duina*?"

"Marnoch and the lords who rode with him named me so. But the goddess won't bless me, and anyway, you're—"

"I'm not fit to be king. I know what I've done, the past ninety years, even if Catairanach chose to ignore the irony in her fine speech to Hicca's folk. Catairlau—is dead. Ahjvar's no king and would be better hanged. But what do you *want*?"

A horse and a dog and songs. That was all she had ever wanted. To be that . . .

"A singer," she said slowly. "To make songs, and carry them. To put myself into what I do, to be a bard in truth, to learn, this time. Not to be a child, in—in tempers and haste and spite. I can't do what Marnoch does, lead men. I know it. I'm just a banner to them. Marnoch made me queen because he thought it was right to do so and he needed to show his command was sanctioned by a queen, to try to unite the lords. Ketsim stole me thinking he could do the same thing by marrying me, placate the goddess and save his folk from the pox. My brother Durandau will use me to rule the Catairnans. Hicca would have killed me to deny me to Durandau and Marnoch both."

"Ketsim." Ahjvar kept to himself so carefully it was a shock, now that the night was past, when he reached and touched her, a finger resting gentle on the back of her hand. "You all right?"

It took a moment for her to realize what he was asking. She didn't even blush, only shrugged. "There was a wedding. He was ill with the southern pox, fevered. He just—he talked a while, told me about his other wives. Then he went to sleep."

A snort of laughter escaped him. "I wish you better conversation, next time. But Marnoch will talk of dogs and horses and where the deer are moving."

"How do you know?"

"A lord of the Red Hills? Marnoch's a name in that family; I've never heard it used in any other hall. And what else is a lord of the Red Hills going to talk of, but his dogs and his horses and his deer? Some things never change."

"I like dogs and horses and deer."

"Not a problem then, unless he talks all night."

Now she felt her face heating.

He grinned. "Not a queen, but a bard. Whom shall we make king?"

"I can't just—"

"*I* can. And you were acknowledged queen, Catairanach notwithstanding. You have a right to stand aside and appoint your own successor. Probably more than I do. I say, we make a king—or a queen—and damn Catairanach."

"Marnoch," she said. It didn't require thought. A man of the *duina*.

A man the lords, well, most of them, would follow. A person who'd shown himself fit to be a king, by what he'd said and what he'd done.

"You'll not be a queen, but a king's wife?"

"He's never said anything. That's not why . . ." He was teasing, absurdly lighthearted, as if he'd settled something that had weighed him down. She wouldn't have thought he cared so much. She hadn't thought she'd shown so much of what she'd hardly known.

"Ghu!" Ahjvar called. "Come eat. We need to ride."

Ghu was already on his way back, alone, his face expressionless.

"Where's the wizard?"

"Yeh-Lin went back to the *dinaz*. She took one of the horses."

"Why?"

"*Yeh*-Lin?" Deyandara turned the name over on her tongue.

Ghu shook his head when she offered him the soup pot. "I'm not hungry. You two finish it."

He stayed with the two remaining horses while they did so, combing out tangled manes and tails with his fingers. Deyandara washed the dishes and packed them up again. Ahjvar just sat, watching Ghu, putting a fresh edge on his thinned and worn sword.

CHAPTER XXVI

"What's wrong with him?" Yeh-Lin demanded, with a tilt of her head at the blond man, and Ghu said curtly, "He speaks good Nabbani."

"A very civilized barbarian," the assassin growled. He looked half dead and willing to fling himself on her at a word from his master regardless. She felt an uneasy reluctance to have to fight him, though damn, but she wanted to fight something. Or maybe scream and stamp her feet and throw rocks at some blameless, pristine pool of water? Yes, that would be about as helpful. Face it, she was in a temper and a sulk, because that—Ghu, and what kind of a name was that for him to use, a slave's name—had taken her unawares and gotten the better of her. For a little she had been terrified, till she realized he hadn't meant to seal her down for good; it had been only a matter of careful working, to unshape the forces of will holding her. Which had given her a pretty good idea of just what he was. Not, as she had first thought, a young dragon, ingenuously flinging that selfsame accusation at her. No, she had the shape of him, improbable, impossible though that was. Not that she was going to let that intimidate her.

She snorted and turned her back, with a jerk of the head, inviting him to follow. He did. And if he hadn't, she would have looked an utter fool. She took a few long, calming breaths as she walked, stood stretching and breathing, waiting for him, feeling the earth under her feet, an ancient trunk at her back. She leaned against it, arms folded, eyes, for a moment, shut, finding some calm balance again. There was no point to anger and temper. He had gone out of his way not to hurt her. And he had been right to stop her, had perhaps saved her. What could rushing into the mess of Marakand have done? Old comrades, old tensions, old patterns . . . she had chosen to walk away from that. She was not strong enough, she had just proven so by her temper, to resist falling into old reactions, whatever her tree had thought. Deyandara could have died when she so rashly left her, and she had grown fond of the girl.

"So," she asked again, opening her eyes, "Your assassin. What's wrong with him?"

"He's cursed," Ghu said warily.

He might have been able to hurt her, but he would not take her by surprise a second time. She did not think he could defeat her, though a victory would not come easily . . . he was not her enemy and she should not think so.

"Cursed how?" she asked instead.

"He's possessed by the ghost of his stepmother. His goddess has ensured he will never die, to be a vessel for that soul on the earth." He gave her truth, at least, as simple and blunt as if he did not understand what he was saying. But he knew. Indeed.

"Possessed by a heavens-damned vampire of some sort, I should say." She frowned. Deyandara and the man were talking intently, and the girl was pressing food on him. "What does it feed on? Him?"

"On him. On death. On dying."

Her anger boiled up again. With cause, this time. "And you let this go on?"

He said nothing.

"You, who managed to bind me, even for a short while, you let this go on?"

"I couldn't have done anything. Not then. Not when I found him. Now, since I found him again here—not without killing him."

Too much denial, there. She knew the sound of guilt. "Then you should have killed him. Does he actually want to live, like that?"

"No. He wants to die. And I love him."

"If you love him, then you'll let him die."

"He can't die. I can kill him, but he can't just . . . die. He won't grow old, he won't fall to some arrow, a swordsman won't take his head. The arrow will miss or not strike deep, the blade will slip and glance aside. . . . There's not a god in Praitan or the Tributary Lands can or will free him from these curses. He was made what he is with the full strength of this *duina*, in anger and hatred and death. I can't take it away from him and let him go on as he should, to whatever fate comes. I can destroy him as I did the Red Masks. Or not."

"You aren't some small god of Praitan and the Tributary Lands. Turn that thing in him out to die, at least."

"Catairanach won't allow it. She's bound them, till Hyllau can be born a new child, and now that he knows, he won't, of course he won't let that be. I can't see a way to separate them. Catairanach pours herself into this binding, and this is her land. He was her king, born of this land. He is hers. I can't change that or deny it, only tear both of them from the goddess together and hope Ahj will be free of his hag then, for the road to the Old Great Gods. Hyllau's final death will be his as well, at my hand. And I promised him, if she wakes again . . . that I would. She will wake. It's 'when', not 'if.'"

"Every life he's taken since you—since you chose not to be other than what you are—"

"I didn't choose. I was sent. I *am* not. I become. Slowly."

"That's dicing words, child of Nabban. Every death is on you."

"Some of them he would have killed anyway," Ghu protested, and he heard the boy in his own voice again.

The corner of Yeh-Lin's mouth tucked up. "And some you killed yourself," she said. "I see it in your eyes, and you are not easy in that. And some I would have killed and saved you the bother, yes. But you admit it, you know it. Those deaths are all yours, not his."

"Yes. Of course they are. I chose. He didn't."

"You chose for him and god or not you had no right."

"*I am no god.*"

She gave him a long, cool look. "And what do you call yourself, then?"

He shook his head. "Ghu."

"And did they drop you on your head when you were born, Ghu? Are you the simpleton you played for Deyandara?"

He almost smiled. "Yes," he said. "Sometimes. And no. They threw me in the river."

"The evidence," she snapped, "does nothing to deny me. They dropped you on your head first, then they threw you in the river. Idiot. Child of Nabban."

He opened a hand, not denying but letting the words fall away.

"Oh, damn the both of you," Yeh-Lin muttered. "You love him. If you have to kill him, it had better be for his own sake. Lend me a horse? You owe me that. No, you don't, don't say it, my folly left the girl to Ketsim and you owe me nothing, but I'm tired, too tired to bind the winds. I dislike very much being buried, you have no idea . . ."

"Where are you going?" Ghu asked, as she started for the horses.

She didn't look back. "To take on a new sin of my own," she said. "Or expiate some old ones."

He didn't stop her. The horses were muscular Grasslanders, two bays and a dark chestnut. She took the first that came to her hand, with a narrow-eyed glance back at Ghu, still watching. *See, they don't run sweating and white-eyed over the horizon, hah.* The curious chestnut filly did flinch back when she tried to stroke her but let her fasten the

bridle again and tighten the girth. Leading the horse, she slipped away
through the woods, out into the open land, without Deyandara and the
assassin noticing. She didn't want words and demands. She didn't want
to have to pass by Ghu. He hadn't asked anything more. She would have
answered, but he hadn't asked.

The hill-fort smoked against the sky, still and dead, stinking of death.
No people stirred about it. Somewhere inside, a dog was whining, crying
heartbroken. The hedged fields along the brook had a weedy, untended
look, with pigs rooting among the peas and cabbages. Straying horses
and a lone camel grazed a field of green grain. Hay meadows had been
ridden across, and recently.

The folk couldn't all be dead. Fled, more like. She might be watched
from the wooded seams of the folded hills. Yeh-Lin followed the brook,
then the narrow stream that ran down to feed it, the goddess's heart in
the world. The water ran clear and stone-cold; she could smell it, and
she was thirsty, but she didn't drink, though she paused to let the horse
do so. Mint and forget-me-not, creamy curds of waterleaf, touch-me-not
and the broad swords of iris-leaves traced its course. White butterflies
stirred up in clouds before her.

The goddess did not rise to greet her. Yeh-Lin dismounted and left
the horse, walked the last few yards to the spring itself. It was shadowed by three big mountain ash trees, heavy with hard green berries. A
sparrow winged away in silence, frightened from the lush grasses about
the water. The pool was deep and clean, the stones a golden brown in the
leaf-scattered patterning of the afternoon sun.

Catairanach was aware of her, no doubt of that. Yeh-Lin drew her
sword and walked a circle, sunwise, about the spring and its guardian
trees. This would not be human wizardry, but the forms might as well
be, to settle her mind. Best not to go into this in anger, to scar the earth
with devilry more than she had to. She began to trace words of binding

and sleep in the Great Gods' script at the cardinal points, standing within the circle. A white mist rose over the water.

What are you doing? Lady of Marakand . . .

"Oh, I'm not the Lady," Yeh-Lin said cheerfully, letting her tongue do as it would, her mind mostly elsewhere. "Be glad. She would destroy you. Or he. She might be he, you know. I'm merely here as, hrm, a friend of the folk you've neglected and abused over the years."

I have neither neglected nor abused my folk! Any harm done them is laid at Marakand's door. I couldn't fight the Lady.

"I didn't mean that. Not that you put much effort into your defence," she added critically. "You've crippled yourself. Bound too much of yourself into this curse on the vampire soul and the man you've tied her to, I should think."

"I never cursed my daughter!"

"You think she'd say so, if she were whole and in her right mind? Or was she ever? I ask out of curiosity, mind you. I do not actually care. But you don't deny cursing the man Ahjvar, I note. You meant to destroy his very soul, to make him watch himself decay to something unbearable, until in madness he became nothing but a howling in the night and there was nothing left for the Old Great Gods to claim and heal."

He betrayed her. He killed her.

There was a figure now, half-seen in the corner of the eye, mist tinted with human colour.

"Did he? It seems to me there is king's law, in this land, before which even a goddess could bring such an accusation."

He was the king.

"And then there is the high king over him and the court of the seven kings. And of course, outright vengeance and murder. What you have done, however, is obscene. It taints the very earth."

Tendrils of mist reached and touched her, twining about her ankles. Touched the script as she finished the last word and recoiled.

A word of her own, and light like fire poured along the letters, white and golden and cold as ice. Yeh-Lin stepped down into the water. The goddess screamed outrage and boiled up into a column of fog. The spring convulsed in waves like a lake storm-beset.

"What have you done? What are you doing?"

The goddess stood amid the waters, naked, her arms raised as if denying the light, but it did not fail. The waves soaked Yeh-Lin to the waist.

"I have no right to set myself up as a judge of gods—or of men, for that matter. But who else is there, who will call you to judgement for the harm you've done to your land and your folk? To your kings?"

"*My* folk," Catairanach said. "*My* land. *My* kings."

"Yes," said Yeh-Lin. "And that is your only defence? That they are yours? Well, then. So be it."

She caught the goddess by the hand and almost laughed at Catairanach's offended face, startled out of her rage. The goddess had not thought herself so material a form. But neither was Dotemon. Water hissed around her. Yeh-Lin dropped her sword and clutched with both arms, like an embrace, like a wrestler, pinning Catairanach close as water hissed and spat against fire, and she told herself, *Ice, remember the ice and the long sleep of the tree, remember roots and the long dream.* It was not the destruction of the goddess she was seeking. But there was no long dream here, no rooted wisdom she could share, to hope Catairanach could grow wise. And she was not here to inflict an eternity of torment, to drive the goddess to madness, just though that might be, if you weighed your justice in the scale of vengeance: misery for misery, despair for despair, pain for pain. Her tree would never approve of that. "You will sleep," she said, gathering the words she had set. The roots of this, start with the roots, when one would understand. She could see.

A man, charming, laughing, dabbling his hands in the water, a sweep of Northron copper hair, unbraided, a glint of slate-blue eye, calling, and the goddess rising to meet him, afraid and enticed. Yeh-Lin's breath caught. Heuslar. *Heuslar, in the days when he had been only the wizard of Red Geir's hall, or was he Ogada? Wizard wandering or devil? Did it matter? There was fear in the goddess's attraction and the spice of danger, and great daring, that she did not hide herself away. Ogada, then, the tang of something Catairanach did not recognize, yet which was more than human. And? And the waiting. The long years. Wait, he had said. He would come back to her. Years, generations, and the child hung between being and not being, because he would return and take her, show her the world her mother could never see, bound in her little waters, make his daughter a queen, he said, of empires in the north. Lives, steeping in the dreams of something greater than this little land of cattle and sheep on the hills and the smoky halls, though what was the north but more of the same? Long lives, and the mortal child soaked in that waiting, that anxiety, those dreams, and he never came.*

He was dead. Truly dead. And when he had been free, he had not come to Praitan seeking her again. The goddess had finally known it, and had given her child to the world, in love and in hatred she did not even see, for the pain the infant brought, the memory of betrayal.

The mother held her now, still, with the strength of her land. Clung to her, in love and in hurt. She would see her born again, see her live a new life, clean and sweet. It would all be right, this time, all sins forgiven, all pain atoned for, when the child was reborn. If he defied her, refused the girl, the girl who could bear the child, who carried the form and the memory of her in blood and bones, he could be brought to it. Hyllau would hear her. Hyllau would—

"You are obscene," Dotemon breathed in Catairanach's ear, as fire and water became bone and flesh again, and the waters shivered. "I take your Hyllau from you. The roots of this land that hold her, I rip from her. The cord that binds you, I sever, as should have been at her birth. I tear her from you, so that she may be given to the world when there is one resolute to take him from her and from you, for her to perish then on that day to come as she should have long ages before." *You cursed her, because you would not let her go. You made her what no god's child should be, more than half a god, and she had not the wisdom to wear even a wizard's powers wisely.*

She felt the tearing, as if fine rootlets snapped beneath her hand, veins weeping blood, the virtue of the land seeping away, the umbilical that fed the babe in the womb gushing free, draining the mother, washing her godhead from the *duina*. The goddess wept, without cries and wailing, without sound at all, tears streaming. Her hands fell away, and Dotemon caught her as she would have fallen into her waters, fleeing.

"Look at me. Hear me. Know me. I am not wise, but I am trying to be so. I know what it is, to try to shape your child to be what you are not, to live what you could not, to live for you. And I know the cost of that, and the sin of it, now. I pity you, but—"

The goddess rose in one last effort, water and earth, stone, pulling the devil down, but she was not startled and taken unawares. Catairanach was only the little goddess of a little land, and Dotemon was the fire of the stars. She enveloped the goddess and stood unfaltering.

Sleep without dreams, sleep knowing nothing, sleep being nothing, till the end of this world. I say it. I, Yeh-Lin of Nabban say it. I, Dotemon called Dreamshaper of the North, say it. Let the Duina Catairna find itself a new god, and if Nabban has the will to do as he should, let the lost soul of your daughter meet its fate.

The waters of the spring sank and were still, and the sky, where stars had shivered in the blue, grew again clear and hot. Crickets sang on the afternoon hills. The water burbled peacefully, grains of sand dancing in the upwelling between the rocks. But the leaves of the mountain ashes were brown and sere, crackling, falling, drifting on the surface of the water, swirling and settling on the winter-grey grass, and the green berries were withered, never to burn with scarlet ripeness in the rich autumn. The grains of dancing sand settled and were still. The spring still burbled and chimed, but slowly, it fed itself out through its overflow, into the stream, lined with dead and rattling stalks, and its voice was silenced. Water stood in the deepest places of the streambed, but where it had run over rocks, they dried in the sun. The spring was a pool, stagnant and sinking into the stones.

Yeh-Lin groped for her sword, dried it on her sleeve, stretching bones that for a moment felt their age. She stepped out and paused, standing on one leg and then the other, to pour water from her boots, making a face.

"But what," she asked aloud of the sky, "happened to Heuslar Ogada?"

She felt the touch of ice on the back of her neck and shivered.

The chestnut mare had strayed far down the hill. Squelching, Yeh-Lin set out after her.

Halfway down, she turned back. Scowled at the smoking *dinaz*, where that lone, lorn dog still mourned. Climbed the hill, straight to the stone wall east of the tower and drew her sword.

A single stroke that never touched, and the drystone wall fell. She climbed down the ditch and over stone, marched through the trampled lanes, smelling death and roasted meat. Nothing stirred. The folk who had abandoned the place had taken everything living with them, save this one small faith. The dog was silent. It knew her, as beasts did, a thing out of place, a thing that did not belong wholly to this world. But then it whined again, afraid, and lost. It cowered under the broken remnant of a gooseberry bush, where once there had been a garden, and it watched a heap that had been a tent, ash, now, and charred felt and bone, and all still warm. Its eyes shifted sideways to her, and back, and it whined, hackles bristling, and stirred at the same time a tail like a black plume.

"There's no hope here," she told it, and when it cringed away from her, grabbed it up. "Even the goddess is gone. Can't you tell?" It was not a terribly large dog, and fit under her arm.

CHAPTER XXVII

The smashed door had never been repaired, but the bodies of the Red Masks were gone. The crack in the floor that had been a well of dark water held nothing now. Mikki sniffed, but there was nothing of Moth, nothing to smell but earth, and stone, and damp. The well was his way, nonetheless. If he could fit. He couldn't sit here waiting for nightfall, while Holla-Sayan fought a devil in his stead. He had no idea how deep the well went or where it might open out before the bottom; it seemed to drop straight down. He was at home in caves but did not love such straight chimneys. Encumbered by a sword in his mouth, he started down backwards, finding clawholds and small ledges, bracing himself between the narrowing—Great Gods be kind, not narrowing any further—sides. When all light of the dome's eye was lost he began to imagine the devil coming, Holla-Sayan's burned and bloody corpse discarded behind her, to send a cascade of lightning down this shaft on his head.

Then there was no hold for his groping hind paw. Dislodged stone rattled and hit a floor, but what and how far—not water. He would have preferred water.

Moth! he called silently. *Damn you, where are you?*

Nothing.

Ulf? Vartu!

But the sword grew cold in his teeth. He wasn't a man, to hang by his fingers and feel about and pull himself up again if he found nothing. It was drop or stay. So he dropped.

He seemed altogether too long falling.

Demon of the forest. . . . A whisper of the mind, and he was in water. He had not fallen into water; he was under water, water lit by moonlight, and he struck out for the surface, grabbing with a human hand as it sank away from him the sword he couldn't carry now in his teeth, flipping wet hair out of his eyes.

A river, a warm summer night, and the cliff rising over him was, maybe, the edge of the ravine, but neither wall nor houses marched along it. The stars were streaked with scarves of cloud, and the moon was full, burning through.

"Lady of Marakand?"

Mist on the shore, gathering, until there was a dark woman standing under the lea of the cliff, naked and wet. He was naked himself, and not entirely comfortable to be so, swimming about in a goddess's river while she watched in a human form. One of them really ought to have some clothes on. Not much he could do about it, though. He waded ashore, slinging Lakkariss over a shoulder.

"Marakanat," she said. "My name is Marakanat. You . . . fell. I remember. You should not have fallen here."

Lakkariss was very—present, that was the word, cold against his side. Lakkariss was awake.

"Marakanat, then. Where's the devil?" he asked. He did not feel the full and holy weight of the presence of a goddess. She was only mist and memory, diffuse and all about him.

She frowned, held up her hands to the moon, watching the light pass through them. "Did I dream of a devil?"

"You're dreaming now," he said gently. "Lady . . ."

"The Lady," she said, as if remembering. The moon, emerging from cloud, poured through her hands, which were only mist. "The Lady, dying, dreaming, imprisoned within a devil, imprisoning a devil within a dream, within memory. I never dreamed a bear of the north. Demon of the Hardenvald. The devil dreams of you. But she is peaceful enough. Leave her to dream. Leave her to die with me, and so she will be gone from this world where she should never have been."

"No. I want her back. And what about the other, who's destroying your city?"

"Other? Yes, there is the other. I thought I had trapped her, but I was wrong. They were two, and she escaped. But at least I hold one. She showed me how herself. Your devil showed me the dream I dreamed, the strength of the river in the days of my strength. The other I can't stop. I tried. We tried. I remember the dancer, the foolish, brave child, but she gave herself to the devil of her own will, and the devil holds me still, a little of me, though she has let most of what I was pass away into the dream, fading . . . there will be no waking. Even the well fails, the last water draining to the deep earth. It's better so. Even the gods die, you know, as the slow ages turn. The river has been gone a long, long time. I would have gone with it, but the folk called to me so, and the well endured. Better I had gone . . ."

Moth! He could feel himself drifting, caught by the river's murmur along its banks.

"Go back to the north. Go away, demon, and take your hungry sword. There is nothing here for it."

The sword, yes. It knew Moth was here, more surely than he. Mikki drew it. Tiny crystals of frost edged the blade. The goddess, mist strengthening, backed away.

"Don't," she said. "That has no place here. No place in this world."

"I know it. The devil you hold is named Vartu. Let her go. She's needed."

"She will sleep, unwaking, and sleep in my dreams when I am gone.

She welcomes it. She embraces it. She wants to sleep and to never wake. See? I haven't harmed her. I'm no killer, as the devils are."

Fog rose from the water. In it he saw stone. Then there was a tree, a ghost of a tree, a ledge, a cavern, a river high in flood, washing above him, and the cavern again, filled with dark water. He saw Moth, turned on her side, head on her arm, eyes half-closed, unmoving, as the shape of the Lady's dream shifted and flowed about her, water, stone, night, day. She faded into the stone, might have been stone. Water seeped down the wall she lay against, carrying a skin of stone.

"Moth!" he shouted.

"She hears only in her dreams. They're pleasant dreams," the goddess said. "She ought not to dream so. She ought to carry her sins and suffer for them, but she dreams of you instead. She might wake, otherwise. Besides, I do not want to overhear what nightmares she might have."

"That, you do not," Mikki growled. "But maybe you should. It's happening here, in your city."

"Not here. Not now."

"Because this is a *dream*. You're there, in your city, whatever is left of you, possessed by a devil who is oppressing your folk, killing in your name, attacking the very *gods* in your name, making you a nightmare and a terror."

"Yes. This dream is all I have left, and it will fade soon, too. The river died long ago."

"Why?" he asked. Not so long ago, as a goddess marked time, surely. There had been a city here then. And so long as she kept talking, she did not remember to draw the vision of Moth away.

Lakkariss had found a way here, even sheathed and sleeping. He had only followed where it took him.

"The mountains shifted and fell. The Marakanat flows south now, beneath stone, under ice. She whom I once was loses herself in rivers of the south, and the lakes, and the waters Over-Malagru have forgotten her. Forgotten me. I almost forget myself."

So the Lady even before the devil came to Marakand had been not a ghost, exactly, but the cast-off remnant of a goddess, enduring in a reservoir of her waters because she had folk who needed her, dwindling, fading, while her true full self had her focus elsewhere. That explained, perhaps, her weakness, and perhaps how she had so easily found the way to ensnare Moth, living herself in past longings.

Lakkariss had brought him here, *ya*, and Lakkariss wanted Moth's hand to be hunting the devil. Or to hunt her souls. Moth talked to it, sometimes, saying, *Not yet*. She thought he didn't hear. Lakkariss breathed tendrils of cold fog, and they crawled towards the dim dreaming sleeper, reaching through the vision into that other place, other time, into a natural cistern of the Lady's waters. The sword's ice-exhalation was pale over the water, fog-fingers touching Moth where she lay.

The Lady of Marakand put a hand on his arm. "Let her sleep," the goddess said.

Mikki jerked away. "The devil Tu'usha still feeds on you. I smell her breath in your words."

The night river shivered, rose, lapping his ankles, first harbinger of the spring freshet from the mountains, thundering down. The goddess reached to hold him, and he hurled the sword, cutting the air, roaring, "Wolf, catch!" Flung himself after it, into a cavern of darkness and fog.

All light vanished, but daytime had taken him again. He surfaced in a cold and stagnant pool, and his frantic paddling forepaws struck a rim of crackling cat-ice. It was dark as a mine; blind, he could find no shore, and the sword's empty sheath looped about his leg tangled him.

"Mikki? Over here." A hand caught a fistful of his ruff and tugged. His paws found solid stone beyond the ice. He heaved himself up, sneezing, shoved hard against Moth, warm and living woman pressed against him in turn, with an arm around his neck.

Sometimes he thought he must have been born a fool, or mad, perverse at least, to have fallen in love with what even he could admit was a youth's imagined woman spun of songs and sagas and old bones in a cave. But then he smelt her, touched her, tasted her, or she could look at him with laughter chasing the weight of old sins from her sea-grey eyes, or the fires of her soul turning her half to light and flame, and he could not doubt himself. She and no other: earth of his moon, sun of his day, and the half of his soul.

Tongue found her face, her seeking mouth. Eventually she let him go, fended him off to cut a rune into the rock with Lakkariss, which was excessive, but that was Moth, and *Fire* glowed like an ember, rose in firefly sparks to the roof, reflected, a dancing swarm, on water still rippling from his fall. The ice that fringed the pool was melting.

Moth grinned at him, tipping water out of the scabbard and sheathing Lakkariss. "I don't suppose it'll rust. Where did you come from, cub?" A frown. "Where did I come *to?*"

"You've been lost not quite a month."

"So little? *Where* kept changing, though it was always here, I think. The river, sometimes. And then, hah, then . . ." She looked away, which was evasion, and he wondered what had truly held her here. She shrugged. "I feel asleep. But I thought it was years."

"Old Great Gods prevent, I hope not. What's left of the Lady claims she trapped you in—she says a dream. Memories of her past, maybe. Are we still there? There was no water in the well when I climbed down."

"Climbed down. In daylight?"

"Yes."

"Gods, cub, that was—what if you'd gotten *stuck?*"

"I took the sword myself because I thought it could find you. Wanting you as it does. Nothing else could. The devil's fighting the Blackdog."

"Why?"

"Because you're not there, my wolf," he said tartly, "and someone has to, and Holla-Sayan is a fool who thinks he has to carry the world. He doesn't walk away from anything. Tell him he's needed—he's got a wife and a child on the way, but tell him he's needed and he's fighting—who, Yeh-Lin?—with his teeth and a Grasslands sabre, because there's nobody else and this morning she tried to kill the gods."

"If Yeh-Lin decided to rule a city again she wouldn't make such a mess of it. The Lady is Tu'usha, but the body isn't Sien-Mor's. Kill the gods how?"

"By burning the life of the land away, like that horror along the Kinsai'aa." He hesitated. "Or the valley above Hrossfjord of the Geirlingas." Which had been Moth's doing. "Ivah had been working on a spell to free them for the loyalists—there's been an uprising against the Lady's rule—something as many-layered and complex as that thing of her father's we found on the Grass, that he used to transport his horde into the mountains, and she must have had some part of it right, because the devil tried to kill her too, or maybe capture her, to make a new Red Mask. She survived. But her work's destroyed."

"Ivah won't do it on her own. She doesn't have all the words and couldn't speak them if she did, being human. But she might weaken it, if she stops hobbling herself with hearing her father's voice." Moth let him go to pace the length of the ledge. "Doesn't matter. Alive or sleeping or annihilated from the world, we can't help them now and they can't help us here." Mikki watched her, feeling oddly at ease. Pacing, the growth of anger, hot or cold, was reassuring. Moth was all too capable of leaving others to fall to their own damnation, as she would say, when action of hers might save them. Anger set her in motion.

And which would Gaguush prefer from Holla-Sayan, who was only a young man, not yet weary of the world, and yet left her to spend blood and risk life for causes not his own, because some stranger, some enemy even, cried for help? Would she really have him turn his back on the falling, the failing, if it meant he remained hers and safe?

"The deep well," Moth said at last. "We're still in the deep well."

"There's nothing overhead. No crack." Though since he'd ended up in a river ages past, what did that matter?

"No stairs, you mean. This is the cave of the well, or it will be, not the cavern of water below. We may have a very long wait. At least until the next earthquake. Could be centuries. And who knows if the city even exists above us yet?"

"I've told you before, you have a knack for annoying gods. You're supposed to leave talking to them to me." And this trap was half Moth's own shaping, he was sure; she was always seduced by passive withdrawal, by the choice of inaction. Safer for the world, maybe, than the restless King's Sword who had united all the north in her brother's name and led them south. . . . "Find us a way back, then. I trusted you could when I came for you. I left Holla-Sayan fighting *that* alone."

"Don't natter, cub. The sword brought you into the Lady's dream. We're still there. It's left a, a weakness in the fabric, say. A trail I can follow." With Lakkariss, she cut runes along the ledge, shoving him back when he trod closer to see. "And don't drip."

"How," he asked, "do you expect me not to drip?"

Water, was obvious, and *Need*, and *Journey*, in a line, and *Devil*, above and below. Then *Sword*, cutting through them all. He did drip, and the water froze to ice in the lines. She sheathed Lakkariss, drew her own sword Keeper and cut her arm, matter-of-fact, tracing every line with blood. The ice smoked away at the touch of it, and the cut dried swiftly.

A hand dug into the deep fur of his shoulder again. She spoke a word, soft, but his mind couldn't hold it. It echoed like the whisper of harpstrings catching some stir of air, no hand laid on them, ran around the cavern and riffled the still water. Stone shifted and tilted beneath them, and the light became dim daylight. There were the stairs rising from the chamber, the ashy, moist earth, the damp stone and the crack of the empty well between. There were his own tracks, crossing the muddy patches, going to the well.

"Hah," Moth said, with some satisfaction. He didn't snarl that she could have done that any time. Even the leaf falling from the tree in autumn takes some final push of air to set it free. Light in the doorway above them flared white. They ran. She was first to the stairs.

CHAPTER XXVIII

Sword.

Ice. It whispered of ice.

She had dreamed it, and the Voice of the Lady had warned.

White sky, copper moons.

Fire within the ice.

Here.

No.

Zora blinked, dazzled by dreams, by seeing.

This dog was no one of the seven, but he came to kill her. He was *sent*. He must have been. Jochiz had opened the hells without her, Sien-Shava needed her no longer. Her brother sent the dog-man to kill her.

Sien-Shava Jochiz had already killed her. She forgot. Silly girl.

She could kill his servant the dog. She could take the sword.

The dog-man hid the ice. She couldn't see. She felt its weight taken from her and drew breath again.

But such a sword could kill her brother. Such a sword could . . . what veil between worlds could it not cut, with a great enough will and need behind it, and a hand strong enough to hold steady in the face of what must follow?

She swayed, eyes shut. She could be so strong. Yes.

And she could kill her brother. Ulfhild had murdered hers; it was easily done.

The bear ran for the deep well. Let him go. A demon was a little thing, and he would not find the Lady there. The Lady slid beyond reach, and soon even her dreams would end. She was the Lady.

The dog charged her. She did not see his sword. If he burned, she could take it from him. No fire of hers could harm it. So she flung fire at him, but she forgot—he was her brother's so he could not be weak she was her brother's she could not be weak he despised her weakness. The dog flung the fire aside. Fangs tore her and threw her and the foolish girl was afraid but she was Tu'usha and this thing was hers to kill yes it was hers and she would take the sword.

But there was only a sabre in his human hand and she had dreamed the sword.

She had not. Her own sword she called to her hand, and the fire lit his eyes and coursed through his marrow and danced on the sabre's edge. He backed away, fearing her, as well he should. Silent.

In silence, then, she struck.

He bled most satisfyingly like a human man.

CHAPTER XXIX

Sien-Mor without Sien-Shava. She was always his shadow and his echo. Moth could see him letting his sister run on a leash, to be his puppet and mask before the world, but not to such folly, such failure as this. Architect of her own ruin. If he were here, he would have put her aside long before now and made an empire, and be scheming still against the unreachable heavens. Sien-Mor, for all her undoubted skill in wizardry, had always been strange, child in a woman's body. Grown crooked, leaning on her brother, hidden under his shadow, unable to stand on her own. They had not known, then, how a human soul shaped a devil's, once two became one. If they had—would they have dared that loss of self, that merging, even for the world?

They would certainly have rejected Sien-Mor, found some other to seduce. Tu'usha had been secretly inclined to Jochiz even before. Vartu had not wanted Jochiz with them; he had followed after as the rift of the hells closed. She would not have brought him willingly, no, nor turned him loose in a world for which she had a use, she and Jasberek. But Tu'usha had called him with them, and he had been willing, had seemed willing, to accept that in this venture, his was not the captaincy. But then Jochiz had chosen Sien-Shava, the two drawn to one another, and Sien-Mor had been given to Tu'usha, the weak to the weak, the latter Vartu's decision. Ruthless. Not so ruthless as Jasberek, who had said, between the two of them, that they should destroy Jochiz rather than let him take a wizard's soul. The wizard Anganurth had tempered the devil Jasberek, in the end, taught him patience and stillness, but . . . but he had been right. Or maybe it was that they should have slain Sien-Shava and found another man to bear Jochiz, saner and weaker.

Could one of the seven take a new host? She would have said no, the Blackdog notwithstanding. That had been possession, slavery, however willingly the dedicated warriors of the mountains had gone to it, at least until Holla-Sayan. He was a single being united now; he could no more become another than she, killing the self, not merely the body, but ripping soul from soul, destroying the self that had been born of the union to become . . . someone else.

Moth didn't know this girl who had become Tu'usha. She didn't know what this new conjoined being, younger in the world than even the Blackdog, might want. Perhaps Tu'usha didn't, either. But it had been Sien-Mor, or memory of Sien-Mor, who had fought her when she first went into the deep well.

The morning was clear and bright as she emerged into the courtyard of the well-house. It was Sien-Mor who fought now, her style, her very sword, when there was a human body that fought at all. The girl coursed with fire, faded, and returned. No wizardry, though; she had only the sword and the devil's will, the devil's fluid reshaping of the world. But the Blackdog stumbled, fading into fire, silver and dark, and Tu'usha's fires ate at him, weakening him. If unwounded and both reduced to humanity, he would probably be the abler swordsman and certainly the physically stronger of the two. Now, though, Sien-Mor's sword was swifter than his tearing fangs, swifter than his sword, as he shifted from one shape to another, unconscious of it, Moth thought, running across the courtyard, vaulting the wall that divided it from the greater yard where the massive domed hall had stood. Mikki loped after her. Holla-Sayan crouched, torn and bleeding and burnt, blade a shield, catching Tu'usha's; he had no shield, no armour, and when he ducked aside and struck for her the air burned bright and stopped his blow as if it had been the good linden wood. Tu'usha rocked back, too, as if that had been so and she had felt it, not firmly braced. A gaunt, bony wisp of a thing, starving, she looked, huge-eyed and desperate, hardly able to hold her blade up steady with her scrawny arms, but her mouth grinned.

"Holla, get out!" Moth called. They fought halfway down a slope of loose masonry, huge blocks precariously balanced, black, sharp-edged fissures between. She leapt stone to stone, and Holla-Sayan rolled away. Great Gods have mercy, which they would not, half his face was a mask of blood, a cut laid bare to the bone across forehead and cheek and eye. He slithered down to Mikki on four legs again, spun to crouch snarling. When his enemy did not follow, he sank down flat, unmoving, except for the heaving of his flanks. Mikki put a worried nose against him.

Tu'usha's eyes found and followed Lakkariss.

"*There*," she said. "*You* had it. I thought he. . . . But it was you, not Jochiz, you all along, you who sent enemies against me, you—*That* has no right to exist in this world. How did you dare shape such a thing?"

"I didn't," Moth said.

"Give it to me." Childish, imperious, and spoken as though the demand were utterly reasonable, in a voice high and breathless.

"Why?" Moth asked, cautiously circling to find better footing. "What would you do with it?"

"What will you?"

"What I must. Tu'usha, what have you done with Sien-Mor? Who's the girl?"

"Sien-Mor's dead. She went mad when her brother burned her. She died. He killed the demon, and the fire ate her, blood and bone, all gone to ash. It's better she died."

"Maybe she didn't," Moth suggested.

"He burned me! Even the Old Great Gods have more mercy. He burned me because I wouldn't go with him again. The goddess hid me—"

"And for that kindness you destroyed her."

"She was weak. She was too weak. I had to hide. I had to be the Lady, to make Marakand strong."

"You destroyed that too. And you've made this girl, this priestess, mad. Her heart's not strong enough for this, Tu'usha. She can't carry you." Neither could Sien-Mor. They should have seen that. Sien-Mor had walked on an edge, always, a harpstring over-wound. Such must snap, sometime. Tu'usha had brought no tempering to that, had not been strong enough herself. Weak to the weak. Sien-Mor had made Tu'usha mad.

"I'm sorry," Moth said. Because she had led Tu'usha to this. She had given Sien-Mor to this. But they had all lost their way, and there was no road back, no undoing of what was done. Only ending.

Lightning gathered about them, unborn. It piled higher, thicker, heavier, burning in Tu'usha's heart, fed on rage and—and pain, and grief. Feeding, too, on the life of the world.

"Tu'usha, do you remember, there's a reason we mostly work human wizardry in the world and are so cautious what else we do? Can you remember?"

"Don't talk to me like I'm a child and an idiot. I'm not mad. It was Sien-Mor, and she's gone. The Voice was mad."

"Do you want to destroy all Marakand? Do you remember the wars, before you were ever Sien-Mor?"

I am Zora! Sien-Mor is dead and burnt and you betrayed her, you left her, you shut your eyes to her misery and you left her to burn—

Vartu did not remember clearly, herself; it was dream, something that strayed into mind on the edge of waking. Even Hrossfjord she did not remember entirely, and that had been she, not that other Vartu, long ago. What she had she offered Tu'usha. *A rent in sky and stone, and white light pouring through. The earth's pain, the dying of its small gods of hill and water and they themselves, the ones who willed it, drowned in the gods' agony*

and despair, even as their fires drank the life of land and gods and all. . . . Dead
lands about Tiypur in the west, where all the gods had died.

"Don't do this," she said. "Already you've left scars on your city that
will never live again. Zora, do you want to destroy all Marakand?"

The girl shrieked and loosed the lightnings, leaping down on her.

Lakkariss in her left hand, Kepra—Keeper, guardian of the hall—in
her right. The demon-forged sword that had come with Ulfhild from
the Drowned Isles was the leading edge of a fire, with no body behind it,
only a dark flame, but the cold edge of Lakkariss she held behind. Fires
broke from the air around them with the sound of thunder and the earth
shook beneath them. Shards of stone flew, great white sheets of lightning
wrapping the pair of them, and the mound of rubble burnt. She could
devour the heart of this weakened devil as a forge-fire eats charcoal, as
the devil had devoured the life of the land. But that was not the death
the Old Great Gods demanded, and Tu'usha should be no such easy prey.

"Let me go!" the girl screamed. The lightning wrapped and held her
but did not burn. "Let me go. Please." She cowered, clutching herself,
rocking on her knees. "Let me go let me go let me go it wasn't me I
didn't mean I didn't want the city I didn't want the city I wanted it safe
I didn't know."

Sien-Mor's sword lay abandoned on the stones. Moth drew the
burning air into herself, a dizzy exultation in it, and the girl didn't
resist, only raised a tearstained face spattered with blood that was probably Holla-Sayan's. "I didn't know. I was afraid."

But the sword still lay there. It was no real artefact of the world
as Keeper was, heirloom left behind and returned to Ulfhild after long
years. Sien-Mor's sword was a thing shaped of Tu'usha's will and Sien-
Mor's memory. And what did a cowering little girl need with Sien-Mor's
sword, that it endured here in the world? It was will made it; it would
not exist without active will to hold it real.

What did either of them need with swords, come to that?

Mail heavy on her shoulders, familiar and hardly felt, certainly not needed. Reminder of who Ulfhild was. They were not what they had been. But it was not her own self the Marakander remembered in Sien-Mor's blade.

"Afraid of what?" Moth asked.

"She would have made me her Voice." A whisper. "Enslaved me, possessed me, made me mad. But she promised that if I gave myself of my own will instead . . . but it was lies."

"We lie," said Moth. "So do you humanfolk, even to yourselves."

"She was afraid." And which did Zora, Tu'usha, mean had been afraid, the devil or the girl she had threatened to possess? Small wonder they were so badly joined, so disunited in will and infirm in mind, a bond forged under such a threat. "She was so afraid, to be made mad, to be a prisoner, to watch helpless. He is coming. He will make all the world his and destroy the road to the heavens. You know he will."

"Jochiz?" Moth asked. "Do you know where Sien-Shava Jochiz is?"

"He burned me. No. He burned her. I wasn't even born then. But after, I was in the temple. I was, my father sent me to the temple to hide and to spy, but he was dead then. He was the last priest of Gurhan. I should have been a priestess, but I can't hear my god. I don't have a brother, but my brother is always in my thoughts. You should have killed him. You should have known what he was, how could you not know what he was, you should have killed him for me set me free you were my friend you left me—"

"Sien-Mor was no helpless child! She could have acted for herself. No one would have called it an unlawful killing. Or you could have brought an accusation in the hall and sought the King's Sword for the king's justice. But you came, the two of you, so very foreign from so very far away, and your ways were never ours, your sins not ours, for all we knew, and you never acted nor spoke to say it was not your will as much as his. You were no child."

"I want to go home."

"We all want to go home."

"Let me go. Please."

"Is it Zora asking?"

The sword on the ground dissolved at last like frost struck by the noon sun. The whisper was so faint she barely heard. "I don't know anymore."

The question was meaningless anyway. Two rivers flowed together, and maybe one carried the sediment of a different soil and hawk's eye floating over might still see it flowing, braiding, blending, but she could not cut one from the other again.

"I kept her from burning the city," Zora whispered. "I didn't let her kill Nour and that other wizard. I didn't let her kill Hadidu. I sent the captain of the Red Masks my champion her champion away from her, sent so many of her Red Masks away where the gods of Praitan might— might do what they could, what they did, something did, something took the Red Masks from her, set them free. I didn't destroy the city, I didn't call fire to the senate palace steps when the senate declared against me and they met there and they talked and they talked treason and they prayed for the freedom of the gods. I didn't. I hated them, and I didn't. I said, wait, the captain will come you I we sent him to take Praitan so the army from the east will come so we will be subtle be quiet win by force of arms and my brother will not see will not suspect I'm here but it wasn't true, was it? They didn't come, the mercenaries knew in their hearts she was weak and a god took him the captain the assassin from her and the Red Masks were released set free set me free even to perish my soul to perish to end. The Lady true Lady ghost of the Lady whispered inside me so I danced I danced and danced and caught her, trapped her in the temple waiting and never doing. I did, didn't I? But then because the Red Masks were taken I no she wanted to destroy the gods. Please, let me go. Like the Red Masks, let me—"

Moth had come too close, with that poor sick helpless thing crouched there, at war with herself, having tried to destroy her own body, it seemed, all bones and staring, sunken eyes. The girl rose to her feet in fire, spreading wings of flame to engulf her, to devour, curling burning tongues over Moth's hand on the hilt of Lakkariss. She was borne back, blind, for a moment, and burning, hand seared to the bone. Tu'usha reached into her as if to seize her beating heart—

Moth was a column of nacreous light, spreading to winglike white flame, towering high, and she flung Tu'usha from her and was Ulfhild again, still wrapped and shadowed by cold plumes of light. If it was white bone that gripped the black sword's hilt, a skeleton's hand, what did that matter? Flesh was necessary, and yet illusion, though the body might scream with the pain of it. Stumble and sway unsteady, trapped in it, weakened by it, fall fainting of it. Not here. Healing was hers. Flesh and sinew were hers, for her willing it.

The girl's dark eyes stared up at her, with Tu'usha's fire running through her veins, and she rocked and rocked her body.

Flesh, sinew, skin made whole, though streaked with scarring, because the body, also, had its memory. The leather wrapping that hid the inscriptions on Lakkariss's black hilt was burnt away and it was cold in her hand. Moth clenched her teeth on pain and stilled her shivering.

"I heard them, you know," the girl said. "Dying. The guards in Gurhan's valley. The folk in Sunset Market. The priests. I hear them now. They scream. Am I going to hear them forever?"

"Tu'usha knows that answer."

"I hear him, too, now. Do you?"

"Sien-Shava?"

"No. My god. I thought I'd killed him—" Words tumbled faster, slurring together, in haste to be spoken. "She'd killed him she wanted to burn Gurhan from the world I wanted him gone if he could not be mine as he should have been not served by a godless wizard freed by the godless wizard so he burned as I burned. But I failed I was too weak I was too merciful and *I hear him.* He says, the road is long, very long." Tears began to streak her face. "There is no forgiveness only pity no mercy only sorrow no going back only the road. I shouldn't have let her I shouldn't I shouldn't have given up I shouldn't have but I did I did try I did we did the Lady whispered and I tried you know I tried. You know what she is what I am mad but not so mad you know what I could have done to this city these rebels to you this folk these gods you know I didn't. I only wanted to save them, to fight Jochiz when he comes."

"That, I know."

The girl's face hardened. "He won't be so easy to kill as I, Vartu."

"No."

Light flickered behind Zora's eyes. "The girl is too half-hearted, a broken little thing. She was a child, never tested. She never had a chance to grow strong in the world. My mistake. I saw her and I saw myself in her, but I didn't truly know her. I should have waited. If I'd won that Grasslander wizard to be mine . . . she was one fit to bear a devil."

"Ghatai's daughter? She'd have been too strong for you."

Fit to stand with them, yes . . . no. Don't even think it.

"So arrogant. So certain. You and Jasberek both. Arrogant. Cold. We were only ever weapons you thought you could use, not comrades in the fight. Don't pretend that isn't so. But at least here in this world, now, it's you who'll pay for my failure. I was right, you know, Vartu. Jochiz will come, and he'll kill you all, you and your demons and your gods and the folk of all the gods, and he'll climb over them to the heavens, with your sword of the cold hells to cut his way. But . . ." She looked down at her hands, writhing together, looked up again. "If you weren't alone, if you had allies against him, strong allies . . . what if I came with you? I could join your train, with your demon and your dog. We could find others, you could call others, like this dog, if you've found the way . . . I'd be better, you know, if I had someone, if I had you, to follow. I always was,

I always needed that. Someone to help me but no one ever helped me no one ever asked ever spoke ever told me—" Her teeth snapped together, eyes blazing. "Sien-Mor is *dead*. I do not hear she doesn't speak—no!" She gasped, clenched fingers on the stone, squatting splayed like a frog. "It is only that I remember, she isn't in me any longer, she isn't she burned he burnt her I watched her let her burn . . . Zora might learn strength from you."

"No."

The devil stared. "So kill me, then, if you must. My brother will avenge me. You were always afraid of him, King's Sword."

"Zora, he doesn't even know you. Sien-Mor is dead, you say. Remember? You said he killed her, his sister. What's Zora, to Sien-Shava?"

"My name is Tu'usha," she screamed, pushing herself up as if to spring, and a dark fire flickered where her hand touched the stone. "Sien-Mor is nothing. Zora is nothing." *I am Tu'usha—and Vartu, you brought me to this.*

I know. No forgiveness, only the road.

Abruptly calm, Zora dropped back, kneeling, arranging the torn skirt of her gown to modestly cover her bleeding thigh, folding her restless hands in her lap. She looked up with Sien-Mor's closed and knowing smile.

"You will take me on that road, companion, ally, or bondwoman, because otherwise you will have to kill me kneeling before you. I am through with fighting. You will have to kill me so, unarmed, submissive and surrendered. Can you? Can Ulfhild?"

Sien-Mor should remember, Tu'usha. I suspect she does, if you do not. The King's Sword was also the king's executioner. But I'm very sorry for this priestess you've seduced and betrayed. At least she heard her god.

Moth brought Lakkariss around left-handed, and the girl's eyes had time to widen in purely animal fear before the edge of the obsidian blade struck. Tu'usha howled, shrieked, torn to streaks of light—

—and a second voice echoed hers, a scream of rage, of fury and loss, and a will reached after. It found nothing to hold. There was nothing but the empty body, soul or souls all stripped from it. The watching, waiting thread fell away. His cry dwindled to the howling of the wind, but it was a wind that in that moment knew Vartu and cried her name—

—the sky burned white and the black cliffs of ice rose to meet it. Lakkariss was a rift in the veils of the worlds. The ice sang loud in Vartu's ears, deafening her to the faint sounds behind, reaching to tear her soul from soul, hungry, to devour her, make her ice of ice, unknowing, unthinking, unfeeling, the death that is the void of the self, all fires quenched.

Don't bloody listen to it! Mikki shouldered into her, a paw slamming down on her wrist. Moth drew a breath, and the air bit with the sunless winter cold of Baisirbska. She was on her knees amid blocks of stones run and fused glassy together, with the white frost creeping over it in lace-edged spears. The girl was dead, gone, and if Lakkariss left any human soul to take the road to the Old Great Gods it was a mercy beyond her knowing. She doubted. She let both swords fall and buried her face in Mikki's deep fur, looked up only when Holla-Sayan's hand gripped her shoulder. He sank down on his heels with a sigh.

Thunder again, a slow, long groan. The Dome of the Well collapsed inward, a half of its courtyard sliding down after it, and the barracks beside crumbling, and a house, out of which a score of priests and guards and serving-folk ran shrieking, to cower along the walls, staring at ruin, as the dust rose and silence fell.

And so died the true Lady of Marakand, at the last, worn-out and weary and choosing, maybe, to end, freed of Tu'usha. The deep well was dry. The temple folk were, comically, trying to scramble over a head-high wall into another courtyard, each pulling the other back in his or her efforts, no mutual aid, all selfish panic. Sickening. Wearying. Moth took a deep breath, but the Blackdog thought she roused herself against the priests.

"Don't kill them. Let's just, just go. Find Jugurthos, it's all his problem now."

Jugurthos, whoever he was, wasn't her problem, either. The cut across Holla-Sayan's face was crusted black now, his eye . . . she hissed in sympathy and put a hand over it. He was devil; the body did restore itself, though not so swiftly as she might, weaker, less certain in himself. Even that eye would see again. In time. But it was an ugly wound and the pain of it would be mind-numbing. She eased that, at least. For the rest, he could find his own way. She was . . . hurt. And was going to hurt worse.

Blackdog, she said, not for Mikki's hearing. *Zora, this girl, the devil, was Tu'usha the Restless, who had been Sien-Mor. Sien-Mor was destroyed, though I think a part of her soul must have endured in Tu'usha, broken and insane. I did warn you, a devil could be killed. But even rootless in the world Tu'usha didn't die with Sien-Mor as she should have; she fled somehow and lived off the fading Lady, the true goddess, until she found a willing human to bond with again, this poor Zora, who wasn't strong enough for such a union. It was her brother Sien-Shava who had destroyed Sien-Mor, her brother and her lover, and he still had some bond with Tu'usha. I don't think she knew it. He felt it when Tu'usha died. He was here; he knows she is dead, and he knows me. So.*

"Bad?" he asked aloud.

Sien-Shava, Jochiz Stonebreaker? Yes. He was—I don't think I can withstand him. Not alone. But if I go seeking the others, and not to slay them . . . the Old Great Gods will come to know. They will.

They expect you to be able to defeat him, sometime, though.

I don't suppose they care so very much, which of us kills the rest, so long as Lakkariss takes us all in the end. And I'm running out of enemies, Holla-Sayan. Should I flee from Sien-Shava and start hunting my friends? She had never had any plan for that but to delay and delay and put off the inevitable choice.

Gaguush is pregnant and has bought a caravanserai, the Blackdog told her. *I'm tied to Marakand, for her lifetime, even if I go to the road again. So you'll know where to find me.*

I told you to run from me, dog. I told you.

"Then *do* something," he said aloud. "Fight them, instead. We did . . ." He shook his head. "I don't remember, the dog doesn't remember and the thought's right there, I can almost—"

"Leave it. And I can't! *You* know I can't."

"Do what? Can't what?" Mikki asked. "Fight who?" When neither answered he growled, "Devils, hah" and nosed at her. "All right, princess, up. Time to make ourselves scarce. I left Ivah in Gurhan's cave. You and the dog can argue your secrets there, if you must, and we can see if there's any hope of Marakand's gods."

She stood, sheathing Kepra, taking up Lakkariss again as well. It shed flakes of frost as she shoved it home.

Nothing she could do. Nothing but run. Sien-Shava, once he made up his mind that someone was his enemy, which she had carefully never openly been, had a foul, cruel streak that would never hesitate to use whatever means he found to inflict hurt. Fighting Jochiz only put Lakkariss into his hands; she had always known he must be the last, because he would be the death of both of them. So put no victims into his hands to use against her now, not Ivah, who could have been but was not her daughter, not innocent Holla-Sayan, who stood too clearly aligned with her despite their brief acquaintance, not his Gaguush nor his child. And not Mikki.

Blood-soaked head, Mikki's head, toothless, eyeless, in a Grasslander cult niche. She had dreamed that, when they lingered in the mountain winter, where they had fled, ostensibly so that Mikki could sleep and recover from his near-death of heat and bitter water in the Salt Desert. Mostly, though, she had been putting off the descent to Marakand and what she did not want to face. Not, perhaps, the warning from the Old Great Gods she had thought, but vision of another threat altogether.

It was not as though they watched her every thought and every act. They could not. The world was too remote. And in the end of the wars in the north, when the Old Great Gods had intervened to bind the seven, the road between the human earth and the distant heavens had been barred to them, to be taken only at the cost of great suffering, so for the Old Great Gods to act in the world, now, was too difficult and painful a journey, except in the most urgent need.

They would pay that price, if need be. One had been sent to bargain with her, if you could call it that, for the wielding of Lakkariss. They would most certainly fulfill the threats that they had made, then, in that dark night under the unreachable stars.

She could not make their threats empty, but if there was distance, if there was . . . time, perhaps the Old Great Gods would believe their threats had become empty. Or they would become empty of their own accord. Or perhaps not. A wound might heal to a scar, or to an abscess. But at least if she stood alone, then Sien-Shava, hunting her, would find no one else to hurt. Because he would hurt someone, that was certain. Even the ghostly memory of Sien-Mor in Tu'usha had been his, and what was his, no one else should touch, even after he had thrown it aside.

"Mikki . . ." She traded a long look with Holla-Sayan—he knew, and he turned away. She took Mikki's head in her hands, ran them down his neck, leaned her face against his long muzzle a brief few heartbeats.

"What?" he said. "My wolf, what's wrong?"

"Mikki . . . go back to the north. Go home to the Hardenvald, if you love me. Go be what you should have been."

"Moth . . ."

She backed away. "*Go.* I don't need you following me any longer." She drew the feather-cloak from her belt, grey silk shingled with forest gleanings, eagle, hawk, falcon, owl, and lammergeier and raven of the mountains, recent repairs. Swept it around her shoulders.

White gyrfalcon, spiralling high. She climbed, until the city swung below her, scarred and small and pale, and only the Pillars of the Sky stood tall against the sun. She wheeled south into them and did not circle back.

CHAPTER XXX

"Ulfhild, damn you—" But she was gone, lost against the dazzle of the high snows, and roaring at the empty sky did no good. "And you—" Mikki wheeled on Holla-Sayan, teeth bared. The man dropped into the dog again, blood-matted and half-blind, and he couldn't take out his temper on one who'd got those wounds for Moth's sake. "Cold hells take you both. Again." Mikki turned away. "I'm sorry. Come on. Out of here."

Holla-Sayan, human again, though he ought to have known by now four legs were surer when you could hardly stand upright, limped after him, caught up and walked with a hand on his shoulder, letting Mikki take his weight when the ground betrayed him.

"Tell me," Mikki said at last.

"I—Great Gods, Mikki, what can I tell you? I think she isn't coming back."

Mikki stopped but didn't look around. Stone before him, ash drifting over paving-stones. They had done nothing about the crumpled body and fallen head of the young priestess, or whatever she had been before she was a devil, but she wasn't theirs and he didn't care.

I know. Mikki had seen it in her eyes. His wolf in tears. "Why?"

"I swore not to—"

"Tell me, damned dog, or—" He sighed. "Just tell me."

"Lakkariss."

"What about Lakkariss? A bargain for a weapon to destroy Ogada, who murdered her brother and slew my mother, that she'd bring justice to the others, that's what she wants me to think, but she didn't need that damned shard of the hells to kill Heuslar Ogada. She didn't need to go hunting Ghatai, or Tu'usha, at all."

"You'd have left Ghatai to make himself a god, destroying Attalissa, a real goddess, not some imposter like the Lady? To do—whatever it was he intended, after that?"

"*I* wouldn't, though there wouldn't be much I could have done about either. But Vartu—yes, probably. Maybe. I don't know. So what about Lakkariss, dog? I'm not an utter fool. I know this wasn't some change of heart and a chance to serve the Old Great Gods. I've asked. She slides aside from answering and over the years I've learnt not to ask. Press her too hard and she walks away. Always comes back, though," he added under his breath. "Never looked like that. So," more clearly, "Why has Vartu become the headsman of the Old Great Gods?"

"You're their hostage against her."

Mikki shut his eyes, which didn't help. Moth, Moth, *Moth.* He ached with the loss of her, already. After a moment he started walking again.

The tunnel, the whole cliff-wall of the sunken dell of the temple, had collapsed inwards. Priests and temple guard milled about where the tunnel to the gate had been, shouting uselessly at one another, but they scattered away when they caught sight of the bear. Mikki showed his teeth to hurry them on, and picked a way up the unsteady slump of fractured stone, the—dog now—following.

And she said, Sien-Shava, that's Jochiz, I think, will be hunting her, now, for killing Tu'usha. She—I don't know, Mikki, she seemed afraid.

"Huh." A haze of dust hung over the ward, yellow in the morning sun. Part of the wall between the wards had fallen, and several houses. He needed—to be out in the wild places, away from men and their unending noise.

There were soldiers in the street, but they wore the black scarves of the loyalist militia or the grey tunics of street guard, and he recognized a few of the captains as Jugurthos's men, and there, Jugurthos himself. The Warden of the City shouted and waved down the overexcited boys who'd been setting arrow to string, turned his pony their way.

Holla-Sayan, human, sank down on the dusty blocks of the fallen gatehouse as if he were simply too tired to go on. "What now?"

"Here? That's Hadidu's problem, and Jugurthos's and the senate's, not yours and not mine. You belong to Gaguush and your child. Marakand's had enough from you."

Holla-Sayan nodded once. He was grey with weariness. "Mikki, what are you going to do?"

"Find Moth," Mikki said. That seemed obvious, once voiced.

"Where?" asked Holla-Sayan. "How?"

"I don't know where, yet, but how not, when she holds my heart?" He set his muzzle on the devil's shoulder. "Go to your wife, Blackdog."

"Yes." Holla-Sayan looked up. His left eye was swollen and filled with blood, unseeing, but that was an improvement over what it had been. "Yes."

"Blackdog, Lord of Forests." All Marakand had picked up that title from somewhere, but Jugurthos knew Mikki's name. The formality was for the benefit of the Clothmarket captain, riding cautiously up beside him. Jugurthos waved the man irritably away. "What's happened in the temple?"

"What's happened in the city?" Mikki countered.

"Ilbialla's slain. We came to—I don't know what we came to do. We took Templefoot Ward easily, they couldn't surrender fast enough. It seemed almost every second man was a deserter from the temple guard or even a priest or priestess, and all saying the Lady was an imposter, and mad, or knew one who had told them so. We found the fires down about the temple and the gates open, but I wasn't certain I wanted to order my people inside. Certainly not once the lightning struck. Or whatever it was. It's quiet now?" He made that a question.

"The Lady and the devil who took her name are both dead."

"Dead. The devil. But then—" He rubbed a hand over his mouth. "Then, it's over."

"For us. Not for you. Your city. What about Gurhan? Ivah?"

"We're not sure. Nour and Hadidu have gone up there, and the senate is—they all came hurrying to the palace steps after the second blast . . ."

"Cattle," muttered Holla-Sayan. "All standing under the one tree on a hilltop. In a thunderstorm. Idiots."

"I did think so. I ordered them to scatter till we knew what was going on, or—or, I don't know what I thought could come. But Beni Sessihz stayed, sitting there in his chair. To be a sign, he said, that this time the senate stood for the gods, uncowed. Silly old—coughing so he can hardly breathe. He should be home in bed. He'll make himself a legend yet." Jugurthos watched Holla-Sayan warily. "The priesthood of the Lady, the temple guard. Are any of them left in there?"

"I didn't do any of that, it was the devil."

"Yes," said Mikki. "Some have survived. And think what you do next, Warden. It will shape what your city becomes. Dog . . ." *Ivah's fine, or she should be; I left her safe in Gurhan's cave and there's been no second attack on it. But we need to get out of here, before the Warden mistakes us for gods and makes this whole mess of a city our problem.*

A nod, no more. Mikki waited, until man slipped into dog again and the Blackdog had loped, still limping, down the street. Leaving the Warden of the City without any further word—and the man only bowed and did not call after them—Mikki followed so far as the open space of the Greenmarket, where camels and carts came with cut fodder for the household goats and the beasts of burden kept within the city walls. It was deserted now, save for a patrol on guard about the market blockhouse.

You all right, bear? Holla-Sayan asked suddenly, then, looking around.

"No," he said. "But I will find her. Go to your wife."

I'll see you again, then. Sometime. Sayan bless.

He watched the dog running, gone. He wouldn't see Holla-Sayan again, not in Marakand. He wouldn't go back to find Ivah, either. She would be fine. She was safe in the god's cave; she would emerge to find her friends, her allies. She didn't need him, an unlikely step-step-father, to watch over her shoulder. He was going. Leave everything, his axe, his carpenter's tools, even the damned horse-skull; he couldn't lug such things about with him. Just—go. To where he belonged. Which wasn't the Hardenvald. Demons hid their hearts, it was said, in the land that gave them being. Hah. He'd left the Hardenvald behind long ago. It wasn't stone and hill and forest that anchored him.

CHAPTER XXXI

They rode slowly, letting the horses walk. Ghu did not speak or even look either of them in the eye, and Ahjvar, without question, took Deyandara up behind him, though she had always had the impression he wanted her as far from him as possible, before. Now she knew why, and he seemed to have stopped caring. Or maybe a granddaughter wasn't a woman, didn't stir up nightmares by her closeness. It was oddly comforting to lean against him in her weariness, to be a child with a grandfather, safe. Their course took them winding through valleys, keeping low, below the horizon. Though they passed a pair of dead Grasslanders, Ketsim's messengers to Durandau, maybe, both with arrow-wounds, a token handful of earth thrown over them as a blessing, they saw no sign of Hicca's folk. There were few signs of anyone, though there were villages, folk whose lord had been the queen direct, in this region. Ghu was choosing a course that took them by the remoter pastures. The murrain hadn't hit the cattle here. Those, they did see, and sheep, and an occasional distant shepherd who usually vanished at the sight of them. Twice their winding crossed the track of many riders.

"Where are we going?" she asked, eventually.

"There was a battle fought at Orsamoss. Just last night. Do you know it?" Ahjvar shook his head. "Seems like years . . ."

"Yes."

"Your folk aren't all traitors. A force under some of your lords came in time to save the high king, when the Red Masks and Marakanders broke his army and put it to flight. How they knew to come—maybe they were coming to meet him anyway."

"What happened to the Red Masks? Ghu told Lin—"

"I did." Ahjvar laughed. She didn't think she'd heard him laugh before; this raised the hair on her arms. "The Lady made a serious mistake there. I hope someone's able to take further advantage of it in Marakand."

She waited, but he only said, "I'm thinking it was your Marnoch who led the Catairnans to Durandau."

"Not *my* Marnoch. But probably."

"Our Marnoch? I hope he lived."

They were both sober and silent as Ghu after that. She fell asleep leaning against Ahjvar's smoky back, feeling the heat of him even through his coat. She slept soundly as she ever had in her safe bed, till he woke her, reaching back to tap her hip.

"Down," he said.

She didn't see any danger, but she did as he said. They were in a valley bottom, below a brush-covered hillside, with Ghu circling back to them.

"Ahj?" he asked.

"Something I have to do," Ahjvar said. "Before sunset. In case it's too late, later."

He left them both standing to roam up into the scrubby trees, moving slowly, stiffly, putting out a hand now and then to steady himself against a trunk. Deyandara looked to Ghu for an explanation.

"Too late for what?"

He shrugged.

Ahjvar wasn't gone long. He returned with a handful of long, leafy switches.

"So . . . Granddaughter. This curse of mine. You still going to call it a story?"

"I—they didn't die because I went to the *dinaz*, Cattiga and Gilru. They didn't. Did they?"

"Great Gods, no. If anyone . . . but that's a lot to blame on one curse. We never had the southern pox in the land in my day, though."

"Winds change," said Ghu vaguely.

Ahjvar gave him a strange look. "Yes," he said, and knelt down, offered a hand, and drew Deyandara down facing him.

"Your stories tell you I was a wizard?"

"Yes. Of course. You couldn't have cursed the *duina*, otherwise."

"Throwing poison into the headwaters," he said. "Of course it's going to taint all the watercourses flowing from there, in some way, greater or lesser. On and on. We could make a blessing-piece and bury it, but it's all gravel here, no clay, and I think this will do it, with you here, queen of the *duina* still, and last child of Hyllau." His voice was rough on the woman's name.

"It's a spell?"

"Of a sort. Ghu? Here. The third. For witness."

Ghu knelt down carefully, so they made, between them, a triangle.

"It's simple," Ahjvar said, and if she didn't doubt it was possible, she might have thought he sounded defensive about that. "But to the point." He thrust his dagger into the soil and sliced the grassroots. "Now. Birch," he said, putting one long, smooth-barked twig into her hand. "Hawthorn. And hazel." He clasped both her hands around the twigs like a nosegay of flowers, folded his own over them. But the base of the hawthorn had been stripped of thorns. She could feel how his hands shook, then, and they felt fevered, dry and burning. But his burns had gone scabby already. ". . . which are new life, and kingship, and purification," he said. "I, who was Catairlau, say, let the evil and the ill-wishing I put on the son of Hyllau and the children of Hyllanim and the land of

Hyllanim, witting or unwitting, be past and done with . . ." His grip on her hands was crushing. ". . . and never return upon them."

He brought her hands down to the earth, and together they laid the twigs in the slit in the turf, pressing it down over them, burying them. And with their faces so close together, he kissed her forehead, still holding her hands.

"So." Let her go and sat back, with a brief flash of a smile. "Since I don't remember what I said, being busy dying at the time, that'll have to do."

She wasn't sure what she could say, so she took her time about wiping the earth off her hands and standing. Did she feel lighter? That was simply having lost the feeling Ahjvar was about to shout or strike out at her in some disdainful impatience. He looked—she wanted for a moment to wrap him in blankets and smooth the hair out of his eyes, tell him it was all right, everything would be fine in the morning, as her nurse had done when she was small and ill. Ghu was still looking at the flattened grass. He put his own palm over it. Ahjvar didn't see, head down, eyes shut. When Ghu raised his hand, there was a bright-green shoot of spring there, forcing through the grass. Birch, hawthorn, hazel? Deyandara couldn't tell, not from the small furled leaves.

Ghu rose and walked away, leaving Ahjvar there, unmoving. She touched his shoulder, warily, and when he looked up, eyes bloodshot and grey-shadowed, offered her good hand. He took it and almost pulled her down, as if he truly did need her weight to brace against in rising.

Ahjvar still didn't suggest she ride with Ghu when he brought the horses up to them, holding Ahjvar's stirrup as he mounted, boosting her up behind.

Deyandara told herself she had to stay awake, because she thought he might be sleeping in the saddle and she'd end up with worse than a shoulder out of joint if they both fell together, but she must have dozed, because she twitched awake at the shifting of muscles as Ahjvar turned to look at something. She looked around herself and saw a rider on the skyline above them. Her heart lurched, but then she recognized the slim shape, the long hair blowing. Which made her think again, *Yeh*-Lin? The rider turned towards them, angling down a sheep-cropped hillside.

"We've decided," Deyandara said in haste, before she lost her nerve to speak at all. "I'm going to name Marnoch king over the *duina*."

"Oh? Did *he* decide that for you?" A jerk of the chin at Ahjvar.

"No! *I* decided."

"Are you sure?"

"Leave her alone," Ahjvar growled. "Or were you planning on ruling Praitan through her? Not much of an empire, after Nabban, but I suppose you'll have to start somewhere to build it all up again."

"I am not seeking empires or dominion in any form. And I certainly wouldn't start with the Praitannec kingdoms if I were. You're doomed. The Five Cities will eat you all, in the end. Speaking of empires."

"Not while the clan-fathers of the cities keep having one another's throats cut," he said. "And emperors have ridden over cities from out of the wild lands before."

She sniffed. "I have better things to do with my time. Deyandara, I brought you a gift. It's around somewhere." Lin—Yeh-Lin—looked about, as if expecting to see whatever it was hovering mid-air.

Her tutor was one of the—"Seven devils?" Deyandara whispered, just to have it given words, if only for herself, but Yeh-Lin waved a dismissive hand. Neither of the men seemed to care.

Ghu still said nothing, but he pointed. His dogs were away up the hill, with a third, smaller, long-haired and black, in the centre of a knot of sniffing.

"Ah, there it is." Yeh-Lin whistled, and the dog, slinking a little, broke away from the others and came to her, wary and crouching. "I can't help the way I smell," the devil said, a little defensively, Deyandara thought, to Ghu. "I like dogs."

His own followed and stood watching her, not bristling now but definitely watching.

When Deyandara swung a leg over and slid down the horse's flank, the dog came to her, pressing close, wriggling, licking. It smelt of smoke, and for some reason that made the tears stand in her eyes.

"It's all right," she found herself murmuring to it, into its fur. "It's all right now. Little black fox, it's all right." Foolish. It had been all right, since Ahjvar had seized her from the fire. And she and the land were no longer cursed.

Ahjvar watched her for a time, then turned his horse nearer, offered a hand to her uninjured arm.

"Up," he said. "We need to make a king."

Ahjvar only wanted to lie down and sleep, and let Praitan tear itself apart in fighting over rule of this *duina* if it wanted to, but he couldn't. He had gone beyond hurting, beyond exhaustion, into some floating dream, like a fever. He needed to stay awake. Things he had to do, before the darkness came. Something had changed, though. He didn't know what, but the world felt off-kilter. Maybe it was having unwound that ill-wishing from the land, having found some place in his heart that wanted to do so, some crumbling of a rage that had turned long ago to stone. Or maybe it was only himself, the wizardry so long buried seeping into its old channels again. His. The hag's. He could feel her, as if she dreamed too, floating in the same uneasy haze. Not *it*, not sated, sleeping, a curse he could push from his thoughts for a day, a week, months, but *she*. And even in their floating dream, she wept, wailed, like a lost child. The sun was standing towards the west. But there were things that must be finished, first. That thought kept returning. For a moment he couldn't remember what he had to do. The curse on the girl. Not that. Over. Better. He wished Ghu would at least look at him.

A king for the *duina*. Marnoch of the Red Hills.

The devil, surprisingly, did not argue or try to bully the girl out of standing aside for Marnoch, saying with apparent approval, "Good. She's never wanted to follow that road." And Ghu gave Yeh-Lin his own nod of approval at that, which Ahj took for a sign of truth in the devil's words.

"Catairanach . . ." Yeh-Lin said hesitantly, then, watching Ghu.

"Damn Catairanach," Ahjvar said, eyes shut. "I'm not asking her."

"No, you won't be. Will you make a new god of the *duina* as well, assassin? Catairanach is gone."

Deyandara clutched at him. Ghu didn't look surprised at all. Ahjvar was dizzy. His ears rang, and the hag's weeping . . . she knew, she had felt it, she . . . he should be dead. He should be dead with her, Great Gods, Catairanach was gone and her curse went on, and Ghu would die, Ghu might kill Red Masks but he was not a Red Mask and the hag would kill his friend . . .

"Ahjvar," Ghu said softly. "It's all right."

What was?

"Dead?" Deyandara asked. "The Lady killed her?" She sounded simply bewildered.

"Catairanach is sleeping," Lin said. "Forever, I do hope. She was no fit guardian for a folk. Sleeping and dreamless, though. I am not a torturer." She sniffed. "Buried, and rather deeper than—"

"That's enough," said Ghu. "Good. Gone," he continued firmly. "So leave the new king to find his new god."

By luck, though Ahjvar did not believe it was mere luck, Ghu led them so that the first warning they had of the high king's camp was a picket of scouts Deyandara said were Marnoch's folk. They spread out in an arc, arrows on the string, even after Deyandara shouted to them, calling one of them by name, that it was all right, she was safe and well, Lady Lin was no traitor. Faullen, she called the grizzled man who seemed to be the leader of the four of them, and he rode forward alone, warily, while the others hung back, guarding.

"Ketsim's?" he asked.

Lin snorted. "Don't make me kick you in the head again, boy." Her appearance had changed at some point as they rode; her hair iron-grey and cut above her shoulders, her face elegantly weathered. Not an illusion; Ahjvar would have noticed her working any spell so complex. Yeh-Lin. Well, Ghu seemed not to mind; at least, whatever had pushed him so inward did not seem to be fear of the devil. If anything, the wariness ran the other way.

"The high king," Ahjvar said. Speaking hurt, and his voice croaked hoarse in his own ears.

Deyandara, interrupted in her explanations—admirably concise and simple, all things considered—of abduction by false Red Masks, the falling-out between Grasslander factions and then between Ketsim and the chief of his Praitannec allies, rescue by old companions of the road, took a breath he felt against his back and said, "Yes. We need to see my brother. And Lord Marnoch, if he—is he . . . ?"

Her breath caught and she sighed with relief as Faullen said, "He'll be wanting to see you, too, my lady. By your leave, I'll come back with you myself. I'm still your man."

She nodded.

Ahjvar listened, drifting half into dream again, to Faullen telling the girl all that had happened since the night she had been captured: how Marnoch had rallied his folk and they had put the mercenary attack to flight, and Lord Fairu was wounded; how, not knowing where the supposed Red Masks had taken Deyandara, they had grimly continued their march to meet up, they hoped, with the high king, knowing, or so they thought, themselves too few to prevail in any assault on the *dinaz* on their own. How scouts had told of the new gathering of Marakander allies, Praitannec traitors, and its core of Red Masks, and the desertions had begun, men and women slipping away.

"If we'd had a longer march," the scout said cheerfully, "there'd have been just the lords left, maybe. But as it was, two days after you were taken—we knew we'd come up with Durandau in the next day, and we knew the damned Marakanders were somewhere near, the new ones, and we'd crossed the trail of what looked like a force come from the *dinaz* to meet them—Mag, she's a wizard of Marnoch's household, my lord," he added aside to Ahjvar, who managed to remember to nod, as if that mattered . . . and to stir to thought again enough to wonder where *my lord* had come from. Nothing Deya had said, circumspect at last. "She's been, well, odd, since that drawing of the wands that went so strange. Quieter. Twitchy. Has dreams. We were lying up for the night on a hillside, no fires or anything, naturally, and planning to be in the saddle again in the foredawn, and those that could sleep were doing so, though I doubt that was many. Then Mag started crying that the king must ride. 'Ride, ride, ride for Orsamoss,' she said, 'or the high king falls and Praitan with him, in the wars of the kings and the quarrels of the tribes,' and she was so wild, so intent, Marnoch and the lords just sounded the horns and roused us out, before anyone really thought and asked, 'The king must ride?' And when they did start asking, some took it for a sign you were dead, my lady."

"Ah," was all Deyandara said to that.

"But riding in the dark, no matter how well you know the hills, and there weren't that many who did, it can all go a bit like a dream, half-asleep and first you're afraid and then you're thinking, we're going to die, and then . . . there were fox-lights running over the ground, and we took our guide from them. And then we didn't need them, we heard the battle, more a running pursuit, north of that swampy ground they call the Orsamoss, and I guess the goddess of the place had sent the fox-lights, and maybe the dreams to Mag, too. They'd been fighting up on the ridge where the kings had fortified a camp, fighting in the dark, if you can imagine. There were Red Masks, and they had the high king put to flight. They're saying the Red Masks had overtaken him and he was surrounded, a little knot of his household folk about him, when a pair of demon wolves—or dogs, I've heard both, or dragons, even—creatures made of shadow and mist and moonlight, with eyes of fire, came up out of the grass and attacked the Red Masks, and let him break away. I don't know, there are always stories, you know. I didn't see any demons myself. *We* came up just about then and the kings came to Marnoch's—to your banner, I should say—and Lady Elissa, the high king's wizard, was saying the Red Masks were all slain and the land itself was eating their corpses. That cry was going about, and the Marakanders must have known it for truth, because they started to fall apart, as if they couldn't fight without their priests. The Grasslanders did better, but even they broke when Marnoch and Durandau rode against them . . ."

Faullen's tale of the battle turned then on the aftermath, sur-render, flight, the dead and wounded. Names, old Lady Senara dead, who shouldn't have ridden to battle at all, young Lady Dellan gravely wounded, the wizard Hallet dead, and Lord Launval the Elder, the high king's champion, slain by the Marakanders' red-priest captain, and his kinsman Launval the Younger, the high king's wizard too—Yeh-Lin made some sound of grief then, and he thought the girl was weeping, silently, against his back, at the names—and the king of the Duina Galatan and his brother too . . . and they'd found wizards, prisoners, all bound and hacked to death, bodies still warm; the Marakanders denied them rescue even as they broke and fled.

Ahjvar really did stop listening, then. He thought he fell asleep, trying to shut it out, but he woke at the horse's sudden jinking side-ways and Deyandara's squeak of alarm at it, caught his balance as he was falling and looked around, hand on his sword. After a moment he knew the shape of the horizon. They were in a valley north of the Orsamoss ridge, where another height rose, crowned with tents and banners, ringed with disorderly camps like a constellation of infant villages. At least they kept a good watch; the horse had been excited by a skein of mounted spearmen cantering up to challenge them.

He could hear the crows and ravens over Orsamoss, even from here, and there were vultures floating in the distant sky, drawn over who could know how many miles.

Faullen rode ahead, across the shallow waters of Orsa's brook. There was a brief exchange of words, with much excited gesturing, before he beckoned them on and the riders parted to let them through.

"Lord Marnoch's with the kings, my lady, my lord," he said. "They're planning their attack on Ketsim at Dinaz Catairna. And arguing. Durandau's for waiting here."

The kings and queens were meeting in the high king's pavilion at the crest of the hill, where the banners of the seven *duinas* and the eagle of the high king flew. There were more challenges, but Faullen dropped his avuncular manner and sang out gravely, "The queen of the Duina Catairna comes to take her place at the conclave of the kings" without a hint of his satisfaction, till he glanced back and winked at Yeh-Lin.

"Ahjvar . . ." There was a hint of panic rising in Deyandara's voice. "What do I do? What do I tell them?"

"Ketsim's dead, the war's over, it's Grasslander gangs and lost Marakanders they need to deal with." His head throbbed. His chest hurt. Finish this, and he could sleep.

"Not that. Marnoch. Is there even something that *has* to be said? I don't know any stories of how it goes, I don't know any words. Nobody's going to listen to me if I say I'm standing aside for Marnoch. My brother will just do what he wants over me, refuse to accept it, say I'm distraught or hysterical, appoint one of my other brothers regent."

"Stand aside—?" Faullen asked in a whisper. "My lady, there's no need for that, even if Ketsim did—"

"Oh, do shut up," said Lin. "No, I'm sorry, Faullen, but it's her choice and her right, she's not a child and she knows herself and her own mind, and what the *duina* needs now—"

"Shut up, all of you," Ahjvar snarled, and Ghu turned his horse to make himself a barrier against Lin, and Faullen, and everyone, put a hand on his shaking arm. He needed to get away from here and it wasn't even the curse and the hag he feared in this moment but his own exhausted loss of reason. Easier just to kill the damned high king and ride away. Find a ditch to crawl into and sleep, and if the hag woke when night fell—Ghu had promised. Old Great Gods, let it be soon. Let it be over. But he would like to sleep, first.

At a sign from the escorting riders they dismounted before the high king's pavilion.

"I'll let the high king know you've returned, my lady, and ask if—" one began, and Deyandara, bent to fondle the little black herding bitch Lin had brought from the *dinaz*, straightened up to interrupt.

"Not a truant child," she said, though her voice was unsteady.

"Is the queen of the Duina Catairna excluded from the council of the kings?" Yeh-Lin purred. The tent flaps were drawn back. She simply swept through as of right, Ahjvar following with Deyandara and her dog scurrying by his side. The spearmen tried to flank them, disorderly, uncertain. Faullen trailed unnoticed.

The high king, a man of about thirty or so, sandy-haired, with dark Nabbani eyes from some colony ancestor, sat on a folding chair, although he looked as if he would rather be standing with his back to a wall and not looking up at the men and women who stood around, the last harsh words of debate trailing off as a blond man with a bloody bandage around his brow said, "—which you would throw away, and if you'd come sooner we . . . my lady!" And then, deliberate, with a deep bow, "My queen."

"Lord Fairu." Deyandara nodded to him, but she was looking around. No need to ask which was Lord Marnoch. A dark-haired young man's strained face lit at the sight of her, and she made a sudden movement as if she would dart to him, checking it even before Lin's restraining hand could do more than rise. But he smiled as if the sun had come out, and whispered to the woman at his side, who came around behind the lords to them, her bard's ribbons blood-stained.

The high king was before her, striding across to take the girl by the shoulders. For a moment he had looked about to hug her but had checked the impulse at the last, fool, when being a brother before a king might have done him more good in the eyes of all, not least his sister. "Deyandara, where in the cold hells have you been?"

She flinched and pushed back from him. "Later," she said unsteadily. "It will make a long tale. I've come from Dinaz Catairna—"

"Lady Lin, you were to find her and bring her to me," Durandau interrupted, shifting his grip to Deyandara's injured arm, as if he thought she might run off. She winced. "What were you thinking, to take her into the *duina?* And now you're accused of being Ketsim's ally, which I don't believe, but—"

"The former was my lady's wish, the latter, a misunderstanding, my lord," Yeh-Lin said. "There was a matter I thought I had to see to. But my lady would—"

"Misunderstanding! From what I hear, you handed her over to the Catairnans and they promptly lost her to Ketsim. Great Gods, Deyandara, you've *come* from Ketsim, haven't you? I should have expected that. Trust you to make a bad mess worse. I suppose she's been sent to make terms for him," he said to Ahjvar. "It won't do the damned Grasslander any good, or the rest of you traitors either. Who are you, anyway? One of Hicca's men? The girl's my mother's bastard, yes, but there's no proof her true father was the Catairnan prince. She has no claim any but the desperate would acknowledge, and you can take that word back to your master Ketsim yourself without her, she's certainly not going back to his bed."

Did he hear himself, and wasn't he planning to use her Catairnan blood himself? Desperate, hah, Durandau should be that.

Deyandara yelped with what sounded indignation as much as pain as her brother turned, dragging her, towards his chair again. Ahjvar caught his wrist.

"Let her go."

Durandau did so, and Deyandara sprang away, hugging her left arm close against her chest, white-lipped. Grant that the man looked shocked as much at his sister's recoil and pain as that someone had laid hands on him. Lords Marnoch and Fairu both came pushing through to stand behind her with the bard and Faullen, Marnoch almost as pale as the girl, which was smothered rage, Ahjvar judged. He let the king go and backed a single deliberate step before the spearmen could make up their minds quite what was happening. Useless bunch. If he had been Ketsim's, sent to negotiate, he'd have given up on talk and handed the Grasslander the kingship he wanted by now. The high kingship and the heads of half the kings at the very least. Durandau certainly wasn't going to be able to hold his title after this. Down in the Five Cities it was said Durandau had only ever been the compromise that prevented all-out war between the Duina Galatan and the Duina Noreia over the high kingship, the choice nobody really wanted and whom nobody really saw as a threat.

"Ketsim is *dead*," Deyandara said. "Hicca is dead. *Catairanach* is— gone. This is *over*."

That made a long moment's silence. Marnoch broke it to ask practically, "Who holds Dinaz Catairna now, my lady?"

"It's empty. Burnt. A pyre for Grasslanders dead of the southern pox," Deyandara said. "Those who didn't die there rode to Orsamoss." She had been paying attention to the signs of the land as much as Ahjvar, then, or more, given the haze he'd ridden in. "You know better than we what became of them." A bard's cadences for the hall, but her smile was for Marnoch. Deyandara was finding her feet, though she herself might not yet have noticed it. Even Durandau didn't interrupt. "Those of Hicca's folk who remained fled the goddess's wrath and are suffering her punishment, even now."

"But Catairanach?" asked the bard. "My queen, you say *gone?*"

"Lost to us," Deyandara said carefully. "But her sacrifice has freed the land."

"The Red Masks failed," said a woman who still stood at the high king's empty chair. "They all died and fell at one time. You mean, the goddess gave herself to destroy them?"

Deyandara glanced at Yeh-Lin. If she gave any sign, Ahjvar didn't see it.

"Catairanach is gone," Deyandara repeated. "Marakand is defeated. The *duina* is free, all Praitan is safe."

Save for the pox and the murrain and the Old Great Gods knew how many lordless Grasslanders and lost Marakanders roaming the borders of the road, to be preying on whatever travellers and lone steadings or small villages they could.

"Well," said Durandau, "that makes things easier. Deyandara, tomorrow we'll ride to Dinaz Catairna to see for ourselves. I'll appoint you counsellors; perhaps Lady Elissa, for now, could take you in hand, since I am not pleased with Lady Lin's—"

Marnoch stirred. "My lord, the queen has no need for you to name guardians over her, like a child, and the high king has no right to order who sits in a *duina*'s councils."

Deyandara bit her lip and looked at Marnoch. "Am I your queen?"

"My lady, if we'd known you were carried to the *dinaz*, we'd never have left you. We thought they must have taken you to the captain from the city; we thought Ketsim would be with him and that if we had any chance of saving you, it was in joining Durandau to defeat this army. If we'd known . . ."

She moved to take Marnoch's hand, and a deep breath with it. Durandau frowned.

"My brother the high king would make me queen of a folk who have already named me their queen," she told the tent at large, the lords and the wizards and the bards, and two sandy-haired young lords who might be more brothers. "It's not for him to decide that. It's not for you, my lords and ladies of the *duinas*, only for the Catairnans and Catairanach, who is gone. I was Queen Cattiga's only heir to survive this past year. I've seen Ketsim slain and the traitor Hicca, and witnessed Catairanach's judgement on the traitors for this *duina*, as its queen, but to be lady of this folk and this land isn't the road the Old Great Gods have laid before my feet. I know it. I would name Lord Marnoch to be king of the land and the folk that were Catairanach's."

And she had the judgement of words to stop there, to not lay all the arguments in his favour out, but to wait.

"Deya!" Marnoch protested, a whisper.

"It's right," she said, with another glance at Ahjvar. But maybe she could carry it on her own.

Maybe not. "Andara give me strength!" Durandau burst out. "Deyandara, you can't just hand kingship over like an outgrown toy." He grabbed for her again, as if she were six and he meant to march her from the tent for private chastisement.

This time Ahjvar put himself between them. His sword didn't, quite, touch the high king.

"No," he said, and stood where he was a moment, till the world stopped tilting. Old Great Gods prevent he didn't fall on his face. Not yet, at any rate. Maybe this was dying at last.

Maybe this was a month with next to no sleep. If he was being a fool, drawing a blade on the high king in the very council of the seven kings . . . Ghu wasn't here to say so. He hadn't followed into the tent.

"If this man is one of yours, Marnoch, I want him out of here now," Durandau said.

"He seems to be my lady's," Marnoch said evenly.

"Cairangorm's champion," Ahjvar declared. "Cairangorm's heir. You did not make Deyandara queen and you will not deny her right to step aside for another, and you will not deny me, in this land that was my father's, the right to add my voice to hers. The kingship falls on Marnoch of the Red Hills. It's time the leopard and the bull both were set aside, and Durandau, you can face me in the circle if you want to contest this, or name a champion to do so, but you do not manhandle your wounded sister as if she's some captive brigand while I am still on my feet."

Durandau's hand was on his sword. Damned gods, he did not want to kill Deya's brother in front of her, but the man wasn't in a temper for a fight to mere blooding. It wasn't going to go to the circle and any formality of law anyway. Durandau was going to attack him as an outlaw in the hall, and they would have a bloody free-for-all before it was done.

But the man, breathing heavily through his nose, slowly took his hand away from his hilt, waved back his bench-companions and spearmen. Not, after all, a fool. Of the kings and lords, other than Durandau's own, none had moved in to back him. The high king had laid hands on a queen of the folk in violence, and most were not sure, quite, but what Ahjvar had the right to stand where he stood.

"I don't intend my sister any harm," Durandau said, sounding more baffled than angry. "How in the cold hells could you think that? But I don't see by what right you speak for her, whoever you are."

"By what right do you?"

"She's not of age."

"She's travelled a longer road than you, alone, across the Tributary Lands and to the skirts of the Five Cities, and to Marakand itself, taking on a bard's duties all untrained for them, when there was no one else the goddess could send." Words grated. He felt as though he were still swallowing ash and soot. "She's seen more blood shed in this war and endured more trials for her land's sake than you. And my lord, you sent her away from your *dinaz* and her own god with only a lone woman to accompany her, like any young apprentice, and you made no effort to find what had become of her, after that. You made no provision to guard her on her road. You never gave her another thought, until you realized the Duina Catairna was without a king and that she might have a claim, and even then you didn't rush, coming as you thought to put her where she had already been put by her own folk. She's proven herself a servant of this land and a woman fit to know her own mind by her deeds, as the goddess of the land would attest, were she still here to do so." He could still lie kingly when he had to. Ghu hadn't corrupted him from that. "*You've* only shown yourself a neglectful guardian."

An older king who had been whispering with his spearmen stepped forward. "As her maternal grandfather, I have a voice in this as well. And my grandson the high king, with respect, is only her half-brother. I will claim guardianship—"

"Why haven't the Five Cities overrun you all yet?" Ahjvar muttered, not quietly enough. Someone snickered, away behind the high king's back. "My lord of the Lellandi, we can argue this till she does come of age, but—"

There had been some other whispering debating going on behind him all the while, women's voices. Deyandara and the bard, with deeper interjections from Marnoch, mostly consisting of negatives. Now Deyandara ducked around him. Ahjvar checked his impulse to fling her out of harm's way, lowered his sword instead, and leaned on it. The girl put herself deliberately where stepping back a mere few inches would have her shoulders against his chest. The little black dog gave a sharp bark and bounded forward. Yeh-Lin raised a finger, pointed at the ground, and it sat, quivering, eyes fixed on the high king, but its teeth were bared. Comedy, the high king defied by a cattle-dog, but no one was watching it.

"I'm a widow," Deyandara said tersely. "And that, my lord brother, gives me my majority and the right to speak for myself."

Durandau looked, for a moment, uncommonly like a fish, gaping at flies.

"Who?" he demanded indignantly. "You had no right marrying without my permission, and especially at your age."

"Well, nobody asked you!" she snapped. "Or me either, if it comes to that, but married I was, and widowed by the next morning, and if you want witnesses, I'm sure you can hunt down some of Hicca's men who were at my wedding feast, as my lord Ah—Catairlau didn't kill *quite* all of them.

Thank you, Deya. Three, was it, he had slain? Hardly any. And it was hardly a legal marriage: abduction and intended rape, no god bearing witness and even if it had been otherwise, unconsummated—but if she could carry them past all that unquestioned. . . . Once get Marnoch acknowledged by even some of the kings . . . it would be so much simpler to settle it in the circle, by the sword's edge. Which was why he was no fit king, certainly, such thinking. *Catairlau?* he heard whispered by the Catairnan bard, who had let *Cairangorm's heir* pass unremarked, or had missed it. Forget that. How many bards were here, how many voices who knew the law? The one at his back was not asking the questions a speaker of the law should, at this point.

"You married *Hicca?*"

"I was married to Ketsim the Grasslander, and my lords and ladies, and my lord brothers, and grandfather of the Lellandi, if you *all* hadn't sat so long in your tents waiting and hoping the pox would do your work for you, there would be many fewer widows and orphans in my *duina* now. I will speak for myself. I have bloody well earned that right—"

Not bardlike, that phrasing. Keeping bad company lately. He saw Yeh-Lin's lip twitch, out of the corner of his eye. Also not true, that lives would have been saved if only they had acted more swiftly. The Red Masks would have broken them and left the lands kingless, if Ghu hadn't come for him. But shame them, yes, she had the right idea there, because there was still Marakand, and the temple might yet raise a real army from the city, without relying on the necromancy of its false god, and the iron road from the forest still crossed Praitan to the Five Cities.

A crane flew in the open door of the tent, silencing Deyandara. The white wings shed a silver light over them as she landed, rustling and settling her plumage.

"Orsa," he said, and bowed. That much courtesy he could find.

"Catairlau. And Deyandara. Who speak with full right for this land." Her voice was human enough, soft and high, and gave the words an ironic twist as she bobbed her head to them and turned to give Durandau a long, head-tilted look along her beak. The high king did not bow but dropped to his knees.

She reared back and beat her wings. Everyone there went down on their knees, save Ahjvar himself and the devil. He wasn't kneeling to the gods who had turned their backs on him, however well-disposed they might be now, and the devil merely folded her arms and looked sardonic. The look the goddess gave her was equally so, though how a crane could convey that much expression . . .

"The goddesses of this land have spoken through the web of waters, and the gods through the deep bones of the hills, and *they* affirm, Marnoch of the Red Hills will be king of the *duina*, as Catairlau who was king has said and Deyandara who is queen has said. Marnoch will speak with the gods of the hills and the goddesses of the waters, a new god will be chosen to give his name to the land. The high king will acknowledge this, or there will be a new high king, for even Praitanna of the Avain Praitanna, the great river, the goddess of the Duina Praitanna, the heart of the seven kingdoms, even she says, it shall be so. The folk of this *duina* have suffered the neglect and disdain of their chosen goddess long enough. Catairanach is gone. Let no one call her back."

Feathers drew out like tendrils of mist, still glowing as if caught in sunlight, and she drifted, a shadow-bird, then a form like a child, to Deyandara, putting arms about her, with the kneeling girl's head bowed to her shoulder. If the goddess spoke to her it was in silence, for Deyandara alone, but then she raised solemn silver eyes to Ahjvar.

"Your place is not here, Catairlau," he heard, but the goddess's lips did not move.

"I know," he said roughly. The black dog wagged its tail, all adoration of the goddess, but nothing else stirred, as if they all hung in the dream of a moment, stretched long.

"I am sorry," Orsa said. She raised one hand towards him, didn't touch, but he could feel the damp, cool air of dawn about her. "There is too much death in you, and no peace for you here. Catairanach is sunk deep in forgetting, but the thing that you carry lives without her and is still beyond us. Go."

He sheathed his sword, fumbling. It took several tries. Bent to kiss the top of Deyandara's head. He didn't think she knew he was there, to know it was farewell. So the gods took that, too. "Be well, granddaughter," he wished her. A breeze flapped the tent door and stirred Deyandara's hair, touched Marnoch's where he knelt, his eyes fixed on Deya, not the small goddess.

"You," he said, because it wanted saying even if the man couldn't hear, "do well by her. And come the winter solstice, they'll be electing a new high king. Durandau can't hold it after this. None of these here have proven they deserve such a place. You see it's you. Time it came back to us."

"And you accuse me of wanting to make emperors," Yeh-Lin said. "I'll tell him. I'll tell *them*. I," and she raised eyebrows at Orsa, "am not going anywhere, yet. I swore to serve Deyandara. I think I shall do so. For a little longer." She grinned. "If only to tease these little gods."

Orsa did not look best pleased at that.

Good.

So he left them.

The long shadows were falling from the west, and away from the pavilion of the high king's council, the business of the camp was going on, loudly, both in mourning and triumph. The captains of the kings would be pursuing the Marakander survivors, disarming them, chiv-vying them to the road. If they wanted less trouble, they should see their enemies had mounts and food and give them escort, Marakander and Grasslander alike, till they were well into the rising hills before the pass, but that wasn't Ahjvar's affair to order. Nobody paid him any attention. He felt slow as an old man, clumsy as a drunk, and sick with he didn't know what. Weariness. Hurt. He would call curses down on the gods of all Praitan, except he had given up cursing and he was too tired. He didn't know where Ghu had gone.

But the dogs found him, nosing in one from each side, as if he needed herding, and then Ghu was there, a shadow battered and smoke-blackened and hollow-eyed as he himself must be.

"Sleep," Ahjvar said with weary relief. "And if I don't—you promised."

"I know."

He could feel the sunset, the darkness, a weight pressing on him. He could feel the hag, too, still wailing for her mother and the shattering of her world, twisting, a worm in his heart. He stumbled at hollows and tussocks. If he fell, Ahjvar was going to lie where he landed, and the Praitan army could damn well go around him. A few dogs came alert and watched them, and horses turned, prick-eared and nostrils flaring, but the men and women didn't look, except maybe one or two, wizards, perhaps, who looked, and frowned, and looked away. They were shadow, that was all, and the mist of Orsa's swamp; the little brook that wound between the hills was filling the valleys with fog. Ahjvar followed Ghu down into it.

CHAPTER XXXII

Holla-Sayan went to the suburb through the Riverbend Gate. Dust hung thick and high over Sunset, staining the sunlight. Crowds of folk pressed that way, patrols of street guard trying to send them to their homes. Fire, earthquake, a fireball from the sky . . . rumour was rife in the air. The death of Ilbialla and, already, the death of the Lady had somehow run ahead of him, though that last must be speculation, and no one retelling the news seemed to know if they meant the true Lady or the devil. He might wonder if they even remembered there had been a true Lady of Marakand at all, or how long it would be before it was forgotten. Greenmarket and Riverbend did not seem much affected by the destruction of the holy places, beyond yet more cracked plaster and on the main thoroughfare, paving stones humped and rippled into odd ledges, as if the earth sank beneath city's weight. Even four-legged he stumbled at them, one-eyed, vision gone flat.

Captain Hassin of Riverbend Gate came tearing out of the tower guardroom after him, shouting for news, but he jogged on, pretending he didn't hear.

Holla-Sayan was through. Let the captain wait for messengers from Jugurthos Barraya. Making the city free again was what Jugurthos and Nour and Hadidu had planned for, been raised for, the younger two, all their lives. It was up to them. They didn't need him or shouldn't, and he didn't want to be needed by them. He was no magistrate, no captain.

The dog killed. That was all. He was only a caravan mercenary, a camel-driver, and his wife owned camels and half of the least-profitable cara-vanserai of the suburb.

He caught scent of Gaguush before he saw her, but then he found her amid the shadows, sitting on the ground at the caravanserai gate in the shade of the draggled incense cedar. Just sitting, chin on her knees. Hurt, he thought, and then, disaster come to the baby . . .

She looked up, found him, and surged to her feet, into his arms as he shifted to meet her.

"Are you all right?" he asked, but of course she was, the light that had come to her face when she raised her eyes to his . . .

"Am I all right? Am *I* all right?" Her hand cupped to his face, didn't touch. "I am now. Bashra damn you, can you see at all?"

"It's getting better." It didn't hurt so drowningly as it had; that had to be better, didn't it? "The Lady's dead, the devil."

"I didn't mean you had to go and—"

"I didn't. I'm afraid the city's going to say that, though." Holla-Sayan thought of Lissavakail, where the priestesses and the folk of the town had seen the death of the Lake-Lord at Vartu's hands, and still the stories ran up and down the road, now, that the Blackdog had saved them. "Again. What were you doing out here?"

"Waiting," she said. "What did you think? Just waiting. It's what the wives of heroes do in all the tales, isn't it? Come inside. I'm putting you to bed, and I'm going to sit across the doorway with a naked blade to make sure you stay there, this time."

"Don't you dare."

"And why not?"

Because he wanted to hang onto her. He wanted to burrow into her warmth and be wrapped in her arms and legs and never move again. He didn't know what she saw in his face, but she took his head in her hands, carefully, and backed him up against the wall and kissed him, pressed hard, body to body, for all they were out on the public street. She did let him up to breathe, after a while, when someone leading a skittish camel colt by paused to make remarks, which were, on the whole, approving.

"Come inside," she said. "Idiot." That, amiably, to the boy with the camel. "Come inside, Holla. We'll clean up your face. And there's tea."

CHAPTER XXXIII

In the cave, time passed. The earth, sometimes, trembled, but only as a faint wave rippling over a calm lake. Ivah felt fear ebb. Maybe it was the cool twilight, lit by the one small high windowlike opening in the stone wall behind her. It was not so large a cave that it could hold any deep darkness, with the morning sun outside, but she made a small light and let it drift. The cave was dry and empty, clean of the debris of animals and birds, but then, it had been sealed from the world for thirty years or so, and a holy place tended by priests before that. Exploring in the dim far reaches—it ran maybe forty feet back and downwards, no more—she found tarnished silver lamps set in natural niches in the wall, not symmetrically arranged, just here and there, where a ledge or a hollow gave place for them. She set light on them, though any oil was long since gone, and they made a star-scatter around the walls.

Mikki had said this mountain, dwarfed to a hill by the Pillars of the Sky beyond, was wormholed with caves, but there was no other opening into here, not the narrowest crack for a fox to squeeze through. She did not think she would have had the courage to explore into any tighter and darker place, anyhow. It was not as though the god were locked in some physical space, which she could find and rap knuckles against for a signal. *Knock twice if you're still alive.*

She settled herself and watched the silvery lights until they seemed to float, and the rocky wall beyond to swim into mottled cloud, a cloud of tiny suns burning through. She could hear water, distantly running. Imagination. She put thirst from her mind, and the pounding of her head. After a while she fished in her pocket for charcoal and wrote on the uneven, clean-swept floor, in long, vine-curving tendrils, the word she had become certain was the name of the god Gurhan, in the script from the tombs that no one could read.

After another while she cut a left-hand finger and began to shadow the black lines in blood.

Nothing changed. The light of the lamps dimmed with her weariness, that was all, and as the sun climbed higher over the ridge and the dust of the air outside settled, the daylight grew stronger.

But did the silence of the cave grow stronger, more aware, listening?

How much of the inscription on the cave had been the actual spell, and how much merely its defences, the killing words to protect what lay within? Had it been symbol of the thing, or the thing itself? Focus of the wizard's active will, like a sign calling light, which was nothing once one's mind was off it, or something set to endure beyond her death? That mattered. If the former, then the damage was only minor; it might weaken it a little, but not be the start of any great unravelling. If the latter, then the wizardry lay in the words, and they were flawed, now, a hole knocked through by the devil's own attack.

"Gurhan?" she tried. "Gurhan, your people need you. Can you hear?"

There was nothing, except that the cave did not feel empty. But it hadn't when she crawled—was shoved—into it, and that might be imagination. Mikki would have noticed; he was demon, kin in nature to the gods of the earth.

Mikki hadn't come inside.

"Gurhan, what do you need me to do?"

There was a listening air to the silence, and was the water louder?

She set hands against the stone floor, either side of the name, and let her lights go out. The shaft of sunlight slanted golden, dust-dancing, over her shoulder to strike the far wall.

There was thunder, and the earth shuddered yet again. A cascade of pebbles rattled down the far wall, and grit rained from the roof. Ivah hunched against it, heart jumping, but the hill did not come down around her.

A crack had opened in the far end, or something cast a shadow, black, narrow, and the sound of water was suddenly loud, a bright chiming stream over stone. She didn't dare move. If shadow, it stood behind her. But it broadened, split, and there was still a fissure into darkness, and a shape that came forward. First it drifted, being shadow, and then dust-motes golden against the dark, and then a man in a white caftan, bare feet silent.

He crouched down, still silent, and took her hands. His were cool, like earth merely shaped to mimic flesh and bone. His face was not an old man's, though his hair was silver-white.

He said nothing. She could not speak, but she felt as though he drank, somehow, from her, all the memory of what had been, and yet withdrew his seeking and delicately looked away when she felt burgeoning all the life that had brought her to Marakand. He leaned brow to brow and then kissed her forehead, let her hands go to brush a trail of tears from the corner of her eye with his thumb, though she had not known she was weeping.

"The devil is dead," the god said then, in a voice that was soft, and deep with the colours of the earth, and yet not so deep as Mikki's. A singer's voice. "The devil is dead and her works undone, but the Lady Marakanat my sister is dead, and Ilbialla, beautiful Ilbialla is burnt from the world. My poor Mansour's child is dead and gone to her long, long road. But there is still one priest who thinks of the good of the folk in this city, and honest and honourable men and women who will seek to bring justice to its laws and its rule again. Daughter of the Great Grass and Nabban, come with me to find them."

There had been no place in Jugurthos's foray to Templefoot Ward for a caravaneer still too weak to walk even half a mile without sitting down for a rest, or a wizard whose chief strength lay in minor wardings. Or for Hadidu, still stunned and devastated with his grief, too wounded for mourning. Nour and Hadidu stayed, sometimes joined by Tulip, watching the patrols go to and from the ruin of the market, couriers clattering up, getting occasional reports. They heard how the valley of Gurhan's cave had been swept by fire before ever Ilbialla was attacked, the details of Fleshmarket's bloody night and victorious morning, with the temple forces pushed out once again. The Red Masks had all been mysteriously destroyed in the night, as well, and the old menagerie keeper murdered, and a gang of priests and temple guards badly disguised as caravaneers were found slaughtered to a man far too near the library for anyone's peace of mind. Extra patrols of the militia were sent to the hill. They heard how Jugurthos, forcing the barricaded gateways into Templefoot easily, had found the ward mostly undefended, but the temple itself a battleground for—he didn't know what, his confidential messenger to Tulip and Hadidu said, and so he held back, waiting, uncertain at the last.

But the fires died, and after one final concussion that shook the city and set the dogs and babies howling, there was stillness, and only a golden haze, like the aftermath of a sandstorm, in the bright noon.

Nour had just spotted one of the couriers again, the woman with the piebald who tended to have the more personal of the verbal reports for their ears alone, when Hadidu, who'd been kneeling, eyes shut and head cradled on his arms in the crenel of the tower's battlements, lurched to his feet.

"Gurhan," he said, almost whispering.

"What?" Nour took his arm, thinking he was drowsing and might topple over the edge.

"Gurhan! Did you hear him?"

Nour didn't accuse him of dreaming then. Hadidu's eyes were fixed somewhere else, remote, shadowed with grief and yet no longer hopeless in defeat. Seeing—Nour couldn't imagine what, something beyond Ilbialla's death, that was certain. And he'd had nothing stronger than sweet coffee.

"No. Hadi, wait—"

But Hadidu was running down the stairs, leaving Nour to follow.

CHAPTER XXXIV

The scent of smoke was strong in the air, but that was drifting over from the Praitannec camp; it was nothing to do with the ghost. Or maybe it was their own hair and clothing. The smell of corrupting bodies was only his imagination, though the crows still squabbled and the ravens cried harshly, on the ridge over the Orsamoss. Ghu would have gone farther, but Ahjvar, who had gone down to hands and knees in the brook to drink, heedless even of his sword, had simply collapsed again as Ghu tried to take him along a folded furrow of the hills, away from the smell. Ghu had dragged his arm over his shoulder, forced him to walk a little farther, just a little, to where a thicket of juniper poured down a steep and stony bank, and there he had fallen again, crawling in under the spiny boughs. It was shelter enough. There were no fugitives here, and they had passed through and beyond the roaming Praitannec pickets in the fog.

"Food?" Ghu suggested, crawling in after him and sitting by his side, back against a trunk and branches brushing his hair. Jui and Jiot settled a little away, each curled into a knot, sleeping the moment they lay down. Food. Not that they had any. He would have to make a raid on the camp and steal a couple of waterskins while he was at it. Maybe find Deyandara and make his farewells. She would be all right, now. Ahjvar's curse on her ancestors was cleaned away, and she was among friends. The death he had felt lying over her was lifted. Even Yeh-Lin meant well by her, though how long that would last. . . . And the goddess Orsa had gone to the kings. Praitan could save itself, now. "Bread, Ahjvar, if I can find any?"

Ahjvar, lying with his head on his arm, didn't answer.

"Ahj?"

He stirred, just enough to roll over. "No. Don't go anywhere."

"Food and drink. You look like a dead man." He did, frighteningly so, gaunt and grey.

"I am a dead man. Don't leave me alone."

Food and water and dry clothes. Ahjvar was soaked from his plunge into the brook, and shivering, but his skin burned, not a good sign, Ghu thought. He unrolled his bundle and wrapped the blanket around Ahjvar.

"Catairanach's gone and I'm still here. It should have ended. She should have ended. We should have died with the damned goddess."

"Yeh-Lin didn't kill the goddess."

"She should have killed me."

"Ahj, no."

"You will kill me. You promised you would. When the hag wakes again—before she wakes again, Ghu, Great Gods, please."

"If—"

"You can. You didn't lie to me, gods, you didn't. Because she'll kill you, she'll kill you first of all, and Ghu, I can't, she's a wizard again, with all my strength and her own will, and you can't just tie me up this time." His voice rose, panicked.

"Hush, hush. I haven't lied to you, Ahj. I don't lie."

"You don't tell me things."

"Sometimes I don't. I'm sorry. Sometimes I don't know things. I don't see myself."

Ahjvar's hand was on his wrist, fingers digging in like claws. "You're not another devil."

"No."

"Who are you, really?"

"Ghu."

"*What*, then?"

"Nabban," he said, reluctant, as if the words alone made it true and if he could hold them back, they might still find the ruin on the coast of the Gulf of Taren again, and the sea, and the south winds on the downs. "I am . . . becoming . . . Nabban. But I don't always see that. I forget it, for long times. Believe that, Ahj. I don't—didn't, always know. Yeh-Lin says . . . but I could not have saved you, when I sat on your garden wall in the rain. I only knew I wanted to—to be some light, in your shadows and your pain." A breath. "You drew me like a fire," he whispered.

There was no retreat. He did not think he could go back to not seeing himself, to drifting, simple and wide-eyed, waiting, not knowing what he waited for. Some step had been too far. When he freed the first of the Red Masks, maybe. When he pulled the dogs to him, into the current of becoming, and they forged ahead on his road, looking back, tails wagging. *Hurry up, then, if we're going this way, things to do. . . .* When he killed a man for a horse, for Ahj. That was not his road, but it fractured the shell of innocence, left him no retreat. Or when he put a devil of the north into the earth, even if only for a little, because she threatened what he had taken it upon himself to protect.

His. He did not want to become like Catairanach, destroying what he most desired to hold.

"The sun's setting."

"Yes, I know. Come here."

Ahjvar rolled over, laid his head in Ghu's lap like a weary child. Ghu pulled the blanket over him again, fingers in his hair. He burned, and shivered.

It had been so easy to thrust the broken souls of the Red Masks out of the web the Lady had made. They had no real bond to the husks of their bodies any longer; they had yearned to be free, even though the soul itself was broken and decayed, the self lost, the road of the Old Great Gods beyond reach. It was so easy to kill a man. Not Ahjvar, though. Catairanach had made him to endure in the world, and if Ghu did not unmake that, he would so endure. Maybe Ahjvar was right after all, and he had been dead these ninety years, and was only a thing, shaped by the goddess's curse to be a vessel for the entangled souls. Simple, perhaps, if not easy, to pluck them free and cast them to the road to start their long journey. But together? He had no idea. What if Hyllau still battened on Ahjvar, still clung, rooted in him? What had Yeh-Lin said, If you have to kill him, let it be for his own sake?

"Ahjvar? I could—send you to the road. Both of you. I could."

"I'm tired, Ghu."

"I know. I know." He stroked his hair, soothing.

"I don't want to wake up wondering who I've killed. No more mornings."

"I know."

"She's not going to let me go, this time. She's strong. The Lady—"

"Hush, Ahj. Ahjvar, if I—"

Too late. Ahjvar shuddered, and dogs both came alert, growling, as the man rolled over and the eyes glared up at him, but Ghu held him, fingers touching the lips, the other on his heart.

"No," he said, and turned his hand, closed his fist. He had her, a grip on her, at least, and he held Ahj. "He won't be yours, tonight. Ever again."

Rage. No fear. She was more than the Red Masks had been; she was will, and memory, but, he thought, as an animal's memory. Emotion and urge. Did she have a voice he could give back to her? He didn't think so. She had never spoken when she had Ahjvar's tongue to use. Perhaps her thoughts no longer ran in such shapes; he had no way of knowing, if she could not or would not speak. He would not step within her soul to see what truly lay there. And what could she say? That she had a right to survive? Not over others' lives. She had slain herself in spite and arrogance, destroying the life she could have had in her greed and pride. Hyllau had destroyed herself; she had no right to take Ahjvar with her. No defence.

It was not so simple as to drive a broken soul from a broken body, out of the knot of the Lady's necromancy. Not so simple at all. He had slowly to tease out the strands of Hyllau's soul, gathering them, a great, mucky, rooted thing, that ripped, sometimes, and tore, and if souls could bleed, he thought Ahjvar bled. It was not seeing but a feeling under his hands, and the scent of smoke and burning flesh. Ahjvar for him was sea air and thyme, and the sound of waves below the cliffs, but under that Catairlau was old, frail bone and ash, and the hag clung to him, new tendrils latching on as fast as Ghu could draw them out. Dreamless Catairanach held her victim close, the goddess's will still wrapped round him, as a dead man's hand still gripped his spear on the battlefield, or a slain mother her living child; the goddess bound him to be the shelter for the child even such a desire as hers had not been able to save. There had been nothing of Hyllau to remake save teeth and a few charred shards; Hyllau's fire had fed on herself first of all, bursting from within, before it reached for her lover.

Ghu could wish he had not seen that, felt that death.

Better to let them go together after all. Ahj *remembered* that, felt it, still, in his dreams.

Hyllau's desire, poisonous, prompting him to cut them both away . . . oh, she was sly. She still held what she claimed for her own and would deny it to anyone else.

The devil Yeh-Lin Dotemon hadn't slain Catairanach, though she could have. Maybe she chose not to kill for her own reasons; maybe she had learnt mercy and temperance, as she said. Maybe she had seen there was no life in Ahjvar, but what the goddess shaped for him.

Yes, it was better Ahj at least die free of Hyllau. There was a horror for endless nightmare, that what Ahjvar called the hag might feed on him, even after the death of the body, even as his soul sought its way to the Old Great Gods.

Hyllau struck suddenly for Ghu's throat, breaking free, but he caught the hands and folded them back down. Ahjvar might be the stronger man, but not tonight.

"No," Ghu said, holding her. He shut his eyes, and reached.

The mountain and the river. Always there. All he had ever had to do was let them take him.

No more wandering.

Black water, the lightless depths and the unmelting snow that burned against the sky, the stone that bound them, running under all the brown land, the green land, from the deserts of the north to the sea. This was Nabban.

She cowered, clung, but he followed her easily now, traced every root and every thread, loosed every claw and gathered her into his hands, and he walked Catairanach's sleep and slid himself where she had been, edging her out of what she had shaped, the will that, even unconscious, held Ahjvar to the world.

Not what he had promised.

But I love him.

So had Hyllau.

No. Desire of possession was not love.

He drew the last threads of Hyllau free, held in cupped hands. Open-eyed, what did he see? Fire, with darkness at its heart. He would have cast Hyllau away, even Hyllau, with a blessing to seek the Great Gods' road, but she turned and dove for Ahjvar's heart, burning as she had burned then, and the junipers were lit with flame.

Ghu closed his hands over her, like a man catching a butterfly, felt her fluttering there, and crushed.

His hands burned. When he opened them, there was nothing to see in the moonlight but a little ash, sifting away. He blew, and a wind took it, so that it did not land on Ahj. The branches above him were scorched and dead. When he laid a hand on Ahjvar's forehead, the skin was cool as he'd expect of a man in damp clothes lying out on a nighttime hill, and no warmer. He breathed, sleeping, a heartbeat still to be felt in the hollow of his throat.

Mother Nabban, Father Nabban . . . prayer had no words. He had done what he had done. The east pulled him. Ahjvar muttered, whimpered in his dreams, grew quiet when Ghu spread a hand on his chest. He watched him a long while, sitting, stroking his hair in silence, keeping the dreams at bay as the swelling moon drifted, throwing silver through the naked branches. Finally, though, he bent over, whispered, calling him. He wanted to let the man sleep, to watch him sleep, to wait for the dawn, but that was not what he had promised, and to take more ungiven—he could not.

"Ahjvar."

Ahj twitched and woke and reached, found his hand and looked up at him.

"Not morning."

"No, it's still night."

There was fear, clear even in night and shadow. The curse had been rising, the hag waking, and now he was awake . . .

"Ahj, no. You've been here. With me. Safe. Hyllau is gone. She did die in the fire, ninety years ago. What was left is burnt away. She is gone from you."

Ahjvar looked as if he did not understand, but maybe empty was how he felt. Lost.

"You said I could die," he whispered.

"I know. I know. I don't lie. But I wanted, Old Great Gods forgive me. Ahjvar, I wanted—I ask now. She is gone. You are made clean. You won't kill for her again, and your nightmares will be only nightmares. Memories. I promise you, it is over. But what Catairanach made you, you are still. I took her from you, but Ahj, I've put myself in her place, to hold you. Because you died too, that night. You were always right, you were dead. In some degree. Not so dead as she . . ." Not so utterly destroyed, not past saving, body or soul. He put fingers to Ahjvar's lips when he would have spoken. "No, wait. I want to ask you this, promise you this. I will let you go. Now. Or whenever you desire it. I swear to you, by the heart of the mountain, the waters of the river, by all I am and will be, I swear I will let you go, when you ask it. This night, now, or any time to come. But you are *free*. I know you are tired, and I know the world is too heavy, but please. I have to go to Nabban. It pulls me, now. I can't stay here. I want to ask . . . try living, again, first? Come with me, a while yet? As long as you will? Only as long as you will. Please. Neither to be my champion nor my captain, nor my assassin." He laughed, half a sob. "Nor my lover. Just, come to keep me company. I am afraid of this road. I can travel it alone. I expected to. I'd rather not."

Ahjvar didn't speak, pulling himself up slowly, as if every bone ached, sitting shoulder to shoulder, his sword pulled across his legs. His fingers traced the gilt leopard's head, but Ghu thought he had his eyes shut.

"God of Nabban," he said at last.

"Not . . . quite. Not . . . yet."

"You do promise. When I ask."

"Yes."

Ahjvar rested his head against Ghu's. "I don't like gods much."

"That's all right."

"Or men."

"Did I ask that?"

"Hah. Do you not? I just want to sleep, Ghu. I can't think. My head hurts."

"I know. But we're very close to the Praitannec camp, and maybe we should go farther, before anyone comes looking for—"

"For what?"

"I don't know. The ghosts of dead kings?"

"Yes. Do I have to walk? Where are we going?"

"Nabban."

"Not tonight, we're not." Ahjvar sat up straight again and rubbed his face. Both dogs jumped up, expectant, tails stirring. "So?"

"So, then?"

"So, we go far enough to boil some coffee in peace. That's all. And you're in charge of horse-stealing. We have no money."

Ghu did, Ahj's money and Ivah's, which he had taken with her scroll-case and blanket that he had salvaged from the street, after the Red Masks took her, but he didn't think a man looking like one of Ketsim's folk was going to find a very friendly market for buying horses in the Praitannec camp.

"I'm sure I used to own some good horses," Ahj muttered. "Someone gave them away, though."

"While you were with the kings, I talked to a groom named Rozen. She has our horses. She thinks they belong to Deyandara, but we can't take horses across the eastern deserts anyway. They'll be happier here, but I do have to go back to Nabban. That means the sea or the deserts. I've been a sailor. We could—"

"I get seasick."

"Do you really?" Ghu grinned. "Have you ever ridden a camel? Some find it's just as bad."

"I don't want to go back to the Five Cities. I don't want to go anywhere I've been before."

"We'll cross the deserts, then." Ghu laughed, leaned against him again, just for a moment. "These Praitans have captured a lot of the Marakander mercenaries' beasts. Let's go steal some camels, Ahj."

CHAPTER XXXV

Nour and Hadidu wanted Ivah to stay in Marakand, of course. Strange there should be that in her thoughts, *of course*, as if she could think she had earned it. A place, if she wanted it. A home. But Talfan was sharp and bitter in her grief, and blamed Ivah for Varro's death, as fervently as she'd held her Nour's saviour, and that bitterness hurt Hadidu.

She didn't want to see Hadidu hurt.

They had burned Varro's body in the Northron way, out on the edge of the desert, given his bones to the desert and the ashes to the wind. His sword, though, had been gone by the time anyone had had the time to go reclaim his corpse. Talfan, she thought, harboured dark suspicions of Ivah on that point too, though the apothecary had the lingering courtesy not to voice those, at least. Ivah thought of the missing temple guardsman, the one who had come with Ashir the Right Hand, his ally in betrayal of the Lady. He had offered to help, and had disappeared into the woods when she refused. Maybe he'd gone back to his fellows, to join in their butchery of the poor old man and his bear, and had been cut down by Mikki's axe. Maybe he'd gone up the ridge and was dust with blessed Belmyn and her patrol. But maybe not. Maybe there was a Marakander mercenary gone to the road with a cursed and kingly sword.

Mikki had not come back. Ivah had no idea where he had gone, once the Lady was dead. Moth had left him, Holla-Sayan said. More to it than that, which the Blackdog didn't think her concern, and she was surprised how it hurt her, to think of the demon heartsore and alone. She wanted to divine for him, to follow him, but resisted the impulse. He wouldn't want company. Not hers, not anyone's but Moth's, and if she did find the demon and intrude on him . . . what then? Nor would Gaguush welcome her to Rasta's caravanserai, seeking Holla-Sayan's companionship. Aside from Varro's funeral, where she'd kept back and silent, she'd seen the Blackdog once, only the once, since the Lady— since Tu'usha fell. He kept out of the city, busy about the caravanserai's business and putting together a new caravan for At-Landi, Nour said.

Ivah had a place in the library as a scholar, if she wanted it. She lived there, now, in a small room with Moth's horse-skull set in the lamp-niche, the clay lamp balanced on its head, and Mikki's heavy axe and a set of carpenter's chisels carefully wrapped in oiled leather under the bed. She wasn't sure why the devil had travelled with a horse skull, which sometimes seemed to watch her in the night, or why Mikki had not at least come back for his tools, but she felt she needed, somehow, to care for them. Awkward, useless remembrances of—of, she didn't know what. She'd been making a bad joke when she told poor lost Ghu that Moth was her stepmother. They weren't family, hardly even friends. But Ulfhild's daughter had been Ivah's sister; her son, Ivah's brother. That was a strange thought. Dead long ages, but siblings. It was a bond. It meant she needed not to abandon some—some memory of Moth and Mikki. To hold something, to draw them back to her, or so that if they came back, singly or together, she could say, *I thought of you, see? I worried, damn you.* Which was what true families did.

The librarians, those that remained, and the young, Nabbani-trained wizards drifting back from the Five Cities, were deferential. Ivah had defeated the Lady in the first battle against her, destroyed the Red Masks, freed the god Gurhan . . . denial did no good and began to seem too fervent a false modesty.

She began to dream of horses, and falcons, and waves of grass under the sun. Of a mountain she had never seen, snow-peaked, hung with patches of dark woodland, and a great slow-winding river, pewter-grey under rain. Marakand wasn't her place; Gurhan, for all his friendship, not her god. She didn't belong here, and she didn't know where she might, ever.

Nour came seeking her one day, as she worked at a copy of *The Balance of the Sun and the Moon* to replace the one lost when the Red Masks took her. It was scribes' work, and there were a dozen scribes eager to do it for her, but she wanted the book—and it would be a bound codex this time, not a damned unwieldy scroll—in her own hand, with her own notes incorporated, and not her mother's ghost in every commentary.

"Kharduin and I still have a living to earn," he said. "We're heading out for Nabban. You were a caravaneer, once, Holla-Sayan says. Come with us?"

EPILOGUE

*T**here is a story-tellers' cycle of tales, and they begin like this:*

Long after the Old Great Gods had made the world and left it for the Lands Beyond, in the days of the first kings in the north—who were Viga Forkbeard, and Red Geir, and Hravnmod the Wise, as all but fools should know—there were seven devils, and their names were Honeytongued Ogada, Jasberek Fireborn, Vartu Kingsbane, Tu'usha the Restless, Jochiz Stonebreaker, Dotemon the Dreamshaper, and Twice-Betrayed Ghatai. If other tellers tell you different, they are ignorant singers not worthy of their hire.

Now, as all should know, the gods and the goddesses live in their own places, the high places and the waters, and aid those who worship them, and protect their own. And though the demons may wander all the secret places of the world, their hearts are bound each to their own place, and though they once served and once defied the Old Great Gods and are no friends to human folk, they are no enemies either, and want only to be left in peace. But the devils have no place, and walk up and down over the earth, to trouble the lives of the folk. And the devils do not desire loving worship, nor the friendship of men and women. They do not have a parent's love for the folk. The devils crave dominion as the desert craves water, and they know neither love nor justice nor mercy.

And in the days of the first kings in the north, who were Viga Forkbeard, and Red Geir, and Hravnmod the Wise, there were seven wizards. And two were of the people of the kings in the north, who came from the western isles, and five were of other tribes, of the Grass and the sea, and from the eastern lands far from the forests of the kings in the north, but the seven were of one fellowship. Their names were Heuslar the Deep-Minded, who was uncle to Red Geir; Anganurth Wanderer; Ulfhild the King's Sword, who was sister to Hravnmod the Wise; Sien-Mor and Sien-Shava, the Outcasts, who were sister and brother; Yeh-Lin the Beautiful; and Tamghiz, Chief of the Bear-Mask Fellowship. If other singers tell you different, they know only the shadows of the tales, and they lie. These wizards were wise, and powerful. They knew the runes and the secret names, and the patterns of the living world and of the dead. And the stories of their deeds are many, for they were great heroes among their peoples. And these all can be told, if there be golden rings, or silver cups, or wine and flesh and bread by the fire.

But the seven wizards desired to know yet more, and see yet more, and to live forever like the gods of the high places and the goddesses of the waters and the demons of the forest and the stone and the sand and the grass.

And the seven devils, having no place, had no body, but were like smoke, or like a flame. They hungered to be of the stuff of the world, like the gods and the goddesses and the demons at will, and as men and women are whether they will or no, and having a body, to find a place. So they made a bargain with the seven wizards, that they would join their souls to the wizards' souls, and share the wizards' bodies, sharing knowledge, and unending life, and power. But the devils deceived the wizards, and betrayed them.

The devils took the souls of the wizards into their own, and became one with them, and devoured them. They walked as wizards among the wizards, and destroyed those who would not obey, or who counselled against their counsel. They desired the worship of kings and the enslavement of the folk, and they were never sated, as the desert is never sated with rain.

So the kings of the north and the tribes of the grass and those wizards whom the devils had not yet slain pretended submission, and plotted in secret, and they rose up against the tyranny of the devils, and overthrew them. But the devils were devils, even in human bodies, and not easily slain. They were bound, one by one, and imprisoned—Honeytongued Ogada in stone, Jasberek Fireborn in water, Vartu Kingsbane in earth, Tu'usha the Restless in the heart of a flame, Jochiz Stonebreaker in the youngest of rivers, Dotemon Dreamshaper in the oldest of trees, Twice-Betrayed Ghatai in the breath of a burning mountain. And they were guarded by demons, and goddesses, and gods.

And there are many tales of the wars against the devils, and of the kings and the heroes and the wizards, and the terrible deeds done. And these can all be told, if there be golden rings, or silver cups, or wine and flesh and bread by the fire.

The kings and the wizards believed their war with the devils was over, and that their sons and daughters could lead their folk in peace. But time weakens all bonds, and men and women and even wizards forget, and only we skalds remember.

It is said that the seven devils did not sleep but lay ever-waking within their bonds, and they worked against their bonds, and weakened them, and they worked against their captors, and they slept, or they died, as even gods and goddesses can die, when the fates allow it.

But from the skalds of the north the winds from the north come bearing new tales to the road, and from the Western Grass to the ports of Nabban the bards and the storytellers repeat them: they say that the devils are free in the world, and the sword of the ice is hunting them.

ABOUT THE AUTHOR

Photo © Chris Paul

K. V. Johansen was born in Kingston, Ontario, Canada, where she developed her lifelong fascination with fantasy literature after reading *The Lord of the Rings* at the age of eight. The love of landscape and natural history that appears in her writing also traces to an early age, when she spent countless hours exploring woods and brooks with her dog. Long family camping trips back and forth across the country (and the continent) may have had something to do with the epic scale of the journeys on which she sends her characters. Her interest in the history and languages of the Middle Ages led her to take a Master's Degree in Medieval Studies at the Centre for Medieval Studies at the University of Toronto, and a second MA in English Literature at McMaster University, where she wrote her thesis on Layamon's *Brut*, an Early Middle English epic poem. While spending most of her time writing, she retains her interest in medieval history and languages and is a member of the Tolkien Society and the Early English Text Society, as well as the Science Fiction Writers of America and the Writers' Union of Canada. Her previous works for adults include *The Leopard: Marakand Part One*, the Sunburst-nominated *Blackdog*, and the short-story collection *The Storyteller*. She is also the author of two works on the history of children's fantasy literature and a number of books for children and teens. Various of her books have been translated into French, Macedonian, and Danish. Visit her online at www.kvj.ca.